The Wicked Kiss

Book Two of the Alexa O'Brien Huntress Series

Trina M. Lee

The Wicked Kiss

Trina M. Lee

Published 2009

ISBN 978-1-456-30257-3

Manufactured in the United States of America

Published as an e-book by Liquid Silver Books

Editor
B. Leigh Hogan

Cover Artist
Dawn Seewer

4

Chapter One

I stared at the creepy nightclub across the street. The Wicked Kiss isn't the type of place I especially enjoy walking into. Inside, you feel as if you've just become the latest tasty item on the menu. Being a werewolf made it no different than if I'd been human. I was food in this place. The vampire bar may have been fascinating to some, like the many donors who risk it nightly, but to me, it's just plain scary.

I had only been inside the club once, years ago, and I'd heard they had renovated the place since. Probably so they could add in some secret passageways or hidden torture rooms. Just a guess.

Trying to calm the nervous butterflies in my stomach, I gave my hair and makeup a final and unnecessary check. My smoky black eyeliner was still perfectly framing my dark brown eyes. I'd worn bold red lipstick, which wasn't the usual for me. Considering the location, I'd planned on blending in the best I could. I had to admit to myself that I looked pretty hot.

I ran my fingers through my long hair and took a deep breath. The chunks of dyed gold that I'd had blended into my light, ash blonde hair had faded out over the past few months. Always one to have fun with color, I'd replaced it with an amazing fire engine red. The alternating layers of blonde and red that framed my face did wonders to play up my eyes.

Now that I was at The Wicked Kiss, I really didn't want to go in. And, I never would have even considered it if Kale hadn't been inside. He'd been missing for three days, and he wouldn't likely be anywhere else for that length of time. Because he was my colleague and my friend, I was willing to withstand some discomfort. That, and because if I didn't go in there and drag him out, Kylarai would, which couldn't possibly go over well.

Kylarai Kramer, my passive-aggressive best friend, had been

seeing my danger-seeking vampire colleague for the last three months. However, they had been coming to realize that their relationship wasn't going to be too cut and dried.

One of the reasons I didn't want Ky going into The Wicked Kiss was because she wasn't comfortable with Kale taking blood from the donors there. Unfortunately, blood is a vital part of a vampire's existence, and Kale, being a product of vampire torture, preferred the donor set up to the kill. Feeding for a vampire can be very intimate and often includes more than blood alone. Kylarai knows it's part of being with Kale, whether she likes it or not.

Steeling myself against the nerves that threatened to keep me in the car, I double checked my shoulder bag for my cell phone and opened the door. I paused to adjust my cleavage in the tight-fitting, black corset I wore. It looked great paired with pinstriped dress pants and my favorite four-inch heeled boots. A strategically placed leather choker was my way of hiding my neck. No open invitations here.

Bumping the door of my red Dodge Charger Daytona shut with my hip, I locked it with a beep and crossed the street. I scanned the parking lot of the bar for Kale's slick 1973 Camaro. Sure enough, there it was near the back. I was somewhat surprised to see that his rims were still attached to his car. This wasn't a good area of town. Although, anyone who wants to live to see another day wouldn't touch a car in this lot.

If I said I wasn't scared to walk through the doors of the club, I'd be lying. I was somewhat reassured that both Kylarai and Jez knew where I was. If they didn't hear from me within an hour or two, they were supposed to come in after me.

Of course, if I was dead or forced to be somebody's plaything by then, it wouldn't matter. There were rules in this place, as far as I knew, but, I mean, we're talking vampires here.

Nobody lingered outside. Two heavy wooden doors opened into a small foyer. A cashier stand stood off to one side where a female vampire waited to take my cover charge. She was new, as in, a new vampire; the energy rolling off her felt tainted with human. At least the smell of death had faded.

How many vampires woke up to their new life in this place? I shuddered at the thought, but my curiosity was piqued.

A few feet away from the cashier stand was a tall, beefy

bouncer. He, too, was a member of the undead as was most of the staff in this place. He gave me a critical once over before nodding his head towards the cashier chick.

"How much?" I asked her, fully aware that I sounded like a total newbie.

"Ten bucks," she replied, making no attempt to hide her wonder as she ogled me. Werewolves are not nearly as common or easy to become as vampires. This happened often.

Handing her a ten dollar bill, I turned away to pass the big vampire blocking the entry into the club beyond. He crossed his big arms over his chest and looked down at me from his tall stance.

"Sorry, but anything coming in here that isn't human is subject to being searched." He smiled, but it didn't reach his eyes.

I was wearing a freaking corset and slacks, where did he think I could possibly be hiding something? Sighing, I allowed him to give me a quick pat down and low and behold, he never even tried to grope me. Good for him.

When he was satisfied that I wasn't carrying a stake, or whatever else he was looking for, he moved aside and let me pass into the main bar beyond. Of course, little did he know that my biggest arsenal was on me at all times. Having the ability to conduct and manipulate energy often meant I didn't need a physical weapon, especially since my power had grown due to my bond with Arys, my vampire lover.

Loud Goth rock music greeted me as I stepped inside. The only lighting in the place was a series of black lights strewn about and a few large strobe lights that illuminated those on the dance floor to my right. The bar was to my left, and I went there first.

The place was not expansively big, but it was on the larger side. Framed classic horror movie posters adorned the far wall behind the dance floor, and a glass-encased candle burned on each of the tables scattered around. A DJ booth was tucked away in the corner behind the dance floor as well as a fireplace and two red velvet couches near the bar where I stood.

It wasn't hard to tell the humans from the vampires. Other than their obvious energy difference, the humans seemed to be wannabe vamps more than anything else. An assortment of heavily made-up men and women in dog chains and fake leather were everywhere. The scent of blood was mixed with that of sweat, booze and vanilla candles.

I knew about the private area where vampires and donors could escape to their own room for uninterrupted feeding and whatever else they did back there. The main club was just a front for what lies in the back.

I knew that's where Kale had to be when I didn't spot him. I still wasn't sure how I was going to get back there to him. I considered fabricating a lame story but decided that honesty may be the best bet.

The biker-style bartender slid the whiskey I ordered down the bar without looking twice at me. I'm sure he saw more than enough interesting tidbits in a place like this.

Sipping my drink, I feigned interest in the bodies on the dance floor, which writhed more than they danced. It was downright creepy. The entire place was a swarm of humans and vampires falling all over each other. I was the only Were in the place.

I felt eyes on me before I determined whose they were. A tall, thin vampire in a hockey jersey and jeans was advancing on me fast from the other side of the room. He was longhaired and scraggly, with a poor excuse for a goatee. His power was weak, mediocre at best. I wasn't intimidated in the least.

Oh great, I thought. I couldn't imagine this would be easier than turning down the human jackasses that wouldn't take no for an answer at Lucy's Lounge, my usual hangout.

"You're new here." He didn't bother to beat around the bush. Most vampires don't. "We don't get many werewolves in here."

"Yeah, well I'm just here to have a drink and look for my friend. Don't let me keep you." I smiled and tried my best for polite. I didn't need to piss off every vampire in the place by coming across as aggressive.

"Is that so? Perhaps I can persuade you to rethink that." His serious brown eyes studied me, waiting for my reaction.

"No, thank you. Really, I'm in a bit of a hurry." I finished the rest of my drink in one swallow as if to emphasize my words. The resulting alcohol rush was pleasant but short-lived.

The vampire glanced out, over the small crowd gyrating on the dance floor, before looking back at me. It didn't look like he planned to move along. I began to grow impatient. I didn't have time for this crap.

He actually took a step closer to me, inclining his head in a way that he must have thought was endearing. "What will it take to get you to come back to a room with me? Just for a little taste. Name it. I can match your price."

So, he thought he could buy my precious werewolf blood with money. This was getting ridiculous.

"I'm not here as a donor. I'm sorry, but I'm busy. I'm sure there are plenty of ladies here who would be more than happy to give you a fix." I turned to walk away, but his cold hand on my bare shoulder stopped me dead in my tracks.

"Look," he said, and his tone had dropped to a deadly pitch. "Maybe you don't understand how potent Were blood is to a vampire, but walking in here without being willing to share is something that could get you killed."

I met his eyes evenly, allowing myself a hint of the wicked smile I'd picked up from Arys. "Is that a threat? Or a challenge?"

Without waiting for him to respond, I glanced at the spot where he touched me and focused on it. All it took was a thought, and I pushed power into that spot hard enough to make him stumble back, arms flailing. It wasn't enough to land him on his ass though, lucky him.

It certainly got the attention of a few club patrons nearby. I didn't risk a glance at them. I stared at the vampire, expecting some kind of retaliation. I did not expect the reaction I got.

His eyes grew wide, and he took a few steps toward me but stopped out of reach. "You're Arys Knight's wolf." It wasn't a question.

I bristled at his words. What in the hell was Arys telling people? I didn't belong to anybody.

"What the hell are you talking about?" I demanded, hands on my hips.

"I'm so sorry," he continued in a blubbering rush as if I hadn't spoken. "I didn't know. I swear; I never would have tried if I'd known."

He began to back away slowly, holding his hands up in a sign of surrender. I advanced on him, ignoring the curious looks from those at the table closest to us.

"Wait, I want to know where you heard that." I also had a sudden idea as to how I might be able to get into the back. Maybe I could use this to my advantage.

"I don't know." He glanced around as if looking for someone to save him. "Everyone knows who he is. You're laced with his energy. You have to be the wolf he's bonded to. Right?"

Was no information considered sacred anymore? Or, was it just that obvious to others? I didn't like that my business was getting out and about.

"Right." I nodded. There really was no point in lying. "You know Arys?"

If he hadn't already looked frightened, he did now. "I know that I don't want any beef with him. I said I was sorry."

This might be easier than I thought. "Ok fine, I'll forget all about it if you do me a small favor."

His expression grew suspicious, but he didn't turn and run. So far, so good. "What?"

"Take me into the back so I can find my friend." I nodded at the heavy, black velvet curtain that hung ominously over a door in the back, next to the bar. A piece of bright red hair fell in my eyes, and I gave my head a toss.

The vampire stared at me as if unsure of what to do. After a moment, he shrugged. "Alright. I'll take you back there for a few minutes, but that's it. I don't need to get in shit for this."

"You won't. I promise." After a moment of consideration, I offered him a hand. "I'm Alexa."

He appeared hesitant before accepting. He felt cool and clammy, like he hadn't fed in a while. "Shawn."

"Sorry to inconvenience you, Shawn, but I really need to get back there to my friend. This won't take long."

"I'll get you back there, but I'm not responsible for whatever happens after that." Shawn glanced at the bartender and then back at me. I guessed that was who provided access to the velvet-covered door. "Who is your friend?"

I debated on not telling him but didn't think the information would be that critical. Kale was a regular here anyway.

"Kale Sinclair. I work with him. He's needed for something." I fudged a little on my reasons, but Shawn didn't need to know.

He suddenly had this look of recognition, and he gave a little laugh that surprised me. "Oh Kale, yeah, he's been here a lot lately. I'll take you to his room."

Shawn turned away towards the bar, and I followed him, feeling the eyes on me from behind. The bartender never even looked at us twice before handing a room key over to Shawn. I guess regulars had an all access pass.

Kale had his own room? Was it just me, or was that kind of disturbing?

When Shawn approached the black curtain, my breath caught in my lungs, and adrenaline rushed forth to set my heart racing. I was nervous and completely unable to hide it. This was so not my domain.

Before sweeping the curtain aside, Shawn turned to me, a pensive look on his face. "I'll take you to his room and then go to this one." He held up the key in his hand. "After fifteen minutes, I'm coming out, so you have to make it quick."

I studied him, scanning for any reason not to put my trust in him, at least temporarily. "Thanks Shawn. I appreciate this."

He cast a wry smile over his shoulder at me. "No problem. Just make sure to put me on Arys' do-not-harm list." He chuckled slightly, going silent when he pulled back the heavy curtain.

I really didn't think he was joking though, and I made a mental note to do my best to do just that, as long as he was true to his word and didn't somehow screw me over.

The curtain led us into a small foyer-type area. There were chairs and a small table off to one side and an ashtray and mini bar to the other. A hallway branched off either side of the foyer, a red carpet leading the way.

Wall sconces hung with candles burning to light the way down the dark halls. Paintings hung along the way, but otherwise, the halls were dark and bare. Shawn turned to the right, and I felt my skin begin to crawl.

I followed him down the hall, noting the numbers on the doors. On this side, they were odd, going one, three, five and so on. I assumed the even numbers were the opposite way. Shawn stopped suddenly between doors, his voice low as he whispered.

"Number thirteen is Kale's. I'll be in seventeen. Remember, fifteen minutes." Before I could reply, he had continued down the hall and disappeared into the dark.

The door closest to me was number seven, so I had a few more to go. As I drew closer to Kale's room, I began to get increasingly anxious. I was a fit of nerves when I stood outside, staring at the number on the door. There was a strange energy in the hall that bit at my skin like angry red ants.

The hallway was so silent that I imagined each room to be soundproof. Either that, or there was something going on in these rooms that I did not want to know about.

I steeled my nerves, knowing that it was now or never. I raised my hand to knock but never even came close to landing the motion before the door jerked open, revealing a pale young woman with red hair, clad in a silky nightgown. Her neck was an assortment of red, swollen bite marks.

I stared at her in shock, and my words died before I'd given voice to them.

Chapter Two

I gaped openly at her, my tongue tied as I tried to spit some words out. She eyed me with an obvious disdain, and I resisted my sudden urge to grab her by the throat.

"What do you want?" she asked with contempt heavy in both her tone and expression.

Before I could answer, Kale's voice rang out from behind her. "I told you to let her in." The red head glared at me, but it was a pathetic attempt. I'd seen worse.

Despite the fact that she didn't want to, she moved back to allow me entrance. I stepped into the room, afraid of what I would see. The room was dark, lit only by two matching candles in a fancy iron candelabrum that sat on the small night table near the bed. The air was thick with an aggressive energy that lingered almost painfully.

The carpet was more of the same from the hall. Everything was laid out just like a hotel room would be. A table with two chairs stood in one corner, a bathroom and a bureau adorned with alcohol, bottled water and small snack items completed the room. I didn't like it one bit.

"Kale?" I couldn't hide the worry in my tone. I cast a glance around while his donor continued to give me a death glare. I really wanted to slap her. "We need to have a little chat, buddy."

Kale was lying in the bed amid black, satin sheets and a furry, zebra print comforter. I had never seen him quite like this, and it scared me. He appeared to be nude, the sheets shoved down to his waist. His bare chest was firm, well built.

I didn't like the look he wore. His different-colored eyes bore the look of a junkie soaring as high as he could get. He'd been born with heterochromia iridium, a gene condition that results in mismatched eyes. One was deep brown while the other was a pale blue. The effect was magnificent but, at the moment, a little eerie.

"Alexa, come in. Close the door behind you." At his sudden gesture, the door closed behind me on its own before I'd even moved. This was not quite going how I'd imagined. The energy soaked atmosphere picked at my flesh.

I stared at the vampire in the bed, more than aware that I was dealing with a side of Kale that was not the usual for me. I completely ignored the red-haired woman standing beside me, staring like she knew whom she was dealing with. Of course, being a human, she had no idea of what I was.

"Kylarai is really worried. You need to leave here ... now." I wasn't going to take no for an answer.

My best glare was lost on him. The smile that adorned his handsome face reminded me of every vampire I've tangled with right before he goes for the bite. It was almost as evil as it was predatory, and it did not look right on Kale. It was nerve wracking, and I found myself on the defensive.

"Kylarai worries about everything," he said, waving a hand as if to draw me closer. I didn't budge from where I stood near the door. "I'm sure I haven't been here that long."

"If you don't know how long you've been here, then that's too long. Come on, I'm taking you home." I had to resist the urge to cover my nose. The room reeked of sweat and blood, among other things.

Kale sighed and ran a hand through his short, dark brown hair. It was just a few shades lighter than black and messy, like it hadn't been washed or combed in days. He looked away from me, down at the zebra blanket in his lap. When he looked up again, I saw a semblance of the Kale I knew behind his eyes.

"Jennifer, it would be best if you left now. I'll give you a call." He gave her a look that struck me as odd. It was almost pleading. He was hoping she wouldn't make a scene.

"What?" Her voice was flat, like she couldn't believe what she was hearing. "Just like that, I'm out of here? I spend three days in here with you, and as soon as the next one shows up, I'm dismissed? That's fucked, Sinclair."

I stood back and waited for the awkward moment to pass. I hated being part of someone else's drama. I watched Kale roll his eyes at her, motioning to where her clothing lay tossed on the back of a chair.

I cleared my throat, drawing their attention to me. "I'd just like to say that I am not a donor. I work with Kale. This is about business."

Jennifer scrutinized my tight corset and killer heels before nodding as if she knew all too well. "It's always business with Kale."

She grabbed the clothes off the back of the chair and stormed into the bathroom, slamming the door behind her and muttering a series of muffled curses. I stared at Kale, expecting some kind of serious explanation.

He met my eyes, and I was sure I saw the flicker of total humiliation hidden in the depths of his carefully constructed vampire gaze. It was quickly replaced with irritation.

Something in me did not like this situation. I realized that, though I wasn't afraid, I was wary. Something wasn't right. I again had the sensation of being prey in this place, something the wolf in me detested. I am a predator by nature, even more so since I'd formed a permanent metaphysical bond with a vampire. I didn't appreciate being looked at as if I were lower on the food chain.

The sound of running water and drawers slamming came from the bathroom. Jennifer didn't seem too happy about being asked to leave. I would have been glad to take off right then myself.

"You shouldn't have come here, Alexa." Kale cast a glance around for a robe, which he spotted on the chair a few feet away. "It's dangerous here. You're like a dose of premium fuel in a place that only has regular. Someone will fixate on you in a heartbeat."

I watched him slip from the bed in one fluid motion, pulling the robe secure around his slender but firm frame. Kale was certainly a sweet sight on most days, but right now, I was more interested in my safety than his lean physique.

"So I've discovered. But, it was either me or Kylarai, so be grateful for small blessings." *That you don't deserve*, I added silently.

Now that he was out of the bed, his presence seemed to grow. It was intimidating. I stood my ground when he came towards me, my pulse quickening in my veins.

"Why are you so nervous?" He asked softly, leaning in to reach behind me, to the hook on the back of the door where his finely pressed pants hung.

When he closed the short distance between us, I could feel the energy trickling from him to tickle me wherever it touched. I rubbed my arms but didn't step away from him like I wanted to.

"Why do you think?" I looked up into his intense light and dark eyes, more than a little concerned. "You're wired. Been doing a little binging, huh?"

Kale's pupils were dilated. They shone with a strange, translucent shimmer. He made no attempt to get out of my personal space, and that instantly raised a red flag for me.

"I wouldn't hurt you. You're not food to me. You know I see you as an equal." His words said one thing, but his actions said another. His clothing hung forgotten in one hand; his gaze transfixed on my throat, despite the choker I wore.

"Then why are you thinking about what I taste like, Kale? I think you need to take a step back." I was careful not to move too much, cautious to avoid doing anything to set him off. I wanted so badly to gather the energy at my core in case I needed sudden defense, but if I did, he'd know.

He gave his dark head a slight shake before turning away from me. His energy grew strained; his sudden distress caused the power level in the room to rise further.

"Dammit, Jennifer! Get out of the bathroom and get out of here. I don't have time for your dramatics right now." I'd only heard that vehemence in his tone when we were hunting to kill.

I had a hard time believing he really found the awkward donor thing to be worth the hassle. It made me kind of glad that Arys frowned upon this lifestyle. I don't think I could handle him becoming this involved with random women who were supposed to serve one purpose only.

When Kale glanced my way again, the shame was evident in his eyes. Maybe there was a really good reason he chose this way. I knew he'd been forced into a lot of things in the past, things that were beyond evil. I was clearly getting the feeling that there was much more to Kale's preferences than I wanted to know. He was pushing it with this binging. It was junkie behavior and not at all healthy.

The angry sounds coming from the washroom filled the strange silence. Kale stood staring at the door as if he really didn't know what to do with himself. He seemed to be fighting a battle within himself, one he was bound to lose, again. Perhaps that was it right there; he enjoyed the pleasure that came with giving in.

I could relate to that. After Arys and I had bonded our energy, we'd ended up sharing both our strengths and weaknesses. I'd slaughtered a man during a moment of uncontrollable bloodlust. There hadn't been much left of him when I was done. Of all the things I've ever had to deal with, the affliction of the vampire's hunger was the most terrifying.

Feeling odd, I cleared my throat. "Look Kale, just get dressed, and I'll drive you home."

He banged on the bathroom door, avoiding direct eye contact. "What about my car?" As an afterthought he added, "It's still out there, right?"

"Yeah, we'll deal with it."

The door to the bathroom swung open, and Jennifer strode out, a small overnight bag in her hand. "Have fun with your newest flavor, Kale. Don't call me anymore. You're much too back and forth for me. That's not what I'm here for."

Kale sighed but only muttered, "Good riddance." I couldn't help but wonder about the tension between them. I thought this was supposed to be some sort of business arrangement, like high-class prostitution.

The glare that Jennifer shot me was pure venom, and she even dared to go so far as to shoulder her way past me. I grabbed her elbow, reacting without thinking about it. Before she could reach the door, I had her pressed up against it.

In one blink my brown eyes went from human to wolf and four sharp incisors filled my mouth, two on the top and bottom. I growled into her face, a jolt of excitement filling me as the fear rolled off her skin.

"I am not whoever or whatever you think I am. And, the next time you step out of line with me, consider yourself dead." I smiled as I spoke. "Because I don't stop at just a little."

The color drained out of her face, and she nodded her head vigorously. Her eyes were wide with horror as she stared at my fangs. They were twice as long as any vampire's, a good two inches or more. Vampire fangs are sharp and extend an inch or so longer than the rest of their teeth all the time. Mine only show up when the wolf comes out.

Jennifer didn't dare squeak a word. Though I felt Kale's high-strung energy behind me, he never moved to intervene. Smart vampire.

When I decided she knew I meant business, I let her go and stepped back. She stunk like wounded prey, and I wanted her to leave before any of Arys' temptations got the better of me.

The door slammed in my face upon her hasty exit, and I physically had to resist the instinctual urge to follow her. My body hummed with energy that was quickly growing. I'd need a release soon, like the impact of a good chase, or risk the consequences of building up too much, too fast. Ten deep breaths didn't make me feel much better.

"I am not prey in this place. Don't ever compare me to humans that ask for it again." My voice shook slightly as I rode a wave of adrenaline.

Kale seemed to think before speaking, choosing his words carefully. "Alexa, you know I never meant that. This place can be dangerous to anyone."

"Obviously, Kale," I replied, the words flying off my tongue. "Look at what it's done to you."

Was that a low blow? Maybe just a little bit. But, I was ticked that all of the crazy-ass power in this place was tempting me and his weakness had brought me here in the first place. That, and my concern for both him and Kylarai. I was there because I cared, but that didn't mean that I had to be happy about it.

Without another word, Kale slipped soundlessly into the bathroom and closed the door. I felt like a jerk, but someone had to say it. I'm pretty well known for being the one to say what we're all thinking when everyone else chickens out. True, it didn't earn me many friends, but I'm not the type to fake nice when something needs to be said.

While Kale was busy dressing, I tapped out a fast text message to Ky to let her know I was with him. Then, I placed a call to have Kale's car towed safely back to his house. No way was I letting him out of my sight. Not until he was home and the sun was up.

There was a squeak as the bathroom door opened and Kale stepped out. Fully dressed, hair smoothed into place, he almost looked like the version of himself that I was used to dealing with.

I was painfully aware of the new and strange tension between us. It was both foreign and unwelcome. I had to say something.

"I'm sorry, Kale. I shouldn't have said anything. It's not my place." My apology sounded forced. At least, it did to me.

He waved it away and began to gather his wallet from where it lay open on the table. Money spilled out, and I wondered how much these vampires were handing out for a lame re-creation of the real deal.

I knew firsthand that the true thrill of the chase, the ecstasy and release that came with the kill could never be duplicated. Kale clearly had enough problems without me laying on the guilt trip. He wasn't my boyfriend.

"I don't expect you to understand everything I do. I know how utterly insane this must look to you." His usually melodic tone was listless and dull. "This has been a hard week for me. I think it's the target I killed for Veryl last week." He paused and glanced around the untidy room.

Veryl Armstrong was our go-to guy for the nasty targets that we get paid to take out. Most of what we do involves policing our own supernatural society as it co-exists alongside human society. If sunrise came and some numb-nuts vampire hadn't exposed us all with his thoughtless actions, then we'd done our job. Being touted as fictional has its advantages, and we'd like to keep it that way. The few humans that knew the truth, like the ones here, were clearly little threat: disposable and not likely to be believed by anyone they were dumb enough to tell.

"What do you mean?" I was disturbed by the haunted glow behind his eyes. I was more than ready to leave, but I didn't want to rush him.

The power rolling off him was steady and natural but stronger than usual. It was chipping away at what remained of my self-reserve. All of this vampire energy was stirring the vampire magic that lay coiled like a snake within me, bonded to my very being.

Kale did a final sweep of the room before striding to the door, stopping when his hand hit the cool, solid metal knob. "This vampiress I hunted, she just looked so much like ... her."

His voice trailed off, but I knew whom he was talking about, the one who had turned him. She'd almost broken him. I knew enough of his past to know that it was a miracle he'd come out the other side of it with his sanity intact. His inclination to slake his blood hunger with willing donors had a lot to do with the things she'd made him see and do.

"She wasn't though, Kale. You should have gone to Kylarai." I imagined the predatory look in his eyes when I'd come in and thought better of that suggestion. "Or me or Lilah. But, I do understand why you do this." I gestured to the room before laying a hand on his arm. "I'm the last person in the position to judge."

I laughed lightly in hopes of relaxing the strained mood. It managed to get me a smile out of him, which I took to be a good sign. Kale and I are friends, but we don't share the level of intimacy reserved for extremely close friends. I have that with Ky and sometimes Jez. I was more than a little uncomfortable in this situation.

"I do love her, Alexa," he said suddenly, the door open just a crack as he held it. "Kylarai has come to hold a very special place in my life."

I opened my mouth to tell him that he didn't owe me any explanations. Before I could get a word out, he continued in a rush.

"I just want you to know that. Because I know you only came in here for her." He shook his head slightly, as if searching for a thought.

A loud bang followed by a shriek came from the room next door, and I jumped. Everything about this place was getting creepier by the second. Kale was completely unfazed by it.

"Kale," I said, wanting to get straight to the point. "Don't think for a minute that I think badly of you. I know you're one of the good guys. Trust me when I say, you don't even come close to comparing with some of the assholes out there. Now, let's get the hell out of here before I lose my mind."

It bothered me that Kale worried about my opinion of him. Maybe he needed to do a little soul searching, examine his opinion of himself.

He was absolutely adamant that we leave through the back exit. I can't say I was especially fond of walking through the club again, but his resistance piqued my curiosity.

When we left the room, the first thing I noticed was the horror movie-style quiet in the hall. There was no sign of Shawn or anyone else for that matter. I followed Kale back the way I'd come. Instead of turning to the door with the velvet curtain, he went all the way down to the other end of the even numbered hall.

We had almost reached the exit door at the end, when door number sixteen burst open and a giggling mid-forties woman came out followed by a large African Canadian vampire.

The guy was large enough to bench press my petite frame with one arm, I was sure. I caught his attention immediately as he identified what I was. His dark eyes went from me to Kale, and a grin revealed white teeth, his fangs drawing my eye.

"Kale, buddy. How did you get so lucky?" He winked and nodded at me as if I wasn't listening. "Prime pickings, my friend."

Kale appeared flustered, eyeing the exit door. "Indeed, Justin. However, those pickings are most certainly not mine." He looked embarrassed, and I started to feel my patience slipping.

The big vampire studied me; the brunette at his side, now quiet in speculation. I met his eyes evenly, unafraid.

"What are you?" He asked suddenly, catching me off guard.

"What?" I gaped at him. "You know what I am."

He didn't move, just continued to stare at me. I had the sensation that he was analyzing my energy, much the way one would slowly pick apart a sip of fine wine.

My mind was reeling. I needed out of this moment, now. Nobody had asked me what I was in months. The last man to do so had been my former Alpha, Raoul Roberts. The same night that he'd said it, I had watched as his daughter killed him.

Raoul had been the first man I'd ever fallen in love with. He had also been the first man to break my heart. If that was all he'd done, I could have gotten over it. I'd learned soon after his death that he had been the one that murdered my family after having an affair with my mother. He was directly responsible for the attack that infected and turned me.

Those same words, "What are you?" they haunted my dreams. That question was one of the last things Raoul had said to me before he died. Now, here was this big, scary vampire asking the same thing.

He was looking at me with a mix of interest and confusion. "Oh, I know what you are Huntress." He gave me a wink and a chuckle that made my spine tense. "But, there's something else there. Something undead."

His words almost caused my heart to stop. Shawn hadn't had a clue until I had thrown a little power around. Justin was clearly more perceptive and a lot more intimidating.

I smiled and shook my head. I wasn't going to be coerced into giving up my secret.

Kale cleared his throat and said, "We really should be going."

We made as if to move, and Justin held up a hand. "Tell me."

I did not like the commanding tone he used. Who the hell did he think he was to demand from me?

"Come on, Justin, lay off." Kale reached to draw me closer in a protective gesture.

The hallway was stifling, and I began to crave some fresh air. Justin glared at Kale, and I sensed the unspoken challenge. With an exasperated sigh, I held up a hand, forming a perfect psi ball with little more than a thought. It glowed with swirling traces of my gold and Arys' midnight blue energy.

Justin's eyes widened, but his lady friend didn't react. Only humans with an incredible sixth sense can see energy. I'd been one of them once. It was much the same with Weres. Vampires were the exception, as increased psychic abilities came as part of the package, though it varied by vampire.

I made no further motion, simply showing him the ball and then allowing it to drop. Kale stiffened as the vampire and wolf energy buzzed around us. Together, it created something much bigger than either Arys or I was on our own.

"You shouldn't have done that." Kale breathed the words in my ear. His nervous glance at the occupied rooms around us set my heart to racing as I realized how stupid what I'd just done was.

"Arys Knight," Justin said, nodding as if he'd known all along and had just wanted confirmation. "You're prettier than he let on. I can see why he's been trying to keep your identity quiet. I wouldn't let a tasty little thing like you become common knowledge either."

Was that supposed to be flattering? And, how in the hell did all these vampires know one another? Small world.

"Um, thanks." I frowned, unable to humor him.

"We really need to go." Kale jerked into action, pulling me with him as he pushed open the door to the parking lot beyond. "Justin, have a lovely night."

The bigger vampire watched us pensively but didn't attempt to stop us. The look he wore was so curious, so eager that I felt the grip of panic tighten my chest. Was I safe from these vampires because of my bond with Arys? Or, was I in more danger than I realized?

I gulped in the fresh night air, feeling like I had just escaped prison. "How do these vampires know who I am? I'm sure I don't have a reputation that precedes me." If there was a slight tremor in my voice, it wasn't a coincidence.

The parking lot was empty of people. The tow truck hadn't come for Kale's car yet. The street noise carried to us as we walked toward it from the back of the building. I was so relieved to be out of there.

"That's debatable, but I think you underestimate your vampire, Alexa. To you, he may come off as some small town vamp lurking in the alleys behind your local hangout. But here in the city, he's a bigger player than I think you're aware of." He looked at me almost apologetically, and it made me feel naïve. I had no idea what Arys was up to when away from me, but I had a feeling that I was in the dark on a lot.

"How so?" When he headed towards his car, I steered him away with a gentle hand, back toward the front street. "It'll be towed. I'm taking you home. And, I didn't know you and Arys ran in the same circle. Neither of you mentioned knowing the other before last summer."

He made a noise of exasperation. "There was nothing to mention. Arys is notorious in this city for being the kind of guy you tiptoe around if you don't want to get killed. He has a tendency of making sure everyone weaker than him knows it."

That I could certainly believe. "So, who isn't weaker than Arys?" His cocky attitude was nothing new to me, but it sounded like a recipe for trouble.

Kale fixed me with a serious gaze that betrayed the monster behind his eyes. "For a long time, very few. Since he has been bound to you, nobody."

I couldn't believe what I was hearing. "Really?" We walked around to the front of The Wicked Kiss where we cut down half a block and waited for the traffic lights to change. "Why does that give me a bad feeling?"

The crosswalk light lit up, and we crossed to where my red beast of a car sat. I was itching to talk to Arys now. He was going to get us into deep shit.

"If it makes you feel any better, it's not like he can hide it from the rest of us. Neither of you can. I was aware of it the moment I was in your presence after you forged your bond." Kale paused to watch the tow truck that turned into the lot of the vampire club. I could see the concern etched on his fine features. "I don't think it endangers you as much as it strengthens you."

I was starting to think that my world wasn't as broad as it needed to be. I didn't know nearly enough about the goings on of vampire society despite my romantic and metaphysical entanglement with one. The fact that I was also bonded to nature as well as deeply involved with my fellow werewolf, Shaz Richardson, was keeping me immersed in the world of Were to the point of ignorance.

I unlocked the Charger and climbed in, Kale mirroring my action on the other side. Worry nagged at the back of my mind. I'd been an idiot to think Arys and I had something we could keep under wraps like a superhero disguise.

Kale was quiet during the drive across the city to his south side home. I turned the radio up to break the silence because I really wasn't sure what to say. We'd just come to a stop at a red light when he spoke, startling me in the quiet.

"The things that she made me do, Lex; I can't stop flashing back to it. To how good it felt even as I hated myself for loving it." His fingers gripped the door handle, and he stared out his window, but I don't think he was seeing what lay beyond it. "All I can think about is stalking a pretty young thing, letting the hunger build to the breaking point, the need for release. It's been so many years since I've savored the power of life filling that void deep down. But, sometimes it feels like just yesterday that I bled someone from a vein in every body part while they begged me to stop. And damn, it was good."

I risked a glance at him but couldn't see the expression he wore. Memories could be a powerful thing. Arys' memories had caused me to attack Shaz. They had a tendency to turn up in my dreams more often than I'd like.

I cleared my throat, a nervous anxiety growing in my stomach. "Maybe you should talk to Veryl. Maybe he can help you deal with this."

He laughed bitterly. "Veryl is the last person to go to when it comes to not being ruthless. The guy is a madman. He's already told me what a fool I am for frequenting a place like the Kiss."

Then maybe you should just kill someone and get it over with before you lose your mind, I thought. I refused to give voice to the thought though, knowing it was the predator in me talking, not the humanity.

I wasn't sure if it was a good thing or not that Veryl was currently out of town, along with a few others that we work with. They'd gone to look into some strange activity in a neighboring city, leaving us to pick up the slack and keep each other out of trouble. Hopefully.

"How do you keep from losing it in a place like The Wicked Kiss?"

"With plenty of practice and a few prayers," he sighed and picked at a loose string on the seat cover. "I'd be lying if I said nobody has ended up dead in that place."

"Maybe you shouldn't go there for awhile. Why not pick off a few of the johns that pick up the teenage prostitutes or something? It's not like they're doing society any favors." It sounded harsh, but it's true.

"I know, but I'm not sure I could stop there. The things that bitch did to me; it goes so much deeper than killing. It's all about the joy, the satisfaction of the terror and the screams." Though he continued to stare out the window, I could tell by his tone that he now wore a smile as he spoke. "Oh, the screams, I think that's got to be the part I miss the most."

The first trace of true fear settled into the pit of my stomach. The lilt to his voice oozed desire for bloodshed and death. Goosebumps broke out on my skin, and I took a deep, calming breath.

"Kale? Are you alright?" I hated asking. It seemed like the perfect opportunity for him to say something I didn't want to hear.

A long silence was followed by his voice, low and wickedly smooth. "Did you know your blood smells like pine and earth? And, feels like power? More power than any werewolf should ever have."

If I thought I was already anxious, I was full blown alarmed now. I turned into his neighborhood, desperately trying to maintain my cool. Every instinct I had told me to pull over and get out of the car.

"Power that I'm not afraid to use." I murmured the warning as the small hairs along the back of my neck bristled.

"The best victims are the ones that fight the hardest." He turned to me then, his pupils so huge his eyes appeared to have no color but black. "Please, don't tempt me. Everything in me is aching to feel that hot, wolf energy roll over me. All it would take is one bite."

I met his eyes defiantly. I had no choice. There was no way I was playing the victim. "Don't make me kick your ass, Kale."

"I think you might have to." The scent of fear filled the interior of the car. Kale was afraid of himself. If he lost control, this was going to go from bad to worse.

Another two blocks, and we'd be at his house. Could we make it that far without killing each other?

"Don't." My voice was sharp with warning, laced with the gruffness of wolf. "You didn't come this far to be taken out by a friend, did you?"

The last thing I wanted to do was hurt Kale. But, knowing that he was thinking about hurting me made me ready to do so. We rounded a bend in the road. I could see his house looming dark and foreboding at the end of the street.

"That sounds like a challenge to me," he replied viciously, and I knew that I'd lost him.

Before I could reply or react, he'd crossed the small space between us. His breath was hot against my face, and as I struggled to avoid him, the car swerved from one side of the road to the other, tires squealing. I let out a small cry and threw up a hand to ward him off while trying to control the car with the other.

He fought for my throat; his fingers dug into the arm I held between us. I slammed on the brakes, bringing the Charger to a screeching halt. The moment I tapped into it, the energy rose and, I concentrated on forcing him back with it. There wasn't enough space in the car for a full on attack, and I had no choice but to be physical as well.

Because I was wedged between the steering wheel and my seat, I couldn't move much. He was fighting to bare my throat while I shoved against his chest with all that I had.

"Kale, stop! You don't want to do this." I succeeded in landing a blow to the side of his face, but he never flinched.

His eyes were large and black as sin as they focused in on the pulse leaping beneath my flesh. With both hands tightly squeezing my upper arms, he jerked me roughly to him. The gearshift dug into my hip, and a frustrated growl erupted from me.

In a swift motion, he'd stripped me of the leather choker and tossed it aside. My panic grew as I started to think this might really be it for me. My seatbelt held me trapped, but it also prevented him from dragging me out of my seat.

My mind tried to make sense of the flurry of scents and sensations. Like I'd done with Shawn in the bar, I concentrated and tossed just enough energy to paste him against the passenger door. Once he was off me, I focused the power on keeping him right where he was while fumbling with my seatbelt.

In his blood-crazed state, he took everything I threw at him. When he grasped my wrist and jerked me hard, I grabbed my door handle uselessly with my free hand. Before I could stop him, he brought bared fangs to my wrist, and I watched in horror as he sunk them into my vein.

It hurt, and there was no pleasure in the sting of his needle sharp teeth buried within me. The touch of his tongue brought a snarl from me as he probed the wound. Instinct took over, and I swung my free fist, connecting with his temple.

When I couldn't free my bleeding wrist, the adrenaline pumped hard and fast. The fifth blow I landed was perfect, and the vampire finally slumped over in his seat, unconscious.

I was examining my injured arm when the tow truck pulled up to the house with Kale's classic Chevy.

Chapter Three

The adrenaline rush had me shaking, and the cool October wind bit at my skin. I leaned against the hood of my car, trying to catch my breath.

After the tow truck driver had unloaded Kale's car and left, I'd wasted no time in vacating the confines of my car. I wrapped my wrist in a piece of gauze from the first aid kit I kept in the trunk. The bleeding had stopped, but the pain throbbed all the way to my elbow.

An SUV drove past me and parked in the neighbor's driveway. I ignored the driver's curious look.

Wrestling the dead weight of the vampire inside his house had proved much harder than I'd assumed. Despite having the strength of several humans, I had a hard time getting him to the front door without dropping him on his skull.

A nice bruise had blossomed on Kale's temple where I'd hit him. It wouldn't last long, but I felt bad regardless.

He was starting to come around when I dumped him in his pitch-black basement bedroom. He would be safe. I wasted no time flying up the stairs and out the door before he was fully conscious, just in case.

It didn't take long to reach the main highway that would take me to Stony Plain, the small town outside of Edmonton that I was proud to call home. Deep breaths and good tunes on the radio helped me relax, but there was an unease that would not leave me.

Kale was someone I pictured to be in control, a keep-it-together kind of guy. What he'd done tonight had completely destroyed that illusion, exposing the true struggle beneath that cool persona.

When the classic hair-metal station switched to the next song, a sense of panic gripped my heart. The Cinderella song that came through the speakers now held more meaning than it ever should have. In the last three months, I'd been turning the station when the rock band came on. For some reason, I found myself wanting to leave it on now.

It made me think of Raoul, my former Alpha and lover. I don't like things that make me think about him. It still hurt like a bitch that he had wronged me in so many ways and I hadn't gotten the chance to even the score. And, the fact that Raoul was dead didn't make us even because I hadn't been the one to kill him.

Though I hated him to the depths of my soul, I knew that it was rooted in the love I'd carried for him during my teen years. My inability to get over his rejection was what continued to burn me deep inside.

Everything he had left me in his will continued to sit untouched. I didn't know what to do with it. His house, car and more than two million dollars in savings were legally mine after the police called an end to the manhunt for Raoul. I'd been maintaining the house but ignoring the money that I did not want any part of. I knew I had choices to make regarding both.

I punched the button on the radio, switching it to Sonic, the local rock station. I growled, frustrated.

After a few good modern rock songs, I'd reached the edge of town, and the weight of my dark mood had lifted. Even though I dreaded having to tell Ky about Kale's freak out, I was psyched to see Shaz, my white wolf, my mate. A few days had passed since the last time we ran together, and I longed for it.

The sight of his little blue Cobalt in my driveway gave me a tingle in the pit of my stomach. I couldn't wait to get inside and lay one on him. His presence would also make talking to Kylarai go smoother.

I'd barely gotten the door open in the entryway when the light turned on. Both Shaz and Ky stood there with expectant expressions. Her grey eyes were incredibly anxious while Shaz looked concerned and ready to be angry at a moment's notice. In baggy skater-style jeans and a plain white t-shirt, he still rocked my world.

"Start talking," Kylarai held a hand out for my shoulder bag as I bent to untie my boots. The white bandage on my wrist caught her attention then, and she let out a little gasp. "What happened to you?"

Kicking my boots off, I sighed and gave them a weak smile. "Let's go in the kitchen, and I'll tell you. I need a drink."

They exchanged a look but followed me down the hall to the kitchen. I went the long way rather than cut through the living room. A couple of deep breaths and a glass of red wine was what I needed.

After one long, savory mouthful of my favorite wine, I pressed a warm kiss to Shaz' inviting lips. I had to resist the urge to linger. I could feel Ky's eyes on me like a weight.

I held up my wrist and said, "Kale did this." As Kylarai's eyes grew wide, I rushed on, "But, let me start at the beginning before either of you react."

In between sips of wine, I told them about my trip to The Wicked Kiss. I made sure not to leave anything out, including the creepy vibe and scary shrieks from the room next door. They listened attentively throughout as I recounted my evening.

"And, then he just lost it in the car. I could feel him slipping, but it happened so fast. I could barely fight him off and keep the car on the road." I looked back and forth between the two of them. Ky chewed a fingernail, and though Shaz appeared calm, I could see the storm brewing behind his jade green eyes. "But, Kale's ok. And, I'm ok, so ... everything is cool. Really it is."

They looked at each other as if deciding who would respond first. Kylarai looked totally ill when she spoke, her voice light and breathy. "Are you really ok? I knew I should have gone with you. Maybe I should go to him."

"You definitely should but wait. If not until tomorrow, then at least until the sun rises. Kale's running on junkie mode. He could be really dangerous, Ky." I met her gaze evenly, hoping she'd see the severity of the situation.

She shook her head, her dark brown bob bouncing. Tears welled up in her round eyes. "I'm not sure I can deal with this, Alexa. The last man in my life to suffer from addiction turned me into a punching bag until I tore his throat out. I can't face that world again."

Shaz stirred but said nothing. He patiently waited for his turn to voice an opinion.

"Sweetie, don't think like that. This is Kale you're talking about." I reached out to grasp her forearm in an affectionate squeeze. "He is not that guy. You know that."

She nodded and sniffed. "I know." The doubt in her voice was so heavy. I worried that she wouldn't be strong enough to stand by Kale through this.

I glanced at Shaz who smiled encouragement at me. It warmed my heart, and I gave him a quick wink. "If you don't want to go to him, Kylarai, then don't. You should never feel obligated to do anything you're not comfortable with."

"Me and Lex can go back there," Shaz offered, reaching to pull her close in a loose brotherly kind of hug. "Or, we can come with you if you don't want to go alone."

She seemed to consider the options but shook her head. "No. I'm going to have to stand on my own two feet. No wallowing in the past. Just moving steadily forward." Her seemingly endless positivity often made me envious. Still, I was glad to see it now.

"Ok good. But, if for even a moment, you feel uneasy or you need me, call. Promise?" I gave her a look that said I wasn't kidding. The last thing I wanted was for her to be in some kind of danger and for me not to know about it.

"Promise." She rolled her eyes at my serious expression but grinned. "I should go hit the shower so I can be ready for sunrise. I don't think leaving the house in an old flannel nightgown is going to be too fashion friendly."

When she'd gone down the hall to her room and closed the door with an audible click, I turned to Shaz eagerly. "I have been waiting for this all day." I had only to beckon to him with a finger, and he'd crossed the space between us.

His well-muscled arms slid around my waist, pressing me to him. His warm lips were soft on mine but firm, possessive. I reveled in the taste and scent of him. The pine and musky fur of wolf tugged at my instincts, and the desire to shift forms was immeasurable.

As the kiss deepened, I felt his growing passion and squirmed against him in obvious invitation. My fingers played in the softness of his naturally white-blonde hair. I pulled back to admire his perfect features with a tingle racing to my loins.

Everything about being with Shaz spoke to the soft, sensitive side of me, the side that I really didn't get to access much. He brought out my lovey-dovey nature that I enjoyed with total abandon in the moment but never openly admitted to.

I gently traced the outline of his jaw, lingering over the soft underside near his neck. I had been seeking a lot of solace in him over the last few months. And, I found something better than I'd imagined love could be. The fact that he puts up with my strange and permanent bond to a vampire, albeit begrudgingly, makes him one of a kind.

"This is exactly how I wanted to spend my night off," he whispered, nuzzling me close. His warm breath near my ear tickled, and I giggled girlishly.

"Aw, I hate when you make me laugh like a school girl." I closed my eyes and took another deep breath, loving the scent and feel of him. "I'm glad you're here. I missed you."

He held me close for a moment but then pulled back so he could look at me. "Are you sure you're ok? You don't want me to beat his ass?" His sensual lips twitched in a partial smile, but I wasn't sure he was kidding.

"Cut it out." I punched him lightly in the arm before downing the last sip of wine in my glass. "It's not like you to treat me like a damsel in distress."

"That's because you're not. This is more of a territorial thing." He grinned then, and a slight blush colored his cheeks. "Don't blame me. It's all instinct."

It was stupidly cute when he got like this. I'd be lying if I said I wasn't touched. "You're too cute. And, I love you for it."

"You better." He growled playfully and gave me a light smack on the behind. "He's the only person in the world who would get away with that and not end up on his ass. "We should go for a run. Unless you want to save that for after our naked bedroom romp?"

I laughed and grabbed some grapes from the fruit bowl Kylarai had left on the counter. Popping one in my mouth, I said, "Sounds like you've got your game plan together. I sure hope you factored in adequate time for a sufficient warm up." I winked and reached for a strawberry.

"Oh baby, you know the games never get underway until you say go." He pulled me in for another spine tingling kiss, and I held my berry forgotten. "Mm, you taste so sweet."

The slightest chill crept up the back of my neck as the vampire energy within me seemed to awaken. For a moment, I was afraid. When it came up like this, it was often accompanied by the blood hunger. Not this time though. It just swept me with a wave of cool, undead power that left me quivering.

I had to take a step away from Shaz in an attempt to clear my mind. My senses were on overdrive as I became more focused on the blood pumping through his veins, hot and sweetly Were. My movement was enough for him to take note of the change in the atmosphere.

"What's wrong?" His entire stance changed, and he reached out to touch my shoulder. "You look all sketchy. And, it's cold in here, like it gets when you're all vampy."

I nodded as I began to feel my vampire counterpart. Close ... so close. "Yeah. It's Arys." I breathed the words, groping blindly for Shaz in anticipation of the power rush I knew was coming. "I feel him."

Shaz' jade gaze narrowed in annoyance. "He's here?"

The front doorbell rang, followed by an aggressive knock on the door. What could have Arys in such a foul mood? His negativity was like the sharp slap of a rubber band. It stung in places that were not physical in nature.

"I wonder what this is all about." I turned to the hall and approached the door with Shaz hot on my heels. He hung back near the entrance to the living room, which gave him full view of the door without being obnoxiously close.

"I can just imagine," he muttered but said nothing further. Leaning against the wall, arms folded over his chest, he waited for me to open the door.

I swallowed hard as butterflies set to flight within me, their wings beating hard against my ribcage. I don't like my two lovers being in the same room for any great length of time. In fact, I go out of my way to ensure it rarely happens.

The moment I turned the door handle, a delicious tingle coursed through me. I felt guilty when my heart raced in anticipation, knowing who was on the other side.

Arys stood on the front step looking irate and out of place with Kylarai's decorative flower arrangements. His jet-black hair was a stylish mess, as usual, and the angry look he wore only served to enhance his sex appeal. A black t-shirt and blue jeans may have looked casual on anybody else, but it hugged him like a drool-worthy second skin. He gnawed lightly on the metal ring that glinted off to the side of his lower lip, one of a handful of piercings he had.

"Alexa." He strode inside so fast I had to step out of his way to avoid getting run down. "What were you doing at The Wicked Kiss?"

The vampire didn't even glance at Shaz. His midnight blue eyes bore into me, making me uncomfortable. With the barest twitch of his fingers, the door swung shut behind him.

"What do you mean? I was there to see Kale." As my defenses kicked in I added, "What's it to you, anyway?"

The look he shot me was incredulous, and he flashed fangs to emphasize it. There was less than two feet of space between us. I resisted the urge to take a step back.

"What's it to me? Are you trying to get yourself killed? You should have told me that you wanted to go in there." It was then that he caught sight and scent of my injury. Capturing my arm in his tight grasp, he brought it closer for inspection. "Kale did this. Why?"

For the second time I retold the events of my evening. When I finished, Arys dropped my wrist and swept past me into the living room. He had to pass Shaz in the process, giving him the slightest of nods.

"Why did you let her go there alone?" Arys suddenly rounded on the fair-haired wolf with a blazing heat in the depths of his hypnotic stare. "Have neither of you the slightest inclination as to how dangerous, not to mention stupid, that was?"

My skin began to prickle in response to him. Though I was quickly losing my temper, a part of me enjoyed it.

Shaz merely cast Arys a look of utter disdain. "Oh, please. That's like asking why the sky is blue. It just is. And, so is Alexa. I'm not her keeper, and neither are you."

"No," Arys retorted. "Just the one that feeds her fire and makes her a desirable target. As the one who claims to love her, you do a poor job making it apparent."

"Hey!" I tried to step between them, but Shaz came away from the doorframe fast, angrily stepping up to glare into the vampire's face.

"I'm not the one endangering her here, pal; you are." They both ignored my attempt to get their attention as they stared into each other with a fury I could taste like bitterness on the back of my tongue. Shaz' voice took on an edge I rarely heard from him. "Don't ever speak to me about love. You don't have a clue what it is if it doesn't come with sex and blood. All you are to Alexa is a parasite. A fucking parasite that has done her more harm than good. Never speak to me again about love or protection. You're clearly out of your area of expertise."

The tension in the room was thick enough to suffocate. I realized that this situation was quickly spiraling out of control. It was only a matter of time until these two tore each other apart. I was hoping it wouldn't be here and now.

"Excuse me." I had to raise my voice to get their attention, but neither risked taking their eyes off the other. "I am not someone who appreciates being treated like an object. This is going to stop, or I'm through dealing with either of you."

It wasn't a big threat, but one that had me shaking as it spilled from my lips. Unable to think clearly, I stormed from the room through the adjoining entry to the kitchen. My intent was to leave the house through the sliding glass doors into the backyard. From there, I just wanted to drop to all fours and run like the wind.

Before I could clear the kitchen, a cool hand gripped my elbow and whirled me around. Arys' intoxicating scent of cologne and hair products hit me, and my stomach muscles clenched in response. As mad as I was at him, the power that we shared had a mind of its own when we were together.

"Don't you see how worried you had me? There are so many vampires in that place that would never pass up a chance to hurt me by hurting you." His voice had softened, but the storm in his eyes didn't cease.

"I know that. I figured it out within minutes of my arrival. Although, if you'd bothered to mention it to me before, this conversation wouldn't be happening." I pulled my arm from his grasp but didn't turn away. "So don't come in here and talk to me like I'm a child to be coddled. And, you do not get off talking to Shaz like he's a footstool. Got it?"

Arys clenched his jaw; his hands tightened into fists. "You are so frustrating, wolf. Have it your way … as usual."

That last little shot really picked at me, but I'd save the response I had for a time when it was just the two of us. His comment wasn't missed by Shaz, though, who frowned from where he stood.

"I'm really not in the mood to deal with this right now. Whatever your problem is, it has nothing to do with Shaz, so leave him out of it."

Arys' deathly energy danced around me so that my own power rose up to meet it. I stifled a small gasp when the two energies mingled to make one that shocked me to the core.

"Anything you wish, my love." He whispered the words, but they struck a chord in me anyway. Despite his agreeable tone, there was evident strain in his voice. I knew that he was dying to touch me. I could sense it.

"I need to shift. I'm irritable, and the full moon is only a week away. So, this conversation will have to wait. I'm not about to argue with you over where I'm allowed to be and when." I shoved past him and slid the kitchen door open wide.

"That is not what this is about, and you know it." His voice rose as he followed me out on to the back deck. "This is about you being in serious danger every time you go near that place."

Something about the way he said it piqued my curiosity. I studied him hard, trying to make him squirm. It didn't work. My opponent had been playing this game far longer than I.

"What's going on, Arys? What is it that you don't want to tell me?" I leaned against the deck railing and fixed him with a deadly glare. "Don't screw with me. I know you're packing more heat than any other vampire in the city."

For a split second, he looked uneasy, but a smirk banished the momentary expression. I could tell it was forced.

"Think about it, Alexa. You are the heat I'm packing. You're not safe at The Wicked Kiss. You can't blame me for being concerned."

"Are you really worried about her? Or, are you worried about what will happen to you without her?" Shaz' voice rang out from behind us. He had come to stand where he could look out at us through the open patio door.

I gave him a look, telling him to shut up. Why was he

purposely antagonizing the vampire? He met my eyes and shrugged before looking to Arys for a response.

"You seem to forget who you're dealing with, pup. I'm not going to keep my patience with you much longer."

"Oh, is that so? So, I struck a nerve. Getting too close to the truth for you, huh?" Shaz' cocky attitude was as sexy as it was shocking. I gaped open-mouthed as he practically dared Arys to take a shot at him.

"Shaz, this doesn't concern-," I started to say only to be interrupted by Arys' angry outburst.

"You know what, kid? You don't know shit about the truth." His eyes darkened until they were all pupil. The energy gathering around him was thick with menace, and I was stricken with fear.

Arys stared at Shaz with such hate that it soured my stomach. His fingertips were alive with the gold and blue of our shared power. If he dared to toss it Shaz' way, I was taking him down.

"Arys, don't even think about it," I warned. Shaz didn't look the least bit concerned. In fact, he looked downright amused.

"Let him, Lex," he said. "If he has to use metaphysical power to best me, then he's as much a man as I thought him to be."

The open invitation wasn't lost on Arys. As fast as he'd gathered the energy, he dropped it, causing the air to hum all around us. Stretching his hands out before him, he cracked his knuckles in a loud series of pops that made me wince.

"So you want to get physical with me, pup? I'm surprised it took you this long." Arys' lips drew back in a snarl, flashing sharp fangs. He made a "come hither" motion with his finger, the way one might entice a lover. "Show me what you've got. Unless it doesn't totally eat you up inside knowing that Alexa gets something from me that she can never find in you."

I wanted so badly to interject, but something told me to wait. My instinct was to gather the power close around me so it was ready at a moment's notice.

"She finds more in me than I even need to tell you." Shaz took one step forward, which brought him outside the open patio door. "Because you know. You see it. And, no matter what you think you have together, I'll always have more."

Arys was quiet as he watched my white wolf in careful

contemplation. Tilting his head to one side, he smiled and said, "If you knew the things I do with her, the ways I complete her, you'd never make the mistake of being so self-assured."

My face grew hot, and I stared at the deck beneath my feet. This wasn't getting any better. Though, Shaz was doing a great job shrugging off Arys' jibes; I had to give him credit.

"Keep talking, vampire." Shaz managed a bored expression as he ran a hand through his hair. "We both know where we really stand. Get back to me when you can run through the forest on four legs with this girl by your side, exploring the true pleasures of the earth. Like sunshine."

So, they were trying to outdo one another by playing off each other's weaknesses. Oh geez, I thought, just throw some punches already and get it over with. But, Shaz wasn't finished yet.

"Alexa and I are mates. I don't care how you come into the picture or what you think you have with her. But, I promise you that if a single hair on her head is harmed because of you, you will be truly good and dead."

As my lungs began to ache, I realized I'd been holding my breath. Neither of them looked at me, and I started to doubt that they'd notice if I went for that run.

Arys shifted slightly, a motion that indicated to me that he was ready for a fight. His eyes betrayed no emotion as he stared into Shaz.

"Ah, so quick to make promises." With a clap, he rubbed his hands together as if enjoying every excruciating second of this. He looked like the monster from every child's nightmares when he said, "Don't make promises you will never be able to keep."

In a sudden, unexpected motion, Shaz lost it. Whatever self-restraint had been holding him back snapped, and he moved faster than my eyes could follow.

The sound of his impact against Arys rang in my ears. Shaz hit him full on with all of his weight. I think Arys had been expecting a fist or maybe even some fangs because the body slam sent both of them tumbling down the deck stairs to the grass below.

The small shriek that escaped me mingled with the sound of wood splitting as they successfully trashed the railing on their way down. Shaz' snarl cut through the night followed by the heavy thud of fists on flesh.

I ran down to the bottom step, stopping frozen in my tracks. They each quickly recovered their footing, but the blows never quit.

"Stop it!" I cried uselessly. I wasn't stupid enough to step between them and risk taking a punch. "You guys, stop! Please!"

Every fist thrown had my stomach cramping. The scent of blood hit me, and I identified it as Shaz'. Blood streamed from a cut above his left eye. He lashed out with a steady hit, connecting with Arys' chin in a teeth-jarring smack. His eyes were all wolf; the whites, obsolete. All four of his fangs filled his mouth indicating that he was going from furious to wild. I felt helpless. I wasn't sure what to do, but I had to act before they killed each other. I was debating on whether or not to toss a psi ball in between them and put them both on their asses.

Suddenly, they sprang apart but slowly circled one another like caged animals. Arys licked a drop of blood from the corner of his bottom lip and beckoned to Shaz with both hands. He grinned with the worst wickedness.

"Come on, pup, is that all you got?"

"You'd like to think so." Shaz' voice was growly, and the rage emanating from him was almost hot in its intensity.

"I have had enough of this male bullshit!" I yelled, overwhelmed at how fast I was ready to take a strip out of both of them. Fangs and claws accompanied my instinct to leap in to the fray and physically make this stop.

"Come on now, Alexa," Arys spoke to me but stared into Shaz with a mocking smirk. "Don't tell me you're so naïve as to never have guessed this day would come."

"You are both acting like children." My spine buzzed as power raced through me in accordance to my emotions. I struggled not to actively tap and use it.

Shaz shifted from foot to foot, like a fighter that can't wait for the next round. A fine line of crimson trickled down the side of his face. It instantly drew my eye.

"He's right," Shaz conceded. "This was inevitable. So, let me kick his ass and get it over with. It's time this useless vampire learned his place."

Arys' left fist shot out so fast, Shaz never had a chance to block. He took the hit firm in the nose, which instantly produced another rush of blood. He never paused in his reaction as he followed up by blocking the next punch and delivering a solid temple blow with his elbow. I couldn't watch this anymore.

"Oh my God!" Kylarai burst through the patio door, her dark hair hanging in wet chunks. "I thought I heard a fight." She took one look at me standing uncertainly aside and did a double take. "What are you doing? Stop this nonsense."

Before I could reply, she'd stepped into the action. Shocked turned to impressed as she grabbed Shaz by the back of the neck, using a pressure point to bring him to his knees. With the other hand, she gave Arys a shove that sent him stumbling, arms flailing in an attempt to stay on his feet. Feeling successfully pathetic, I threw up a barrier between them, a wall of power that was as good as concrete with the right energy feeding it.

Kylarai's eyes blazed wolf in the moonlight. "If you two idiots want to kill each other, go right ahead. But, get the hell off our property first. I will smash your skulls together before I let you assholes disrupt our quiet neighborhood." She cast her predatory gaze over each of them in turn. "Now, make like good little boys and beat it before I have to remove you myself."

Shaz didn't even look up from where he kneeled on the grass. He clenched his clawed hands into fists, drawing blood from his palms. Arys stared defiantly at Kylarai but never dared to speak a word against her.

Her eyes came to land on me, flashing with an irritated fury. "You really need to deal with this crap."

I tried to swallow, but my throat was dry. This was my fault. She was totally right. I nodded, but nothing came out when I opened my mouth.

Arys huffed and walked up to my energy barrier, dissolving it with a touch. I gawked at him incredulously. It seemed that this sharing of power was becoming quite the double-edged sword. Pulling a silver key ring from his pocket, he flipped through the keys until he got to the one he wanted.

As he approached me, I sensed both Shaz and Ky stiffen. Arys paid them no attention. His right eye was black and swollen; blood oozed from a gash on his lower lip. My heart sunk. I couldn't believe these dumbasses beat each other because of me.

The mystifying vampire looked down at me from his six-foot-four frame, a fire smoldering in his eyes. In a sudden motion, he practically slapped the key into my palm.

"I'll expect you at dawn." His voice was low and rough. "If you don't show, I'll be back tomorrow night. And, it won't be pleasant for either of us."

It wasn't so much the threat that he uttered as much as it was the drowning black of his pupils. His eyes, more black now than blue, glittered with the driving force of the undead. Hunger for blood, power and control swam in those inky orbs, and I felt my defense die.

"I'll be there," I heard myself say. The urge to lick the blood from his lip was stronger than I was.

As I reached for him, he embraced me just long enough to press his lips to mine in a mind-shattering kiss. The bloody smear he left on my mouth was tantalizing, causing me to crave him like an addiction.

Before I could say or do anything, he turned on his heel and stalked from the yard. Only the sound of the gate that led to the front street indicated his exit.

I looked at Ky, expecting a motherly scolding. When she saw my defeated expression, she shrugged and went back in the house. Shaz remained where he was, and I went to him, dropping to my knees and taking his face gently in my hands.

He tried to resist at first but gave up when I wouldn't be deterred. The gash in his eyebrow was ugly and looked like it might actually scar. It should heal quickly though it continued to ooze slowly. The blood from his nose was drying and flaky. Looking into his battered face was gut wrenching, and the guilt ate at me like a disease.

"Don't baby me, Alexa." He swiped half-heartedly at me but allowed me to look closely at the ugly facial injuries.

"What were you thinking you were going to do to him?" I asked gently, hoping he didn't take offense. "I mean, what if he had fought dirty and bled you dry?"

He looked up suddenly as if I'd slapped him. A slow smile spread across his youthful face, chilling me in its intensity with those razor sharp fangs. The length and ferocity of them looked so wrong in Shaz' twenty-three-year-old face.

"There are a lot of viable possibilities when it comes to how I may bite it. But, it will never be by the hand of that goddamn vampire." His tone ended on a low growl. "Mark my words."

The energy he exuded was extremely aggressive, especially for Shaz. It tantalized my wild side, sending a shot of adrenaline through me. At the same time, when paired with his glazed predator's eyes blinking at me, I was also a little anxious.

"You scared the hell out of me." I searched him for a sign that he wasn't out of his mind. "Don't ever call him out like that again. I can't watch you two kill each other. Please, don't make me."

His touch was soft when he reached to brush the hair out of my face. I leaned in to the warmth of his fingers as he stroked the outline of my lower lip.

"Don't worry about it. We just needed to blow off steam. I doubt either of us is really intent on killing the other. Yet." The way he said it did nothing to fool me. I was starting to think that if he had the opportunity to see Arys in ashes, he wouldn't hesitate to make it happen.

"So, how about that run, hmm?" There was a glint of the wolf within Shaz when he grinned and winked a bruised eye at me. The true beast inside was so much more than the soft, sensitive Shaz that I was used to. It was strong in him now, pressing the surface.

"Are you sure you're up to it?" Looking at his injuries was more painful to me than they were to him. He seemed oblivious.

His t-shirt hit the ground, quickly followed by his jeans. "I've never felt the wolf in my blood as deliciously as I do right this moment. I wouldn't trade it for the world."

He stood against the night sky and stretched. I allowed myself a moment to take in his hard, nude body before accepting his offered hand.

My pulse raced and my face felt flush when he pulled me against him, biting my bottom lip. That act of dominance sent an excited thrill to the tips of my toes.

Shaz certainly had a tendency to get a little extra attitude going on when Arys had been around. But, this cocky edge was new. Though I found it intriguing, I also found it frightening.

"You're all pumped up from that fight. Which I'm sorry about, by the way. It shouldn't have come to that." I motioned for him to unlace the back of my corset, which he was more than happy to do.

"Don't apologize. I'm looking forward to next time." His breath came hot against the back of my neck, and I trembled slightly as the corset slipped free. The night air was soothing despite the fall chill.

Shaz made as if to cup my breasts, but I turned swiftly, capturing his hands in my own.

"Now, now," I said, stepping back to shimmy out of my pants. "Don't let the testosterone make all of your decisions. Do me a favor and don't let Arys get to you so much. I think it just empowers him."

Shaz made a sound low in his throat but didn't respond. His eyes followed my naked silhouette, hungrily and possessively. Even as he reached for me again, his fingers lengthened into massive claws. The change continued until his body was a mass of fur. In less time than it takes to blink, he was the most beautiful, white wolf.

"I'll give you a head start." I nodded to the stretch of field behind the house. A kilometer beyond that, the forest began, and with it, the tree that we always raced to. I was nearly undefeated every time.

His tongue lolled out, and he wore a look of serious contemplation. No sooner had I embraced the change and gone to my knees than Shaz shot past me, through the back gate and into the field beyond.

As the Were energy rolled over me, there was the briefest moment of agonizing pain as bones shifted and reformed, then sudden splendor on four feet. I gave a great shake and a stretch before bounding after the flash of white in the distance.

Chapter Four

I had come to count on watching the sunrise with Shaz almost every day. Those rare mornings that we do not run together feel strangely incomplete. As the sun broke over the horizon, we sipped hot coffee on the back patio.

I knew that Arys would be watching the clock tick until I got there, but I was in no immediate rush. The key to his house was in my pocket where I'd dropped it upon getting dressed into fresh clothing. Leaning against Shaz where we sat on the top step, I almost wished that I could trade Kylarai vampires. Facing Kale would have been easier than dealing with arrogant, domineering Arys.

"You'd better go soon." Shaz didn't look too enthused, but since our run, he had lightened up considerably. "I never thought I'd hear myself tell you to go to that bastard. But, you should go. Find out what the deal is with The Wicked Kiss. And, next time you want to walk into a nest of vampires, I'm going with you."

I smiled as his words warmed my heart. He never even attempted to discourage me from going back like most men would, Arys included. Instead, he offered to face potential danger alongside me rather than tell me what to do. It was just one more thing that set him apart from the rest.

"You know you're the greatest, right?" I nudged his ticklish spot with my elbow, and he squirmed.

"Yes, but keep telling me." With a laugh, he ruffled my hair so that it fell haphazardly around my face. It was something I detested, and I bit my lip in an attempt to resist flicking him in the nose.

"You don't have to leave." I pushed his hand away and finger-combed the red and blonde tangles. "I won't be long ... if you want to wait."

His face softened as he reached to twist a red strand of my hair

44

between his fingers. "Normally I would, but you shouldn't rush on my account. I think I'm going to head home and catch some Z's."

I studied the broken railing where it lay in pieces on the grass. I wondered if either of the fools planned to fix it.

"Alright, well, call me later." I paused, thoughtful. "Jez and I are going shopping for Halloween costumes later this week. What do you think I should be?"

He raised an eyebrow and grinned. "Playboy bunny. And, I'll be Hef."

I laughed outright at that. "You're in dreamland, honey. I wasn't thinking along the lines of something that skimpy."

"But, it's Halloween!" He protested as he rose to go and pulled me up with him. "Oh, I'll be back at some point to fix that railing. You can model it for me then."

"It won't be what you're thinking." I promised, ignoring the mischievous wink I received.

I followed him to the bottom step. He produced a set of keys on a Chevy keychain before leaning in to kiss me. "I'll see you later. If that vampire gets out of hand, punch him in the eye for me."

"Scout's honor." I pulled him in for one more embrace, lingering just a little.

After he had let himself out of the yard, I turned to go back in the house through the patio door. Kylarai was leaning on the kitchen counter with an anxious expression on her finely featured face.

"What's wrong Ky? You know, you don't have to go to Kale. Not if you don't want to."

She held her coffee cup in a white knuckled grip. It wouldn't be the first mug she'd broken that way. "But if I don't? What then?"

"What do you mean? He's a big boy. He'll get over it if you don't show. He may not even be expecting you." I went to the sink, depositing our coffee cups before reaching into my pocket to touch the small key. "I'd trade you vampires if I could."

She laughed bitterly and grabbed her cell phone from the top of the microwave. "I'd love to go tear a strip out of Arys for you. Especially since you won't do it."

"I will, too!" I protested, looking at her sharply.

"Oh please," she scoffed. "You let that one get away with too much. And, he damn well knows it."

It was no secret that, though Kylarai and Arys were on good acquaintance terms, she didn't understand why I bothered with him when I had Shaz. She also didn't understand that I needed him. It might be the way a junkie needs a fix, but it was undying and inescapable. It was as much a part of me as the need for water or air.

"Bah humbug," I muttered, sticking my tongue out at her. I received an eye roll and a middle finger in response.

"I'm going to get moving. If you don't hear from me by noon, send a search party."

"Very funny." I grabbed my shoulder bag and keys and turned to follow her down the hall. "I'll walk out with you. I think I'm more likely to need the search party."

I slipped a pair of casual sandals on my bare feet and locked the front door behind us. Ky's Escalade chirped as she disarmed it with the key fob. I flinched in response; my nerves, already jittery.

I gave her a wave as she backed out of the garage and onto the street. Double checking my bag for things like my phone and wallet was my way of stalling because I really didn't want to do anything but curl up in bed for a few hours. I'd been awake almost twenty-four hours.

I was also embarrassed that I couldn't even follow my own advice. I'd told Ky not to go if she didn't want to, yet here I was screwing around because I wanted to put off more dramatics with my vampire.

ಬಬಬಬ

"I didn't think you were going to show." Arys lounged in a comfy leather La-Z-Boy chair, clad in a black robe made of the softest fleece.

It was dark in the living room. Heavy curtains sealed every side of the window, effectively eliminating any trace of sunlight. The only light came from the glow of the TV. The news played with the volume low.

"You would have liked that, wouldn't you?" I crossed my arms and gave him a sly smile. "A reason to come storming over again to trash some other part of my house? I wasn't willing to take that chance."

His dark gaze followed my movements as I crossed the span of the room, purposely taking the easy chair across from him rather than the couch beside him. His jaw clenched and unclenched, and I knew that he wanted to say something. I figured I would get it out of him easier if I let it come naturally. Prodding would get me nowhere.

The energy rolling off him was heated, like he had been nursing a low-level anger while waiting to see if I'd come. It was tantalizing, teasing me with the promise of bigger things. I had half a mind to crawl up on his recliner chair and straddle him beneath me. The challenging expression on his handsome face only enhanced the urge.

"I suppose I should apologize for tearing your railing off. But, I'm not apologizing for smacking the wolf pup. He had it coming." He studied me when he spoke, as if awaiting my protest.

"You both had it coming. I hope you each got it out of your systems because if it happens again, I'm stepping in." The veiled threat wasn't missed by Arys who grinned as if enticed by it. "I'll be doing a little skull bashing. And, enjoying it."

"I look forward to it." His broad grin flashed fangs, and a shiver crawled up my spine in response.

His bruised eye was rimmed purple, and the cut on his lip was like a target that drew me. I was dying to nibble that soft tender spot, knowing that it would hurt and that he would love it.

"I'm serious Arys. I won't allow you to take another shot at Shaz without having to take one at me, too." My smile faded, and we stared at each other like the adversities that I sometimes felt we were.

He looked absolutely vicious when he bared his teeth and said, "You are so dramatic."

I laughed outright then, long and hard, with as much melodrama as I could muster. "Spare me the hypocrisy, love. Drama is a lifestyle as far as you are concerned."

"Don't pretend you don't love it." He purred like a cat, beckoning me with a finger.

My senses were blazing as they grew in intensity. The light dab of cologne Arys liked to wear invited me to get closer so that I could breathe in the heady scent of him. I resisted the instinctual need to go to him.

After the last few months, I'd gotten used to the power driven needs and urges, though there were parts that I would never get used to. I knew when the energy was the driving force and when it was worth fighting or giving in. I wasn't giving in this time.

"Be straight with me, Arys. Why do you want me to stay away from The Wicked Kiss? Because you've got more enemies than I'm aware of, or because you've got something to hide?" I sat back with my arms crossed over my chest. A toss of my head flipped a lock of hair out of my face and earned me an appraising glance from Arys.

"Perhaps both." He waved a hand in a noncommittal gesture. The sudden shift in the atmosphere had me wary. "But, the fact remains, you are not safe there. And, I won't compromise your safety."

I took a deep breath and braced myself. "It isn't yours to compromise." He narrowed his eyes, and I went on before he could release whatever retort he held ready. "I won't be told where I can and cannot go. I live my life taking risks every night. Risks that I don't see you objecting to. So, I want to know, what's with the sudden change?"

All I heard then was the weatherman giving the forecast for the next four days. Arys sat quietly, and I knew he was weighing his words, deciding what to tell me. There was mention from the TV that we most likely would not see snow until well after Halloween. That sounded good to me. Alberta winters were harsh. Starting late was always a welcome reprieve from icy roads, head colds and frozen paws.

Arys slid from the recliner with a motion as smooth as butter. His robe flashed his broad, taut chest but otherwise stayed together, thankfully. He went to his knees before me on the plush carpet so that we were at eye level. Taking my hand in his, he interlocked our fingers, sending a wave of excitement and power crashing through me. The tingle that burned in the palm of my hand traveled a steady path to my loins, which caused my heart to skip a beat.

"You are a predator that needs no assistance when it comes to you and your prey. The risks you take are of your own choosing. My concern is that you will become the hunted in a place where you're at a disadvantage. And, it will be my fault." He took my other hand then, completing a circuit so the energy flowed freely between us.

The outcome of calling a lot of power had its drawbacks. There were negative repercussions, which is why I make a point to cross the boundary only when necessary. Since Arys' hungers had become my own, I had certainly learned my lesson. The things you put out always come back with a kick in the ass. Energy is the driving force of all magic and supernatural ability. But, every action has to have a reaction, and it's rarely a pleasant one.

"I made the choice to go in there, and I made it out in one piece. It's just a damn vampire junkie bar. Don't make it bigger than it is." I smiled to lighten the mood that had settled. His expression remained stone cold serious. "I never even realized you frequented that place. You always shit talk Kale's patronage."

"I don't frequent that place. I remain firm on my opinion when it comes to feeding from the mentally unstable rush addicts in that club." He leaned in to press a brief but strangely tender kiss on my lips. The metallic ring in his lip was cool against my skin. "Look, Alexa, I'll be frank with you. I have contacts at The Wicked Kiss. But, there are a lot of people that would enjoy wiping me out. They have their reasons. I am the most powerful vampire in the city. You have helped to clarify that. Anyone that wishes me dead has been walking this earth far longer than you have. And, that fills my heart with fear."

It wasn't an easy admittance for him. I could see the strain in his pinched features. He gnawed his lower lip anxiously, grimacing when he bit the healing cut.

It went without saying that anyone possessing great power or ability of any kind was at risk. Jealousy and fear are strong driving forces behind the motives of the weak.

"Who are you worried about? It must be someone specific if you're this upset about me going to the Kiss. What's the deal?" I briefly reflected on the reactions to me when I'd been at the vampire bar. "Nobody seemed to want to do anything but snack on some potent Were blood. Until they realized I was the one they'd heard about. Then it was smooth sailing."

The conflicting emotions in Arys' eyes had me nervous. Was it possible that I'd walked right past potential death and hadn't even known it?

"Then he wasn't there. Thank God." Arys closed his eyes and murmured what sounded like a small prayer. Of everything he'd said so far, that scared me the most.

In all the time I'd known Arys, I had rarely heard him reference the big boss upstairs. Something about it set off an alarm that chilled me.

"Who? Who wasn't there?" Panic gripped me, and I squeezed his hands painfully. He seemed oblivious. "Tell me what's going on. Who the hell am I supposed to be afraid of?"

I wanted to slap him across the face like they do on television, but I was the one feeling hysterical. I'd seen a lot of crazy shit in my life, but I wasn't dumb enough to think that I was the biggest of the bad. If Arys had inadvertently endangered me, I needed to know.

"You've shared my most intimate and personal memories. You know the one vampire that I loathe more than any other." His words instantly generated an image in my mind.

When Arys and I had joined metaphysically, we had shared every piece of our past memories. It had not been pleasant. We all have something we'd never share with anyone. Arys and I no longer had that luxury. At times, we're literally inside one another. Our shared memories were mostly a blur, but the most poignant ones had a way of standing out with amazing clarity.

The image was that of a vampire that had the charm and persuasion of Bill Clinton with the distinguished forty-something appearance of George Clooney. Looks were deceiving though, and I knew he looked nicer than he was.

Harley Kayson. I knew him only from Arys' memories. And, they were far from good. Harley was a vampire with as much authority as a mob boss and about as many connections, too. He was a smooth talker with a penchant for gorgeous men in addition to his harems of women. He was the vampire that had turned Arys.

Arys had been working the streets of New York City more than three centuries ago when Harley's mistress had taken a liking to him. She was the last client Arys would ever entertain. Once Harley discovered the angelic beauty she'd brought home to play with, the greedy vampire simply had to have Arys all for himself.

Harley had envisioned the stunning, dark Arys to be the partner in crime he'd always longed for. But, despite Arys' enjoyment of the vampire lifestyle, it hadn't always been that way. Arys had been a troubled young man that resented Harley for making choices for him, especially the one to leave his human life behind. It wasn't a case of foreboding vampire syndrome but rather the fact that it hadn't been his idea. Arys was too headstrong and confrontational to be what Harley wanted him to be. He was no one's sidekick.

As far as unhealthy predator and prey relationships go, those two had one of the worst. They had parted ways on the worst of terms. Of course, Arys having burned Harley's house to the ground with his vampiress lover inside may have played a role in that.

"Why would he be in Edmonton? I thought the last time you saw him he was living in Vegas." Fear caused my spine to tingle uncomfortably. A knot formed in my throat, and my stomach hurt.

Harley was a sick bastard who divided all people into two categories: those who could be toys and those who were just food. I couldn't help but wonder which one I'd be.

"He was. And, still is." Arys stood up, pulling me with him. "Harley owns The Wicked Kiss, Alexa. That's why I don't want you there. He owns a string of them across the entire country."

I tripped over the question on the tip of my tongue. "He owns it? Thanks for thinking to share that information sooner. Are you trying to get me killed?"

"You're going to get yourself killed. And, I'm sharing it with you now." He reached out for my hand, and I surrendered it but didn't budge from where I stood.

He gave my arm a gentle tug, pulling me toward the darkened hallway and the bedroom beyond. "Come, lie with me."

"Arys, I can't." I resisted, though I wanted desperately to cling to him. "I have to go home and get some sleep."

He never let go of me, forcing me to walk along beside him. "You can sleep here. I won't bite." He raised a dark eyebrow then and grinned. "Unless you ask me nicely. And unfortunately, there's more."

"I'm not doing anything to reward your bad behavior. And, what do you mean, there's more?"

He visibly shuddered. The tangy scent of fear came off him in small traces, but it was still there. On most other people, the scent would have been enticing. On my dark vampire, it was all wrong.

"He's here because he knows about us. Being my sire, he likely sensed the changes in me despite our lack of communication. He's curious to see if I've blood bonded you." He pulled me in close so that my nostrils filled with the wonderful scent of him and placed a kiss on my forehead. "Come to bed. I just want to hold you until I fall asleep."

It was such an unexpected request that I couldn't deny it. I followed him in to the bedroom, which was even darker than the living room. It was always impeccably clean and smelled like scented candles. I knew how soft the thick black comforter was, and I began to anticipate getting under it.

Arys wasted no time dropping his robe over the desk chair in the corner. He looked like a marble statue of some great angel. I let my gaze linger over him as if he were a fine piece of artwork. When he caught me staring, he actually looked embarrassed. That's no easy feat for that vampire.

"For a girl who isn't looking for any action, you've sure got the hunger in your eyes."

My cheeks warmed as I began to take my clothes off. "Just admiring the view." I left my lacy black bra and panties on and climbed on the bed.

We sat awkwardly in the bed side by side. It occurred to me that we had never been in this room together without being in the throes of passion. When we were together, it was usually a combination of metaphysically driven intimacy and the predatory urges and gratifications we desired by nature.

It wasn't that we had no deeper emotion for each other but rather that we had never acknowledged it. The sweet romantic side of me only came out with Shaz. Likewise, the worst of my predatory nature was reserved for my time with Arys.

He moved quickly to pull me into an embrace that was as tender as it was surprising. "This is new for us."

"It is." I got settled against him so that my head was on his chest, one leg thrown over his as I snuggled into the feather soft blankets. "It's ... different."

Arys rested his head against mine, one hand idly stroking my hair. "I like it."

This softer side of him was certainly unusual. Rather than create an awkward moment by making mention of it, I chose to go with the flow. Maybe I was being too analytical, imagining this newfound sensitivity.

My mind was filled with nagging questions that wouldn't go away. Now was as perfect a time as any. When I couldn't take it anymore, I blurted out, "So tell me about the blood bond. Isn't that a vampire thing? Can it be done on mortals?"

Arys tensed beside me; his hand gripped mine tight. "Oh yes, it can be done. With extreme consequences."

I waited patiently for him to continue, flashing him an expectant look when he didn't. He relented, but he didn't look happy about it.

"A blood bond between vampires is like ... a marriage of sorts. It's a true commitment, one that you truly can't escape until death. It forms a permanent telepathic link between both parties. Vampires rarely form blood bonds, especially with mortals."

"Why?" I was intrigued already. He didn't want to tell me this. I could tell. "And, why would he expect you to form one with me then?"

"If a bonded vampire dies, their mate feels it. They may not even survive it. And a mortal, they risk such things as insanity ... and worse." He paused again, and I thought I was going to have to beat the words out of him. Then he continued. "Alexa, a blood bonded mortal is destined to rise as a vampire upon their mortal death."

The shock was audible in my ears, like a beat of thunder inside my head. That was heavy duty.

"But werewolves-," I began, only to be abruptly cut off by Arys' hiss.

"Are still mortal."

"Oh..." I was silent for a moment, absorbing this startling new twist. "But, there has to be a reason why it would be done, why some mortals would find it worth the risk."

My mind was going faster than my mouth, like usual. His frown indicated his unease with the subject matter. I wanted to know.

"I'm sure there are many reasons." His voice grew soft, and he looked away, at the mirror on the bureau that reflected our image back at us. "He expects me to bond you as a life mate, to make you mine beyond your mortal death. To ensure that you cannot die just once. That is why the bond is called the wicked kiss. Which obviously, is where Harley obtained the name for his little blood donor bar."

The words were so simply said, but their weight was enormous. I couldn't breathe for a moment.

"And is that something you would want to do?" I asked the question gently, so he would see that I was just curious.

His penetrating blue eyes were wide with alarm. "I would ruin you."

I swallowed hard and gathered my courage, daring to say what I was thinking. "What if it was the only way? If I were dying or something, or in danger ... you'd never do it? Despite the ways we're already bonded so completely?"

The glare he flashed me stung, and I winced. Why was I asking these things?

"For vampires, the exchange of blood can be a symbol of love or even a matter of convenience. For the living, it is worse than a death sentence. Would you really want me to do that?"

"I want to know that you would do anything I needed you to do, if it was necessary. If I asked it of you."

Though I wanted to push my questions further, the pained mask he wore convinced me otherwise. The tense atmosphere was an indication that my musings were best left inside my head for now.

"Alexa, don't ask me to choose your destiny. You are mortal, and wolf. I can't take that away."

"I'm not asking you to choose." I met his gaze pleadingly, willing him to understand what I was asking and why. "I'm asking you to do something only you can if I ever request it."

Not that I had any intention of sealing my fate so solidly. I was still absorbing the reality of what he'd just told me.

"Look, all you need to know is that I am devoted to you. But, please don't ever ask that of me unless you are more certain than you ever have been about anything else in your life." Arys' lips moved softly against my ear as he gently kissed my lobe. "I don't want to be the bad guy. Not with you."

I couldn't resist the smile that danced over my lips in response to his words. "Baby, you're not nearly as bad as you think you are."

I glanced up to find that his eyes were closed. It wouldn't take him long to fall into a deep slumber. Vampires sleep like they truly are dead. Though there was no coffin for this bed-loving vamp, he was otherwise dead to the world until sundown.

"I have to go shopping for a costume for the Halloween party at Lucy's Lounge," I said, for no other reason than to see if he was still awake. Changing the subject right about now couldn't hurt either.

When he didn't answer right away, I thought he was out. A low chuckle rumbled in his chest, and he said sarcastically, "Pray tell,

Alexa, what are you going to be for Halloween? A werewolf?"

"That's not even worth dignifying with a response. There's nothing wrong with dressing up for Halloween. It's fun." *And, it reminds me of being a kid*, I added silently.

"I suppose it is, when you haven't suffered through as many as I have. They all start to blur together."

His voice was lazy, and I knew he was drifting away. I reached up to gently grasp a handful of his silky, black hair. It slid through my fingers with a softness that created a warm tingle in my veins.

"It's exciting to be a superhero or your favorite TV character. You know, dressing up in a way that you would never do otherwise."

Arys stirred slightly as he turned towards me, his arm going around my waist possessively. "Like a Playboy bunny?" His tone was teasing, and I couldn't help but giggle to myself at the incredible odds.

I snuggled in beside him and gave in to the fatigue that pulled at my eyelids. I had absolutely no intention of telling either Arys or Shaz just how alike they could be. I doubted that it would be very well received.

Chapter Five

It wasn't all that often that Shaz managed to score two nights off in a row. As the best crowd-pleasing bartender in town, his employer's hated having to let him escape their clutches at all. So, even though we had just spent the past two hours in a typical Hollywood chick flick that failed to impress me in any way, it was worth it because we were together.

On our drive into the city, I had told him about Harley. He'd pursed his lips and muttered obscenities about Arys, which had made me reluctant to tell him the rest, about the blood bond. However, he was my mate, my wolf's other half, and so I had to spill it all.

The look of horror on his face had me rushing to assure him that the blood bond was not something I intended to enter. It was just a vampire thing that, shockingly, could be applied to mortals. There had been an anxious energy oozing from him since, and I almost wished I hadn't told. Maybe it just wasn't that important.

The heater was on in Shaz' little Chevy. I angled the vents so that I could put my hands up to the warmth. We were heading out of the city, back to Stony Plain. I flipped down the visor so that I could check my makeup in the mirror. My careful black liner was just as it had been before I left the house.

"What are you looking at?" Shaz asked, a lazy smile tugging at his full lips. "You always look incredible."

"Aww," I blushed, grateful for the darkened interior. "That's very sweet of you to say. It's also a lie."

"Like hell it is. I don't know another woman that could rock those pants the way you do." His attentive gaze momentarily left the road to rove over my tight, black leather. "Hot damn, you are fine."

I laughed then, a bubbly sound that only he could bring out of me. The truth was that I had dressed just for him, knowing he would appreciate the pants paired with a low cut, white top made of flimsy, sheer fabric. It thrilled me to hear how much he really loved it.

"Be careful, babe," I warned teasingly. "If you keep talking like that, my ego will go through the roof."

I felt his sidelong glance and met his jade eyes. He was serious when he said, "You don't give yourself enough credit. I love your modesty though, it's sexy."

My response was to stick my tongue out and make a very unlady-like noise. His compliments felt good, but I didn't know how to take them. I just got all fluttery and weird inside.

Shaz reached to fiddle with the heater control before smoothly sliding his hand onto my thigh. "So, do you want to drop in at the Lounge or just head home?"

The clock on the dash read 12:37 am. It was still pretty early. Even though it was a weeknight, Lucy's Lounge was guaranteed to be packed.

"Let's hit up Lucy's. We'll just stop in for a beer and then head home. I'd kind of like to turn in early anyway." I added just the right inflection to my tone so there was no mistaking my meaning.

"Are you sure you want to go to the Lounge?"

"Yes." I grinned at his sudden change of mind.

Lucy's Lounge was packed when we arrived. Crossing the threshold of the brightly lit building instantly thrust us into a sea of sensations and energies. Most of the metaphysical stuff I could shield out, like the rush of so many human bodies packed into one place. The dizzying assortment of smells and loud noise were not so easy to combat.

Something about amazing heels instantly makes one walk like a sex goddess. As we made our way through the crowded entryway, I felt the eyes of several men on me and even a few ladies, too. Though it's footwear that I don't wear regularly, I had made an exception for an evening out. I appreciated the four inches that it added to my petite five-foot-one.

One of the local bands from the city was rocking out on the stage to the far right. The sign behind them read, "Squeezeplay." They fit right into the laid back, middle-class bar scene with their bad hair and groupie girls gathered around the stage.

Once we got through the traffic-jammed entryway, I was able

to take stock of the entire place. To the left were the pool tables, all of them occupied. The clacking of pool balls was only one of many things contributing to the roar of the club.

The werewolf energy in the club was strong. Zak and Julian were at the pool table closest to us, shooting pool and sneaking glances in our direction. I had only seen them once since Raoul's death. Julian had made it clear that he didn't trust me as the remaining Alpha in this town. Not now that I was so heavily involved with a vampire.

No male wolf in this town had attempted to take Raoul's Alpha status, which made me the top of the heap. Of course, none of them could best me; none matched me in power and ability, and we all knew it. And, Julian didn't like that. He didn't like vampires, and he didn't like me. Too bad for him.

Arys wasn't there, at least, not yet. I was almost hoping that he wouldn't be in tonight. It was too soon to have him and Shaz in the same building.

Shaz clasped my hand warmly in his own, and we made our way to the closest waitress. One plus of having your boyfriend work at the local hot spot was the no-waiting clause. Since he knew everyone, we didn't have to join in the long line at the bar. The ginger-haired waitress smiled and greeted Shaz with a friendly smile.

"What can I get you guys?" She grinned at me, and I instantly liked her. It doesn't take me long to get a vibe for people. Most of Shaz' co-workers were great people that he enjoyed working with.

As Shaz ordered our drinks, I took a moment to glance around again. I could have sworn that I felt Kylarai's spicy energy. I was surprised when she exited the ladies' room and made her way toward Julian and Zak. Sensing us, she looked over suddenly and gave a small wave. What was she doing here with them?

Before she noticed it, I squashed the frown that tried to form on my features. I waved back and smiled, hoping I didn't look as suspicious as I felt.

"Let's find a table," Shaz said, leaning in to speak close to my ear. "I wonder why Ky is with those guys. Weird."

It certainly was. I followed Shaz to a table across the bar from where Ky and the two male Weres shot pool. It gave us a good view of the stage. The lead singer was screaming now, but surprisingly, it didn't bother me. I enjoyed the occasional screaming rock song, when the mood struck.

After the waitress brought our drinks, Shaz turned on me with a grin that shocked me to the soles of my feet. I couldn't help but be awestruck by how sensational he looked. His platinum hair was slightly messy, as if he'd run his hands through it too many times. His green eyes were bright and shone with amusement. He was dressed head to toe in black jeans and a tight black t-shirt, and I was struggling to prevent myself from openly drooling. The creamy white skin of his well-toned arms was taunting me with the need to run my hands over all of his hard curves.

When he gave me a knowing look, I raised my eyebrows in question. He leaned in so that his lips brushed my ear, sending a hot tingle down my spine.

"You have to dance with me. I'm just waiting for the right song."

"What?" A jolt of nervous energy slammed through my system. The thought of dancing didn't sit well with me. I was usually only inclined to do so after many drinks.

"You heard me." He winked and smiled slyly. "Any excuse to get you into my arms."

I laughed nervously and took a sip of my drink. "Oh, come on now, we don't need to dance for me to be in your arms."

He just shook his head. "Nice try, lady. You're not going to get out of it this time. I'm usually stuck behind the bar. I want to take advantage of this."

He had a point. He didn't get to do this often. One dance couldn't hurt, could it? Not if I could manage to avoid tripping over my own feet.

I couldn't help but peek at Kylarai. It didn't take a genius to figure out that she was here with Julian. His casual touches and intense stares weren't missed by me.

"Are you going to go talk to her?" Shaz asked, nodding in Ky's direction.

I considered that scenario. It was plausible, but I didn't want to talk to Julian nor did I want to put Kylarai on the spot.

"Not right now. She'll fess up at home."

It was nice, relaxing in the bar with Shaz, a drink and a live band. I wished that we could do this more often. Of course, if I was willing to accept Raoul's money, we could both live the rest of our lives and never have to work again. I had too much pride for that. And, I'm sure it would get boring.

There was a break in the music, and the singer shouted out that they were about to play the last song of the night. The girls around the stage hooted and hollered. Local bands received a lot of attention if they were good. More than one rock band had gone on to make it after getting their start in a small town like this.

Something kept drawing my attention across the room to the pool tables where Kylarai was. She was at the same table with the guys, but something wasn't right. A completely different guy had joined them, and he was up in Julian's face, too close to be anything but confrontational.

I froze, watching the scene play out before me. The human male was obviously calling the angry Were on. I couldn't tell what had started the altercation. Kylarai made an attempt to come between them, and the guy shot her a venomous look. His mouth moved quickly as he spat a nasty remark at her.

Julian said something in response, and the man shoved him hard. This wasn't going to go over well. I nudged Shaz and was on my feet by the time the first punch was thrown.

A werewolf in a bar fight was always the winner. I didn't want to see Julian break this guy's face. I couldn't let it happen.

Fighting my way through the people that stood between the pool tables and me was a frustrating setback. I managed to cross the distance in time to see Zak pull Ky away from the chaos as if she were a breakable doll. The punches were flying fast. Those in the nearby vicinity were becoming aware of the fight as the guys crashed into chairs and tables in their brawl.

A few bystanders were daring enough to try to split the fight up, but each of them backed off when they quickly failed. Shaz was right beside me; his long legs carried him much faster than my shorter ones carried me. The heels didn't help my speed.

Shaz was a blur of black and white as he leaped into the middle. He quickly tackled Julian, whom he had no problem taking down. Two more bystanders grabbed a hold of the other guy who struggled violently against them. Julian struggled to break free of Shaz' controlling hold. As soon as he was steady on his feet, I was in his face.

"What the fuck do you think you're doing?" I growled angrily. Amidst the music and commotion, nobody could hear me clearly but Julian.

He was breathing hard when Shaz released his arms. A trickle of blood ran from his nose. His eyes were wild, all wolf, daring me to keep talking.

"Have you lost your mind?" I wanted to throttle the life out of him for such blatant stupidity.

"Back off, Alexa." Julian glared down at me from his six-foot-three stance. "This has nothing to do with you."

Fury burned through me, and I felt my control slip. Right then, I just wanted to kill him. "You will respect me as Alpha wolf, Julian. If you want to expose yourself by being an idiot, you won't be doing it in my town."

He eyed me with a smugness that made me want to scream. It took all I had not to backhand the arrogance off his face. "What are you going to do about it? Sick your vampire on me?"

He actually had the balls to taunt me. Big mistake. I could feel Shaz a few feet away, simmering with anger. Kylarai and Zak hovered uncertainly nearby. Everyone else had gone back to their own business now that the brawl was over.

"It isn't him that you should be afraid of." I smirked with a conceit that wasn't the norm for me.

All it took was a thought to throw enough power at Julian to slam him back a few feet. I didn't even raise a hand. He reached out quickly to catch himself on the side of a pool table.

His dark gaze was filled with hate, which I took great satisfaction in. I had something he didn't, and that made me the dominating force.

To say I was shocked when he got up in my face then would be a gross understatement. I was blown away. The dark haired werewolf was suddenly growling down into my face with a mouthful of bared fangs.

"If you want to fucking threaten me, bitch, then you better be ready to follow through on that." He was close enough to kiss, the intrusion into my personal space a blatant show of disrespect.

Before I could take a breath to respond, Shaz was between us,

Trina M. Lee

shoving Julian away from me with a push that would have taken most people off their feet. He followed up with a second shove that had Zak moving to their side, as if he thought he could break them up if they decided to go at it.

The dark fury that blazed in Shaz' eyes, like jade-green fire, almost caused my heart to stop. I had never seen such raw hate written in his gaze as long as I'd known him. It frightened me even as it excited.

"I don't care who you fucking think you are; I will kill you before I allow you to talk that way to Alexa. You're a fucking nobody, pal." Shaz was poised to strike if Julian so much as blinked the wrong way.

"Guys, come on." Kylarai's gentle voice was chiding. She was afraid they would fight. "This is all a misunderstanding."

Julian didn't look at anyone but Shaz. He pulled himself to his full height before snarling through his teeth. "Just because you want to be her pathetic lapdog doesn't mean that I do. I will take you any day, Shaz. Even out back, right now."

My heart surged with adrenaline at Julian's venomous words. A small cry escaped me when Shaz lashed out with a blow, catching the other wolf with a fierce right hook.

"Shaz, no!" I lunged to grab his arm before he could keep swinging. The motion almost knocked me off my feet, but I held him back.

"If that's what you want then, buddy, let's make it official. It has been months since Raoul died. Maybe it's time to appoint a new Alpha male in this God forsaken town," Julian sneered as he rubbed his jaw. My eyes widened when I saw where he was going with this.

Shaz studied the other Were for just moments before replying in a low voice, filled with menace. "Where and when?"

"That isn't necessary, you guys," Ky pleaded, but neither of them so much as looked her way. "It doesn't mean anything."

Zak looked extremely uncomfortable as he shifted nervously from one foot to the other. "I think we'd better leave, Julian," he said, trying to be the neutral party. "Let's grab some beer and head back to my place. There's a fight on pay-per-view."

The approach of a couple of bouncers effectively ended any further incident. With a murderous glare, Julian looked from me to

Shaz. "Me and you, on the full moon."

"Count on it." Shaz practically oozed confidence, and I had to do a double take.

Julian allowed Zak to pull him along by the upper arm, but his eyes were locked on me. A slow smile spread across his lips. He paused to pull Kylarai into his arms, and I stiffened when she let him. My stomach turned when he kissed her.

"I'll call you later tonight," Julian said to her, smirking with the knowledge that I hadn't known about them.

She avoided my eyes, a frown creasing her delicate features. "I'll walk you out."

We both knew she was trying to escape me. Fine. She couldn't avoid me at home.

Shaz turned to speak to the bouncers in an attempt to smooth over the situation. I could hear him reassuring them that everything was cool and we were all leaving now. As an employee, he was risking his job by brawling in the bar. After a moment, the two security guys nodded and returned to their posts.

When Shaz swept me into his arms, I clung to him. "Have you lost your mind? Why? Please, just tell me why."

"I can't believe you have to ask. When he got in your face like that, something inside me snapped. He threatened my mate. And now, I want to kill him." He said it so matter of factly. I searched his eyes for the monstrous rage I heard in his voice but found only tender love.

"I don't want you to fight him." I reached to touch his face, tracing a light bruise that remained from his round with Arys.

"I know that." He brought his face to mine, kissing me with a sensuality that was all wolf. I savored it. Pulling back, he kissed the tip of my nose. "But, I'm going to. I have to. Everything in me demands it, and it's a call that I want to answer, have to answer. You have to understand."

I did understand, but I didn't like it. I pursed my lips and stared at the floor. "Did you hear him though? He thinks this is a battle for Alpha."

"It is ... now." He gently pushed a few tendrils of hair from my face. "If he wants this to be about the top wolf in this town, then that's fine with me. I don't plan to lose."

The DJ took over as the band finished off their set and began to pack up. When the Alicia Keys song, "No One," began to play and the dance floor filled with couples, Shaz gave me a heart-stopping grin.

"No worries, ok? I promise, you have nothing to be anxious about." He pressed another quick kiss to my lips before pulling me toward the dance floor. "Now ... about that dance."

I allowed him to pull me onto the dance floor among the other couples. My stomach was unsettled, and I just wanted him to hold me. All I knew was that I had to talk him out of fighting Julian before the full moon. That didn't give me much time.

Shaz' arms went around me, holding me close. It was easy to get caught up in the music. The heady swoon of the emotional lyrics and the enrapt couples all around us had me seeking comfort and reassurance in his touch. I wrapped my arms around him and nuzzled the warmth of his neck. Pressing my lips to his pulse, I closed my eyes and moved as one with him to the rhythm of the music.

The thought of him fighting Julian scared me to death. It wasn't that I didn't think Shaz could take him; I knew he could. However, I didn't trust Julian to play fair, and I knew he wouldn't go down easy.

In that moment though, it was hard to think about anything other than how good it felt to be in the embrace of my white wolf. The song itself stirred an emotion in me that was gut wrenching in its strength. When the beautiful music ended, Shaz placed a series of kisses down the side of my neck, causing me to shiver.

"Let's get out of here." The heat from his whispered words tickled, and I laughed.

ဆဆဆ

A movie played quietly on the TV perched atop my dresser. I wasn't paying much attention to it, but with a sexy, naked werewolf in bed next to me, how could I?

Shaz and I lay together, a mess of entangled limbs. I always felt the warmth and comfort of the pack when he shared my bed. Our nights apart were less than enjoyable. We cuddled in an affectionate embrace that sparked feelings of giddy love within me. It wasn't something that I was used to by any means. I still had a hard time believing it was real and not some amazing dream I would wake up from, disappointed to find it wasn't real at all.

Kylarai's Escalade was in the driveway when we got home. The door to her room had been closed and would likely remain that way until she was forced to come out. It wasn't like she owed me any explanations, but she was dating my friend and co-worker. Or at least, I had thought she was.

Once Shaz breathed softly and his eyes closed, I thought that was it for him. I gazed absently at the moving images on the television screen, but my mind was focused on how perfectly our bodies fit together. No matter how we slept, we always seemed to mold to one another.

"I really don't like this whole thing with Arys' sire being in town." Shaz' voice came low beside me. Since I thought he'd fallen asleep, I was startled. "And I really don't like that blood bond nonsense. I think you have more than enough vampire influence in your life as it is."

"I knew that was bothering you. I could feel it." I reached for his hand, tracing light circles in his palm with my finger. "It shouldn't. You're right, it is nonsense. And, I'm not afraid of Harley." That was only a half-truth. I'd seen things in Arys' memory that certainly did stir fear inside me. Harley thrived on pain and fear, torture driven energy.

"Why do you think he's here? I mean, why now?"

I pondered that for a moment, not liking anything that came to mind. "He knows about the power that Arys and I share. I think he wants to see it for himself."

The tension that seeped into Shaz caused him to stiffen beside me. I didn't like it. This was supposed to be a place and a time for comfort and relaxation. I rubbed his shoulders, hoping to ease some of the strain.

"Just tell me that you won't go back to that vampire bar alone." His arms went around me, blanketing me in his warmth. "I'm not trying to sound like Arys, that cocky ass, but I need to know you're safe. After Julian's display tonight, I'm feeling madly overprotective."

I gave a small laugh. The truth was that if Arys had acted this territorial I would have been super-pissed. Shaz was my wolf mate though, and that was rooted in something deeper than we understood. I knew that implicitly. His urge to protect and defend me was driven by love and nature. When Arys did it, it was all about the ego boost of saving the damsel in distress.

"You are too good to me." I nuzzled his face with mine before kissing him with undying devotion and passion. "I love it when you're overprotective. But, I don't want it to have you scrapping everybody. And no, I won't be going back to The Wicked Kiss alone. Promise."

The name of the club brought the blood bond to mind. I hadn't known vampires called it that. I also hadn't known that humans could be bonded. The thought sent a chill through my warm insides. I resisted a physical shudder.

"Don't try to talk me out of fighting Julian. I'm doing it, Lex. I'm putting that pitiful excuse for a werewolf in his place, and I'm going to enjoy doing it." He pressed even closer, if that was possible, with his head resting against mine. "I love you. And, I know you want me to let it go. But, I'm running on instinct here."

I sighed but didn't bother trying to dissuade him. That didn't mean I wouldn't try again before the full moon. It just wasn't something I wanted to think about right now.

"I love you, too, babe." I breathed in his intoxicating scent and closed my eyes. "Now promise me that you won't get yourself killed."

Chapter Six

The crumpled edges of a post-it note crushed beneath my face brought me awake to the delicious scent of bacon frying. The note was written in Shaz' messy scrawl. "You are so beautiful when you sleep. I couldn't stand to wake you. I love you ... forever."

I would have once scoffed at the sappy sweetness of the note. Now it warmed my heart and brought a stupid smile to my face. I sighed and took a deep breath of his heavenly scent on my pillows and blanket.

Kylarai was clearly feeling guilty over keeping her fling with Julian a secret. She didn't cook often. It was usually left to my poor attempts and Shaz when he was over. Ky was too busy with work. So, it spoke volumes when I rounded the corner of the kitchen to find her also making her famous omelets, which I loved so much.

"Coffee?" Her first word kind of surprised me. She smiled wide, but it didn't quite reach her eyes.

"Sure, thanks." I watched her fill a mug and hand it to me. I fetched my own cream and sugar. "Good morning, or afternoon I should say." The microwave clock indicated that it was closer to the supper hour than breakfast. Such was the life of a werewolf.

"Did you sleep well? I stayed up reading the latest Nora Roberts novel until my eyes were dry. Had some pretty crazy dreams after." Kylarai bustled around the stove, carefully not meeting my eyes for more than a few seconds at a time.

I took a long sip of my coffee, watching her like a hawk. I didn't have to say anything. I knew her, and she would cave all on her own. "I slept great. There is no such thing as a bad sleep when Shaz is with me."

She took two plates out of the cupboard and began to scoop food onto each with the spatula. Handing one to me, she met my eyes with a guilty half-smile.

"You're not even going to ask, are you?"

That had happened even sooner than I'd expected. I gave her a friendly grin and reached out to pat her arm before grabbing a fork and taking a seat at the table.

"Of course not," I said. "But, that doesn't mean I'm not dying to know."

I took a bite of the mouth-watering omelet and almost had to close my eyes in pleasure. Kylarai was a supreme cook when she had the time. I was going to enjoy this. I'd be fending for myself again in no time.

She took the seat across from me but didn't pick up her fork. "Ok, this is the quick version. Kale and I called it quits over a week ago. I just can't do it, Lex. I can't be with a vampire romantically. Kale has baggage that I can't even begin to comprehend." She shrugged and looked like a lost little girl. "I didn't think it was fair to him. I had to let him go."

"Is that why he was drowning his sorrows at The Wicked Kiss?" I asked between bites. "That makes more sense now."

"And, it wasn't that I was trying to keep anything from you, but then I ran into Julian at Lucy's and one thing led to another..." Kylarai smiled shyly and tucked her hair behind her ear. "I really like him."

I wished she had let me finish eating first. I grimaced inwardly but miraculously prevented it from manifesting on my face.

"Just like that, huh?" I took a sip from my coffee cup, using the moment to think of something positive to say. I failed.

"Well ... the attraction isn't new, but acting on it certainly is." Ky picked up her fork and took a bite of her eggs. She chewed robotically, out of habit rather than desire. "I can't stop thinking about Kale though. He didn't want to see me, when I went to him after he bit you."

I could see how the admittance pained her. Dropping my fork on my plate, I reached across the table to give her hand a warm squeeze.

"Don't worry about him, Ky. Kale will be fine." I didn't sound very convincing, but I'd seen how rough he was. Why didn't he tell me they had broken up?

She chewed her lower lip, her eyes darting between her plate and me. "I just couldn't do it. I can't donate blood to him, and I can't sit by while he gets it from that whorehouse of a blood bar. Everything unraveled really fast."

I nodded in understanding. Kylarai hadn't even been cool with it the first time Arys had fed from me. It was a very personal experience, one that was more intimate than sex. I could understand her inability to be part of that world. And, Kale was the type of guy who needed that in his lover.

"You can't blame yourself. Kale's issues go deeper than either of us realize. I'm sure of it. And, if you aren't able to be with him, then it's better to figure that out now instead of months or years from now." I was encouraged to finish my meal when she began to pick at her food again.

"I know," she nodded and pushed a slice of bacon around her plate before finally spearing it and popping it in her mouth.

We ate in comfortable silence for a few moments. I wanted to ask her why Julian of all people. She could do so much better. That would be rude though, so I bit my tongue against the urge.

"I know it's hard, Kylarai," I said instead. "But, Kale will be fine. And, so will you." As an afterthought I added, "I hope you don't hold it against me for introducing you guys." I smiled to soften the seriousness of my words.

Kylarai laughed then which made me feel a million times better. "Don't be ridiculous, Alexa. I adore Kale; he's a good man. He just isn't meant to be mine."

Her warm grey eyes fixed on me, and the uncertainty in their depths made my heart go out to her. Her energy was very strained and pinched. It stung if I concentrated on it. Too much negativity.

I finished eating and rinsed my dish before stacking it in the dishwasher. That had to be man's greatest invention to date. I went for a second cup of coffee, needing the caffeine boost in my system. There was more that I wanted to say, but I wasn't sure how.

I shook my head and resisted the urge to hug her against her will. She wasn't ready for that though. I could see how hard she was fighting to subdue the depths of her feelings.

"You know I'm always here, right? If you ever want to talk." I wished there was more I could say, but I could only say so much.

Her face lit up then, and she beamed a grin at me. "I know. I love you for worrying about me. You're like the younger sister I never had."

"And you're like the tough-ass older sister I always needed to throw my boyfriends around." I had to laugh when I pictured her stepping in between Arys and Shaz the other night. I wish I could have appreciated their surprise at the time.

"We have to stop them from fighting, Alexa," she said suddenly, and I paused, my coffee partially raised to my lips. "Julian and Shaz, we can't let them do this."

"I know." I nodded and thought back to Shaz' fierce intensity when he spoke of beating Julian's ass. "It's going to be fucking ugly. Shaz refused to listen to me last night. He insisted it's something he has to do as my mate."

Kylarai looked worried; her food, once again abandoned. "And, I wouldn't expect anything less from him. I'm sorry ... Julian isn't the easiest person to understand, but he is a good guy underneath it all."

"Well ... I hope you can talk some sense into him; otherwise, we're going to have one hell of a furry mess to clean up."

"I'll do my best." She searched my eyes then, a shadow of doubt passing in her stormy gaze. "But, if they won't listen to reason, if they still fight, we can't let it go too far. We have to be ready to split them up."

I was pretty sure I knew what she was saying. "Don't worry, Ky. I'll be more than happy to blast them both on their asses."

"I just don't want to see anyone get hurt."

It never ceased to amaze me how she had such a sweet, gentle nature that could unleash into a frenzy of murderous rage at a moment's notice. I was counting on her to use that to our advantage if necessary when those boys went head-to-head. And, I could feel it in every part of me that without a doubt, they would.

I moved about the kitchen, tidying up the counter and starting the dishes. I was looking forward to a quiet night alone. Shaz was bartending tonight and judging by Kylarai's perfectly done makeup and hair, she had plans.

After Ky disappeared to her bedroom, re-emerging in a stylish black cocktail dress, I considered getting dressed. With a questioning brow raised, I asked, "What are you all dressed up for? You look gorgeous, by the way."

"Thank you. Julian and I are going to dinner." She had the decency to blush and look guilty when she said it. "I won't be home until morning. Do you have any plans tonight?"

"Nope. Shaz is working, and Arys is, well, being Arys most likely. I'm going to lie around, watch movies and be thankful that I haven't had to hunt down any vampires all week."

The vampire activity had been reasonably quiet in the city recently. Of course, that could just be the calm before the storm. In all honesty, I love what I do. Hunting rogue supernaturals was necessary. Somebody had to do it if we all wanted to keep our secrets. I had a hunger for the hunt and kill that made me a natural for the job. Having partners, like my friends Kale and Jez, alongside me made it a lot more fun than when I worked alone.

"You haven't done that in a long time. I'm sure you need it." I watched as Ky gathered her things together to leave. She leaned in to give me a quick embrace before turning to go. "Enjoy the quiet time. It's good for the soul."

After she left, I stood in the quiet kitchen, listening to the sounds of the clock ticking and the fridge running. Slipping through the glass sliding doors to the backyard, I was pleasantly surprised to find the night wind to be particularly warm for October. A run would be really nice right now. Just thinking about it brought an itch to my limbs and muscles as the need to stretch out and become wolf grew quickly.

Running alone isn't something I do often. In fact, I can't recall the last time I didn't have Kylarai or Shaz with me. It was kind of a group activity. So imagine my surprise when the first time I do head out alone in a long while, I run in to Zoey Roberts. I hadn't laid eyes upon her since the night she murdered Raoul. Though, that's not to say that she hadn't occupied my thoughts since then.

I was trotting along, minding my own business as I savored the crisp freshness of the night breeze. I rounded a bend in the trees that led to the small forest clearing where several of us meet to run on the full moon. The black wolf caught my eye immediately, my mind conjuring a memory of Raoul. She just looked so much like him. My heart leaped, and for just a moment, I thought it was him.

Then her scent reached me, and the instinctual need to kill was back. Despite everything, I had to lay the blame somewhere, and though Raoul was dead, his vindictive offspring wasn't. A snarl erupted from me, unbidden and unexpected, yet welcome. What was she doing, so close to my house? This was my turf, not hers.

We stared at one another across the distance that separated us. She looked a lot better than she had the last time I'd seen her. How she'd managed to escape death was beyond me. Her once blood-matted fur was now long and silky, the color of sin. The one feature that set her apart from Raoul was the eyes. She had cerulean blues rather than ebony orbs. I was glad that the similarities only went so far.

I waited, not blinking an eye, but she never came any closer. The seconds ticked by increasingly long. How I kept my feet planted is a mystery to me. Maybe it had something to do with the sudden memory of the challenge in Raoul's eyes as he lay dying, allowing Zoe to kill him. He had been willing to do anything to give her the vengeance she felt entitled to, regardless of my feelings, my need for vengeance.

After a long, suspenseful moment that had me shaking in my tracks, she backed away toward the thick trees behind her. When she was sure that I wouldn't give chase, she turned and fled into shadow.

I didn't hang around to see if she'd return. She wouldn't, not tonight anyway. Instead, I beat it home to take a soak in a hot bath while I nursed a combination of guilt and confusion.

I wasn't sure where the guilt came from. Maybe because while I was relaxing in bubbles up to my chin, Zoey was out there trapped in wolf form indefinitely. The confusion was partly due to Raoul's death having only occurred a few months ago. I just wasn't entirely over losing the man I'd looked up to, nor could I accept his betrayal from beyond the grave. That would likely never change. How could it? He had waited until he was dead to reveal to me through a letter that he had been the werewolf that killed my family and turned me. That kind of pain didn't fade overnight.

Since I was alone, I dragged my fuzzy comforter out to the futon in the living room. After making some African red tea and grabbing a bag of chocolate covered pretzels, I was ready to get comfy with a good movie.

I munched on pretzels as I scrolled through the TV channels

with the remote. There was a late night showing of one of the old Halloween movies. With Halloween being just weeks away, I also had three or four other horror flicks to choose from. After eliminating them based on cheesiness and gore level, I stuck with Michael Myers and his shrieking teenage victims.

It wasn't long until my eyelids began to droop. The classic slasher theme played in the background as I drifted between sleep and wakefulness. It accompanied me as I sunk deeper, right into a dream I hadn't had in months.

I was back in my family home, surrounded by the bodies of my dead family. Raoul stood before me as wolf, but this time I knew it was him. The first thing I noticed was that I wasn't my teenage self in this dream like in previous ones, and I was fully aware that this was indeed only a dream. I soon came to realize that though it was a dream, it was not at all the same one I'd assumed it was.

Unlike dreams of the past, Raoul wasn't snarling or preparing to attack. He simply stared into me with calm, coal-dark eyes. I was overcome with the instant urge to tell him what a jackass he was for trying to communicate with me now, after my run in with Zoe. It was always about her.

But, try as I might to say all the things that came to mind, I was unable to give voice to them. I could only look into those dark eyes and feel a mixture of sadness and wonder.

Just when I felt that something was going to transpire, another sensation roused me. When my conscious mind became aware that somebody was in the house, I was wide-awake, on full alert.

My instinct had me swinging before I'd identified the intruder. All at once, I realized it was Arys, but he had already deflected each of my blows, catching my wrists tightly in his grasp.

"Alexa," he whispered loudly. "It's me. But, a word of warning. Don't fall asleep with the front door unlocked."

I stopped struggling against him and sat up on the futon. Arys leaned down over me; his face, more battered and bruised than it had been previously. He released my arms and stepped back as I pushed my disheveled hair from my face.

"What happened to you? That's not from Shaz." I reached out to brush a finger across his bruised eyelid but he caught my hand in his, kissing it softly.

"No. I saw Harley tonight. At The Wicked Kiss." He stared at me with an intensity I felt in my toes.

Arys looked worried, almost afraid. He wasn't the fearful type in any way. He pulled me into his arms, burying his face in my hair and inhaling my scent. I tried to pull away, pushing on his chest so he had to look at me.

"Tell me what happened."

He studied me, his jaw clenching hard. "We had a little confrontation. It didn't go so well."

"You don't say." I cocked my head to the side, taking in his battered appearance. "Start talking, vampire."

He reached out for my hand, and I surrendered it but didn't abandon my stiff position. That had never deterred this vampire though, and it certainly didn't now. Arys advanced on me, tipping my head up with a hand under my chin, kissing me with a fervor that I felt in my loins.

"That's not going to get you out of trouble, mister. Start talking. I want to know about Harley." I managed to pull away though I would have loved to let him continue as if nothing else mattered.

He tensed noticeably, looking away from me to stare at the gruesome horror flick that played quietly. His averted gaze told me plenty. I had to bite my tongue so that I didn't ramble on in an attempt to pry the information out of him.

When his piercing, blue gaze swung back to me, there was an angry fire burning in their depths. He ran his hand through his always bedroom-messy hair, a sign that he didn't want to tell me. I chewed my bottom lip nervously. If he didn't start talking, I was going to burst.

"He's bad news, Alexa. He wants to see what could possibly be so tasty that even I can't get my fill." Arys eyed me closely as he spoke. I felt his gaze like a weight. "He wants to sample you for himself. His exact words were a little more crude, which resulted in the punch in his face that started our little brawl."

I swallowed hard around the lump that had suddenly formed in my throat. Ok, now I was a little nervous.

"You've got to be joking." My hand went to my mouth, and for a moment, I thought I might throw up. "What is it with people from your past wanting a piece of me? Why? What did I ever do to them?"

My voice took on a frantic, high-pitched lilt.

"Oh, Catherine was nothing worse than the jealous-high-school-girl type. Harley is like the evil cartoon villain that never dies. But worse, because he's real." Arys lightly touched a finger to one of the bruises lining his strong cheekbone, a thoughtful expression on his eternally beautiful face. "He seems to think you'd make a great toy. And, I know he's egotistical enough to think he can have whatever he wants. But, he can't have you. I'll kill him first."

I drew him to me, a hand tracing the line of his jaw. "We have nothing to worry about. The very thing that he wants from us is what will give us the upper hand. I'll be ready for him." I pressed my lips to his in a kiss that had him wanting more, if his reaction was any indication.

Arys crawled up on the futon so that he hovered over me on his hands and knees. Each of his legs was on either side of mine, and his hands came to rest on my pillow with my head caught between. The position forced me back so that I had to tip my head back to meet his eyes.

"You can't underestimate him, Alexa." He nipped lightly at my bottom lip. It sent a hot tingle through me, from head to toe. He had a way of always rousing the most savage energy within me. "He's powerful and so fucking sadistic, it turns my guts to think of him touching you."

There was a sharp pain as he bit my lower lip; the blood welled instantly. Before it could spill down my chin, he caught it against his tongue. The warm, moist touch against my wounded lip was heavenly.

"I know that, Arys. But, don't underestimate me. I take out vamps like him all the time." It irritated me that he spoke to me like I was defenseless.

"I'm sorry, Alexa, but you have never dealt with a vampire like him. I guarantee it." He pressed a kiss to my bleeding lip. "And, don't you dare make this into a damsel in distress scenario. You know it's not like that."

The power rose around us in response to the blood and sexual energy. It danced along my body like a strange second skin. His tongue slipped inside my mouth, and I tasted my own coppery blood. It made my heart race, and I sought to pull him closer, needing to feel him pressed against me.

"Don't start with me," I said, even as I gasped breathlessly. "It's always like that with you. I'm not a breakable item that will crumble into dust at the wrong touch."

"Yes," he growled down at me. "You are. I'm not arguing about your safety. Nobody is safe when Harley sets his sights on them."

Just when I loved where we were headed, he pulled back, a serious expression on his face. "I need you to promise me that you'll stay away from The Wicked Kiss. And, watch for Harley. Seriously. Just until I know how far he's willing to take this."

"Arys..." I wanted him to stop talking about danger and getting killed. It was really cramping the mood we'd started.

"I mean it. Don't make me beg." He gave me an imploring look, and it was enough to unsettle me.

"This isn't like you," I commented, trying for casual. "What's with the extreme worry? He's not going to kill me."

His wane smile grew sad and accepting all at once. "That's what scares me most. Harley has a penchant for collecting things, most of them being people. Like me. If he gets his hands on you, that's what you'll be. Another toy. But, what's fun for Harley is never fun for his toys."

The creepiest chill crept over me as he uttered the words. Harley loved torture, and if he got his hands on me, I'd be praying for death instead.

"Stop," I whispered, suddenly afraid to speak any louder. "I don't want to go there right now. You have to leave before sunrise. Let's not spend our time talking like this."

A small bead of blood overflowed from my lip, down my chin. Arys' eyes followed it, and his little finger was quick to catch it.

"Alright." He brought the little crimson splash to his lips; his eyes glazed with the rush of energy, which he openly embraced. "For now, it's all about us."

I smiled when he reached to untie the sash to my silky robe, wasting no time hiking my short nightie up around my waist. I gave a small playful shriek and slapped at his hand when he made as if to slide my G-string to the side.

"Hey now," I said, shoving against his solid chest in an attempt to sit up. "What's your hurry?"

He remained steadfast so that I was deliciously trapped beneath him. He released his hold on my skimpy underwear and kissed me hard. The thrill that shot through me caused me to gasp, and Arys chuckled seductively.

"We don't have much time. I want to make the most of it." He whispered the words against my lips before sliding a hand up my side to cup my breast. "I need to feel you."

His touch was possessive and demanding but had a gentle quality to it that I noted immediately. As nice as it felt, I couldn't help but be anxious. I knew his sudden need for me came from his insecurity regarding Harley. It frightened me to know that it was eating at Arys so badly.

My arms went around his neck as I took a deep breath. His scent was made up of cologne and hair products since vampires generally have no distinct scent. When he was experiencing my weaknesses, he also smelled like wolf.

He leaned into me again; his tongue sought mine hungrily. I welcomed the warm, moist heat of his mouth as he pressed his erection against my bare thigh.

All at once, our bonded power began to grow between us, stretching and reaching for more. It was extremely rare that we made love without it encouraging the flow of our passion.

When Arys broke off the mind-shattering kiss, I was momentarily disappointed. His tongue soon traced wet lines down my neck beneath my ear, causing my body to respond with a rush of blood through my veins and a flood of feminine moisture between my legs. His fingers deftly found my nipple, and I let out a small moan when he rubbed it until it stood firm.

I entangled my fingers in his amazingly soft hair, loving the sensation as he licked and nipped at my sensitive throat. "I need to taste you, Alexa." His voice came hot and breathy against my ear. His request caused me to tense in heart-racing anticipation. It was not often that he really bled me, and it was even less often that he asked.

And, something about his use of the word "need" had me on alert. If I didn't know better, I'd almost think Arys was getting emotional on me. As far as emotions go, it's not something we openly discuss. It's something that somehow plays a part in our relationship but has a tendency to be glossed over.

We were both guilty of pretending we could live without the other, yet, it was a thought I couldn't entertain. There were no claims of undying devotion between Arys and me. That was something that only came out with Shaz. But, if forced to look inward to what I felt for Arys, I couldn't deny that there was something real there.

What it was, I couldn't define, as it had kind of snuck up on me. I hadn't ever intended to feel anything for him. Not really. Ultimately, we don't always choose who we feel for.

Butterflies beat their delightful wings hard against my insides. I was nervous because I was rarely the prey. Allowing Arys to take blood from me took a lot of control on my part. I trusted him, though, and the rush of power swirling around us assisted in my readiness.

Ever so softly, he stroked the side of my face as he pulled back to look into my eyes. The tenderness in his hypnotizing gaze was shocking. I didn't expect to see such vulnerability hidden in those ocean blue depths. I realized in that moment that, though I had become one of Arys' strengths, I was also one of his weaknesses.

It went beyond the metaphysical weaknesses that we shared. I worried that, if he developed deep feelings for me, it would destroy him.

"Do you have any idea what you do to me?" He asked; a tantalizing grin slowly spread across his face. The sight of his sharp fangs had me excited.

In response to his question, I reached down between our bodies to grip his shaft tightly. "I think I have a pretty good idea. But, I'm really not liking all of the clothing between us." I began to unfasten his jeans, and he followed my lead, stripping off his t-shirt.

He then slid his jeans off, freeing the smooth as velvet erection that I eyed hungrily. I encircled it with my hand just tight enough to coax a moan from him. His pupils dilated until his eyes were all black. He only allowed me to stroke him for a moment before pushing my hand away.

With a low murmur, he buried his face between my legs, pulling my G-string aside roughly. I dug clawed hands into my pillow as he directly attacked me with his tongue. As he roughly licked me from top to bottom, I cried out at the overwhelming onslaught of sensation.

My instant reaction was to plunge both hands into his jet-black hair, careful not to gauge him with my claws. I held tight, and a series of groans and growls filled the silence. The orgasm was almost instant, and I shuddered beneath his persistent tongue.

He quickly stripped my thong off and tossed it on the floor. My robe was quick to follow, but he left my nightie on, bunched around my waist. I grabbed for him eagerly when he rose above me, expecting him to enter me. When he didn't, I was surprised to find him staring down at me.

All of a sudden, he hooked his hands under my hips and flipped us over so that he was beneath me, and I straddled him. I couldn't hide the naughty smile that played across my lips.

I immediately gripped his manhood so that I could slide myself down on to it. Before I could do so however, he grasped my left arm in his hand and drew it close. His tongue played over that soft spot in my inner elbow. He traced the veins there, sucking at them until they plumped up nicely. His other hand went to my hip, guiding me so that he was ready at my soft, inviting entrance.

I was more than ready to slide down on his amazing, rock hard length of flesh, but he stopped me with a look. I knew that look. It made my stomach clench.

"You are my wolf." It wasn't a question. Arys simply made the statement, but he waited for a response.

"Yes." I nodded, my voice thick with sex. I rubbed against the head of him, teasing with my slick wetness.

In one swift fluid motion, my dark vampire pulled me down on him so that he slid deep inside me as he sunk fangs into my soft flesh simultaneously. A pained noise escaped me as those needle sharp teeth freed the blood trapped within my vein. It hurt intensely, but every moment of pain was matched with just as much pleasure.

As I lifted up and plunged down on to him again, he gripped my hip possessively as he sucked at my bleeding arm. A trickle of blood escaped him, streaking crimson lines down to my wrist. The sight of it added to the exhilaration of the moment.

I increased my speed on top of him as he thrust up into me, driving himself even deeper still, wrenching a cry from me. His mouth on my flesh sent a shiver down my spine, increasing the pleasure coursing through me. We rode the wave of power that crashed over us with the natural balance that we'd established over the past few months.

I clung to Arys with my free hand, and my nails left angry red scratches on his chest and stomach. I panted his name, and he made an animalistic sound low in his throat. He lapped at the bloody wound. His touch became more than I could handle as another climax began to build.

When it rolled over me, I embraced it in full and felt him tense as he reached his own peak. I felt him spasm inside me, which caused wave after wave of additional pleasure as my body instinctively gripped him tighter. I collapsed on top of him, my face pressed against his chest. He licked my wounded arm again before releasing it and wrapping me tight in his embrace.

Arys breathed my name and pressed a kiss to my sweaty temple. Soreness began to set in from the bite on my inner arm, but it was a welcomed pain, much like the one that would set in between my legs.

The best sexual afterglow was the one that needed no words to perfect it. My head rested over his still heart, the very place he once claimed I had breathed new life into, and I wondered what he was feeling. I gripped him tighter, wishing we could stay like that all day. It wouldn't be long before the coming dawn would drive him from me, taking with him the safety and comfort I was reveling in.

Chapter Seven

After Arys left, I'd promptly fallen asleep on the futon with the TV still on mute and my nightie haphazardly arranged. I'd awoken around three in the afternoon to Ky attempting to work quietly on her laptop at the kitchen table.

After a shower and more than one coffee, I was feeling more alert and almost ready to go hunt down a rogue werewolf.

Honestly, I wasn't in the mood to go out and mess around with an idiot Were that seemed to think he or she was a product of a Hollywood film, butchering hookers in dirty back alleys. Jez was coming along, so I could probably get away with leaving most of the bullshit to her. I'd rather take out a vampire than a Were any day. Killing a mortal could get incredibly messy.

I stood on the back deck watching Shaz as he hammered and banged at the broken railing. He grinned up at me and winked, setting a swarm of butterflies free in my stomach before flashing a disgusted look at the splintered wood.

"I need to get some new two by fours for this railing," he announced. "It can't be fixed like this. I'll do it next weekend if that's ok."

"No problem. Arys can pay for half the cost of the wood. Or, maybe the entire cost since he couldn't be bothered to fix it." As soon as I spoke the words, Shaz' eyes went to the healing bite on my inner elbow. He'd likely noticed it the moment he walked in the door. I felt ashamed and wished I'd worn a sweater.

I tried casually to turn my arm slightly, so that the two puncture marks could not be seen. He made a sudden noise of exasperation and dropped the tools he held to the ground. He took the deck stairs two at a time, coming to where I stood at the top.

"Don't hide it." He pulled my arm away from my side, turning it so that he could see the wound. His warm fingers grazed it, and a flood of pleasure and adrenaline swept me momentarily. "I hate that you feel you need to."

"I don't want to hurt you or make it a bigger deal than it is." I felt foolish and weak and once again wondered why he loved me the way he did.

"If this was something I wasn't capable of dealing with, I wouldn't still be here. You really need to relax." Shaz stared down at the vampire bite with a strange expression on his perfect face. "But, tell me, why do you let him do this? Do you really enjoy it?"

"I guess so," I searched his green eyes, finding a sincere desire for answers. "It's all a part of the energy and the power we call. Of course, there are other aspects." I felt awkward. I didn't want to talk about Arys feeding from me. Not with Shaz.

He looked more comfortable with it than I felt and that struck a chord that resonated deep within me. I expected Shaz to persecute me constantly for the ways that I'd wronged him. And, when he didn't do it, I did it to myself.

Sensing my unease, he released my arm and changed the subject. "So it's really over for Ky and Kale?"

"It is," I nodded and pulled him close for a tender kiss. "She and Julian seem to be an item now. I can't say I'm thrilled about that."

He gave a low growl at my mention of Julian. He didn't seem to have any intention of letting this go.

"I can't imagine what she's thinking," he shook his head incredulously. "She's a knockout and the nicest person in the world. Being with Julian is punishment for women like her. She deserves better."

"She had better." I kept my voice low so that it wouldn't carry. "But, it isn't any of our business. She's our friend, we have to support her."

"I know. I'm just not sure how easy that's going to be after I kick the shit out of her boyfriend." Shaz chuckled, and the wicked sound made my eyes widen.

I couldn't share in his enthusiasm. Unlike him, I was worried sick about that fight. Judging by his gleeful expression, he couldn't wait to sink his teeth into Kylarai's new love.

"Cut that out." I grinned and poked him playfully in the ribs. I wanted to lighten the mood. "Or, I might have to give you a smack or two myself."

He grabbed my finger and pretended to bite it. "I'm sorry, babe. I know you're not happy about this. I can't imagine that Ky is either."

I shook my head but said nothing. I couldn't wait for it all to be over. It was just another thing for me to stress over. As if Harley lurking around wasn't enough.

"I just want time to fly so I can hit up the Halloween party at Lucy's Lounge and unwind. For once." I kissed the end of his cute nose. "And, you better not have to work that night, either."

He laughed and caught my hand in his, pulling me closer so our bodies were pressed together. "Oh, don't you worry. There is no way in this world that I would leave you alone for every guy in the place to drool over. Especially if you're dressed as a Playboy bunny." He gave my ass a light pinch, and I squealed in surprise.

"You know, I think just for that, I'm not going to tell you what I'm dressing up as. You will have to wait and see." I smirked because I had no idea what I was going as. I still had plenty of time to shop.

"Well, if you're not telling, then neither am I." He flashed me that mischievous grin that I so loved, and my knees weakened.

"I guess we'll both have something to look forward to then. I'm actually excited at the thought of getting out. I haven't had much of a social life lately."

"All kill and no thrill, huh?" Shaz pulled back to nibble my bottom lip before giving me a light nip on the neck.

"Well, a little thrill." I threw my head back and embraced him tightly. "Not nearly as much as I'd like." I gave in to the urge to slip my tongue teasingly along the curve of his ear. It caused him to shudder as the nerves tensed and spasmed down his back.

"Stop that! You know I've got to get going right away."

"Yeah well, I've got to leave you with a lasting impression. I need to know how bad your wolf craves me." I wiggled against him briefly before pulling back. I wanted to tease him but not cause him any extreme discomfort.

He groaned and resisted when I went to move out of his reach. "There isn't a time when I don't crave you, Lex. Hot damn, you are such a tease. God, how it drives me wild. I love it."

He immediately closed the space between us so that my hands came to rest against his hard, alluring body. When he kissed me again, the taste of pine and wolf overwhelmed my senses. It stirred the animal inside, and I had the sudden desire to be furry. Everything felt right with Shaz, natural and serene.

When he broke off the kiss, it was with extreme reluctance. "Be safe tonight. Call me when you make it home so I know you're safe."

The genuine affection that he had for me never ceased to blow my mind. There was no question that I loved him, and really, how could I not? He was a dream come true, everything I thought I'd never find. He accepted me in every way, flaws and all.

"You know I will."

Shaz' embrace was the best, most perfect embrace that I'd ever been in. He had this way of holding me just tight enough so that I felt nothing but love and security. The emotion I sensed from him when he held me was one of the most powerful energies that I'd ever felt.

After I'd kissed him goodbye another half dozen times, I sent Jez a text to say I'd be ten minutes late but was on my way. Chances were good that she would still be later than I would anyway.

I went to my bedroom and dug through the closet until I found a red, form-fitting, long-sleeved shirt. The stretchy material it was made from was both body hugging and comfortable. My favorite pair of blue jeans made it a great outfit for fighting and running in. Hopefully, that wouldn't get excessive.

After brushing my long, poker straight hair and staring at it undecided in the mirror, I opted to leave it down but bring a hair tie just in case. Aside from my usual smoky eyeliner and blush, I wore little makeup. I didn't generally go out all dressed to kill someone unless it was part of the plan.

I took a moment to just sit on my bed and feel the pure energy of the earth. It hummed all around at all times but required concentration and willpower to truly experience it. I used my connection to the earth for many things. Right then, I used to it to ground my own energy and attempt to center the combination of wolf and vampire in my core.

It was somewhat of a metaphysical reset button. I was able to cleanse any negative or excess energy or acquire more should I need it.

It wasn't always the optimum power source, but it was pure and steady. Of course, my energy bond with Arys gave me my very own power source, though, that too had its limits.

Kylarai was softly humming a song I didn't recognize when I re-entered the kitchen. She looked up at me with a bright smile as she stacked clean glasses in the cupboard.

"Are you taking off now?"

I grabbed my shoulder bag from the counter beside the fridge and rifled through it to make sure I had everything. "Yeah, Jez and I have a new Were to put down. There's no second chance for this one. It's been slaughtering prostitutes downtown."

Kylarai pursed her lips and shook her head solemnly. "That's terrible. And yet, sadly typical."

It certainly was. The chances of being turned by a werewolf were incredibly slim because, in most cases, victims don't survive the attack. Of those that do, less than ten percent made it through without succumbing to the urge to kill and to have fun doing so. At times, I'm still not sure how I keep from going past the point of no return. This is a thought I have heard echoed by Shaz. I suppose the genetic and mental disposition isn't something that just anyone can adjust to.

"Well, have fun," she said, sounding like she meant it. "I will be here doing paperwork for a case I'm working on."

Kylarai had a tendency to be a workaholic, using work to lose herself. A night of paperwork would likely do wonders to help her sort out her recent thoughts and feelings. Trapping herself in the office for days at a time was common self-therapy that usually had her emerging like a butterfly from a cocoon.

"Don't run yourself ragged. I'll see you later."

The chilly October air was like a slap in the face. I didn't like it, but I didn't shiver. My resistance to the natural elements was stronger than that of humans. It was much colder than it had been the previous night. That was a typical Canadian fall though. I smiled to myself and paused to enjoy the quiet autumn energy.

The moon glowed overhead, round and vibrant against the night sky, not quite full. Its energy radiated down to me, strong when I concentrated on it. The sudden temptation to throw my head back and howl was hard to resist. Instead, I savored the sensations, anticipating that, in just days, the moon would be full and I would be wolf.

෨෨෨෨

Just as I'd thought, Jez still wasn't at the office when I arrived. The funny thing was that she lives closer to it than I do. The building was dark, and the parking lot was empty. I didn't plan on going inside.

The Blue Collar Comedy station on satellite radio kept me chuckling while I waited. I may have even snorted a little during a bit by Jeff Foxworthy. I don't care what anybody says, that redneck humor never gets old.

When I found myself looking at the dash clock for the second time, I decided that if Jez wasn't here in five minutes, I was calling her. Either that, or heading home to watch scary movies and sleep. The sound of a familiar and easily recognizable engine caught my attention, and I turned down the radio to listen. I had to be mistaken.

It sure sounded like the old muscle car to me, but I didn't really believe it until Kale's slick, black ride peeled around the corner at the end of the block. I watched as he turned into the lot with a squeal of tires, stopping a few yards from my car. What in the hell was he doing here?

Kale slid from the Camaro with a strong predatory energy that I could feel from where I sat. I quickly opened my door and got out of the car. I didn't want him approaching while I was still inside.

He was dressed to kill in pinstriped pants and a fedora that made him look like a vampire mob boss. His long duster was part of the badass look, like always. Those two different colored eyes of his sparkled with a devious glint, the one I saw when he killed. I wasn't sure that I liked this.

"What are you doing here, Kale?" I didn't try to hide the suspicious note that crept into my voice. "I wasn't expecting you."

He looked at me as if deciding how honest to be. "I need to kill something, Alexa. Something that still has a heartbeat. I'm coming with you tonight." He flashed me a look that dared me to contest his choice.

I leaned against the back of my car and crossed my arms over my chest. It was the best casual stance I could muster. However, I was overtly aware of the power of the moon above me, and I was prepared to tap it the second he gave me a reason.

"Alright," I conceded. What could I do, argue with him? "Have it your way. Do you want to take my place with Jez? She should be here any minute."

There was no way of escaping the awkwardness that fell like a blanket over us. So, I met his blue and brown eyes evenly, ready for anything. He wasn't prepared for a face off, and he avoided my gaze, looking out onto the street.

"Actually, she isn't coming. I'm taking her place. It's just me and you."

His words rang in my ears, and I stared at him dumbfounded. Please, tell me he was kidding. This was so not cool.

"Look, Alexa," he sighed and forced his gaze to mine. "I need to apologize for what happened the other night. I still can't believe I lost to the hunger like that. I'm sorry I hurt you."

I had expected his apology, knowing him the way I do. Kale is a stand up, respectable guy. I didn't expect the vibe I was sensing from him.

"Thank you. I understand the temptations. I've given in to them, too." I glanced nervously down the street as if expecting Jez' beat up white Liberty to fly around the corner. Of course, it didn't.

I wasn't afraid of Kale despite what he'd done to me just days ago. But, the devilish look in his eyes mixed with the lusty hunger emanating from him sure had me on edge.

"There's more." He took a step closer but stopped a few feet away. "When I took your blood, it wasn't like anything I've ever experienced before. It woke a hunger in me like no other."

I was keenly aware of the subtle changes in his personal energy. It stirred the atmosphere around us, causing me to grow naturally defensive. I had a feeling that I wasn't going to like where this was going.

"Kale," I began. "Let's just let sleeping dogs lie. There's no reason to-,"

"I can't stop thinking about you, Alexa." He forced the words out in a rush, and I shut up instantly as I choked on my own comment. "The power in your blood, the combination of the undead and the wolf is like nothing I have ever felt in my lifetime. There is no living power that compares to what you hold inside you. And, it's all I can think about."

Oh please, I thought. Let this all just be a bad dream. I struggled to swallow as my mind went into overdrive. I was shocked and at a loss for words.

"I don't know what to say to that, Kale. I don't understand." I swallowed hard, my breathing shaky. "We have a dangerous Were to track down. Let's do our job."

"Your blood is like a drug. Ever since I tasted it, all I can think about is tasting it again. You're drawing me like a moth to a flame, and I don't know why."

Alarm rang through me, and I hissed, "Stop it!"

"Alexa..." Kale trailed off pleadingly.

The silence quickly grew strained as we stared at one another. I could feel the glare that adorned my features. His face remained stony, expressionless.

My guts turned when I replayed his rushed confession in my head. A sinking sensation settled heavily in my stomach. I had to fight down the panic that threatened to launch a full-scale attack within me at the thought of Kale obsessing over my powerful blood. Was this something I should tell Shaz and Arys, or keep to myself?

I sighed heavily. "Let's just go do our job. We are friends, and that's not going to change. But, we have priorities, like a bloodthirsty werewolf to stop. And, I have no coherent response for what you just said." There, I was honest.

"Last chance to bail out," Kale said when I turned to his car. After what had happened last time we rode together, I wasn't driving. I wanted both hands free.

"Not on your life. If I don't hunt something soon, my head will burst." I got into the Camaro and put on my seatbelt, turning to him when he got in next to me. "I am stressed to the max right now, and I just need a good fight."

His sexy chuckle tickled the nerve endings in my spine, and I squirmed in my seat. "Careful what you wish for, my dear. I may have to remind you that you said that later."

As we pulled into traffic, I felt a shift in the energy inside me; something was changing. My stomach flipped a few times, and my fangs appeared unbidden. I swore, and Kale glanced at me, his eyes widening.

"Are you alright?"

I had to think about that before I could answer. The power was roiling around inside me like a rumbling volcano. Closing my eyes against it caught me up in a tornado of undead energy, and I felt like I was falling.

"I'll be fine." I ground the words out between clenched teeth. "It's been worse. Arys ... he must not have fed recently."

"I can't imagine how much harder it must be for you than it is for us." He turned down the radio, plunging the car into silence.

"I have given up trying to figure out how it all works. I feel like a pawn to the power more often than I feel in control of it." I sighed and stared out the window. "The stress doesn't help."

He seemed to consider this carefully before tentatively asking, "Do you want to unload? I'm always happy to listen."

I debated telling Kale, but before I could censor myself, it was all pouring out. The past few days of fighting, blood bond talk and scary-ass vampires that wanted a piece of me were too much, and I needed to share with a friend. It was easier with someone that was outside the situation.

The scenery outside the window flew by as we made our way downtown. I was hoping we could pinpoint this werewolf by its energy. If we had to rely on physical senses only, it would take forever.

"That's some heavy shit, Alexa." He let out a low whistle. "I'm sure I don't have to tell you what the blood bond means to mortals."

"No," I murmured. "You don't. I'm fully aware. And, of course, it's not something I'm even considering."

"Why do I sense that there is more to that thought?" Kale's attentive eyes darted from the road to me and back. "Like you left off the words 'right now'."

I paused and stared at him in wonder. My tone had indicated that I was leaving something out. Not in a million years. It had taken me ten years to get used being a werewolf, to love it and embrace it as me. Vampire? No, thank you.

It scared me that he had heard something in my tone that I hadn't intended. Panic shot through me.

"Kale, if you ever hear me say that I want to do it, knock some sense into me. Seriously." I reached out to touch the cool sleeve of his coat, wanting to ensure he knew that I meant what I said. "I'm afraid of myself and what I might do in the wrong situation. I just need to know someone has my back."

It got quiet then, and I reached to turn the radio up a few notches. I waited for his response, aware that he was weighing his words. I trusted him. I wanted to hear whatever he had to say.

"I'll do my best, Alexa. I mean, I'll try."

He sounded so uncertain. I smiled and gazed out the window as we went deeper into the slums. "That's all I can ask of you. Thank you."

Nerves had my stomach in knots as the anticipation began to build. My fangs itched at the gum, burning to pierce and tear.

I snuck a sidelong glance at Kale, judging his mood. He caught me and with a wry smile asked, "Yes? Is there a reason you're peeking at me from behind your lovely blonde locks?"

"Maybe." I might as well ask. "How are you feeling? About the whole thing with Kylarai, I mean. I wished I'd known, the other night, but she didn't tell me."

"Ah," he nodded his dark head in understanding. "How long have you been waiting to ask that? I'll manage, if that's what you mean. I adore her, Alexa, but we're not meant to be. I knew that. Wishful thinking, I suppose."

He sounded too casual. I didn't want to push it, but I was curious.

"So you're really all good? I was worried about you."

The admittance felt strange in lieu of the last time Kale and I had been together, but we were friends, and I truly cared for him.

"Not nearly as worried as I am about you." He smiled tightly, and I had a feeling there was something he wasn't saying.

Well, I sure as heck wasn't going to ask. Flashing back to the night at The Wicked Kiss was enough to get my power humming and reaching out to him. Focusing on taking deep, calming breaths was harder than it should have been.

We parked on a side street, just off the main downtown strip. The negative energy that filled the neighborhood stung despite the fact that I was shielding hard. It was strong here. Murder, addiction and despair, all powerful in their evil.

This wasn't looking too good so far. Judging from the fact that we were in a rundown area, away from the business district, with little to no streetlights, houses or people, I was pretty sure this was going to be a gong show. Either that or so easy, it wouldn't even be fun.

"Are you ready?" Kale raised a dark eyebrow in question as I double-checked the small dagger I had secured to my left wrist.

"You know it. Don't get me killed, or I will haunt the shit out of you. And, my boyfriends will beat you up." I stuck my tongue out at the absurdity of my statement.

He gave my hair a ruffle and then shoved my head playfully before climbing out of the car. I frowned and smoothed the mess back into place. Of all the irritating things...grrr.

"Do we have a plan of any kind, or are we just running blind like usual?" I asked, shivering slightly in the chilly night air. The cold didn't usually bother me, which meant the temperature was really dropping.

"Not a clue," he replied as his large strides forced me to double time my steps. "All I know is that we're looking for a werewolf, gender unspecified, that has been snacking on some of the downtown street folk. If they'd used a little more discretion, it may have gone unnoticed, but the slaughter fest has been drawing public attention."

He stopped suddenly and dug around in the pocket of his duster. "Here. I want you to take the spare key to my car. Just in case."

I gaped at him with wide eyes. "In case of what?"

"After that incident in the hotel with the demon, I don't want you left without a way to take off if it comes to that."

"Are you planning to leave me, Kale? That's not what I signed up for." I accepted the key and tugged on the sleeve of his jacket, encouraging him to keep walking.

"Of course not. I'm sure we can handle a Were. It's merely precaution."

A few months ago, the two of us had unexpectedly encountered a demon during a routine vampire kill. Kale had urged me to run, to leave him behind. I'd refused. And then, it had been too late. We'd made it out, but it was still nice to know if something came up, I wouldn't be stranded in the ghetto without a ride.

As we made our way to the main strip, my heart began to race. I was eager to catch scent of this shifter. Any werewolf lurking around out here couldn't possibly be up to any good.

The neighborhood was filthy. The street was littered with everything from cigarette butts to used hypodermic needles. I wore a disgusted grimace as we passed a series of abandoned shops, each with the windows smashed out. It got slightly better as we progressed to the next block.

Sirens wailed in the distance. A scantily clad woman leaned against a light post, watching us as we approached. Did she have a clue how close to death she was? Of course she did. She thrived on it. Any human that could walk these streets night after night was looking for something, and it wasn't good. Staring death in the face on a nightly basis was as close to feeling alive as some of these people got. It broke my heart.

I was prepared for her glare when we passed, though it was unlikely she could have mistaken me for a working girl. With my jeans and hoodie, I did not look anything like someone out to turn tricks. Hopefully, we would find this rogue wolf before it found her.

The traffic picked up slightly as we went from block to block. I raised my face to the wind, scenting the air for anything animal. A bevy of smells hit me, automotive fumes being the strongest. Mingled along with oil and car exhaust was an assortment of greasy food, garbage and something unidentifiable. I didn't like it though. There was a stench on the air, as if the lack of hope and dreams had grown stale and rotten over time.

For more than an hour, we followed both physical and psychic senses, finding nothing but dead ends. We'd covered a lot of ground, miles since we'd left the car. I was beginning to get frustrated. I didn't expect it to be easy, but my eager anticipation was fading.

When we passed by the entrance to another side street, my senses went on full alert. Everything in me commanded that I follow my instinct. I would find our werewolf.

"Do you feel that?" I turned to Kale with a renewed excitement. "We have to go this way."

I walked fast, a sense of urgency quickening my pace. Kale frowned down at me, his brow furrowed in thought.

"I feel it now that you've drawn my attention to it. I didn't before." The weight of Kale's heavy gaze drew my eyes to his. "I can still just barely make out that Were's energy. Your powers have seriously grown. And fast."

I couldn't be more powerful than Kale. He was older than Arys, for crying out loud. Of course, many other factors played a role in it, such as the fact that Arys killed and derived a lot of pleasure and power from it, whereas Kale was doing the willing victim thing. I turned it over in my head; the realization, shocking. I don't think I fully realized what Arys and I really had going on together.

The street was lined with apartment and condo buildings on either side. Additional side streets and alleys branched off between them. Though there were lights on in many windows, we didn't see anyone. If I were a human living in this part of town, I wouldn't be out at night either.

As we progressed from block to block, my senses began to burn like wildfire. The energy of the Were was strong, thick with the negative lashings of unrestrained primal fury. She was hunting. I could feel it. It caused me to quicken my pace; Kale, hot on my heels.

"This werewolf is hunting somebody," Kale said, keeping his voice low so as not to disturb the silence around us. "Her hunger is so fierce. I hope she doesn't already have prey in her sights."

I knew the werewolf we sought wasn't far. I allowed both my nose and my psychic abilities to guide me. Together, one sense seemed to complement the other so that I could almost see her in my mind's eye.

My legs moved faster until I was almost running. I knew she was close, and I wanted to reach her before she caught my scent and ran. I could feel Kale beside me, moving with the stealth and grace that nothing living could ever possess. Now that we'd located our target, the urgency within us grew. The power inside me seemed to respond to the excitement of my wolf. It began to scratch at me like a dog begging to be let out.

"This way," I announced when instinct and the sudden tangy scent of blood pulled me between two shabby looking apartment buildings.

As we slipped between the buildings, the pale glow of the streetlight behind us fell away. There was only darkness ahead. My eyes quickly adjusted, making out what lay before me. It was a parking lot with an alley running behind it. One single, dim bulb glowed in a streetlight near an overflowing dumpster.

Rounding the building, I already knew what I would see

between the building and the dumpster: our werewolf and what was left of her prey. She hovered over the body of a man, tearing chunks of flesh from the bone with a ripping, squishing sound. She was so engrossed in feasting on the kill that it took a solid five or ten seconds before she looked up at us.

We were too late for this victim, but there wouldn't be another. Her dark wolf eyes landed on us, and the vacancy within them struck me as eerie. She was completely out of her mind. Not a semblance of sanity remained in her murderous gaze. Her face and hands were smeared with blood, so much so that I couldn't tell at first glance what shade her olive skin was. Her long, black hair hung in dread-like chunks to her waist, and her clothing was splattered with blood and gore.

For a split second, I flashed back, seeing an image in my mind of a time when I'd slaughtered a man just like this. After Arys and I had bonded, I'd lost control to the hunger and killed a human who was abusing his girlfriend. She had thanked me later. The gruesome images were never far from my mind. I lived with the fear of losing control like that again.

Then, everything seemed to move in slow motion. Even though it all happened so fast, it was like a slow moving sports replay before my eyes.

Kale launched into action in the same moment that the crazy she-wolf did. I hung back, watching and waiting with a flaming ball of blue and golden energy glowing in the palm of my hand.

She rushed him; her garbled snarl sounded all wrong as it came from between her human lips. He anticipated her blow and easily took her off her feet with one outstretched arm. In a flash, she regained her footing and slashed at him with both clawed, bloody hands.

The craving for blood and power grew inside me. I threw the power I held at the rabid she-wolf, and it successfully knocked the breath from her. She went down on her rear end, choking and gasping for air. Kale stood over her, unleashing blows that would have killed most mortals. It didn't even faze her.

She came up scratching and biting, fighting for his throat even as he beat her back down again. I moved to shadow him in case she gained an advantage, but Kale stunned her with a blast of power at point blank range. It didn't throw her like I expected, though it did knock her senseless for a moment. She stared with wide eyes, and a high-pitched wail filled the night.

I made the mistake of letting my guard down for a split second. I turned to Kale with a question on my lips, taking my eyes from her as her instinct kicked in, driving her to fight harder. Despite Kale's reaction, he wasn't able to block her and searing heat cut through me as three of her claws bit through the material of my sweater. The blood ran from the deep slashes.

"Alexa?" Kale asked, never pausing to look at me as he grasped the Were by the neck and dragged her close. "Are you ok?"

She flailed wildly; her arms beat at the vampire uselessly. He deflected each blow with his free arm, but his eyes now locked on the pulse in her throat. My fury grew with every crimson drop that coursed down my arm. I lashed out with a blast of energy, causing her to cry out in pain. That wasn't enough for me. With a growl emanating from me, I struggled to get in between them, punching at her with a tight fist. I wanted to tear her apart.

"Let me kill her," I cried out, irrational in the surge of rage that swept me.

"No way. She's mine." Kale jerked the werewolf roughly so that she stumbled against him. Kale was in need of a fix, and it showed. His lips peeled back in a snarl, and he sunk fangs into the thrashing werewolf so hard that I felt it like a kick in the gut as I watched.

Blood poured from the wound as Kale opened the artery. The scent was suddenly heavy and thick all around us. As he drank in both blood and energy, the combination of physical power and hunger struck deep in me. Though I suffered the same weakness as Kale, our hungers were rooted in different places.

Watching him drain the werewolf to the point of death made me feel like I was spying on a personal moment, one that I shouldn't be seeing. It was as intimate as if I'd been watching him have sex. I have seen Kale kill but never have I seen him feed.

Turning my back on Kale wasn't something I wanted to do, but watching gave me the same sensation I got when I saw Arys kill: I liked it. I hated that I did, but there was no sense denying it. So, I didn't move; I stood frozen, feeling like a naïve novice. Every time I thought I knew what world I was a part of, I was thrown for a loop.

It was impossible not to feel the powerful energy rolling off Kale as he feasted on the intoxicating wolf blood. It swept me up in its inviting glow.

The wolf in his grasp put up a pitiful struggle, but it didn't take long for her strength to wane. She made a series of unintelligible sounds as if she was attempting to speak. It wasn't long until she was silent and limp as Kale deposited her on the ground at his feet. My eyes strayed to the punctures in her throat and the blood oozing from the wound.

When I met Kale's eyes, they weren't crazed or monstrous. However, they were calculating and watchful. I couldn't help but be affected by him as he crossed the short distance between us. In no way was I prepared for what he did.

Not for one moment did he pause or hesitate as he grabbed my wrist and pulled me to him. There was a strange look in his haunting eyes as he tipped my head up, forcing me to meet his eerie gaze. He kissed me with a depth that instantly transcended physical. I was pleasantly surprised to find blood still in his mouth. I was also shocked at my own sudden eagerness.

His tongue sought my own, and the blood dripped from his mouth to mine. He was ablaze with energy that forced any doubt or reluctance from me. The mix of vampire and werewolf power inside me was intrigued, curious to know what Kale had to offer.

Even as I savored the way the blood scratched Arys' itch inside me, I was drawn to Kale's centuries old energy. It wasn't the same with Arys. I had a bond with him that went to the root of our metaphysical makeup. Instead, I realized that I could feed on Kale's power and use it as my own. I realized that my power viewed Kale as a source to feed from, which was empowering after the night in the Charger when he'd made me the victim. I was fully aware of him drawing on my power as well, but this was different because I had control.

I allowed myself to fall into the power and ride out the wave that held us in its thrall. I tasted him with a selfish abandon that overruled my common sense. My wolf was pressing the surface of my control, and the desire to spill his blood won out.

I bit his tongue, just enough to get a taste of him. Kale's blood was an intoxicating blend of rich, age-old power and time. Power that didn't get exercised the way that it should. My body responded to him against my will as his deathly alluring darkness touched me in forbidden places.

He broke off the kiss and stepped back. I couldn't prevent the gasp that came from me. I stared at him in awestruck wonder as I licked the blood from my lips. In light of what he'd told me earlier, I couldn't decide which of us was the cause of this strange moment.

I searched Kale's eyes for a sign of his reaction. He regarded me coolly, as if he didn't trust himself to speak. Tentatively, he reached a pale hand out to touch the bleeding gashes along my upper arm. I was afraid to speak and break the strange spell as I watched him then lick my blood from the tips of his fingers.

"I'm sorry," Kale spoke softly, a look of shame evident in his contrasting eyes. "We should go."

Now that I'd tuned into Kale's personal energy, I could really feel the sadness and sense of loss. I hadn't been aware he carried it around so strongly. He was a very lost man. Kale needed to find himself. Something I felt I was still only beginning to do myself.

"Don't be sorry," I breathed, unable to make the words come out any stronger. I had to take a few deep breaths. "Don't deny what you are, Kale. And, never apologize for it."

"You make it sound so easy." He eyed the pulse leaping hard in my throat, and I swallowed hard.

"It can be. It doesn't have to be something you deny in order to maintain control. You can't ignore what you are or what you need."

His eyes closed briefly, his dark lashes framing them beautifully. A pained expression crossed his face. "I have to ignore this need, so we have to leave before I do give in."

It frightened me when he said that because I could feel the raw honesty in his tone. After the kiss we'd just shared, my own control was seriously being tested. The energy of the hunger has a way of trying to sway decisions, and it was always about the power.

My tongue held the combined taste of both the dead wolf and Kale. I couldn't resist licking my lips once again, tasting them both.

"Alright, let's get out of here." I nodded toward the dead she-wolf just yards away. "I'll call Fox to deal with disposing of that." Fox Mathews was the resident medically trained werewolf and friend of my small town pack. He dealt with our nasty injuries and took care of things like this, things human authorities simply must not be allowed to discover.

"Thank you, Alexa." Kale nodded and tipped his hat to me like the classy gentleman he usually was. "You are a true gem."

I concentrated on taking deep breaths in order to slow the beating of my thrashing heart. My mind was reeling, and it was all I could do not to giggle foolishly in response to the power high.

As we made our way back toward the filthy street front, I wiped at my bloody arm. It wasn't as bad as it felt. If I thought I'd had worries about what to tell Arys and Shaz before, I sure had them now. I chewed my lower lip nervously as I turned that conversation over in my head. Maybe ... maybe it was better kept quiet for now.

Chapter Eight

I stifled a yawn and took another sip from my paper coffee cup. Jez pulled a skimpy French maid costume from the clothing rack, and I shook my head vigorously in response.

"You wouldn't seriously wear that, would you?" I reached past her to finger the material of a velvet medieval gown.

"I don't know. I could be Magenta from The Rocky Horror Picture Show." She eyed the price tag before putting it back. "It's a cute option anyway."

"You should be someone really badass," I said, moving to another wall of costumes. "Like Beatrix Kiddo."

Jez tucked a long golden strand of hair behind an ear that was adorned with a large silver hoop. She looked both casual and stylish in a leather jacket and biker boots. The blue jeans she wore fit her slender legs like a second skin.

"Mmm," she purred, licking her bright red lips. "That would be a good one. Do you have any idea what you want to be?"

I gave my head a shake, causing my long ponytail to brush against my elbow. I had already turned my nose up at hundreds of costumes. I was getting ready to give up.

"Lex? Why don't you go as something like this? Blow the socks off your boys."

When I looked over to where she stood about thirty feet away, I could barely make out the flimsy scrap of fabric she held.

"Um, what the heck is that?" I walked over to her, careful to avoid the nosy saleswoman that had been after us since we walked in the door.

"It's a Jane costume," she giggled. "You know, Tarzan's woman."

"Oh shit, no way." I laughed but refused to accept the tiny outfit when she extended it to me. "I'd like to wear a little more than

99

that. And, I think I get enough of that "me Tarzan, you Jane" shit as it is from those guys."

"But, it would make your boobs look amazing. Mine aren't big enough to wear something like this." She tried to hold the small leopard print material up to my breasts and I snatched it out of her hand, returning it quickly to its hanger. She gave me a dirty look and said, "Suit yourself, but it would have been perfect."

I wandered aimlessly from rack to rack. From Little Bo Peep to the Wicked Witch of the West, I considered and rejected everything. The sales lady decided she was brave enough to ask me one more time if I needed assistance. I successfully resisted the urge to bare fangs and snarl.

"Alright, you're trying this on if I have to wrestle you into it myself." Jez approached with a gleam in her eye and something black and red clutched in her hand.

"Jez..." I was wary of what hideous outfit she was going to thrust at me now. She grabbed my hand and dragged me unwillingly into the nearest change room.

Once inside she tugged lightly at my black velvet tank top, rushing me before I'd even gotten a look at what she held. "Just hold on a minute here. What are you trying to do to me?" I grabbed the red and black costume from her hand.

A black strapless corset dress laced in red trim along with a silky red cape made me raise an eyebrow in question.

"It's Little Red Riding Hood. It makes perfect sense. You are the big bad wolf so you might as well be the innocent little vixen as well. Just put it on. You'll knock 'em dead if you wear this."

I had to admit that it was a pretty sexy costume without being overly trashy. Jez may not be straight, but she was one of my best friends. So, even though I would never change in front of my guy friends, changing in front of her wasn't as awkward as one might think.

She took my coffee cup and motioned for me to get moving. When I'd exchanged my comfy blue jeans and tank top for the costume, I had to do a double take at my reflection in the mirror. The dress clung to my curves, passing my thighs and rear end but ending well above the knee. My boosted cleavage was certainly eye catching. It looked better than usual. My running shoes didn't look as good as knee high boots would, but I could easily envision it.

The cape was just a little longer than the dress, brushing the back of my knees. It was incredibly soft and a glance at the price tag made me think that for that kind of dough, it had better be.

"This has to be the one. You look amazing. What do you think?" Jez stood beside me; her reflection in the mirror nodded in serious approval. "Just make sure you wear some lipstick on Halloween. Red will really make your eyes pop."

I rolled my eyes at her, watching my reflection as I did so. I loved the outfit and the irony of being Little Red Riding Hood kind of appealed to me.

"I like it," I conceded, and she smiled knowingly. "Does this mean I get to pick something out for you now?"

"Not a chance."

Twenty minutes and nearly a day's pay later, we were on our way out of the mall. Jez had settled on the black and yellow Kill Bill costume I'd suggested. I had my moment of gloating at that. She admitted that I was right. No one else could rock that outfit like she could.

It was dark already; the sun descended long before supper during the fall. Arys sure didn't mind. It gave him significantly more freedom.

The parking lot hummed with the energy of dozens of dimly lit lights. Jez continued to chatter on about the latest hot lady she was dating as we made our way to the car.

"Can you believe that? She actually told me that she's dating two other women as well as me. That's some nerve alright. I have to break it off."

"Hey, hypocrite," I said, pulling out my car keys as we drew closer to the Charger. "Aren't you practically always dating more than one person?"

"No, not always. I'm just trying to keep my options open in case Miss Right comes along. And, don't be tossing ugly words around, Alexa. You'd be super pissed if Shaz or Arys were seeing someone else." She wagged a finger at me, and I ignored it.

What she said was true, for the most part. However, that just wasn't an issue with Shaz. But Arys, I didn't always know what he was up to with his victims. It wasn't something we talked about. Maybe because I didn't really want to know.

"So," Jez continued animatedly. "Are you sure you don't want to come stake a few vampires tonight? I mean, I know you said you don't think it's a good idea to hang with Kale tonight, but we could ditch him."

I looked up at her suddenly in shock, and she was grinning from ear to ear. I'd told Jez all about my recent outings with Kale, much to her delighted surprise. She was always one for juicy gossip.

"Very funny, Jez. If you had been there last night, you wouldn't be making jokes." We got into the car, and I gave her a look. She continued to smile.

"I believe you. I still think it sounds sexy though." She shrugged and tossed her thick, leopard gold mane. "You're the one with all of the vampire mojo going on. I'm surprised you don't want a taste of Kale. And, I mean that in the best way possible."

She held up both hands in mock defense, and I decided to let that one slide. We cruised through the city, headed toward the office. We carried on casual conversation along the way, but I couldn't help but mull over what she'd said.

I'd tasted Kale last night. His strong, coppery blood had dripped inside my mouth so that I could taste him in both body and power. I hadn't known that I'd wanted to until it had been happening, but I had wanted it bad in that moment. The only reason that bothered me was that I'd once accused Arys of being power hungry, wanting whatever he could get from me. It nagged at me that perhaps I wasn't so different. No, I definitely would not be going out on the hunt with Kale and Jez this evening.

Just the sight of the black Camaro parked outside the office set my heart racing. This was ridiculous. I think part of it was that I hadn't told either of my lovers about the bloody power kiss we'd shared. Of course, it helped that I hadn't seen either of them since.

Nobody knew except for Jez. There was no way I was stupid enough to tell Kylarai. It just wasn't worth mentioning. At least, not at this point.

"Don't let him know that I told you Jez." I stopped her with a hand on her elbow. "He really is like a brother to me, and he's dealing with enough right now."

"Of course. No worries." She beamed and blinked bright green cat eyes at me. "Kale will come around on his own."

I followed her inside, took a deep breath and focused on slowing my heart rate to normal. If I didn't have a potential client coming by, I wouldn't have even come in.

At first glance, it appeared that Kale was the only one there. However, upon closer inspection I was able to determine Lilah's spooky energy down the hall in her office. Lilah was both vampire and demon, older than dirt, according to some. I didn't know much about her, but she'd saved my ass, and that made her cool with me.

I couldn't help but miss Lena's presence. I wished that she were here, instead of out of town with Veryl. I always had so many questions for her. The witch was damn talented, more so than she let on.

The front door latched behind us, preventing any unwanted guests from entering at leisure. The sound of it was loud in the quiet inside. Kale lounged in a chair at the table in the small kitchen with a newspaper spread out in front of him. He glanced up as we entered, a shadow of something unidentifiable behind his eyes. He banished it with a smile and a shake of his dark head.

"Hey ladies, how are you?" Kale greeted us with a grin, and I could see that he was forcing casual as hard as I was.

"I don't know about you, honey, but I am ready to take out a vampire." Jez deposited her shopping bag on the counter before digging through the fridge.

"Just one?" Kale raised an eyebrow skeptically. "What about you, Alexa? Are you up for another hunt?"

I had to force myself to meet his eyes directly. I didn't want him to know how nervous he had made me. "No, I'm waiting for a client. You two will have to have all the fun for me."

"I can handle that." Jez produced a container of leftover Chinese food. "Who's is this?"

Kale wrinkled his nose in distaste and fanned a hand before his face. "Does it matter? It smells hideous."

"Not a fan of Asian cuisine, Kale?" She pulled a fork from the drawer and dug into the container. "I hear those Asian chicks taste divine."

"I guess you would know," he shot back at her, winking as he spoke. She frowned upon realizing that his lame joke had been better than hers.

"Do we really have to talk about tasting people?" I dug through the cupboards until I found clean coffee filters. Couldn't anyone put them back in the same place? I was carefully trying to avoid looking at either of them, knowing that Jez would have a grin a mile wide.

Her peal of laughter had me rolling my eyes knowingly. Thankfully, she didn't say anything facetious like I'd been expecting. Kale made a dramatic show of clearing his throat before rising to his full height.

"How much longer will it be until you're done stuffing your face and we can head out? I'd like to avoid cutting this one as close to dawn as last time." He smirked at Jez as he spoke, and her cat eyes narrowed into a glare.

"We did not cut it that close. Besides, it's still early." Jez paused, her fork poised in midair. She hissed softly. "I thought vampires had loads of patience. No need to get your panties in a twist."

Kale merely sighed, regarding her with a cool, unaffected stare. I turned to the sink, running fresh water into the coffee pot. It was more than obvious that Kale wanted to escape my presence as surely as I wanted to be relieved of his. It was just so awkward with that crazy kiss replaying in my head.

I turned to pour the fresh water into the coffee maker, giving Jez a pointed look as I did so. All at once, understanding crashed over her features and a blush colored her cheeks.

"You know, I can get something while we're out. Just let me grab something from my office." Dropping the Chinese food container, she dashed out the kitchen door and down the hall, leaving Kale and I alone.

"How awkward is this?" The words just tumbled out of me, and I cringed inwardly in embarrassment. I flashed Kale a tight smile, feeling my cheeks flush.

Despite the span of the kitchen separating us, Kale's presence felt enormous. His energy seemed to overwhelm my senses once it caught my attention. His power was running strong and steady tonight, not unlike the brewing coffee that I couldn't wait to drink up. I had to shake myself out of that mind frame.

"Come on, Alexa. It's us; it shouldn't have to be awkward,

regardless of what happened last night. Again, I'm sorry."

I shook my head and dared to cross the distance, laying a hand lightly on his leather-clad arm, just for a moment. "No apologizing. This is the world we're part of, and we should know what to expect from it."

He seemed to consider this before nodding in agreement. "You're right. And I, even more so than you, after this many years of existence. No worries then?"

"No worries." I busied myself with fetching cream and sugar, taking care to double check the expiration date before pouring the cream in my cup. "Your friendship means more to me than any of the power stuff that's bound to come up. That's what will keep us sane. I have enough insanity in my life with men. I count on you for normalcy."

His low chuckle was soothing and comforting because it immediately banished the strange atmosphere that had settled. Jez reappeared in the doorway with a file folder tucked under one arm.

"Ready?" Her bright eyes flicked back and forth between us.

After the two of them had left, I beat a hasty retreat to my office for some quiet time alone. I didn't get that very often and even brief moments were worth savoring. I wasn't sure when my potential client was due to show. It could be any time. I didn't even have the client's full name. In fact, I wasn't even sure what gender I was expecting or if this were a human or a supernatural. Had I really agreed to this? I had to start paying more attention.

I passed some time checking email and catching up with various online avenues while waiting for this mystery person to show up. It was likely a run of the mill vampire hunt. One vampire gets ticked at another and outs them for some treacherous deed, gaining them a death sentence. Meanwhile, the original vamp never gets exposed as the one behind it all. Not all vampires were bold and brash. Of course, a cowardly vampire rarely existed for long.

After an hour passed and nobody had shown up, I began to get restless. I wasn't one for sitting around idly. I clicked around in my documents until I found an ebook that I'd purchased last time I'd been stuck waiting for someone. I'd wait one more hour, but then I was out of there. It wasn't that I had anything better to do right then, but I would have rather been slaying vampires with Kale and Jez than sitting on my ass in boredom.

The horror novel had caught my attention easily with gore and slaughter right from page one. I had a penchant for the harsh writing style of most horror authors, a refreshing break from some of the more feminine pieces Kylarai was inclined to bring home. I was so engrossed in the tale of terror that I didn't fully register the sounds when Lilah let herself out of the building.

When the front doorbell rang, I almost leaped out of my skin. A shot of adrenaline slammed through me, and I had to take a deep breath. I quickly bookmarked my spot in the book before closing the file and turning off the monitor. As my legs carried me to the door, I had to fight the sensation that they were made of jelly.

As my fingers closed over the lock, the strangest feeling swept me. Everything inside me screamed not to open the door. I paused and questioned the rationality of that. It just felt like a vampire. And, I had just been reading a slasher novel all alone in a large, dark office.

I forced myself to clear my thoughts and focus on my instinct. It continued to persist that whatever was on the other side of the door was something I did not want to meet with face to face. The bell sounded again, and I stood motionless, uncertain.

Despite all of my instincts, something else was pushing me to open the door. The promise of something big on the other side was almost too much to ignore. Against my better judgment and the cry of protest from my wolf, I unlocked the door and pulled it open. A thousand different words for describing stupidity flooded my brain as I looked out on the vampire smirking down at me on the front step.

Harley Kayson looked just as he had in every memory of Arys' I could recall. To say that I was frightened would have been understatement of the year. I was staring at a monster far worse than what any horror author could conjure up.

I stared at Harley with dread etched on my features. He smiled back at me, knowing he had me right where he wanted me. I swallowed hard but didn't dare speak.

"What's wrong, Alexa? You don't look very happy to see me." He stared at me with eyes so dark they appeared black. "I assume I need no introduction."

He took his time looking me over from head to toe and back again. A shake of his head drew my attention to his short, dark hair.

The barest traces of silver lined his temples. Clad in an obviously expensive suit, he looked as if he had just stepped out of one of Arys' memories.

"You're just like he said you were. But better." If his words were supposed to ease my panic, they succeeded in having the opposite effect.

With a thought, I held energy ready at my fingertips. It didn't seem to faze him. Instead, it encouraged his interest in me.

"So it's true." He nodded more to himself than to me. Before I could consider slamming the door in his face, he shoved past me, glancing around at the empty office. "You can relax though. I'm here to talk ... this time. Is there somewhere that we can sit? Or, would you prefer to stand?"

My mind raced a mile a minute as a series of horrific images flashed behind my eyes. This monster was beyond vampire, he was pure evil. I stood my ground as he slowly circled me, getting a good look.

"What the hell do you want?" My voice shook with fear, and I swallowed hard.

He studied me pensively. "I haven't decided yet."

"Yeah, well I don't have time for this shit. You really should be going." I wanted to toss the power I held ready, but something was sapping my confidence. He was giving me a daring look; he wanted me to do it.

Harley cleared the remaining few feet between us in less than a second. I gasped when he stood close, gazing at me with open, raw hunger. I swear I felt my heart come to a stop.

Before I could react, he grabbed my hand, ignoring the dancing blue and golden yellow within it. I almost choked on my fear when the power I held fell flat. He took it into himself with a touch, as easy as if I hadn't been resisting.

A smile of pure pleasure crossed his face as he tasted my energy. "I'm sorry, darling, but I'm not about to spar with you here. You and I are going to have a little chat. It's your choice how much of that chat is talking and how much of that is power games."

I obviously had little real choice in this matter. Of course, the last thing I wanted to do was battle it out with Harley. I sighed and crossed my arms over my chest. "What do you want to talk about?"

"What do you think? There seems to be just one thing we have in common."

"Arys."

"None other."

"What about him?" I narrowed my eyes suspiciously at the intimidating vampire.

"I want to know more about what you have with him. He wasn't inclined to do a lot of talking about that when he took it upon himself to defend your honor, which I have yet to truly threaten." He raised a dark eyebrow and grinned. That action seemed to be threat enough for me. "You are not like any other werewolf, human or vampire. You seem to have a little of every world, and my dear Arys is somehow connected to you. It's only natural that I am curious."

"Of course." I nodded, hating that he referred to Arys as his. Arys had never been his. I had to bite my tongue to keep from saying so. "I'm sure you know we've bonded our power."

"What have you gained from that?" His eyes remained on mine, but I could feel his analysis of me on every level.

"I'm still not entirely sure. It's come with a bit of a learning curve." I was choosing my words carefully, and from the dark look he gave me, it was apparent.

Harley paced a very slow circle around me so that I had to turn to keep him in my direct line of sight. His coal-black eyes were eerie; a chill coursed down my spine as they peered deep into me. I felt myself falling into them before I could stop it. The next thing I knew, he had me up against the wall, a hand on either side of my head. It was dizzying, and I struggled to clear my mind.

He pressed close, so that I had to keep staring into those drowning pools of black. I gasped when he brought his lips to mine, a gentle press that I couldn't deny while gazing into those hypnotizing eyes. Though I knew that this was his allure as a powerful vampire, I couldn't combat it.

I expected him to deepen the kiss, but he didn't. The press of his open mouth on mine was enough for him to draw my energy directly into him, intimate but not entirely invasive. I was stricken with fear that he would bite me. I didn't want him tasting my blood. He never did though.

Harley tasted sweet, like forbidden candy. My resistance burnt up like a flammable substance until it was nonexistent. When I found myself reaching for him, I came back to myself with a start. I began to struggle harder against him, and he stepped back with a strange smile pulling at his lips.

I felt ashamed of my weakness and inability to resist him. My hand flew to my mouth, touching my lips as I pondered what had just happened. Harley laughed, low and smooth. My stomach clenched in response.

"He hasn't blood bonded you." Harley ran his tongue over his lower lip, tasting me. "It's incredibly easy to see why he was drawn to you. You are damn powerful."

I had to concentrate on the mechanics of breathing. I shook my head and choked on my words. I gaped at him for a moment. "You stole the power right out of my hand. How powerful can I be?"

"That has nothing to do with it. I merely took what you were freely giving. It was idle power, fair game." He shrugged as if it was common knowledge. "What can you really do?"

I thought back to what I'd done to the vampiress that I'd killed with Arys. I'd forced power into her until her heart exploded. Telling Harley about that couldn't possibly work in my favor. I was glad mind reading was a selective ability for vampires, much like energy manipulation. Some were better than others.

"Nothing," I answered blankly. "I'm just a werewolf." I feigned the best, vacant-eyed expression possible.

"Alright, Alexa, have it your way. I won't be put off that easily. You have successfully made Arys more powerful than even he would have dreamed possible. And, if you think that's going to go unnoticed, you'd better think again. I won't be the only one crawling out of the woodwork to get a taste of you."

I shuddered at his words, hating the feeling of him on my lips. What I hated most was how badly I'd wanted to taste his power as well. I glared at him with all of the hate I could muster.

"Why are you here, Harley? What is it that you really want from me?" I came away from the wall with my hands balled into fists.

He nodded thoughtfully, a slight tilt to his head. "I want to know what Arys has that I don't. I want to know what is so important that he is willing to destroy anything that dares to threaten you. Clearly he loves you, yet he chooses not to bond you." Harley's voice was low, contemplative. "I want to know what joins him to the most powerful werewolf alive."

I stared at him fearfully as if he were mad, which I was pretty sure he was. This was all about what Arys had that he did not. Was it just a vampire's need to dominate or was there more to it?

"All I can tell you is this, whatever Arys and I have, it's meant to be. It's bigger than we are and try as I might to find my way out, it is here to stay." I saw no harm in divulging that much to Harley. I was hoping he would see it for the truth it was and leave me alone.

He remained motionless, but his energy sparked hot around me. What I wouldn't have given to have Lilah walk in right then.

I felt myself shrink beneath Harley's sinister gaze. True terror struck me when his power reached out for me, battering my personal shields.

"I created him, wolf. Arys is mine before he will ever be yours." Harley took an unsteady step toward the door, and I knew he was fighting the urge to hurt me. Or worse. I knew better than to argue with him. "And whatever is his, is likely to be mine, if I should will it."

My breathing effectively stopped then as his words squeezed my heart like a vice. I stared into those inky orbs, the blank expression on his stony face stealing any response I would have had. His threat was clearly spoken, leaving no room for confusion. I began to pray silently that he would just leave before this situation could get any more fucked up.

"I just had to see you for myself," he continued, edging closer still to the door. "And, I see what a rare and powerful beauty you are. So much so, that I do not trust myself to stay another minute without tasting your blood. I'm afraid our visit is much shorter than I would have liked. I promise you that next time, we will get to know one another a little better."

He winked then, his self-satisfied smile unfading. The moment he disappeared through the door, I was moving. I slammed the door closed and secured the locks before backing into the kitchen, a hand over my mouth as I asked myself what the hell had just happened.

Oh, I knew what happened, but I couldn't believe that it was real. Harley Kayson had set his sights on me. His intentions were clear. Just as Arys had feared, Harley had taken an unhealthy interest in me. And, his obvious jealousy was something to be concerned with.

I sat in the kitchen, shaking in both fear and revulsion. When nobody came back to the office, I paced anxiously until sunrise was so close that I knew I was safe.

No vampire had instilled this kind of fear in me in almost a decade. It was humiliating, and a part of me wanted to cry. It swept me back in time to when I had been a frightened teenage werewolf coming to grips with the urge to shred living things with my bare hands. This was worse, much worse.

Chapter Nine

Shaz was practically having kittens by the time I made it home. Making the mistake of leaving my cell phone in the car had resulted in half a dozen missed calls. I was feeling both stupid and ashamed when I pulled up at home to find his car sitting out front. He probably thought I was dead after being MIA for so long. I wasn't looking forward to sharing this news with him. My overprotective mate was likely to become even more so.

"Where in the hell have you been?" The look on Shaz' face was so stricken with concern that I couldn't even laugh it off like I'd hoped. "I've been calling you since I got off work."

"I know. I'm sorry; I forgot my phone in the car." I went to him immediately and slipped into the safe confines of his warm embrace. "I had an unexpected visitor at the office last night. Harley couldn't wait any longer to get a look at me."

My white wolf lost it then. He pulled back so he could take a good look at me, checking for anything amiss. "What? Why didn't you call someone? Where was everybody? Did he hurt you?"

I shook my head and smiled in spite of his worry. It was just so sweet. "No, I'm fine. I promise. He just wanted a little taste of my power, which he took against my will. Then he threatened me and left."

I gave Shaz the instant replay of what happened, walking down the hall to my room to change as I spoke. He followed closely, asking questions here and there. His tone was frantic, and I knew that no matter what I said, he was going to go all territorial male on me.

"I knew that Arys was going to put you in danger. It was just a matter of time." He ran a hand through his white hair, causing a tuft to stand up haphazardly. "I'm going to fucking kill him, I swear it."

"Oh please, not that again. I need you to stay calm. Freaking out isn't going to put me in any less danger from Harley." I shed my clothing and shrugged into my silky, leopard print robe. "I need you, Shaz. If you go crazy, you could get yourself killed."

He scoffed but didn't reply. He knew I was right. Crossing his arms over his firm chest, his green eyes followed me around the room as I brushed my hair and piled my laundry in the corner.

After a long moment, he sighed and said in exasperation, "Arys was adamant that he hear from you. He came by Lucy's Lounge last night. He was worried when I mentioned not being able to reach you during my last break."

"I'm surprised you mentioned it at all." I smiled teasingly, but he wasn't in the mood. His jade eyes remained serious.

He crossed the room, his footsteps falling softly on the beige carpet. With the gentlest touch, he lightly traced the scabby claw marks that ran down the side of my arm.

"I know there are some things that I can't save you from and others that I don't have to. Still, I can't help but feel the need to try." He smiled softly and bent to press his lips to mine in a tender kiss. "And that godforsaken vampire is just one of them. I'm sorry."

I kissed him back with a desperation that surprised even me. My wolf was eager to cling to him and the comforts of pack. "Don't be sorry. I love everything about who you are. Even when it makes me crazy." I laughed softly in between kisses with my hands entwined in his downy soft hair.

Shaz slipped his tongue between my lips, tracing a moist path along my lower one. I sucked his tongue into my mouth, loving the taste of wolf and pine. Closing my eyes against the daylight streaming through my window, all thoughts of Harley were swept away. As the kiss deepened, Shaz' strong arms went around me, and he slowly walked me backwards, to the bed.

I thought he was going to drag me down with him but instead he pulled back. "You better call that damn vampire and get it over with. I want to enjoy you, uninterrupted."

His touch fell away as he turned to get the phone from my bedside table. I rolled my eyes when he pressed it into my hand, but I dialed Arys' number anyway. He answered on the tail end of the first ring.

"I know you saw him, Alexa. Tell me what he did to you."

Arys cut straight to the chase, not one to waste time on meaningless small talk.

I sighed and took a deep breath. "You were right. Harley really does want a piece of me. He scared the living shit out of me tonight." A litany of curses was Arys' response to that before demanding that I tell him everything. After doing so and taking care to leave nothing out, he immediately demanded that I come to him.

"I'll be there at sunset." I watched Shaz who sat on the end of my bed, waiting patiently. Nothing could pull me from his side right now.

"You're with the wolf."

"Yes. Is that a problem?" My tone was daring, and he knew better than to push me.

"Of course not." He laughed outright in my ear, and I realized he'd been worried that I simply didn't want to see him. "I'll expect you at dusk."

"Happy now?" I asked Shaz, replacing the phone on the receiver before turning to him expectantly.

He grinned playfully before his arms went around me, and he tackled me down on the bed. "Almost. I'll be happier once I'm inside you. I can't tell you how bad I've been aching for you."

His words instantly brought both a blush and a smile to my face. If my wolf could get away with never leaving his side, she would never part from him. Regardless of the need we had for each other all the time, it was considerably stronger with the approach and rise of the full moon. Just knowing how bad he wanted me had the heat rushing between my legs.

I lay beneath him as he nuzzled my neck. Shaz' hot breath tickled, sending a delicious shiver down my spine. I pulled him closer, inhaling his scent deeply into my lungs. It stirred me to life inside, and I hungered for him.

"You make me crazy, Lex," he whispered, dragging his teeth over the sensitive skin of my throat. His tongue was quick to follow, and I squirmed in excitement. "If I had it my way, I'd never let you out of my sight."

Drawn to touch his bare skin, I reached under his t-shirt, sliding it up so I could run my hands over his perfectly hard body. A sigh of contentment escaped me. "I love you, wolf boy. I wish we could stay this way forever."

Shaz rose up on one arm so that he could look down into my face. The look in his eyes was intense, as if he could see into my soul. Maybe he could. He kissed me suddenly, plunging his tongue deep into my mouth. Things tightened low in my body as moisture rushed to my tingling sex. I made a sound of pleasure, and Shaz nipped at my tongue and lips.

"My mate," he murmured, tugging on my lower lip lightly with his teeth. "My love ... you are my other half. I'd die without you."

The soft touch of his hand as it slipped inside my robe had me anxious to rush ahead, needing to feel more of him against me. Though I noted his strange choice of words, I didn't want to inquire about them and risk stopping our building momentum.

The truth was that I agreed wholeheartedly with his emotional words. I felt them to the tips of my toes and the depths of my very being. A surge of feelings swirled like a tornado inside me, and I clung to him. In light of last night's events, I feared my time with Shaz would be cut short now more than ever.

Shaz trailed a hand over my ribs, up my side to my breast. When his fingers deftly found my nipple, I moaned softly and bit at his bottom lip. I wanted to taste his blood, something I rarely did. I was suddenly aching for his hot werewolf blood. With fangs, I carefully bit down, drawing just enough blood to coat my tongue. He made a small pained noise, but his growing erection pressed against me indicated how much he enjoyed my bite.

His touch grew in aggressiveness along with his desire. I tugged at his shirt, wanting him to be rid of it. I needed to feel his skin on mine. I ached for it.

"I need you," I panted, pulling at his clothing. Slow and savory wasn't what I was in the mood for. However, Shaz seemed to have his own ideas. He pushed my hands away, kissing me as he did so, deep and thorough so that I had no choice but to give in.

"Slow down. What are you in such a rush for?" His tongue dipped in and out of my mouth, playing along my sharp fangs. When he kissed and licked his way down to my breasts, I knew it was going to be his way whether I liked it or not.

He drew my nipple into his mouth, swirling his tongue around it in a way that started a fire burning in my loins. It quickly grew into a flame that caused my power to rise. Though it was subtle, it was undeniable. Every single piece of me was in need of him. Shaz' head came up suddenly; his eyes fixed on me as he felt the sensations of the energy as it hummed around us. He raised an eyebrow and then shrugged, nuzzling his way into my robe.

I was more than willing to let him pull it out from under me, glad to be rid of it. Shaz pressed his face against my flat stomach, inhaling deeply. His tongue dipped into my bellybutton, and I giggled. Placing both hands on each of my hips, he held me perfectly immobile as he licked his way down to the edge of my black thong.

I bit my bottom lip, careful with my dangerously pointy teeth. He was my mate, and right then, I needed him to act like it. Sensing this, his touch seemed to grow rougher as he quickly stripped me of the flimsy underwear. When it had landed on the floor with my robe, he turned back to me, a fire smoldering in his sexy stare.

The direct eye contact as he lowered his mouth to me was exhilarating. As Shaz dipped his tongue into my wetness, I shuddered and clawed the bed sheets. His touch was soft as he licked me lovingly. His hands gripped my hips, controlling my movements, holding me still beneath him as he worshipped me. Though Shaz was naturally a very gentle man, I absolutely loved it when the wolf in him came out to dominate me.

I reached down to entangle my hands in his hair. I moaned and writhed beneath him. When he bit at me, the touch of his fangs sent a thrill racing through my veins. I practically melted as the orgasm steadily built in response to the rough licking. The sensations quickly became overwhelming as the waves of amazing pleasure washed over me. When I climaxed it was with a shattering intensity that had me crying out between gasps for breath. He never ceased his oral love, not until I had ridden out every descending wave.

I couldn't have formed words if I'd tried to. All I knew was that I wanted him inside me, to fill the emptiness and ease the throbbing ache. He bit lightly at the inside of my thighs before pulling my legs open wider.

When he rose up over me, I repositioned so I could take his deliciously smooth shaft in my hand. I stroked the rock hard length of it, wanting to feel him throb in my mouth before taking him into my body. Shaz closed his eyes as I ran my tongue along the sensitive head of his cock before sucking him deep into my mouth. He moaned softly, and a small growl rumbled in his throat. I smiled to myself, loving his response to me. It wasn't long before he begged me to stop, wanting to climax inside me instead.

I lay back as Shaz kissed and bit his way along my neck and shoulders. He positioned himself between my legs, and I was eager to have him fill me. Wrapping my arms around him, I held him close as he teased me with the head of his velvety erection. I squirmed against him, coming undone by his teasing. Just when I thought I would surely scream for him to take me, he slid deep until he was completely buried inside me.

A cry broke from me, ending in a growl. He responded with a similar sound as he thrust into me with an urgency that I felt in my soul. Wrapping my arms around him, I held him close so that my breasts were crushed against his hard chest.

Shaz moved slowly at first, teasing me on the inside with soft, deep strokes. Though I could feel him shaking with the exertion it took to hold back, he was adept at doing so. My need for more was undeniable. I gripped his lower back, feeling him move in and out of my body. We moved together as one. It was so perfectly natural, as if we'd been made for one another.

Moans and growls filled the silence around us with a delectable array of sounds. Shaz' pace began to quicken as his own need overwhelmed him. My hold on him tightened as he plunged as deep as my body would allow; my muscles clenched around him, holding him buried to my womb.

I grew frenzied as the waves of climax began to build. Love making with Shaz was always an emotional experience. I was suddenly overcome with love for him, and I hugged him close, biting lightly at his neck.

He reached up to tangle a hand in my long hair. With a bruising kiss, he increased his speed until I was moaning into his mouth. The sweat rolled off each of us to create a slippery layer on our skin. The orgasmic sensations were even better with him joined to me than it had been before. As he kissed me with a heightened fervor, the pleasure became too much to take. When the orgasm crashed over me, I threw my head back and howled.

My body automatically tightened around his shaft, holding him deep. He joined in my howl, causing a shiver to race down my spine. Every pulsing climactic wave wracked my body as he filled me with the warmth of his seed. We remained joined together; savoring the moment until at last, he rolled off me, curling his body around mine.

We rarely needed words in these moments. Everything that needed to be exchanged already was. Both the wolf as well as the woman in me was comfortably sated. Snuggling up against Shaz was easily at the top of my list of favorite things. I sighed and allowed the magic of the afterglow to sweep me away. Resting my head against his chest, I closed my eyes and allowed the steady beat of his heart to lull me.

கூறுகூறு

Arys scowled down at me from his tall, lean frame. He stood in the doorway to his house, glaring out at Shaz and me. I'd known he wouldn't be pleased to see the white wolf at my side, but he had insisted on coming with me.

Looking over my shoulder to Shaz, Arys said, "What are you doing here, wolf? This doesn't concern you."

"Like hell it doesn't. My mate has been threatened because of you." Shaz shoved past me, daring to shoulder his way past the vampire that was shooting daggers at him with his eyes. "Don't worry, Arys. I won't be here long. I have to work in an hour. But, I want some answers."

I shrugged meekly and followed Shaz into the house. Arys gave me a dark look that promised things to come that I may not enjoy. I just wanted to get this over with. Shaz was in a real territorial fit since the incident with Julian. Harley's visit to my office greatly disturbed him, more than he was really letting on.

"I don't need you getting up in my face about Harley. I'm going to deal with him." Arys followed us into the kitchen, his arms crossed over his chest. He leaned against the counter and fixed his ocean-blue eyes on Shaz, then me. "I promise you, Alexa, I will not allow any harm to come to you."

Shaz scoffed but said nothing, instead waiting for me to speak. I shuffled uneasily from one foot to the other. Arys seemed to be waiting for me to either show my trust in him or outright admit that I had none. I didn't feel this was a matter of trust. It was a matter of me wanting to stay alive and knowing that would take more than trust. With a ruthless bastard like Harley, staying alive might just be the beginning of my troubles, what with the way he liked to play.

I hugged myself tightly as fear stole through me. "I know you mean that, Arys, but this is a big deal. He could have killed me last night if he'd wanted to."

"He doesn't want you dead." Arys nodded knowingly. "And for now, that means you're safe."

"He tasted my power, Arys." My voice rose to a pitch that was almost shrill. "He drew me in, physically pressed his lips to mine and tasted me. I can't remember the last time I was that terrified." Ok, that was a lie. I could remember it. But, I didn't want to. It had been when Raoul attacked me, before I'd known it was him.

A pained expression crossed Arys' face. Shaz stood motionless, patient but irritated. The dark vampire eyed me, a questioning stare on his handsome face.

"Did he bite you?"

"No. He left because he was afraid he would go too far." I swallowed hard and watched the pain flicker through Arys. "He doesn't want to do that ... yet. He clearly has other plans for me. But, his biggest concern was you. He doesn't want to share."

The rage that filled Arys then oozed throughout the room as his energy burned hot with anger. "That infuriating mother fucker," he swore, pacing the length of the kitchen. "How dare he think that I belong to him after all of these years?" A sound not so far off from a growl rumbled in his throat, and my eyes widened.

The look on Shaz' face said everything that he was thinking. When Arys' back was turned to him, he made a dramatic show of rolling his eyes. I frowned and shook my head once.

"Look, I won't be letting him catch me alone like that again. Let's all just relax and think this through coherently." I went to Arys, grasping his forearm, forcing him to look at me. I went stone cold when he shrugged me off. I took a step back, slightly hurt but incredibly confused.

Shaz cleared his throat from behind me. His tone was firm when he spoke. "You clearly have issues of your own with Harley, and I think that needs to be addressed." He didn't flinch when Arys turned his icy stare on him. "I'm just saying that this isn't personal, this is about doing what it takes to keep Lex safe. And, if that means never leaving her side, I will do it. You have to do your part."

The two of them faced off, and my heart began to race. Arys' energy steadily increased until it began to hurt. I had no way of shielding against it. It was literally inside me as much as it was around me. Shaz appeared uncomfortable but otherwise could not feel it. Not the way I could.

"Watch yourself, wolf. I won't be cowed by you. Not now, not ever. I can deal with Harley ... and I will."

"I didn't come here to go for a second round with you, Arys." Shaz' voice rose as his usual cool self began to grow hot-tempered. "Just cool it. Is it really so impossible for us to be civil? If anyone should be acting like the jealous boyfriend, it's me."

My guts twisted at Shaz' words, and I had to fight the grimace from my face. I tensed, waiting for the snarky response from Arys that I knew was coming. He surprised me.

"You're right in that regard," he relented. "But, both of you need to realize how great a danger Harley is. And, I won't be bullied into handling it any way other than my own." He raised an eyebrow, giving Shaz the opportunity to dispute him.

I knew how dangerous Harley was, and I did not intend to let him get that close to me again. Shaz seemed to contemplate Arys, the two of them staring at each other as if I wasn't there. If they did fight, I was walking out and leaving them to it.

"Fine." Shaz tilted his white-blonde head in a slight nod. "Do whatever you need to do. In the meantime, I will do what I need to do."

Neither of them said another word. From the way Arys' jaw was clenching, I knew he wasn't happy. Clearing my throat, I made them both look from each other to me.

"And, if you both choose to pretend that I am not at the center of all this, I will be smacking your heads together." I put my hands on my hips and mustered my best "take no shit" expression.

Shaz held his hands up in a sign of surrender and flashed me his spine-melting grin. Arys made a noise of disgust and muttered, "Dramatic." I beamed a smile at him, hoping to enrage him just a little.

"I'm going to take off to work. Will you come by later?" Shaz came forward to slip his arms around my waist, kissing me quickly. "If you don't, I'm coming to your place right after."

I couldn't help but sneak a glance at the vampire who glared at the floor. His energy was beginning to simmer down, but it didn't cool completely. I returned Shaz' embrace, following when he made his way back to the door.

"I might come by tonight. If Kylarai is out, I'm not sure I will be up for staying home alone." I shrugged, embarrassed at the admittance of fear. It felt so unnatural to feel it on this level. Harley had awakened a side of me that had long been dormant, and it pissed me off.

He hugged me to him once more; my scent lingered on him, mixing with his to make a delectable wolf scent. He pressed a warm kiss to my temple before turning to go. "I love you, babe."

I gave him a small smile, keenly aware of the weight of Arys' eyes on my back. "I love you, too. Don't worry about me, ok?"

"Impossible." Shaz pushed the door open, never once looking back at the vampire. "I'll see you later."

When his blue Cobalt pulled away from where he'd parked near my car, I closed the door and turned back to face Arys. He didn't look any happier.

"Thank you," I said, approaching him slowly. "You know, for not getting into it with Shaz."

He sighed and pulled me into his arms. "Only for you." He sniffed lightly and wrinkled his nose in distaste. "You reek like him."

I frowned but let it slide. I couldn't be drawn into the testosterone war between the two of them. Whether Arys liked it or not, he had been the one that pushed me into Shaz' arms months ago, claiming that I needed the love only my white wolf could give me. And now, it seemed that Arys was regretting that in some ways.

"I need to get really serious with you, Alexa, and you may not like it," he continued, forcing me to look into his heavenly eyes. "You have to keep that pup away from Harley, at all costs, or you risk losing him."

I felt the blood drain from my face. I shook my head, momentarily confused. "What do you mean?"

He studied me carefully before stroking the side of my face. "If Harley learns about him, and how much he means to you, he won't hesitate to hurt him." ...*Or worse*. I could feel the part he was leaving out.

My mouth instantly went dry at the thought of the sadist vampire touching Shaz in any way. I'd give myself to him before I'd allow that to happen. "Oh God. That can never happen." I felt like I couldn't breathe. The reality of the danger we were in hit home with a heaviness that made my vision spotty.

"Are you ok?" Arys put a hand out to steady me when I rocked away from him on my heels, unsteady. "It's going to be ok, Alexa. I promise you, I will do everything in my power to prevent any harm from coming to you ... or the wolf pup."

Try as I might to speak, nothing would come out. I felt the warning sting of tears and fought them back. There was nothing to cry over, not yet. I'd be damned if I was giving into the weakness that fear was stirring inside me.

I finally managed a deep breath. "I'm ok. I just can't breathe." I attempted a smile, but it was a poor one. I pushed a lock of red and blonde hair out of my face. He responded by reaching out to grasp it, twirling it around his finger.

"Your wolf is right about one thing. I don't feel right about leaving you alone, either." The concern that pulled his sensual lips down into a frown warmed me.

"Don't be ridiculous. I'm pretty sure I'm safe for now. He made it seem like he wants to drag it out."

Arys pressed his lips together. He clearly didn't believe my claim. I watched him twist my hair, the two different colors creating a candy cane effect. The close proximity made the effects of his energy stronger. It no longer felt angry. Instead, it felt hungry.

The blood lust rose up then, engulfing me in one giant swallow. It clawed at me like a rabid dog fighting to get out. My gums tingled, and my fangs were suddenly there, large and sharp in my mouth. The need for blood was overwhelming.

"I need to feed before it tears you apart. I can feel it raging through you." Arys looked torn, as if he wasn't sure what to do.

"It came on out of nowhere." A hand to my head, I went to the cupboard that I knew held dishware and fished out a drinking glass. Going to the kitchen sink, I ran the cold water until it was icy. After taking a long, refreshing swallow, I deposited the glass in the sink and turned back to my vampire. He looked anxious. "It isn't fair. It never eats you up the way it does to me."

"I've had centuries to learn to deal with it. Of course, it won't be so easy for you." He shook his head and a familiar expression of self-loathing played along his features. "I wish this didn't happen to you."

"It's not like you escaped unscathed." I waved a hand dismissively. I didn't need his guilt right now. Since we'd joined our power three months ago, we have each suffered the other's weaknesses in the worst of ways. Though it was getting fewer and farther between, the strength and urgency of it, when it did occur, seemed to only increase.

"You're better at taking care of that than I am. I don't deserve you." Arys ran a hand through his hair, messing it further. "I need to feed. Will you be alright for awhile?"

"Yes, of course. Do what you must. Don't worry about me." I struggled to appear cool and confident though I was never that good an actor.

"Why don't you head to Lucy's, and I'll meet you there later?"

I debated arguing that and accusing him of thinking I couldn't take care of myself. I restrained the urge with great difficulty. I couldn't always give Arys the run around for trying to keep me safe. True, it got annoying when he did it in situations that were so mundane and every day, like when I got hit on by a guy that wouldn't take no for an answer at Lucy's Lounge. But, I knew he meant well. I wasn't sure why I always busted his chops when I would never do so to Shaz. They were different men, and I was a different person with each of them. They drew out different sides of me.

"Alright. Don't kill anybody that doesn't deserve it." I winked when I said it and received a sexy little snarl from him in response. He bared his fangs at me, and my body reacted to it against my will as a thrill shot through my veins. When Arys sensed the changes in my body, he smiled wide, satisfied.

"I'll see you at midnight then." He pressed close; his hard frame against my soft, feminine form felt like magic. "Stay alert, and don't get caught out alone. I don't think Harley would come to Lucy's, but I can't say for sure. If he wants something bad enough, he'll go to any lengths to get it."

"I'll be fine," I murmured against his lips as he bent to kiss me.

He tasted like power, tangy and savory. I closed my eyes and allowed it to wash over me. It was similar to the sensation of falling into Harley's power only this was welcome, which made it so much better.

After much contemplation, I pulled away from Arys and turned to go. He walked me to the door; my body reacted to his as he shadowed my movements. Just being in the same room as the smoldering hot vampire stoked the fire inside me. It also caused my power to rise to a dangerously uncontrollable level, especially when the blood lust was strong.

"See you in a bit." I fought back an unexpected wave of nausea and kissed him quickly on the cheek. I hurried down the front step to my car, eager to get away from him so that I could think. It wouldn't make the blood hunger stop, but his presence was feeding it.

I started my car and pulled away from the curb. It was still early. I planned to go back home before heading to the Lounge. Kylarai had been home before Shaz and I had left the house. I'd had time to fill her in on my visit from Harley while she ran around getting ready for another date with Julian. Was I a bad friend for wanting that whole, sordid relationship to dissolve? She was my best friend, and I adored her. I wanted better for her.

I was singing along to an Ill Scarlett song as I crossed town to my neighborhood. Passing one of my neighbors, I raised a hand in greeting. When I turned the corner on to my street, my expression froze on my face. A black SUV that I recognized as Julian's was parked in front of my house. Why did I get the feeling that this was just the beginning of a bad night?

Chapter Ten

I made a face of disgust to nobody at all as I turned the doorknob, letting myself into the house. Kylarai's laughter rang out, tinkling like wind chimes, and Julian's low murmur came in response. I let the door slam shut behind me, a little harder than necessary, but I wanted to make my presence obvious right off the bat.

I was hoping that I could bypass the living room where they sat and escape down the hall to either the kitchen or my room. The square layout of our house had the hallway running past every room as it continued around the house. It wouldn't be all that hard to sneak past the entry to the living room, would it? Hopefully, Ky would know better than to stop me.

Unfortunately for me, the voice that called to me as I hurried past the living room entry was not Kylarai's. I cringed when Julian's low, husky tone caught my attention. His hurried, loud whisper of, "Alexa!" had the hair on the back of my neck standing on end. I shuddered and turned towards the living room, unable to resist as Arys' blood lust rode me.

I appeared in the doorway suddenly. Kylarai actually jumped, which I found both odd and surprising. Crossing my arms over my chest, I mustered my best bored expression and said, "What do you want?"

Julian held up both hands in a mocking show of surrender. The smile that played along his lips was more than a little malicious. I stared at him and instantly saw him as prey to be hunted and bled. I think I may have licked my lips as the sound of his steady heartbeat alone suddenly outweighed any other sound in the room.

My eyes went to Kylarai. She was curled up against the corner of the sofa, sipping from a steaming mug. He sat next to her, an arm slung loosely about her shoulders. Though he attempted casual, there was no missing the way he looked me over. I'd caught him doing just the same thing at Raoul's once. That time it had appeared sexual, this time it was the sign of a wannabe Alpha wolf sizing up the competition. I smirked openly at him.

"I'm not here to get into it with you, Alexa. I just want to spend some time with my girl here." Julian nodded at Kylarai, and I had to fight down the bile that threatened to rise up in my throat.

"Then why did you call my name when I tried to successfully ignore your wretched presence?" I felt Kylarai cringe more so than I saw it since I was staring down the pathetic excuse for a werewolf beside her.

"Alexa," she piped up, her voice gentle as she tried to draw my attention to her. "I didn't know you would be back tonight. Is something up?"

I studied her for a moment before replying. She wore a long, black robe and had her long bob pulled back into a ponytail. Her grey eyes were filled with anxiety. I hated that she was caught in the middle of all of this.

"No, not at all." Though I looked at Ky, my senses honed in on Julian, sharper than before. "I just had some time to kill before I head to Lucy's. I didn't mean to interrupt."

Her ponytail bounced as she gave her head a vigorous shake. "No worries. It's your house, too. We're just watching some silly ass Freddy Krueger movie on the Scream channel. Want to join us?"

Julian seemed to await my response as if he thought I might really say yes. I couldn't resist the urge to look at him, his scent tantalizing my blood hunger as I did so. It seemed to grow stronger when our eyes met. The spice and pine of Were blood assaulted my senses, and the wave of demanding bloodlust rocked me. It was all I could do not to cross the room dividing us and bleed him.

"No," I replied, a slight shake to my voice. I swallowed hard; confused at the way I was reacting to Julian. "I won't be here long. You won't even notice me."

I turned to leave the room before the growing, sickening hunger could affect my choices. Julian cleared his throat, and I knew he was going to speak before he did. I closed my eyes and took a deep breath, counting to ten. I was not going to murder him in my own house.

"I just want to say something quickly, Alexa." When I turned back to face him, he wore a serious expression. "The whole thing with Shaz ... no hard feelings, ok?"

Was he freaking kidding me? He looked so damned serious, but I just didn't buy it. My hands clenched into fists at my sides, and the surge of anger that hit me directly fed my hunger for living, pumping blood.

"Remember that you said that when he wipes the forest floor with you." The words came tripping out of my mouth before I could stop them, not that I wanted to. A wicked smile graced my lips then, and I knew it was Arys' smile. Julian may not recognize it, but Kylarai would.

She stiffened noticeably; her mug smacked the coffee table loudly, and her mouth dropped open. Julian looked like he didn't know what hit him. I took great pleasure in his shocked expression. I found it somewhat surprising that he hadn't expected it from me. He recovered fast though, his typical smirk back in its place on his scruffy face.

"And, if he doesn't? What then, Queen Alpha? Are you going to accept me as your second fiddle in this town or take me on yourself?"

"Julian, that's enough!" Kylarai warned as her cheeks grew flushed with angry heat.

"I won't hesitate to run you out of this town with your tail between your legs like the pathetic dog that you are. You will never be a dominant to either Shaz or me, so keep dreaming. Dreams are all you have, little boy." Something moved inside of me, and Arys' power slammed through me.

It was Julian's reaction that alerted me to the fact that my eyes were Arys' startling blue, not my own deep brown. It was something that happened when the vampire's power was strong, pressing the surface of my being. It was also something I would never get used to. I avoided mirrors like the plague when my eyes turned the eerie vampire blue.

"Holy shit," Julian breathed. He sat frozen next to Kylarai who just looked plain worried. She thought I was going to kill him. I could see it all over her face.

"Don't say another word," she hissed under her breath. Of course, I could hear her as if I'd been standing beside her. To me she said, "It's cool, Lex. Just calm down ... okay?"

Try as I might, I couldn't shake the snake-like grin from my face. "Trust me. I am calm."

I wasn't trying to scare Kylarai, but her face paled, and she ever so slowly got to her feet, motioning for Julian to stay seated. He watched me with dark chestnut eyes that had gone all wolf, leaving no trace of white. It was only natural that his wolf would go on the defensive. It only encouraged the cool energy dominating my focus.

"Maybe I should call Arys for you?" Her tone implied a question, and I realized she was afraid of me, not just the situation. If I hadn't been so wired right then, I would have been saddened by that.

I could remember the first time this had happened to me, right after I'd lost it and attacked Shaz. That had been the first morning Ky went to bed with her door locked. Did she really think I would hurt her? I shuddered at the look of horror on Shaz' face, my mind conjuring the image of when I'd rushed him as Arys' tortured memories drove me.

"Arys is hunting." My voice sounded hollow, even to me. "I said I'm fine. I can't help it if obvious prey inside my own house triggers the bloodlust." My smile vanishing, I turned to Julian. "You think you're something to be feared?" I flashed my sharp fangs at him, blinking my blue eyes slowly a few times for effect before a vicious laugh bubbled out.

It took everything I had in me to turn toward the hall and put one foot in front of the other. I knew how badly I'd massacred that first victim, the woman-beater, and I knew I'd do the same to Julian if I put my hands on him. One foot in front of the other, and I finally entered my room and managed to close the door without going back for a fight.

I didn't want to be in my room though. I wanted to get the hell out of the house. This was so not good. My best friend and the werewolf I detested, dating. Ugh. Was it wrong to hope they wouldn't, as gross as it was, fall in love?

Against my better judgment, I went into my ensuite bathroom and very quickly looked over my appearance. I didn't get any closer to the mirror than necessary, unnerved by my unnatural blue orbs.

The black, hip-hugging jeans and equally black halter-top made my hair look so much blonder than usual. The shirt was one of my favorites. It held my breasts perfectly supported so they both felt and looked great, and the fabric that fell around my waist was sheer, longer on one side than the other, and jagged-cut. I didn't wear jewelry when I knew I'd be shifting, but today I had slipped on a silver charm bracelet that Shaz had given me for my last birthday. If the Hollywood rules about werewolves had been true, I never would have been able to wear it.

After running my brush carelessly through my waist length hair, I tossed the red streaked locks over my shoulder and turned back to my room. It had gotten incredibly quiet out in the living room. If I couldn't sense their heartbeats, I would have thought they'd left.

Before leaving my bedroom, I grabbed a pair of black ankle boots from my closet so that I wouldn't have to go back for my shoes at the front door. Silently, I slunk down the hall to the kitchen and let myself out the sliding door into the backyard. I crossed through the yard to the front where my Charger sat large and red against the dark backdrop of night.

I revved the engine a few times before putting the car in gear and driving away. I wanted to make sure they knew I'd left. Arys likely wouldn't be at Lucy's for some time yet, but that didn't mean I had to sit at home with two chicken shit werewolves feeding my fire. I needed to burn off some of the aggressive power I'd built up before I dared to step foot into a bar filled with tantalizing humans.

Turning onto the main drag, I headed for the north end of town and the beautiful little fountain park that also served as a both a tourist attraction and information center. It would be empty at this time of night, perfect for unleashing some negative energy. By then, hopefully, Arys would have appeased both his hunger and mine.

ഇഇഇഇ

As expected, the park was cast in darkness. A few strategically placed streetlights illuminated the path that led to both the gazebo and the path that wound the circumference of the large fountain pond. I parked in one of the many vacant spaces and got out of the car, breathing in the crisp night air.

Thick, luscious trees and brush surrounded the park on all sides except the one with the large hill, which led up to the highway on the edge of town. The sound of vehicles passing by was distant. If I turned away from the hill, it was as if I wasn't even in town anymore.

I passed the community bulletin board, glancing briefly at a flyer advertising a way overpriced, used Mustang for sale. I chuckled to myself, knowing the guy would never unload it on anyone but a sucker. Passing the gazebo, I continued down the path, headed toward the bridge that spanned the length of the pond.

As I drew closer, the darkness seemed to grow thicker. The fading light behind me was soon no more than a pale glow. The bridged loomed large and spooky beneath the silver moonlight. A chill spilled down my spine like ice-cold water when a memory surfaced, unbidden and unwelcome.

I had come here the day that Arys gave me the letter from Raoul, the one he'd found addressed to me, Raoul's confession. It had been one of the most horrifying and enlightening days of my life. Everything had changed that day: some for the better and others not so much.

I stepped onto the bridge, light and silent on the wooden planks beneath my feet. I followed its U shape up to the peak of its height, reaching out to the metal railing to steady myself. The water below looked absolutely black. I knew it was filled with thick, dangerous weeds and was actually very deep in places. The glint of the moonlight reflected off the dark surface, catching my eye.

Despite the perfection of the scene around me, the vampire's bloodlust scarcely waned. The need for the kill was deep in my core, riding me hard. Hadn't that damn vampire fed yet? Where could he be? At most times, the differing power of the wolf and the vampire co-existed somewhat peacefully within me. Now, they seemed to be battling for control. The approach of the full moon encouraged my wolf's dominant and controlling nature as it warred with the cold power of the undead.

A visible spasm wracked my body, and I gripped the railing tighter with both hands. The warm living energy of my wolf fought to battle the blood hunger, but something else appealed to my instincts. My head snapped up suddenly as the night air carried the scent of werewolf to me but not anyone's scent that I knew.

My eyes instantly searched the surrounding darkness; my every sense, on full alert. I was standing in the middle of the bridge, and my

The Wicked Kiss

instincts screamed at me to both fight and to run. I inhaled deeply, pinpointing the scent to my right, the way I'd just come. I only smelled one Were out there lurking around. His energy was livid, and he was out to kill.

I sprung into motion, moving slowly but steadily along the bridge, towards the other side. I didn't want a confrontation on top where I could end up going over the side. I couldn't imagine who this werewolf was stalking me or why. I'd be lying if I said I wasn't scared shitless.

Judging the distance back to the Charger, I knew I'd never make it in time if this Were was intent on attacking me. Ever so slowly, I made my way down the other side of the bridge, grateful when my feet were back on solid ground. I could feel his energy grow stronger in its intensity as he advanced on me. I had yet to see him in the darkness. I could feel him though, getting closer with every step.

I tapped into the hungry power I held inside, bracing for the attack that I knew was coming. His scent was musky and strong, as if he had been in wolf form for a long time. I was praying he wasn't on four feet now, or he would easily have the physical advantage. We never saw foreign Weres in this town, not like this.

Everything seemed to move in slow motion. The shape that came across the bridge then seemed to be nothing but a blur. I gave a small cry, throwing my hands up, the power rushing from me so fast that I almost collapsed. The rush of gold and blue hit him dead on, throwing him back. I turned to run, sensing only one but fearing more than that.

I had barely made it ten feet when a clawed hand reached me, digging into my shoulder and down my back. I felt the blood spill from the gouges before the scent reached me. The adrenaline blasted through me so hard, I almost stumbled from the onslaught of it. I was afraid, but the bloodlust was quickly stripping that away, and I turned to fight him with all I had.

A snarl broke the silence, and everything seemed to speed up again. In the pale glow of the moon, I could see that he had long, dark hair, stringy and matted. His eyes seemed to glow deep amber brown, and his large fangs flashed as he rushed me.

My breath whooshed out as his weight slammed into me, taking me down beneath him. His fangs snapped just inches before my

131

face, and I struggled uselessly to make my lungs work. I lashed out in defense, raining blows like bricks against his face. He seemed to be unfeeling as he took every one with little protest. His eyes were locked on mine as his clawed hands wrapped around my throat.

He squeezed so hard that my vision blurred and white spots danced before my eyes. For a moment, I truly thought I was dying. The power of the undead saved me. It wasn't afraid to die because it was already beyond mortal life. It wanted to taste this fiery werewolf, to drain everything from him slowly and completely. I reached out metaphysically first, drawing his energy to me.

At first, he didn't feel me drawing him into me, absorbing his strength, his very life. Then, awareness brightened his eyes, and he tried to pull back. I gulped in the air when he released my throat, grateful to be able to breathe again. I reached for him as he scrambled backward, suddenly desperate to put space between us. He thought that would make a difference.

I leaped to my feet with my fangs bared and a loud growl rumbling in my throat. I wanted to taste his musky wolf blood as I drained his life energy away. My mind wanted to ask him what the fuck he thought he was doing, but my instinct just said kill.

"Vampire." The word came from him like a hiss. I almost wasn't sure I'd heard it. His shock didn't last long. He flew at me again, and this time I hit him with a psi ball that left him panting, but still, he didn't stop. "You killed her. You killed Olivia!"

Uh oh. It all made a little more sense now. He took another clawed swipe at me, this time painfully close to my throat, grazing my upper chest. It seemed that Kale and I had failed to consider that the she-wolf we'd taken out had a mate. Like any mate would be, he was hell bent on my death as retribution. And, knowing Shaz would be the same, I couldn't blame him.

"It wasn't personal. She was endangering all of us." I didn't doubt for a moment that he had been a willing partner in Olivia's rampage. I would have given anything to be in wolf form right then, but it just wasn't possible, not unless it got really ugly.

I tapped Arys' power and threw the wolf clear, sailing through the air to land against a thick pine tree. He immediately tried to get up, but he was dazed and moved slowly. Running, I crossed the distance between us, landing on him with a series of power-fueled blows that snapped his head back and forth. I just knew that I couldn't let him gain the advantage again.

Despite the blows that resulted in a series of crunches and cracks and plentiful blood flow, he didn't cease his assault either. When his body beneath me began to turn furry, I knew I was a goner if I didn't get the hell out of there. I didn't want to shift in the park and be trapped, unable to get in my car and leave. I had to get to the Charger.

I went for his throat, but he successfully blocked me with an arm that was instantly a furry front leg. Leaping off him, I turned to run, feeling ashamed but knowing I couldn't take him here and now. The sound of his paws hitting the ground behind me had my heart leaping into my throat.

I threw up an energy wall between us, buying myself some time. He'd either have to wait for it to dissolve or go back across the bridge and around the pond the other way to catch me. Glancing back, I saw him slam right into the barrier and go down. I poured on the speed; my feet barely touched the ground as I ran.

Fear drove me to move faster when I saw the large wolf scramble to its feet and take off the other way, across the bridge. I was closer to the Charger than he was, but he had twice as many feet as I did. I could taste blood in my mouth from a cut I'd sustained during our scuffle. The pain was beginning to set in as my injuries throbbed in time with my pounding heart.

As I drew closer to the car, I fumbled my keychain out of my pocket. With a loud jingle, it dropped to the grass, and I had to jerk to a halt. Cursing, I snatched the keys from the ground and continued sprinting to the car. A large shadow was barreling around the other side of the pond, drawing closer with alarming speed.

Thanking God for the remote unlock feature, I literally threw myself at the passenger side of the car, since he was coming up fast on the driver side. I had just gotten in and slammed the door shut behind me when his two hundred pounds of aggression crashed into the driver's side of my car. Scrambling to get into the driver's seat, I jammed the key in the ignition and felt absolute relief when the engine roared to life. I'd been afraid he would have done something to strand me here.

Slamming the car into reverse, I pressed the gas to the floor, and the car flew back in a wide half circle. If he was stupid enough to get in my way, I was going to run him down. He backed off though when I put the car in gear. In a blur, he darted out of my path and in amongst the trees. I didn't stop driving until I was across town, safe in the parking lot of Lucy's Lounge. Rather than park at the end of the lot as usual, I double-parked next to Shaz' car in the staff spaces near the door.

My heart had barely slowed in the five minutes it had taken me to cross town. Flipping down my visor, I studied my face in the mirror. I could have screamed when I saw my face and the tangles and filth in my hair. My eyes were still Arys' shocking blue, but that was the least of my worries right now.

There were small, bloody punctures on my throat from where he had grabbed me. Crimson stained my bottom lip, and I could only imagine how bad the deep, long scratches down my back were. I'd need a full-length mirror to see it all.

Finger combing my hair was almost useless, and I had to arrange it carefully so that the marks on my neck were hidden from the humans at least. Anything supernatural would know I was injured immediately. At least I wouldn't have to deal with Julian here, since he was at my house, in my personal space.

Taking a deep breath, I opened the car door and scented the air before getting out. Call me paranoid, but I wasn't taking any chances. I reached the door in record time, nodding briefly to the bouncer just inside. He raised an eyebrow but waved me through.

My first instinct was to look for Shaz at the bar. I knew I should go for the bathroom to get cleaned up, but I needed to see him. I had come close to biting it at the hands of a crazed werewolf intent on revenge.

Before I'd even made it halfway to the bar, my white wolf's head snapped up as he scented my blood. With a word to Tawnie, his partner behind the bar, he was moving through the crowd to get to me. My bottom lip trembled as he drew closer and when he pulled me into his arms, I choked back a sob.

"What in the hell happened to you? Don't tell me this is about Arys or Harley." Shaz' expression grew venomous, and I shook my head vigorously. He pushed my hair back, scrutinizing the marks on my neck before dragging me back towards the staff hall at the back of the building.

"No," I said, clinging to his heavenly warmth with relief. "It's not that at all. It's a wolf that Kale and I killed ... her mate attacked me in the park." Saying it sounded so ridiculous. I hadn't considered this outcome.

With his interest piqued, Shaz scented me closely. His jade eyes widened as he got past the blood and nightclub scent, picking out the musky odor of the wolf who had dared to touch his mate. When he looked up at me again, his eyes were all wolf. "Where is he now?"

"No! You are not looking for him." I touched his cheek, forcing him to look at me. "He's out of his mind. Please, don't."

"Alexa, you've got to stop this. You can't shelter me anymore. I'm not a kid; I'm your mate, and I am going to make it clear to every wolf that I am the Alpha male in this town. You can't deny me that. It's in every part of me." His chin lifted in defiance, and a gleam lit his eyes that I'd never seen before. Still, I couldn't back down.

"You can kick the living shit out of Julian and anyone else in this town if you feel the need to. But please, don't go looking for this wolf right now." I pressed an urgent kiss to his lips, forcing him to respond. I felt the fight go out of him as his shoulders sagged, and he deepened the kiss until it was hot and passionate.

Arys' blood lust honed in on Shaz and I had to pull away. Looking into my blue eyes, he nodded knowingly. "You want to bleed me right now, don't you? That son of a bitch isn't supposed to let this happen to you." His anger teased my senses, bringing a smile to my lips though I didn't find it at all funny.

"Don't freak out about it. He said he was going to hunt." I breathed deeply, savoring the delightful aroma of living, breathing humans. My fangs had disappeared upon leaving the park, but my gums tingled in anticipation, and I ached to sink teeth into something soft and full of life. Shaz' intoxicating Were energy was both painful and pleasurable.

Shaz scoffed but didn't spit out the retort that I knew he had. "Stay put. I'm going to get you a warm cloth or something." His hand lingered, tracing the outline of a bruise on my jaw.

"He got me good, right down my back. I'm not sure how bad it is." I turned so that he could lift my torn hoodie and shirt to examine the wounds. He swore softly, and a second later, his gentle touch against the stinging claw marks made me jump in sudden pain.

"Sorry," he murmured, carefully replacing my clothing. "It's deep, but you'll be fine. I'll get you some ice."

When he'd disappeared from sight, I leaned back against the wall near the staff hall. It gave me a clear view of the door and my vampire, should he walk in. His hunger didn't dominate my focus as it had earlier, but it did continue to gnaw at me.

I didn't have to wait long. My dark lover strode into the Lounge with a cool energy that reached out to touch me before our eyes met. He didn't look anywhere but straight at me, and my heart raced for an entirely new reason. The hunger dissipated, and a cool wave swept the heat of it away. Unable to deny the need, I reached for him.

Arys swept me off my feet, pulling me close in a possessive embrace. "What happened to you, my wolf? Your car looks like it's been side swiped."

"Shit! I just ran for my life from the mate of a wolf Kale and I killed. I should have seen it coming." I enjoyed the feelings that ignited in me at his touch. The heightened power within me reached out to him, entwining so that I felt like I was falling into him. The illusion was shattered when he began to look me over. "I'm fine, really. He just caught me off guard."

"And what does the wolf pup say about this?" Arys' eyes narrowed, and I knew what he was thinking.

"Don't you dare start with him. I do not need that shit right now." I glanced around for Shaz, expecting his return at any moment.

He gave me a look that said I was being ridiculous. "I mean, that I'm sure he has no intention of allowing this werewolf to get away with an attempt on your life. Simmer down, Alexa. I fed an hour ago. Why are your eyes so blue?"

"I begged Shaz not to go after him. That wolf was out of his friggin' mind. It was Kale and I who caused this, and we will have to deal with it." I crossed my arms over my chest and frowned, confused. "They've been blue for awhile now."

If I hadn't sensed Shaz' approach, I would have known it by the look Arys instantly wore. He looked as if he had the taste of something bitter in his mouth. I rolled my eyes and ignored him when he muttered, "I bet he just loves my eyes on you." Men, I so did not understand them.

I accepted the warm towel Shaz held out to me with a smile and turned so that he could place a cloth filled with ice against the wounds on my back. I sighed with relief as it eased the burning. Shaz' energy grew to mirror the aggressiveness that Arys was putting out, but he didn't so much as antagonize the vampire.

Arys seemed to avoid my gaze purposefully, and I knew why when he blurted out, "So, are we going to go hunt down this son of a bitch or what?"

My mouth dropped open, and I stared in shock at Shaz when he met the other man's eyes and said, "You read my mind."

They stared at each other because neither of them had the balls to look at me. Swiping the ice-packed cloth from Shaz, I spun around to confront him. "Excuse me?"

"Well come on, Lex, you have to be serious here. Independence is one thing, but this is my place as your mate. You can't handle everything yourself." Shaz shrugged and a glimmer of pain passed over him. "You don't have to."

I made a noise of disbelief and wiped my neck wounds with the warm towel. "You two, together? You're more likely to kill one another than that werewolf."

Arys snorted and chuckled. I ignored him and stared at Shaz. He looked incredibly uneasy, and by the way his eyes darted around, I knew it was because of my eerie blue eyes. Sighing, I turned to wipe the bloodstained skin of my back. I was unable to reach, and Shaz took the towel from me, cleansing my tender skin with a loving touch.

"I wish you wouldn't be so uptight all the time," he admonished. Arys met my eyes and gave me a wink and a nod, as if in agreement with Shaz. I wanted to pout and stomp my feet over the fact that he was saying this stuff in front of the cocky vamp, but I huffed and puffed in silence as he continued. "If we don't take him out now, he's just going to keep coming after you."

I hated that he was right on that count, but it wasn't worth it to me to risk him for anything. However, I also knew that he was right about one thing. I couldn't keep treating him like the kid that he used to be. Shaz was nothing if not a man. I just couldn't help but be protective of him.

"I know that. I just don't like it." I scowled when I caught Arys smirking like a cat with a mouse. "And, I don't like the idea of the two of you running around in the dark together."

"What are you afraid of, Alexa? That we might actually get along just fine? I think that would scare you more than if we were trying to tear each other apart." Arys ran his tongue lightly along the metal ring in his lip, drawing my eyes to it. I had the sudden urge to tug on it with my teeth.

What really sucked was that I couldn't deny that he was right. A part of me didn't much enjoy the idea of my two men alone together without me. I guess I didn't trust them, or rather, I didn't trust Arys. I didn't think he would hurt Shaz, but I didn't trust him to keep his opinions to himself, either.

Shaz looked frustrated. "I just want to get this guy before he makes it out of town. I can get Tawnie to take over the bar for awhile. Let us do this, Lex."

The thought of him going out there without me turned my stomach. "Not without me."

"Out of the question," Arys piped up. "You smell wounded, like prey. You will only endanger yourself if you go looking for him." When I stared hard at him, willing him to shut up, he shrugged and said softer, "We'll have each other's back, alright? No harm will come to your wolf."

"You can't go back out there." Shaz nodded, but I could see in his eyes that he hated agreeing with Arys. "We'll be fine. I promise. Why don't you head home?"

I gritted my teeth, fighting back the urge to lose my temper with both of them. I didn't want to feel like the wounded female, dammit. I was the Alpha in this town. "Julian and Kylarai are there. I could have torn his face off earlier."

Shaz immediately perked up. "Julian is there?"

"Don't even think it."

Arys watched our little exchange with mild amusement. I think it intrigued him, the aggressive side of Shaz that rarely surfaced. I seemed to be seeing a lot of it lately. But, what could I really do? Put up a fight and tell him he wasn't going? That wouldn't end in my favor.

I sighed, the exasperation authentic. "I don't want you going after that wolf. But, I won't try to stop you. You're both big boys."

Relief washed over Shaz, and it was so obvious he'd been expecting a fight that I felt foolish. Arys glanced between us, turning toward the exit. "Shall we then?"

A lock of platinum hair fell in Shaz' eyes as he pulled me close. With a quick kiss, he whispered, "I love you." Before I could reply, he had turned to follow the vampire, striding smoothly for the door.

I watched them go, wishing I could call him back. Why was this so hard? I wasn't used to having someone willing to step in on my behalf, let alone two of them. As long as they refrained from turning on each other, maybe, just maybe, they would be ok.

Chapter Eleven

Pouting made me feel like a child, yet I felt justified in doing so. It greatly wounded both my pride and my ego to have my two lovers hunt down the werewolf that had attacked me. I should have been able to handle it myself. And, the fact that they had gone together, united in a cause, had me beside myself with discomfort.

The midday sun beat down through my window, warming my toes where it fell upon them. I was waking up to the local lunchtime news with a coffee in hand and worry at the forefront of my mind. Tonight was the night of the full moon. Shaz and Julian were going to fight it out, and Kylarai and I would have to watch. The thought froze me with fear.

It hadn't taken Arys and Shaz long to find the Were that attacked me. Within an hour, I'd gotten a call from Shaz telling me to come out to the parking lot. He had been too blood covered to risk walking inside.

They'd found the wolf alright, still near the park. He had been smart enough to stay where there was little light and zero human activity. Perhaps he had simply been regrouping before he came after me again. I didn't get a lot of details. All I knew was that Shaz wore a loopy grin from ear to ear, and Arys looked sated, like a dog with a bone.

Perhaps what threw me the most was the relaxed atmosphere between the two of them. They weren't being friendly in any way, but they showed less of the animosity I had seen recently. Killing together had somehow united them. Was I supposed to be reassured by that?

Though neither of them had wanted to leave my side, I had insisted on going home alone. I was shaken and uneasy and greatly in need of some alone time. I knew Arys well enough to know that no matter what, he was still feeling the need to be a bigger bad than my white wolf. And, Shaz, if anything, was playing nice because it was easier than constantly bickering. Despite killing together, their casual complacency was somehow more worrisome than when they'd been throwing punches.

The weather forecast called for a surprisingly warm day for this time of year. This close to Halloween, there were rarely soaring temperatures. It would make for a nice night.

Sighing, I set my coffee mug down and stretched thoroughly before hitting the bathroom. Thankfully, Julian's SUV had been gone by the time I'd gotten home. I'd almost cried upon getting a detailed view of my damaged driver's door. That nasty wolf had smacked it good, denting it in so that it crumpled beneath his weight. I would likely need a whole new door. Shit!

I kept my clothing simple, knowing I'd be shedding it later in favor of fur and four feet. Tight black leggings and a plain white tank top were both comfortable and practical. As usual, I left my long hair down so that it fell past my elbows and abandoned the idea of makeup. It wouldn't be necessary tonight.

The sound of Kylarai shuffling around in the kitchen reached me, and for a brief moment, I wondered if I should tell her about Kale. It seemed irrelevant, but it also seemed wrong to hide it. Was not telling the same thing as hiding? After all, she had decided that she couldn't share her life with him. He was my friend, and what we'd shared was ours, regardless of how messed up it was.

Shoving the thought aside, I retrieved my mug and went to the kitchen for more caffeine. I was completely expecting Ky's apologetic smile, which she turned on me at full blast. I waved it off before she could even speak.

"Don't apologize for having Julian here, Ky. This is your house, too." Grabbing the coffee pot, I pulled it out of the machine too hard, and a few drops fell to sizzle on the burner. I beamed a smile at her so that she wouldn't feel guilty.

She shrugged and looked guilty anyway. "I know, Lex, but it's a bad situation. I never considered the possible outcome of him being here. And, tonight is going to be a gong show."

I noted the way her face fell when she said that. Apparently, Julian hadn't changed his mind either. "I know. I didn't sleep worth a damn last night. Of course, the attempt on my life in the park may have had something to do with that."

Tossing two slices of whole wheat bread into the toaster, I pulled the strawberry jam out of the refrigerator. Turning to the cutlery drawer, I was disappointed to find that there were no clean butter knives.

"What are you talking about?" Ky whirled around to fix me with a mothering look. "What happened?"

I began to wash a knife off in the sink since the dishwasher was still stacked with dirty dishes from the previous day. "Kale and I took out a she-wolf a couple of nights ago. Her mate came looking for me, and somehow managed to find me last night. He totally lynched me and destroyed the door to my car ... but Arys and Shaz went after him, and he is no longer a problem."

"Wow," Kylarai remarked, her warm grey eyes watching my movements as I dried the knife and tapped my fingers on the counter in front of the toaster. "That's outrageous. You always have the craziest nights."

I had to do a double take when I heard the longing in her voice. Was sweet, good girl Kylarai getting tired of the same old day to day?

"Yeah well, now, I have to pay for door repairs and somehow accept the fact that Shaz and Arys teamed up to save me." I made a quotation sign on the words "save me" in the air with my fingers, though the butter knife in my hand messed it up.

She nodded and watched me thoughtfully. I could almost guess what was running through her mind. Her features were drawn, and if I didn't know her so well, I would say that she was closed off. I could see through that. She was afraid.

"Are you worried?" She asked me suddenly, confirming my suspicions. "I mean, about tonight. Do you think it's going to get out of hand?"

I didn't know what she wanted to hear so I told her the truth. "Oh yeah. I can't remember the last time I dreaded something as much as I dread tonight."

"I tried to talk Julian out of it, but he wouldn't even let me finish an entire sentence. He can't wait to fight it out with Shaz. It turns my stomach to think about it."

My toast popped, and I turned away to spread jam on it, glad that she couldn't see the frown I wore. "I know. It kills me that I have to accept Shaz as the man that he is and not the boy that he was when I first met him. So much has changed." There was a forlorn note to my voice that I hadn't anticipated. It felt all wrong.

Kylarai surprised me by laughing. "That boy you speak of has been a man a lot longer than you give him credit for. If anything, what he did for you last night should prove that."

My cheeks warmed as I bit into a piece of warm, strawberry toast. I thought of the previous evening, how he had gently cleansed my wounds, willing to heed my pleas as I begged him not to go after that wolf. It had been against his instinct to ignore that urge, and he was willing to do it for me. Until Arys came along...

Whether I liked it or not, Shaz was the most dominant male wolf in this town. He had to prove it, and I had to play my role as his mate and back him.

"Yeah, yeah, I know. I'm just not sure how far I should let it go before I stop it. If we let them determine that, it won't end until somebody's dead."

Ky made a noise of disgust. "Men! Can't live with them, and you just can't kill them."

"Says who?" I winked and munched away on my toast. I paused, just then noticing her dressy attire. "Are you working today? On the full moon?"

"I have some papers that have to be delivered in person for a client. I won't be gone long." She began to put away some of the coffee accessories, a nervous habit on her part, one she could do without. "And don't tell me that I work too much. If I don't keep busy, I'll be a nervous wreck all day."

I smiled in response, keeping my opinion to myself. I was nobody to talk about work. At least her job wasn't going to get her killed. There was a likely chance that mine could, if my personal life didn't catch up to me first.

I glanced at the clock. Shaz would be coming by later. We would be heading out to the forest behind my house together. In the meantime, I had a few mundane tasks to take care of. The large H on the kitchen calendar caught my eye, a reminder that Halloween was just days away. If we all made it to the party at Lucy's Lounge intact, it would be a miracle. I was actually looking forward to getting out and having some fun.

After Kylarai left, I gathered my laundry together and threw it in the machine. Whenever I wanted to do chores, I knew my anxiety level was up. I had to give both Kale and Jez a call before it got dark. Jez didn't run with us wolves often, but she would tonight. I'd asked her to come and back me up. I didn't entirely trust either myself or some of my fellow wolves.

Kale wouldn't be up for hours yet. I wanted to bust his chops for not knowing our target had a mate. The gashes down my back had scabbed over nicely but still pulled and stung as I moved. Shifting later would be less than pleasant but would aid the healing process.

Picking up the phone, I punched in Jez' number and waited. I hung up when it went to voicemail. She would see that I'd called. Wishing that I could stop time and knowing it would never happen, I turned my attention to my jewelry box for costume accessories. Hopefully, forcing myself to show interest in what I was going to wear for Halloween would take my mind off the fast approach of nightfall.

I stared into my closet, eyeing the Little Red Riding Hood outfit that Jez had found for me. Whereas a few days ago, I wasn't feeling all that confident about wearing it, now I just hoped that I would still get the chance. Everything that could go wrong lately had. And, I could only wonder what else lay ahead. I couldn't escape the feeling that the worst was yet to come.

めめめめ

"I'm telling you, Lex, there is nothing more to say about last night. We found him, fought him and killed him." Shaz shrugged like it was all in a day's work. He had been in an incredibly chipper mood since he'd arrived. His energy was blazing with a feverish heat as he mentally readied himself for a fight.

"So by that, I can assume that you dropped him and Arys bled him."

"I insisted. I thought it might make a difference, for you and the bloodlust."

Maybe that was why Shaz had been so quiet about the details of their shared kill. He'd seen Arys feed. It was nothing if not disturbing. I wanted to keep pestering for details simply because I hadn't been there and it bothered me. It wasn't worth it, though, in

144

light of what was coming.

I literally had to bite my tongue to keep from begging Shaz to reconsider this scrap with Julian. The determined look on his face made it clear I'd be wasting my breath. The sun had set; Jez was on her way, and Shaz was antsy to get moving. His continued glances out the kitchen window into the backyard had my guts twisting into knots.

I didn't miss the way his green eyes followed me as I moved restlessly around the dining room table. When the doorbell rang, I literally jumped as my skin prickled with anxious energy. I called out for Jez to let herself into the house. Rubbing my arms did nothing to ease the sensations of Shaz' feisty energy, and I frowned when he reached out to grasp my hands.

"Would you stop twitching out? What's up with you?" His eyes searched mine, concern etched in their jade depths. "Your eyes are brown, and you don't feel vampy."

"You know damn well what's up with me, Shaz. I'm freaking out because I don't want you to do this. And, I know that's not going to stop you. So, I'm just trying to keep my mouth shut and get this night over with."

The sound of the door reached us, and Jez called hello from the front entry. Shaz pulled me closer, his warm hands running up my cold arms to entangle in my hair. "You know why I have to do this. You would do the same." He pressed a tender kiss against my forehead, and I sighed as my wolf rose to the surface in response to his, flooding my body with heat.

"Please, just don't do anything stupid." I whispered the words, leaning in to lay my head against his chest. "I need you, wolf boy."

"I'm not going anywhere, babe. You'll see. And then, don't you dare doubt me again." He followed up with a sound smack on my behind as Jez entered the kitchen.

She raised an eyebrow and shook her head, causing her long golden waves to shimmer and bounce. "Save it for later, you two. I'm no voyeur."

Shaz chuckled, and I shot her a playful glare. "Help yourself to anything in the fridge if you need a drink or something," I offered, attempting to be the accommodating host.

"No thanks, I'm all good." Her cat eyes slid from me to Shaz as she studied us. "I'm ready to head out whenever you are."

She moved to the sliding glass door, her slender frame lithe and graceful. Looking out on the bright moon, she cast a coy glance over her shoulder at me. I watched as the green of her eyes spread to obliterate the whites. When she smiled, she revealed four dainty fangs, sharp as razors. Like mine, she had both two on the top and the bottom.

It was clear that I was the only one not at all ready to head out into the night and the forest within it. Influenced by Jez' intense Were energy, the wolf was strong in Shaz, and he gazed at me with wolf eyes that blazed with fire. The power of their beasts taunted me, luring me in despite my attempt to resist it. It's what I was, and my resistance didn't last long.

With the hot, searing power of my wolf forcing my limits, I turned to Jez, nodding for her to open the sliding door. As we made our way into the backyard to disrobe, I told myself to keep a level head. Though no blood lust afflicted me, anything could set off Arys' undead power, waking it from where it slumbered so quietly inside me. I had to maintain control because Shaz was going to lose it. One of us had to keep it together.

I had barely descended the patio steps when Jez went to her knees, having quickly stripped off her skirt and tank top. In a heartbeat, she was a shockingly gorgeous leopard. With a shake of her body, she loosened up her muscles, stretching and flashing me a look that told me to hurry up and ditch the human body.

Shaz had removed his t-shirt, and the moonlight danced along his finely sculpted body like chocolate drizzled over ice cream. At least, my mind saw it that way. Before I could reach to pull my shirt over my head, he turned to me, his hand closing on my wrist possessively.

"You know how much I adore you, right?" He waited for me to answer, his gaze heavy and intense.

"Of course." I nodded, aware of Jez padding silently over to the gate to give us space.

"Then please, trust me. Don't stop this until it's truly over." He gave me a hard look, knowing me far too well. "I mean it, Alexa; let me finish this."

His use of my whole name indicated his seriousness, and I didn't like the monster I saw lurking behind those jade orbs. "I stop it when my instinct tells me to. I can't promise anything other than that."

Silently, I fixed him with a look that dared him to argue. Taking a deep breath, he sighed and pulled me into his arms so that I was pressed against him. "You really are a pain in the ass sometimes." His hand stroked my hair, and I snuggled into his comforting warmth. His scent stirred parts of me that had never been human. I wanted nothing more than to wrap myself around his naked body. Unfortunately, now was not the time.

Jez scratched lightly at the gate, a quiet indication of her impatience. I ignored her and kissed my white wolf with all of the emotion and wild need I held inside. Slipping my tongue between his lips, I hid a satisfied smile when he moaned softly.

The taste and scent of him filled my senses to overflowing, and I gasped when he bit my lower lip; the moist heat of his tongue followed to soothe the delicious pain. It was a dominant move, one that both antagonized and enticed. The need to be wolf coursed through me, and I broke off the kiss when my fingernails became claws.

"Let's get this over with," I murmured, slipping out of my clothing and tossing it on the deck stairs. By the time I turned to face him again, he was already wolf, stark white and beautiful against the backdrop of the moonlit night.

I fell to my knees and embraced the change, enjoying the flash of pain that was always followed by a sensual kind of pleasure. After stretching languidly, I went to Shaz' side, closing my eyes in enjoyment as he nuzzled me. When Jez' spotted form took off across the field, heading for the tree line, I didn't attempt to keep up. She could easily outrun us.

I smirked to myself, imagining the look on the faces of the other werewolves when she broke through the trees into the clearing where they would be gathered. Upon further thought, that could lead to trouble. I quickened my pace until I was at a full out run. Shaz ran at my side, his playful nature absent with his darker intentions.

It took just a few minutes for us to enter the forest, cutting through the trees with a natural rhythm that allowed us to move without being caught by twigs or fallen logs. I felt him at my side and at times just behind me, a shadow that moved perfectly in synch with me. The dread in my core continued to build.

Upon breaking through the trees into the clearing, Jez' golden fur caught my eye immediately. Less than a dozen werewolves filled the clearing, most of them in wolf form. Kylarai and Julian sat among them, together. Part of me felt betrayed by that, though I knew it wasn't my place to feel that way. She should have been with us, not him. Even though it was a show of support to her new lover, she was selling us out in a way.

More than a few of the gathered wolves eyed Jez uncertainly. Her long tail slapped the ground beside her, moving like a snake. I went to her side, making it clear to anyone wondering that she was there with me. Shaz slunk along slowly behind me, his eyes already locked on the shaggy brown wolf next to Ky.

Before either of them could move, I placed myself in the center of the clearing, drawing all eyes to me. It would be up to me to give the signal for Shaz and Julian to go at it like the testosterone-charged animals that they were. However, before I did so, I had every intention of making them both submit to me. I was Alpha and if I demanded it, they would have little choice.

I fixed my eyes on Shaz first, communicating easily without words. He blinked a few times as if disbelieving what he read in my gaze. I inclined my head and pawed lightly at the ground before me. Slowly, he came towards me, careful not to look at anyone else. The energy of every other Were there seemed to hum as they watched with collective interest.

As Shaz drew closer, he dropped lower to the ground so that his belly almost touched the fertile forest floor. Our connection grew in strength as we stared into one another and my personal power rose up. Desire filled me when he rolled over at my feet, baring his throat to me in absolute submission.

This was love. It really was. How many men would be willing to say with actions everything that this said?

I bent my head as if to gently bite his throat but instead, I licked long warm lines across his snowy white face. I wanted to nuzzle him but drew back before the others could see the tenderness. He scrambled to his feet and backed away; his eyes followed mine to Julian.

The sandy-brown wolf glanced at Kylarai, unease plain on his features. She continued to look straight ahead, at me. He was left to make his own choice. Ever so slowly, he made his way to me. He seemed to drag his back feet as if wishing he could drop into a hole in the ground. This must be killing him. If I could have smirked with glee in his face, I would have.

When he dropped down on his belly, satisfaction slid through me with a cold and slimy sensation. My wolf instantly identified him as lesser, insignificant. He glared up at me with hate shining in his dark eyes. I had never forced anyone to submit to me. We were people first, after all. Raoul had though. And, looking down at the whelp of a wolf at my feet, I understood what he got out of it.

I waited, staring Julian down until at last he gave in and rolled to expose his throat to me. I could feel every set of eyes on me, waiting to see what I would do. I believe a few of them expected me to tear his throat out, eliminating the need for a fight. Everything that was vampire within me cried out for his intoxicating blood, but I would never do that to Shaz. This fight was his.

Julian's scent filled my nostrils when I bent to his bared throat. Ever so gently, with all of the control I had within me, I placed fangs lightly to his skin. I never so much as grazed his flesh though everything in me demanded that I unleash the tightly bound wolf inside.

I drew back, stepping away from him to clear my head of his scent. He got to his feet in a motion so fast that I braced, my defenses on autopilot. He never made the mistake of coming any closer. He turned then, facing Shaz who stood just ten feet away.

I launched into action, moving between them. This wasn't starting until I was damn sure that Shaz was ready for him. I looked between the two of them, my question apparent. When a low growl began in Shaz' throat and was quickly echoed by Julian, I knew it was on.

Reluctantly, I backed away. I looked at Shaz, hoping to meet his eyes, but he saw nothing but his foe. No sooner had I moved out of their space than they flashed into action. The sound of their furry bodies hitting was like concrete on concrete. I ground my teeth together as I watched them meet in a flurry of snapping jaws. Fear coursed through me, and I shook my head slowly.

Kylarai came to my side, her grey eyes mirroring the terror I felt. The two wolves snarled and growled, their angry sounds echoing throughout the clearing. The energy of every wolf watching seemed to ring in my ears. I could feel it well, but it didn't have the same influence it would have had if I'd been in human form. The thought suddenly occurred to me that if I needed to tap metaphysical power to stop this fight, I would likely have to be in my other form.

Julian and Shaz moved so fast, it was hard to keep an eye on the details of what was happening. They lunged at one another, testing each other's limits. They started with a lot of defensive movements followed by feinting and circling. I was dying from the suspense, wondering when they would really try for the kill.

Time seemed to stop when Shaz got a hold of the brown wolf's shaggy neck fur. He bit deep, shaking his head as he did so. A strangled sound escaped Julian, but he twisted and struggled in Shaz' grasp until he had squirmed free. He didn't hesitate, lunging at Shaz in an attempt to throw him off balance. It worked.

Shaz went down with the brown wolf growling and snapping in his face. I saw Julian's fangs sink deep into my wolf, felt it as if he'd bitten me. The blood instantly stained Shaz' snow-white fur a deep red. It took all of my inner strength to resist surging forward. I needed to go to him.

But, Jez' watchful gaze stopped me. She was paying more attention to me than to the wolf fight. I think she was planning to take me down if I tried to rush in there. It would be for my own good. I could get myself killed doing something so irrational.

I couldn't breathe, watching them lash out with all they had. The blood flowed from each of them as the blows were exchanged. It was just as I was considering changing forms that I felt a cool presence in my mind. Arys.

'Are you ok, my wolf? How is our pup doing?' His voice was a soothing sensation as it echoed through my mind. This was something we could only do when I was in wolf form. It seemed to be our power's way of compensating for the loss I suffered by changing forms.

'This isn't the best time, Arys. It's getting bloody.' I jumped when the two wolves managed to gain a secure hold on one another. They wrestled in the dirt and grass, each of them now bleeding profusely. I didn't know what to do. I had to stop this, but the winner had to be obvious to everybody present.

Arys' presence was there but quiet, as if he wasn't sure what to offer me. If he'd been hoping to hear that Shaz was down and out, he was going to be disappointed.

'That's not fair,' he chided. 'I would never wish such a thing on him. I'm selfish, not petty.'

That was reassuring. And, most likely untrue. As I watched Julian sink fangs into Shaz yet again, this time in the meaty part of his shoulder, the vampire's power rose, and I tried to tap it. My body seemed to shudder and a sharp pain stabbed through my abdomen. The wolf was as much a part of nature as the earth's energy running strong beneath my paws. Yet, I couldn't access both of them fully at once.

The agony became too much, and I fought to maintain control and keep my eyes on the fight before me. Kylarai bumped against my shoulder, a question in her eyes. I shook my head, backing away. I willed the change to come, and it was brutal. My wolf was confused and unwilling to give in to the human side of me. I was insistent though, and it was going to happen.

A cry broke out of me when I was gasping on my knees, digging my fingers into the dirt. I shivered at the sudden temperature change from fur to skin. The sound of my pain was something that Shaz could not ignore, and the moment he took to look my way gave Julian the advantage.

The large, brown wolf threw himself on Shaz, pinning my mate beneath him. He fought for Shaz' throat, believing the end was within his grasp. My wolf was nothing, though, if not determined. He effectively angled his head so that his throat was hidden, twisting his body to throw Julian's balance off. He was unable to maintain his hold, and Shaz grasped his sudden opportunity, throwing himself right in the brown wolf's face.

Though Arys' voice was now absent from my mind, the power we shared soared up inside me, forcing me to my feet. I was shaky and pained from the sudden shifting, but I was not going to let them kill each other. A few of the wolves around me moved uncomfortably at my quick change.

Shaz was in Julian's face with jaws snapping too fast to see. Julian was surprised by the move and fell back, losing his footing in his attempt to backpedal. It gave Shaz all he needed to get on top of the other wolf, successfully pinning him. Everyone seemed to be reacting to the urgency in the atmosphere. The anticipation of the end was heavy.

My hands grew hot as I tapped the roiling mixture of undead and living energy inside me. Shaz gained a clear shot of Julian's throat, and he took it. Only Kylarai's tiny whimper reminded me why I was willing to stop this. Shaz' fangs sunk into Julian's flesh; in the same moment, I let a blue-tinged gold psi ball fly.

It was enough to knock Shaz off his feet without hurting him. Before Julian could get up, I threw up an energy wall between them. When he didn't get up, Kylarai rushed to his side. Shaz growled with a low rumble at the barrier that separated them.

Everything had happened so fast. My heart pounded louder than any other sound. It was over though. And, they were both alive. Angling my body so that most of my nakedness was shadowed; I went to them and kneeled next to Ky.

The blood pumped steadily from the wound in Julian's throat. However, it wasn't a fatal puncture. He would live. And, I couldn't help but wonder if that would be something both Shaz and I would regret allowing to happen.

I made eye contact with my beautiful white wolf; my heart broke in response to the many red splashes marring his fur. He looked both proud and relaxed. Confident that he wouldn't try to finish Julian off now that he was down, I dropped the barrier.

Leaving Ky and Julian, I went to Shaz, kneeling before him. Though I was still in human form, I bared my throat to him anyway, acknowledging him as Alpha male. My breath sucked in as his sharp fangs tentatively touched my skin. His breath came hot against my flesh and a rush came over me when I longed for him break the skin.

Shaz' touch was nothing less than gentle and loving when his teeth grazed me. I closed my eyes and leaned into him, my hands reaching to entangle in his filthy, matted fur. A swell of emotion erupted like hot lava coating my insides. My eyes filled with hot tears, but they did not fall. I wasn't sad, yet a melancholy feeling enveloped me. I had only kneeled before one other man, claiming him as my Alpha. That man was dead. Was this nostalgia or something else entirely?

Slowly, I got to my feet. I was startled to find a line of werewolves behind me, each waiting their turn to show respect to their new Alpha. I watched them, one by one, as they kneeled and gave Shaz their throat. It caused my heart to swell with pride. He was so much more amazing than I even knew yet. Everything about him told me so.

Julian finally struggled to his feet, leaning his weight heavily against Kylarai. He was in pretty bad shape. When at last they were the only two left to acknowledge Shaz, Ky moved to do so and Julian hung back. He was unwilling, which meant he forfeited his place and protection within our pack.

The silky smooth leopard fur rubbing against my thigh drew my gaze to Jez. She had been such a quiet observer that I'd almost forgotten she was there.

"Thanks Jez," I whispered for her ears only. "I appreciate that you came here tonight." I said a silent prayer of thanks that she hadn't had to tackle me as I feared. With Shaz' control compromised, I'd worried for my own.

She made a noise low in her throat, something between a purr and a growl. With a chuckle, I added, "You so better not be checking out my ass." She hissed at me then, her tail flipping around wildly. I knew it was only because she had no voice to blast a retort at me.

Finally, Shaz padded over to me, pushing his muzzle into my hand. I smiled down into his enchanting face, that strange sadness welling up again. He actually didn't look too bad. Julian was in worse shape.

"I'm not feeling up to running tonight," I told him, my voice low. "If you feel good enough, stay and run with our wolves. I just need some time alone."

He studied me, confusion and worry written all over his dirt-stained face. I smiled and kissed the tip of his wet nose. With a sigh of relief, I allowed the wolf within to have her way, and I once again embraced the change. Shaz nuzzled me, rubbing his side along mine. We were the mated Alpha pair. It seemed so surreal to think of it that way.

When he was certain that I meant what I'd said, he glanced around the clearing. Shock shone in his eyes upon noticing that the other werewolves awaited his command to run. Giving me one last reassuring nudge, he loped out of the clearing with every other wolf close behind.

When even Jez had sauntered off into the night, I turned and headed back the way that would lead me home. Leaving Julian and Kylarai in the clearing didn't feel at all right but staying would only wound his pride further. I trotted in between the tightly woven trees, listening to the voices of my pack, raised together in spine-chilling harmony as I went.

Chapter Twelve

The door creaked as I pushed it open. I'd had it repaired since the last time I'd been here. I'd broken it when I'd kicked it open. That had been months ago. In some ways, it felt like years and, in other ways, like it was just yesterday.

Despite the fact that he'd been dead for three months, Raoul's scent hit me as I stepped into his house. Closing the door behind me, I counted to five and then turned around. I honestly wasn't sure what I'd see.

Everything looked completely normal, as if nothing had been out of place. The furniture was the same. Everything was the same. The wolf tapestry that had once hung over the fireplace was gone though. Zoey Roberts had destroyed it.

Closing the door, I slipped off my shoes and crossed the front room until the kitchen came into view. The breath was crushed from my lungs as I took in the sliding glass door that led onto the patio. Though the glass was brand new and the mess long since cleaned up, I could see it in my mind like I was reliving the night Raoul died.

For a moment, I couldn't think or make sense of why I was there. Something had drawn me. If anything, I needed to be at Raoul's. I had put off coming here since Zoe killed him. But, I couldn't shake the feeling that I was supposed to be here now, if only for my own sanity. I'd thought that leaving the forest would upset my wolf, but being here, in Raoul's house where I'd once spent a portion of my life, I felt at home.

Since he had left the house to me in his will, knowing his death was imminent, I had kept it maintained. I'd also refused every offer from those interested in buying. I had no intention of giving it up. Did that make me crazy, nostalgic or just unable to let go?

I flicked on a few lights as I went, flooding the space around me with a warm glow. I came to a stop at the bottom of the stairs that led up to the bedrooms. Shaking my head, I continued on to the kitchen. I hadn't been upstairs since Zoey murdered one of Raoul's lovers, a fellow pack member, and I didn't feel inclined to go up there now. New carpet and paint wouldn't wash away the negative energy left in that room.

Raoul's small den was just off the kitchen. It was where we had shared our first and last truly intimate moment. The door stood open, but it was pitch black inside the windowless room. A hot tear streaked down my face, and I touched it to be sure it wasn't a vampy blood tear.

Turning on the kitchen light, I squinted against the sudden illumination. A quick glance around the kitchen showed me that it looked as if nothing out of the ordinary had ever taken place there. The beam of light shone into the den, and I followed it, pausing in the doorway.

I looked toward the couch in the corner. I could barely see it from where I stood. Crossing the room, I turned on the lamp that sat on the corner of the desk, the same desk where Arys had found the confession letter Raoul had left me.

Against my better judgment, I pulled open the top desk drawer. It was filled with typical desk clutter like pens and post-it note pads. I closed it and went on to the next one. It had nothing but file folders for Raoul's real estate business, which was nothing of extreme interest to me.

As I reached for the handle on the third drawer, something told me not to open it. Of course, that only made me want to get into it even more. Pulling it open harder than necessary, I was surprised to see that it was filled with photo albums. There were three of them. I couldn't help but reach for the first one, the pages creaking uncomfortably as I opened it. Clearly, nobody had looked at it in awhile.

The first page held a very old photo, a young woman with smiling brown eyes and a head of hair to die for. The caption beneath it said, "Naomi". I was astonished and began to scrutinize the picture closer. This was Zoey's mother, the human woman Raoul had loved. One of two anyway.

Flipping through the pages revealed more photos, some of Raoul and Naomi together. In all the time I'd known him, I had never seen him look at these pictures. It must have hurt him too much.

Now that I knew about the two great loves of Raoul's life, one of which was my own mother, I could better understand why he chose the bachelor lifestyle he had lived until his death. It didn't make it any easier to accept though.

The entire photo album was photos of that time in Raoul's life, before me. I put it back and reached for another one. Flipping open the cover, I was strangely surprised to see photos of Shaz and myself, among other wolves, from when Raoul had taken us in. It was strange to see a much younger version of me. Looking at the teenage version of both my white wolf and myself, I couldn't help but think of everything that had changed since that time.

For one, my loss of innocence had gone from learning how to deal with the change to becoming more of a monster than I had ever dreamed possible. The uncertain smile on the face of the teenaged me spoke volumes, and I slammed the album shut. I didn't bother opening the third one. I didn't want to take this trip down memory lane.

Casting a glance around the small office, I put the photo album back in the drawer and kicked it closed. I sat heavily on the end of the couch with Raoul's scent puffing up at me as I did so. I leaned back so that my head rested against the back of the soft, worn sofa. Running my hands over it, I instantly became lost in a memory, one that refused to leave as easily as it had come.

It had been in this very room, oddly enough. The very first time that Raoul and I had made love. My skin flushed hot with the memory of his hands on my body. I had been so young, a virgin. He had been the man of my dreams, the one who had saved me in so many ways.

I had been in the den here, crying after an especially traumatic night. A fellow wolf had tried to take advantage of me, and Raoul had kicked the shit out of him. He'd found me in tears on this very same couch and pulled me into his arms, pressing moist kisses to my temple, cheeks and eventually my lips.

The memory ensnared me until it was as real as it had once been. Raoul drew my face to his with a warm touch, and I melted, hungry for what he offered. Our lips met, and my heart raced in disbelief. I had spent so many nights imagining this moment and all of a sudden, it was happening.

He had never been one to take it slow. Once I responded to Raoul, kissing him back, biting his lips and tongue, he'd been quick to take it a step further. Pressing me into the back of the sofa, his long black hair fell around my face, and his scent was all I could breathe in. Intoxicating and overwhelming, I was flooded with heat between my legs as he buried his face in my hair and nipped at my neck.

I reached to pull him closer, needing to feel him against every part of me. He growled low in his throat, and my wolf leaped in response. It was both frightening and awe-inspiring. I gasped when he bit me harder, a shot of pleasure going straight to my groin.

The next thing I knew, I was naked and begging him to take me. His silky, soft, ebony hair trailed over my skin as he kissed his way down my body. He kneeled before me on the floor, his dark eyes peering into mine as he spread my legs wide. When he tasted me, I thought I had died and gone to heaven.

My fingers were lost in his hair as I pulled him closer. A strange growl bubbled out of me, and I writhed under his expert touch. I orgasmed with an intensity that tore a series of cries from me.

Raoul stood beautifully nude, like a Greek god. I ran my hands over his hard stomach, boldly reaching to stroke his hard and ready shaft. Though I was inexperienced, I wasn't completely naïve. He looked down at me, his coal-black eyes watching every slick motion of my hand. With his hands on my shoulders, he slowly pushed me back so that I was lying on the couch. Raising one of my legs up over the back of the couch, he moved between my thighs so that he was positioned at my entrance.

"Are you ready, Alexa?" His voice was powerful, touching me in the pit of my stomach so that I had the urge to squirm.

I tried to speak, but the words wouldn't come out so I reached for him instead, my clawed fingers creating red scratches on his forearms. He leaned down so that my breasts pressed against his hard chest. Wrapping my arms around his neck, I let out a little yelp when he pressed forward, slowly but surely, until he was fully sheathed inside my tight warmth.

"Sorry," he murmured, his breath hot against my ear. "I figured it would be better than inching my way in."

A blush colored my cheeks, and I bit my lower lip when he

began to move, building a steady rhythm. The pain eased, replaced with pleasure unlike any I could have imagined. Desire had me moaning with every one of Raoul's thrusts; the animal inside me was truly unleashed in this act. I welcomed it, wanting more, needing to feel him deeper and fuller.

I couldn't be still beneath him. My hips moved as my body instinctually sought to pull him further into me. We grew slippery with sweat as Raoul increased his speed until he pounded into me harder than I ever would have guessed possible. My body received him willingly, opening up to accommodate both his power and size. The sensation of an approaching climax started, deep inside me.

Each wave built until it was bigger than the last. I gasped for breath, my hands on his ass to hold him immersed in my body, fearing he would stop.

Raoul pulled back to nip at my breasts and throat. A low snarl deep in his throat caused my heart to surge with adrenaline. He wouldn't hurt me, would he?

Just when I thought surely I couldn't take anymore, my muscles clenched and tightened around his cock. I cried out when the earth shattering orgasm rolled over me. Every wave drew a cry from me, but it was edged with the hint of a growl and sounded like somebody else.

He tensed and then spilled his hot seed inside me, throwing his head back. He moaned, and the sound was chilling in its husky maleness. I stared up at him with a mixture of wonder and awe in my eyes. I could feel the adoration spill out of me as I looked at him. He was my Alpha wolf, and I had given myself to him, no regrets.

With the curtain of his hair shadowing his face, Raoul spoke softly. "Are you ok? I didn't hurt you, did I?"

The sincerity in his eyes had been heart stopping. If only it had been real.

As I reclined on the very same couch, lost in the past, those words echoed in my head. *Yes, you did hurt me, Raoul*, I thought. If only it had been physically instead of emotionally. But, I have to forgive you, or I will never be able to move on.

The overwhelming urge to cry struck me, and it was more than I could take. The tears spilled down my cheeks like a waterfall. A sob broke the silence around me, and I felt ashamed because a part of me would have given anything to relive that night. The pain that Raoul had caused me back then ran too deep, I couldn't completely let it go. Yet, I knew that I had to.

I practically leaped off the couch, feeling like it had burned me. The strangest sensation struck me, the feeling that I wasn't alone. A chill stole down my spine, and I shivered. I didn't like the idea that something could be there with me, something like ... Raoul? I wasn't keen on ghosts; I really wanted nothing to do with them. Despite everything that had transpired with Raoul, I hoped that he would have gone on to something better than that.

Feeling uncomfortable, I left the den and descended the stairs near the kitchen, to the living room below. I turned the TV on and let it play quietly while I curled up in an old easy chair in the corner. I didn't want to leave the house, and that was both comforting and frightening.

ജ്ഞ്ജ്ഞ

I didn't know that I was dreaming. All I knew was that Harley had me pinned beneath him, and I was struggling to fight him off. He wanted to bite me, to draw my blood deep into him while I fought him. I knew that, and I knew that I had to stop it from happening.

This wasn't about him trying to kill me. His intentions were darker than that. Whatever it was that he intended, it was worse than death. It hit me all at once. I knew what he wanted from me. He wanted to claim me so that Arys never could: the blood bond, the wicked kiss. I couldn't let it happen.

The dream broke into fragments and as I fought him, it all began to fade away, as fast as it had come. I woke with a scream on my lips, staring into the worried blue eyes of my dark vampire.

Arys took a step back, waiting for me to come to my senses. I gasped and blinked at him, uncertain if I was really awake or still dreaming. When I focused in on the rest of Raoul's living room surrounding me, I knew I was awake.

"Arys?"

He scowled in response to the inflection in my voice. "What happened to not leaving the door unlocked? We've been over this. Do you have a death wish, Alexa?"

"How did you know I was here? What time is it?" I shook my

head in an attempt to clear the cobwebs from my brain. I felt disoriented and confused.

It was still dark beyond the windows, but there was a shimmer to the air, invisible to human eyes, which indicated dawn's approach.

Arys watched me closely, and I felt scrutinized under his heavy gaze. Lifting an eyebrow in question, I shot him an irritated glare. He crossed his arms and cocked his hip in a way that was both sexy and told me that I was being analyzed.

"I'm surprised that you have to ask." He glanced around before answering me. I had the strangest feeling that he was nervous. "I could feel you. Your pain ... it drew me. I had to get to you. I don't think I could have denied that need if I tried."

Staring into his eyes, I saw the truth there and with it, love? No. I had to be imagining the emotion swimming in the abyss of his gaze. I was reminded then of two things: One, Harley stating that Arys must truly love me, and the other, another time in this house when Arys had tuned into my pain. Raoul and I had an emotional confrontation, and I had cried. Arys knew it without laying eyes on me. What was this all about?

"What?" My throat was dry, and I coughed. My dream came rushing back to me, and I was suddenly much more alert. "Arys, I dreamt about Harley. He was trying to blood bond me, and I was fighting him. So hard." My eyes closed as I saw the image again, Harley's fangs flashing in the light as he used his weight and power to hold me.

Arys' expression grew dark, and his energy was alive with rage. "He wouldn't dare." His fingers clenched into fists, and I grew warm from the heat of his anger. There was something in his anxious manner that betrayed his words.

"You know he would." I reached out to him, needing to feel his cool skin, his power mingling with mine. "He's not going to let me have you."

Arys grabbed my hands and pulled me to my feet. His arms went around my waist, pressing me against him. I looked up at him, and he bent his head to capture my lips with his in a breath-stealing kiss. I was sucked into the magnetic draw, falling into him with no resistance. The power we shared sought to control us, and I wanted to allow it. After the torrent of emotions I'd already dealt with tonight, I wasn't afraid to let the power lead us. I wanted to feel the freedom and release that only came with surrender.

He paused, despite my insistence. Looking down into my eyes, he placed a hand beneath my chin and forced me to look deeper into him. My heart skipped a beat when he whispered, "You already have me."

Unmistakable human emotion filled his eyes. Try as I might to deny it, something was there, something more than I had ever expected from my vampire lover. It frightened me; it truly did, even as it excited me. I already held Shaz' heart in my hands, precariously at that. Could I honestly say that I didn't love Arys, in some way?

I don't give myself to any man without reason. Perhaps the power had joined us, but it wasn't what kept me coming back. Not entirely. Was it possible to be in love with two men, albeit very different ones? I wasn't sure. All I knew was what I felt when I was with each of them.

It wasn't the same. What Arys brought out of me was unlike anything I had felt with Shaz and vice versa. They each held a part of me that was all their own.

"That's what I'm afraid of," I admitted, my lips brushing his as I spoke. I paused to nibble the silver ring in his pouty lower lip. He made a sound that was a combination of a sigh and groan. "I don't know how to love you."

Arys ran a strong hand through my hair, balling a handful in his fist. The extremely possessive gesture spoke through dominance to the wolf in me. "You don't know how to admit it." The room felt alive with energy as our power danced around us. My skin almost burned with the need for release as the pressure built.

He was right. I hated when he was right. His firm hold kept me still as he dipped his tongue into my mouth, tasting of me fully. When his fangs drew blood from my lower lip, it was no accident. Sucking on the tiny wound, he pressed harder against me so there was no mistaking that his need was as great as my own.

The coppery taste of my blood in his mouth was delightful as it stirred the desire building within me. When his fangs grazed my throat, I gasped, and the adrenaline blasted through me.

"My beautiful wolf ... you don't even know what it is you mean to me." Arys maintained his gentle but firm hold on my long blonde locks as his other hand slipped beneath my top. His cool touch was soothing. I clung to him, desperate to get my hands on any part of him that I could.

The sharp points of his fangs came to rest lightly over my jugular vein, and I could feel the sudden urge to kill rise up in him. He would never do it though. I trusted him completely, only realizing now how deep that trust went. Every time we were in a moment like this, I allowed him the choice to take my life. Dear God, I did love him. How else could I willingly do something so bold and possibly so stupid?

"Then tell me," I replied, needing to hear now more than ever what I meant to him. "Tell me what I mean to you, Arys. I need to hear you say it."

I didn't miss his hesitation. Lifting his head to look at me, I was shocked to see that his eyes had gone all wolf, the whites' now solid blue. Some things about our bond, I would never get used to. The hand that held my hair loosened but didn't let go. We faced one another with an open, raw emotion that made me feel uncomfortable and exposed.

Arys gently touched the side of my face, stroking it with an affection that stole my breath. His eyes went to my bloodied lip, and he ran his tongue sensually over his fangs. My own curiosity was piqued. What would Arys taste like? His blood had to be overwhelming, like way too much of a good thing. How bad did I want to find out?

"Alexa, I have never been more alive in the past few centuries than I am right now, with you." He paused, second-guessing himself, and I turned to plant an encouraging kiss in the palm of his hand where it continued to stroke my cheek. "You are the only light in my dark world. All I see ... is you."

I closed my eyes, the emotion overcoming me in its immensity. His next words came low, barely a whisper. Yet, I heard them as clearly as if they'd been shouted at me.

"I love you. I know it's wrong, but I do. You have given back to me everything I thought I'd lost forever." His voice carried the sound of defeat. I opened my eyes to find him staring at the floor, shame evident in his expression.

"How you feel, Arys, it's not wrong." I placed my hand over his, drawing it to my chest where my heart beat steadily. "And, it isn't one sided. Arys, I-,"

"Don't say it!" He looked up suddenly, his eyes filled with hope and fear. "Don't say it," he repeated, placing a finger over my lips. "You love the white wolf."

Knocking his finger away, I rose up on tiptoes to look him directly in the eyes. "I do. And, he has his own place within me that can never be touched by another. As do you."

He wanted to believe me, but Arys didn't know how to be loved any better than I had just a few months ago. I understood how hard it was to trust fully. I'd been there.

"I'll never let Harley get his hands on you. I will kill him before he can do anything to separate us." Arys kissed me then, a hard bruising kiss that spoke of his need for solace. His desperation was evident by the pained energy that rolled off him.

"He wants to bond me, Arys," I managed to get out between fevered kisses. "I would rather be dead than be bound to him."

Arys began to slide my clothing off, a simple task since I'd been lightly dressed for shape shifting. His hands caressed my stomach, sliding up to cup my breasts firmly. "Nobody is going to harm you, my wolf. I swear it."

Lowering his head to my breasts, he ran his tongue lightly over one nipple and then the next. A soft moan escaped me, and my knees went weak. His arm went around my waist, holding me up as he sucked and nibbled at my breasts. I threaded my fingers into his soft, perfectly messy hair. He still held a tangled handful of my own long locks.

Arys' touch held a tenderness that he'd never shown me before. It caused a tightening low in my body and a quickening of my heart. Nobody had to tell me this time would be like no other before it.

I tugged at his t-shirt until he quickly discarded it. I was already making short work of his jeans when he brushed my hair from my face and kissed me again. He pulled me down to the soft carpet, allowing me to get comfortable before slipping between my thighs. I instantly grew moist when his erection pressed against my soft folds, instinct drawing our bodies together. Yet, there was something else drawing our souls together, and seeing that love in his eyes as he leaned to run his tongue along my collarbone completely boggled my mind.

My arms went around him, and I hugged him close. I wanted to feel him on every inch of me. Arys rose up over me so that we had to stare into one another. It demanded more boldness than even I possessed. The intimate nature of it had me shaking in anticipation.

Arys grinned knowingly, and I flushed from head to toe. The embarrassment was washed away when he pressed closer, guiding his hard shaft to my entrance. I expected him to thrust into me immediately, so when he ever so slowly slid inside while pressing his lips to mine, the rush and tingle that filled me was overwhelming.

Emotion fed the power humming and growing all around us. Arys buried himself as deep within me as he could possibly get while I fought the urge to cry from the metaphysical effects of the emotion in the power between us. It was so strong, more than I could take. When he pulled out and thrust into me again, I moaned and wrapped my legs around his waist.

Not once did he take his eyes from my face. He watched me as he forced the soft cries from me with each stroke of his body locked deep inside mine. His eyes held a sense of wonder and intrigue as we rode the waves of energy fueled by love and desire, rather than just desire alone. It was stronger, this power, and I felt it penetrate every part of me.

If I thought I was afraid, then Arys had to be downright terrified. He was clearly as swept up in the sensations as I was. I felt the shudder that rippled through him as he also struggled with the onslaught of power that seemed to beat at us with newfound strength.

I ran my hands down his body to his lower back, losing myself in the feeling of him moving in and out of me. He went achingly slow, tenderness in every stroke. It was a pleasure unlike any other I'd known during our usual frenzied, sexual encounters. This was not about the desperation for release. It was about coming to terms with a deeper need and affection for one another. One that I couldn't deny as Arys loved me with such careful and perfect precision.

The building waves were strong, and I knew they were going to crash over me hard. I gasped for breath and growled when his pace quickened. My body clenched around him, holding him tightly, wrenching a strangled groan from Arys. The sound heightened my senses, and I moved in time with him, my fangs tingling at the gum.

Again, the thought crossed my mind, what would Arys taste

like? As the orgasm approached, I threw all inhibitions to the wind, careless and wild. The wolf was strong in me but so was Arys' own undead power. My fangs were ready, and I didn't think, I just acted.

I went for the spot between his shoulder and his neck, careful not to sink my fangs too deep. Mine were much longer than Arys' were. He made a sound that was both surprised and pained as I broke through the surface of his smooth, porcelain skin. His blood hit my tongue, hot and tangy, and the most powerful orgasm rocked me to the core.

I cried out; the sound was muffled against his cool flesh as I tasted the bright red vampire blood. It hit my system like a narcotic, and I instantly had tunnel vision. The waves of undying pleasure continued, building towards a second climax. I felt like I was falling, plummeting head first toward the earth at an alarming rate. Arys' blood was almost sweet on the back of my tongue. I wanted more, and I sucked harder at the wound.

Arys moaned and thrust into me hard as he climaxed. My body welcomed it, gripping his shaft as it twitched and jerked inside me. His release flooded me with heat and a fire that consumed. I drew back from the bloody punctures and met his eyes. I will never forget the exposed emotion I saw there. It was so vulnerable compared to the guarded expression he usually wore. I studied it, wanting to remember it always.

He raised an eyebrow, a sexy grin spreading across his face. "Why are you staring at me, beautiful lady?" His tongue darted out to capture a drop of blood at the corner of my mouth.

My lips quirked in a half smile. "No reason. Just enjoying the view." I reached to run a hand through his hair, reveling in every part of touching him.

Arys rolled off me and curved his body alongside mine. It was somewhat strange to be lying naked on Raoul's living room floor. It also felt incredibly free and liberating. And anyway, this was my house now, and I needed to start treating it as such.

"Speaking of the view," Arys pointed lazily toward the window where the darkness was thinning fast now. "I'm not going to make it home. That means you have to stay here with me all day."

That sounded like a great way to spend the day to me. I wasn't ready to leave him yet. "Ok, we can take some blankets downstairs to the basement. It's furnished." A thought struck me, and I added, "I have to give Shaz a call though. He's going to be looking for me."

I expected a grimace or dirty look of some kind from Arys then, but his expression remained neutral. That raised my suspicions, and I was suddenly dying to ask him about his little hunting excursion with Shaz.

"Alright, you go call him. I'll get us set up downstairs." He trailed a hand over my back and down my behind as I got up, sending a shiver through me. I was glad to see that I had escaped without a rug burn.

As Arys rummaged in a hall closet for blankets and pillows, I went to my purse for my cell phone. It wasn't quite dawn yet, and I got Shaz' voicemail, as I'd expected. I left a quick message telling him where I was and not to worry about me. I was almost relieved that I could prolong having to face Kylarai in the light of day. I dreaded that conversation.

Against my better judgment, I went to the kitchen and opened the fridge. It was pretty bare. I had little selection so I chose a can of Pepsi and headed back down the stairs. Arys had already vacated to the lowest level of the house as the sun beams started to creep in.

I gathered myself, prepared to take on Arys and, hopefully, get more out of him than I had from Shaz. Was my curiosity unnatural? Maybe, but it was driving me nuts to know they had shared an intimate moment, hunted and killed together, and I didn't know any of the details. Arys was more likely to share things that Shaz would gloss over. And, I had all day to get it out of him.

Chapter Thirteen

I stared uncertainly at my reflection in the full-length mirror on my closet door. The Little Red Riding Hood costume did wonders for my physique. Unfortunately, it also nagged at my insecurities. I didn't mind showing a little skin, but I usually had a higher clothing-to-skin ratio than this.

My cleavage was more than impressive in the black, strapless corset dress. The red lace trim grazed the top of my thigh high fishnet stockings in a barely there way. I decided to pair the costume up with leather knee-high boots that had killer five-inch heels, sharp enough to take out an eye.

My few accessories included silver bracelets that jingled when I moved and a black ribbon tied like a choker around my neck. The little red hooded cape was my final accessory. Kylarai assured me that it wasn't too short from where she sat on my bed, watching me do my makeup. I'd gone a little heavier than usual on the dark eyeliner and, after hesitating, had even added the red lipstick Jez had insisted on when I bought the outfit.

Things hadn't been as awkward with Kylarai as I'd expected. I had said a prayer of thanks when I arrived home to find that she was there alone. We hadn't said much about the fight between Julian and Shaz. Shaz was Alpha, and there wasn't much more to be said about that.

I was dying to see him. After getting virtually nothing out of Arys, I was frustrated and ready for an evening out. All Arys had been willing to share was that he and Shaz had formed an unspoken understanding and that I would be wise to stop picking at it. Well ... fine then.

I so rarely got the chance to enjoy some cheap entertainment. I had also come home with a ton of ideas and plans for redecorating

Raoul's house. It was still hard to think of it as mine. That would come with time.

I'd enjoyed being there, more than I'd thought I would. I had expected to feel out of place in the house filled with both good and bad memories. Instead I had felt calm and at peace. Strange but true.

I turned to face Kylarai, loving my height in the high-heeled boots. She was dressed as the green fairy, better known to some as the absinthe fairy. Clad in a long, forest green cocktail dress with a slit from floor to hip and the cutest sparkly green wings, she looked like she'd just stepped out of a fantasy novel. Green eyeliner would never have looked so perfect on me. Her grey eyes were dazzling.

"Should I leave my hair down or put it up?" I asked, ignoring the part of me that felt guilty as soon as I met her eyes. Some combination of Julian's loss and the kiss I'd shared with Kale nagged at me.

"Leave it down but use some mousse and blow dry it upside down to give it that wild look with lots of volume," she said. "That would look sexy."

"Are you sure you don't mean trashy?" I laughed and scrutinized my appearance one last time before ransacking the bathroom for mousse.

"You look amazing. Now stop fussing. The trick-or-treaters will be coming soon." She slid off my bed and smoothed her skirt down. "They're going to be so cute, all dressed up."

I couldn't help but smile in response to her enthusiasm. She genuinely adored the innocence of children.

"Alright, just let me find my blow dryer, and I'll be right out."

The doorbell rang then, and a chorus of small voices called out, "Trick or treat!" Kylarai let out a little squeal and ran for the door. Her inner child really came out during holidays of any kind.

After blasting my hair with the blow dryer to increase the volume, I arranged the pieces of red and blonde around my face and called it done. I left my bedroom before I picked apart my costume any further.

In the kitchen, I poured myself a glass of red wine. The excited chatter of kids reached me along with Ky's exclamations. After savoring a long sip, I joined her at the front door. She waved goodbye as the small group exited the yard.

Groups of kids could be seen down the street heading this way. Ky's genuine joy made me wonder if she wished she'd had kids of her own. I wanted to ask, but now wasn't the time.

Children weren't something that I thought about much. Since the attack as a teen, it was something I'd come into adulthood accepting wasn't for me.

"Oh Alexa, look at the little princess!" Kylarai had the door open before the next group of kids had even made it up the walk. "You guys look awesome!"

My eyes widened when I noticed the size of the handfuls of candy she was giving out. The big smiles on the painted faces peering at her with wonder warmed my heart in places that felt foreign to those cozy feelings. I instinctually gravitated closer to the doorway.

A princess, two superheroes and a ghost all called out a happy, "Thank you!" Their mom stood at the end of the walk waiting for them, and I raised a hand in greeting. I couldn't help but feel deceitful. These people had no idea they were sending their kids to the door of two vicious killers.

By the time we'd had twenty-seven kids come to the door, I was finished my first glass of wine. Not intending to go overboard but needing to take the edge off, I poured another smooth glass of cabaret. I think I was a little nervous about walking into a party where both Shaz and Arys would be. If there was any fighting tonight, I was leaving.

It was almost nine o'clock when the trick-or-treaters stopped coming. The big bowl of candy was almost empty; only a few lollipops and chocolates remained. I'd nibbled more than a few during the past hour. After a third glass of wine, I was ready to go to the Lounge.

Kylarai was permeating a positive, happy vibe as she spritzed on some perfume and gathered her purse. I was still too nervous to ask her if Julian would be at Lucy's Lounge. She'd volunteered to drive tonight because of an early business meeting. So, I had the liberty of sipping cocktails and socializing. I was looking forward to it. I needed to get out more. Hunting and killing didn't count as a social life. Did it?

When we were cruising through town in Ky's white Escalade, I began to feel an anxious flutter. I couldn't shake the feeling that it was going to be an eventful night.

That feeling didn't ease when Kylarai said, "You're definitely going to have those two at each other's throats dressed like that. Better be prepared to deal with some drama."

"You have my full permission to smack their skulls together if they start any trouble," I replied as I flipped the sun visor down to look in the mirror on the back. How is it that celebrities make red lipstick look so easy and perfect? It's much harder to maintain than any other shade.

"Remember that you said that when the time comes. You look fine. Stop looking in the mirror."

The drive to Lucy's Lounge took less than ten minutes. My senses went into overdrive the moment I got out of the big Cadillac. As we crossed the parking lot, a group of guys whistled at us. It boosted my ego immensely. They also cat called to the three girls that walked a few paces behind us, but that was beside the point.

The club was filled with a delightful array of costumes. It was nice to see that so many people had decided to dress up. The typical blockbuster movie characters were there in full force. No Halloween party was complete without the Joker and a Jedi or two.

Of course, the classic horror costumes from devils to Lugosi vampires were everywhere as well as sexy cops, angels and celebrity recreations. It never ceased to amaze me how creative some people get with their costumes.

One of the local bands from the city was dominating the stage. It looked like the bar staff had made a half-assed attempt at decorating. Black and orange streamers hung from the ceiling. Matching candles adorned each table. Otherwise, it was the same drab yet welcoming environment as always.

Arys was not there. At least not yet. I couldn't feel his presence, but it was early yet for him. I didn't expect him until later, after he'd take care of the blood hunger. If he neglected to do so, there was going to be trouble. The bloodlust and a crowd like this could make a deadly combination for me.

Once we got through the traffic jammed entryway, I was able to take stock of the entire place. The werewolf energy in the club was strong. I could feel Shaz as well as Zak, which likely meant Julian wasn't far. I ignored the urge to cast a glance around for him.

Kylarai's head came up suddenly, sniffing the air. Wherever Julian was, she had found him. I spotted him a moment later. He and Zak were each dressed as characters from a superhero movie. I think it was X-Men, but I'm not much of a movie buff myself. Zak crooked a finger to beckon us over. I was eager to get to the bar for a drink so I could see Shaz. I was dying to see how he was dressed. And, the last person I had words for was Julian. I still wasn't sure if I should force him out of town or not.

"I'm going up to the bar. Do you want a Coke or anything?" I gestured toward the dark-haired Were that drew her attention. "I know you want to go over there. Feel free. I swear, I don't mind."

Impulsively, she hugged me tightly, and I almost lost my balance on the extreme heels. "You really are the best, Alexa. You're so much more understanding about this than I would be." Before I could reply, she was gone, flitting off across the bar to her brown wolf.

I shrugged and turned toward the bar. The large line-up prevented me from getting a glimpse of Shaz until I got closer. When at last I caught sight of his platinum hair, my heart increased in tempo. The anticipation was eating me alive.

I laughed despite my sudden speechlessness when I finally laid eyes on my white wolf. He was dressed as Billy Idol, complete with a badass leather jacket. A punk rock style chain hung around his neck.

As the people ahead of me received their drinks and moved aside, I could see that he wore jaw- droppingly tight leather pants. Holy crap! I don't know what I'd been expecting but this wasn't it.

Shaz' white blonde hair was a mess of spikes and gel. Combined with the barest smudge of black around his jade green eyes, the look was so sexy on him that I was instantly flushed. I would have fanned my face with my hand if it would have made any difference. He had only minor bruising around his left eye from his scrap with Julian. He looked damn fine.

Though he had yet to see me, he knew that I was there. I was impatiently waiting for the four women ahead of me to get their drinks and get the hell out of the way. Knowing my wolf was so close yet out of reach was making me crazy.

All at once, the crowd seemed to disperse before me, and I sauntered up to the bar with a look that oozed sexuality. Our eyes met, and Shaz' mouth literally dropped open as he took in my attire. The watchful wolf inside me did not miss the sudden increase in his heart rate.

I flashed him a playful smile and a wink. I was playing it cool, but my guts were twisting in knots. He looked good enough to climb over the bar for in front of all of the people waiting behind me. I couldn't help but feel like I was staring at him stupidly.

"And, what can I get for you?" Shaz' eyes roamed over my body, lingering on my fishnet-clad thighs. He swallowed hard, and my pulse raced. "Other than the extreme fucking I am dying to give you."

His boldly uncharacteristic statement had me literally tripping on my own tongue. I couldn't get over how delicious he looked. Punk rock was a really good look for him.

"You are so sexy right now. I could just eat you up." I licked my red lips teasingly. "Red wine, please. And, please tell me this is a joke. You can't be working now. I have to have you."

He raised an eyebrow, and a mischievous grin spread across his luscious lips. "I love your costume. It's so perfectly you. The wolf disguised as the innocent." He turned away momentarily to grab a fresh bottle of wine and a glass. I gazed hungrily at his leather clad behind. "It really makes me want to bend you over one of these tables. I'm abandoning ship here as soon as Tawnie gets in. Don't disappear on me."

He pressed the wine into my hand, refusing to let me pay for it. What a sweetheart. I didn't want to move, but the line of people pressing behind me gave me little choice.

"I'm not going anywhere, baby." I blew him a kiss and left the bar.

The glow that filled me just from that brief interaction with my white wolf had me buzzing. Waiting for him to be free of his responsibilities was going to be torture. Every instinct I had as both woman and wolf demanded that I touch him the way I so desperately wanted to.

No sooner had I turned away from the bar than I both sensed and saw the tall, lithe leopard enter the Lounge. Jez looked gorgeous, dressed to kill as Beatrix Kiddo from Kill Bill. She looked deadly in the yellow outfit with black stripes, replicated from the film. She even carried the notorious Hanzo sword on her hip. Impressive. Her golden hair hung long and silky straight down her back. I was instantly jealous.

She spotted me right away, and I moved to meet her. "You did the red lips like I told you to. It looks so hot." The first words out of Jez' mouth shouldn't have been surprising, especially followed by, "I love those boots."

The crowd continued to grow as the next wave of partygoers started showing up. So much freely exuded positive energy was more potent than the red wine in my hand.

She grabbed my arm and pulled me along to the nearest shooter girl. I assumed it was to hit on her, but then she thrust an oddly colored shot into my hand. Drinking was one thing but shooting drinks was another.

When I eyed the blue concoction, she leaned in close and said cheerfully, "Here's to being carefree for a night. Happy Halloween, wolf girl. Bottom's up!"

She tossed it back like a trooper, and I followed her lead, grimacing in response to the sour taste. I should have known. Leave it to a cat to choose a Sour Puss as her choice of shot. I preferred the wine.

We walked around the lower floor, from one side of the large building to the other. Jez wanted to check out everyone's costumes and send out her "single girl" radar. I was more than happy to take in the entire place.

I experienced a flash of disappointment when Jez asked a passing waitress to bring us drinks. I wanted to feast my eyes on Shaz again. Seeing him from a distance was an absolute tease. In the back of my mind, I could think about nothing but touching his rock hard body.

We paused on the edge of the dance floor to wait for the waitress to return. The crowd on the dance floor appeared to be having a great time. I was eager to join in.

"Do you think Kale will show up?" Jez asked as she openly admired a tall brunette in a Roman goddess costume. "I invited him."

I glanced over to where Kylarai was shooting pool with Zak and Julian. From where I stood, I could see bruises marring Julian's skin. It brought a smile to my face.

"I kind of hope he doesn't. That wouldn't go over very well." I sipped my drink and glared at the lesser wolf, the one that dared to think he could ever be Alpha anything.

When I looked back at my cat-eyed companion, she was giving me a knowing look. "She doesn't know he kissed you."

"She doesn't need to. They're not together anymore. And, that was personal."

She clearly didn't believe that's all there was to it. "If you say so."

I had to avoid the temptation to step on her toe as the waitress walked up with our drinks. Jez passed her a twenty, and she put up a hand in refusal.

"I have strict orders from the bar not to let you two pay for anything. I will happily take a tip though." She beamed and giggled, despite looking uncomfortable dressed as a French maid.

Jez gave her the twenty anyway, making her promise to keep an eye out for us. "Free drinks all night," she quipped to me. "You must be giving it to that wolf good."

Her comment warmed my cheeks, and a fire started in my stomach. "Trust me, I am waiting very impatiently to do just that."

Her musical laughter peeled out like ringing bells. "Come on, let's hit the dance floor. I have energy to burn."

Jez was naturally graceful and seemed to move like a willow tree caught in a breeze. Dancing in heels didn't feel as natural to me as she made it appear. I felt eyes on me and looked up to find a dark-haired pirate giving me the eye. His attention was flattering, but I was grateful when he danced on by. I didn't want to give anyone the wrong idea.

The waitress made good on her promise and came back to us. Despite my higher tolerance, I found myself to be getting quite tipsy. I had to cut back before I did something to embarrass myself in these boots.

After three or four songs passed, my foot developed a cramp, and I begged Jez to use her additional height to find us a table. Miraculously, a couple vacated one nearby almost as soon as we started looking.

I sat down with a sigh of relief after shoving all of the empties to one side. I could see most of the club from where we sat. The stage was in front of us but against the opposite wall. Diagonally to the left was the bar in the center of the room, the staircase behind it and the pool tables to the direct left. The entry and those passing in and out to smoke were between both sides of the room.

Shaz' hair was visible from a distance but the constant line up at the bar prevented me from getting a good look. I wondered how many girls had already tried to slip him their number.

Jez dug into her tiny purse and pulled out a lipstick and a compact mirror. "This place is really hopping. If Kale doesn't show up, I'm going to kick his ass. He always misses out."

I watched her reapply her perfect lipstick without the slightest smudge. No fair. "I just hope he doesn't go to the Kiss. That place is going to ruin him."

"No shit. I've been telling him for ages to just kill something already and stop torturing himself with that dive."

We chattered on, watching the activity of those around us. I wasn't surprised when a fight broke out on the other side of the bar between two drunken fools dressed like Batman and Captain Jack Sparrow. I shook my head at their human foolishness, glad they weren't my responsibility.

Like usual, Shaz reached them before the bouncers did. It didn't take him long to separate them. I watched closely, my heart beating out a tense rhythm. No sooner had the bouncers taken over than he beamed a grin my way and headed over.

Jez kicked me lightly under the table and said, "That's my cue to go chat up that beautiful brunette dressed as Cinderella. I'll catch up with you later." With a wink, she bumped her glass against mine in a "cheers" motion and sauntered off.

Shaz' scent filled my lungs as he approached. I could have breathed it in all night in absolute splendor. He closed the distance between us, kissing the end of my nose lightly. "Give me fifteen minutes, and then meet me by the staircase."

Before I could reply, he had jogged back to the busy bar. I watched him go, in those butt hugging, leather pants, with a goofy smiled plastered on my face.

Rather than make myself a lone target for the single guys, I figured I would mosey on over to the staircase to wait for Shaz. I was halfway there, carefully picking my way through the crowd when I felt him. My dark vampire had arrived.

Chapter Fourteen

I turned to the front entry, waiting expectantly. Everything that made me more than human was on full alert as that cool, dark power approached.

When Arys emerged from the sea of people lingering near the door, my heart paused and dropped into my feet. I wasn't sure what I'd done to get so lucky, but as his blue eyes fell on me, I didn't care. The tingle that swept me with a warm glow woke the power curled up within my core.

I honestly hadn't expected him to show up in a costume. Not after the comments he'd made about Halloween. So, I was definitely taken aback to see him dressed to the hilt as Johnny Depp's Sweeney Todd. It couldn't have been a more perfect fit.

He had the outfit down to a tee. I had never seen him dressed like that. He looked as if he had stepped out of another time.

Desire slammed through me. His hair couldn't have looked hotter. It was still typically mussed up but with a strategically placed style. Down to the white streak in the front, he had it. He looked sensational.

From the moment his eyes locked on mine, I was frozen in place. Nothing drew his attention from me as the distance separating us fell away.

"You are easily the most heart stopping creature I have ever laid eyes on." He greeted me, his velvety smooth voice tantalizingly beautiful.

"You're insanely gorgeous yourself." I reached up to brush a strand of hair away from his eye where it had fallen. "I can't believe you dressed up."

He grinned and leaned in to kiss me softly. "Only for you, my precious wolf."

Everything about him tested my control. The inviting power of our bond enticed me to sink into the pull, to allow it to control us. It was agony to resist.

"I'm glad." I beamed up at him, my hand clasped in his. It was warmer than usual. That was a good sign. He slid a hand beneath the front of my skirt where it trailed along the edge of my thigh high stocking. The breath was knocked out of me, and I blushed.

"I knew you'd look sensational. I couldn't come underdressed." Despite his neutral tone, the heat from his hand on my thigh caused a rush of blood to flood the private place between my legs. I sucked in my breath and quivered uncontrollably. This brought a smile to his lips, revealing fangs.

Between him and Shaz, I wasn't sure how I could handle this much smoking hot man flesh. I wanted them both with an equal ferocity but for very different reasons. Was that even possible? I forced the thought from my mind, scoffing at the absurdity of it.

I couldn't help but look over my shoulder, towards the bar where Shaz had gone. "I seem to have my hands full tonight."

Those entrancing eyes gazed at me with their perfect frame of silky black lashes. "Is that so?" He followed my gaze to the bar before looking back at me. "Do you think you can handle both of us?"

The blush that warmed my cheeks was instant. Only this bold vampire would head down that trail of thought.

"That's not what I meant," I laughed nervously and looked away. "Though I can't say that I wouldn't love to find out." It was something that slipped out freely, something I never would have said to Shaz.

I felt Arys studying me, enjoying my discomfort and embarrassment. He leaned in close so that his lips brushed my ear, whispering, "Be careful what you wish for."

A jolt of electricity slammed through me from where his lips touched me, all the way down my spine. His words were shocking due to the passivity of his tone. There was a lot about Arys that I had yet to understand.

When he pulled back, he wore a strangely disconcerted expression. I felt the shift in his energy as if it had been my own. His instant wariness had me glancing around suspiciously.

"What?" I asked him, a little too fast. I didn't sense anything amiss. "What do you feel?"

He looked over my shoulder to where Shaz now waited in front of the staircase. A petite redhead dressed like a cop was showing him her handcuffs.

"I'm not sure. Go to your wolf. I'll come find you." He was gone in the time it took me to blink, moving rapidly through the crowd in search of something I could neither see nor feel. A chill stole over me in his sudden absence.

I went to Shaz but couldn't deny the urge to look over my shoulder. The redhead looked up at my approach, vacating promptly when I boldly kissed him full on the lips, sliding my tongue between them.

The passion he kissed me back with matched my own in its fierceness. When he pulled back and gazed deeply into my eyes, the first question out of his mouth was, "Where did Arys go?"

I'd kind of hoped my kiss would have swept the vampire from his thoughts. I was feeling the lively pull of the moon. I'd just have to get his mind to focus on other things.

"I don't know. It doesn't matter." I didn't hesitate to run my hands over his hard chest the way I wanted to. "So where do you want to go?"

Shaz trailed a hand through my hair, entangling it in his fist. A playful smile danced along his lips. "You've got to be kidding me. Here?"

"Here." I nodded, ignoring the curious looks from those going up and down the stairs. "I just have this ache inside me that I need you to ease."

Between the moon, the power I shared with Arys and my own wanton desires, I was ready for him. I had been since arriving.

Shaz appeared to consider it. It didn't take long. "Where would you like to go?"

"Anywhere you want."

He surveyed the club before saying, "Let's go out back."

Honestly, I'd expected more resistance from Shaz. It was clear that the rousing atmosphere was stripping away his inhibitions and riding him hard, too.

He entwined his fingers in mine and pulled me along toward the back exit. Nobody used the exit except for staff. The back door led into a dark alley that just led to another alley and the back of the neighboring buildings.

Outside that door, Arys and I had wiped out a crazed vampiress that had tried to kill me. I used our bonded power to destroy her, forcing the energy into her until her heart burst. That entire scenario had been utter madness, especially since she had been trying to employ my services. She'd wanted me to kill Arys.

I didn't notice either Ky or Jez as Shaz and I snuck down the long back hall past the washrooms, to the door at the end. I did wonder where Arys ventured off to, but I trusted that he could take care of himself.

I was wild with anticipation when we slipped out into the night. The sudden change in atmosphere was like a slap to the senses. It was so quiet, only a dull roar could be heard from inside. The stars twinkled overhead. The one, lone streetlight stood yards away, casting a pale glow just beneath it.

I allowed Shaz to lead me away from the door to the far edge of the building that was draped in darkness. He pressed my back against the cold brick, taking a dominant role right off the bat. The intrigue that that one action instilled in me was adrenaline inducing.

"Are you sure you want to do this?" He gave me one last chance to reject the impromptu setting.

"I can't believe you have to ask." I maintained eye contact with him as I ever so slowly lifted the front of my skirt up.

As I revealed more flesh, his eyes darted to my thighs and what lay between. "Forget I asked."

His first response was to thread a hand into my hair so that he held my head tight, a display of control that thrilled me. His lips and teeth immediately sought my throat. The generous erection that he pressed against me was perfectly outlined by the thin leather. The material felt cool and smooth where it touched my bare skin.

I reached down as if to pull my panties off, and Shaz caught my hand in his. I was happy to relinquish all control to him. I loved it when the wolf was as strong in him as the man. The cold felt soothing through the flimsy red cape, despite the fact that I was leaning on bricks.

When he looked at me again, his eyes were all wolf, and his four fangs made his young face achingly beautiful. His energy was running strong, and I reveled in it. In that moment, it was just the two of us and the moon.

Shaz nuzzled my neck, the tip of his warm tongue darting out to trace the edge of my earlobe. I remembered how Arys' lips had just been in that same place, and the fire grew within me.

When he dropped to his knees before me and reached up under my skirt, I gasped in delighted surprise. My breath caught as he hooked his fingers in my thong and dragged it down my legs. After stepping out of it as daintily as I could, I quickly untied the cape and tossed it aside.

Shaz looked up at me with emotion in his green wolf eyes from where he kneeled at my feet. The sound of people in the parking lot on the other side of the building carried to us. On our side, it was quiet. Nothing moved but the slightest breeze.

Without warning, he broke eye contact and turned his attention to my inner thigh. The touch of his tongue and then his fangs brought a whimper from me as I tried not to go weak in the knees.

His hands curved around my hips as he licked and bit his way between my legs. When he brought his mouth down on me with a hungry, probing intensity, I automatically buried my fingers in his hair.

I let my head fall back against the building so that I looked at the stars. There was nothing commanding my focus except for the moist heat of Shaz' talented tongue and the sharp point of each upper fang that occasionally grazed me. It heightened the pleasure immeasurably.

Soon, he brought me to orgasm, and I quivered against him. A cry broke from me, and he silenced it by rising and pressing his lips to mine.

Before I could request it, he freed his throbbing, rock-hard cock from the tight leather pants. I licked my lips with anticipation and reached to stroke it. He astonished me by grabbing my hands and pulling me away from the wall.

With one swift motion, he picked me up and switched us so that his own back was against the wall to support our weight. He had a hand under each of my thighs, and I wrapped my arms around his neck eagerly.

He slid into me with a slick thrust. I was positioned so that I could move up and down on him rather well as he supported my weight. The excitement of what we were doing and where only added to the overall intensity.

In this position, we were directly face to face, almost forced to look into one another's eyes. And, I loved it. The carnal look in Shaz' eyes as he buried himself deep inside me was both frightening and enticing. I fell into the mesmerizing pull of his jade orbs as well as the natural rhythm that we had together.

The atmosphere crackled all around us as the power of our union drew on the energy of the moon. It all felt so natural, like it always did with Shaz. Two wolves and the moon, united. So, the sudden rising of the undead power inside me was both unexpected and surprising.

As Shaz and I moved as one in the dark outside Lucy's Lounge, I felt Arys. He was close, so very close. Amidst the throes of passion, the awareness did little more than stoke the inferno raging inside me.

My heart raced with the barest trace of fear when I felt those dark blue eyes on us. If Shaz felt it too, he gave no sign. Instead, he kissed me with total abandon so that I could taste myself on his lips.

I knew the exact moment Arys emerged from the dark behind us. Like a ghost, he seemed to materialize from thin air. Because my back was to him, it was Shaz' face that he looked into.

I watched him as he stared into the vampire behind me. Shaz' pace slowed but never stopped. I was willing to bet he'd been more aware of Arys' approach than I thought. The look he wore was challenging, but it lacked menace.

The next thing I knew Arys was just there, his hard body against my back. I'd be lying if I said I wasn't a little nervous pressed between the two of them. I flashed back to Arys' question before he left me in the bar. Could I handle both of them? Was it even wise to try?

Part of me fully expected Shaz to withdraw from the situation. But if anything, he liked it. He thrust into me harder, forcing a small cry from me. All the while, he stared over my shoulder at the vampire.

Arys moved slowly; his energy, strong and enthralling. He reached one hand under my thigh, careful not to touch Shaz. I realized he was helping to support my weight between the two of them. Shaz looked suspicious, but he also had a curiosity that I could read in his eyes like a book.

With his other hand, Arys reached up to sweep the hair away from my neck. He stroked a finger ever so gently along the sensitive skin beneath my ear. I realized exactly what his intention was then, and my heart sped so fast I could hear it thundering inside my head.

The two men shared a look, and I could sense what it was they were not saying. I risked a glance back at Arys. He stared at Shaz with heat in his gaze and more. There was nothing friendly in the look they shared. The rise of power that enveloped us then was enough to force a moan from me. I was amazed to hear Shaz echo it.

As Arys' lips and tongue touched my neck, I shuddered and moved faster on Shaz. I saw my white wolf give the briefest of nods, his eyes locked on the vampire as fangs sunk deep into my flesh.

I let out a pained cry as my blood spilled and the power responded. Though I was tempted to close my eyes, I wanted to watch Shaz' face.

He stared at the place where Arys' fangs were embedded in my flesh. There was a combination of horror and intrigue on his youthful features. However, I couldn't help but notice that he increased the strength behind every thrust so that a moan escaped me with each one.

A trickle of blood began to run down my neck and chest with Shaz' eyes following it. Arys licked and sucked at the wound, feeding the energy that seemed to captivate us all.

I was hurtling fast toward climax. The sensation of being between the two of them was so spicy that I couldn't believe it was real.

As I'd suspected he wanted to, Shaz gave in to the urge to lick the spilled blood from my chest and collarbone. For the briefest of moments, his head was just inches from the vampire's.

I watched his face when he pulled back. He leaned his head against the building, but his gaze landed on me and Arys, drinking from my throat.

The effect the power was having on him was evident by his huge pupils. Having a third party was something our power seemed to like. As we all fed off each other, the rush of white noise grew loud around us.

I hit that crucial peak without warning, and the orgasm rocked me to the core. As Shaz' climax accompanied mine, he let out a series of growls and snarls. Even Arys gave a low moan as he tongued the punctures in the side of my neck.

I was soaked with sweat, and I clung to Shaz as the aftershocks and waves racked me. With one arm, I reached back to Arys, my hand brushing against the side of his face. He promptly placed a kiss in my palm. A faint bloody smear remained.

Power hummed around us, cloaking us in a blanket of it. Of all the things I expected to feel right then, the urge to cry wasn't one of them. Hot tears threatened to fill my eyes as I was overcome by the energy and my own personal emotions. I blinked quickly, but it was too late.

The tears fell to my cheeks, and I saw shock spread across Shaz' features. He caught a drop on his finger, examining the crimson tear. He knew just as well as anyone that only vampires cry blood tears.

Arys took a step back, bending to gather my things. Shaz lowered me so that I could get steady on my feet again. I tugged my dress into place, smoothing it anxiously. My legs felt like jelly.

"Alexa, are you ok?"

I smiled at my white wolf as Arys draped the cape over my shoulders. That silly wolf worried about me too much. He was high as a kite on my blood and power, and all it took was a few tears to snap him back to reality.

"Yes, Shaz. I promise I am." I wanted to ask how he felt but didn't want to put him on the spot in front of Arys.

The vampire stood quietly to one side, observing Shaz but acting as if he weren't. No sooner had I tied my cape securely than the back door of the Lounge burst open.

Chapter Fifteen

Tawnie stood illuminated in the glow from inside, casting a frantic glance around. It didn't take long for her to spot our small group huddled in the dark. If there hadn't been three of us, she may not have noticed us at all.

"Shaz," she called frantically. "We have a pretty bad fight going on in here. We could use your help."

"I'll be right there Tawnie. No worries."

Shaz' eyes never left my face as he replied to her. The power that belonged to Arys and I was clearly manipulating him. He'd tasted me both physically and metaphysically, and it had affected him. The dazed expression on his face seemed to overrule his struggle for control. I smiled when he actually gave his head a shake as if to clear it.

Tawnie disappeared back inside. Arys maintained a safe distance as if unsure what to expect from Shaz.

"I love you," Shaz whispered, nuzzling the side of my face as he would in wolf form. "I've got to run, but I'll find you after."

I didn't want to let him go, not before the afterglow had begun to fade. He didn't look at Arys as he made his way to the door though he had to have felt those vampire eyes following him. Knowing the taste and feel of my blood lingered on him drove me crazy with curiosity. I wanted to know what he was feeling.

When we were alone, Arys turned to me with a satisfaction in his eyes that reminded me of the cat with his paws in the fishbowl. I trembled in the breeze as the sweat cooled on my skin. He swept me into his arms in a swift, smooth motion.

"The wolf pup certainly surprised me." He spoke soothingly, my head tucked beneath his chin. "He is bolder than I ever would have believed."

"You don't give him enough credit."

185

"He loves you madly."

Arys' observation hung heavily as if suspended in the atmosphere around us. It struck me as a strange thing to say just then.

"I know," I murmured. My hand went to the place on my collarbone where Shaz had licked the blood from me. "I don't deserve him."

"Nonsense. You're both so young with so much yet to experience. Enjoy what you have while you have it. Don't learn the hard way that there is no time for regrets."

I pulled back to study his face. He raised an eyebrow and gave me a playful smile, but I wasn't fooled. He clearly spoke like someone who knew firsthand.

"What's up with you, Arys?"

"What are you talking about?" He fidgeted then, something extremely uncharacteristic. I tuned into our energy and focused on him, the vibes of his emotions. He was trying to shield what he was feeling from me. I could sense it.

"What's with the cryptic remark? And, all of a sudden, you're encouraging my relationship with Shaz. You tend to be very back and forth on that."

"Yeah well, I'm an asshole. But, I'm also realistic." He shrugged and held out a hand, playing with the psi ball that rapidly formed. Like always, it was a gaseous vapor swirl of blue and yellow, the color of our energies.

"How realistic?" I laughed when he gave me a dirty look. He dropped the ball, and I felt the energy reach out to us as well as the natural elements before it ceased to be.

"We should get back inside before your lady friends start to think you've abandoned them." With a warm hand, he steered me towards the door.

I didn't miss the way he scanned the area before turning his back to it. He seemed more alert and wary than usual. I didn't sense anything when I mentally searched the night around us.

The moment we stepped inside, my senses had to readjust to the volume and the many smells. I winced against the onslaught. All of my senses were heightened after our power play outside. It was a little unbearable.

Before we reached the end of the staff hall, I paused near the ladies room, gesturing for Arys to go on without me. I needed a personal moment to refresh and check on my appearance. I also had a wound that oozed two matching drops of blood.

Thank goodness it was Halloween. With all the fake blood in the building tonight, no one would notice a splash of the authentic stuff. But, the wound looked incredibly real. I'd worn enough to know. I used my hair to hide it as I ducked into the washroom.

It was pretty busy inside. The majority of the stalls were taken, and four girls crowded the mirror. Shit. I recognized one of them right away.

Amanda caught sight of me reflected in the mirror behind her. She was studiously trying to fix fake eyelashes.

"Hey Alexa!" She called over the noisy din of chattering women. "Great costume. Are you having a good time?"

I smiled at her, but my focus was on grabbing an empty stall and escaping conversation. "Yeah, it's really pumping out there. How are you? I love the Cleopatra look. Very hot."

I rushed by before she could stop me, slamming the door of the stall behind me. I willed them all to leave. I didn't want to come out and get roped into a conversation with Amanda.

The girl is a total sweetheart, but ever since I'd slaughtered her abusive boyfriend, she had developed a strange fascination with me. She didn't know exactly what I was, but she'd seen enough with her own eyes to know it wasn't human.

I closed my eyes and counted to ten, thinking hard. When I reopened them, the washroom was quiet. Incredible.

When I came back out, no one was there. I couldn't believe the projected power of my influence had driven them out.

I wasted no time in wetting some paper towel and wiping up the bloodstains on my neck. After washing my hands, I arranged my hair so that the bite couldn't be seen. It was sore but pleasurable in the raw pain.

There would be no hiding it from Jez or Kylarai. They would smell the fresh wound right away. My face was especially pale, and I pinched my cheeks in an attempt to bring some color back. After a few minor make-up touch ups, I went to brave the teasing and ridicule of my friends.

It took me a minute to pick them out of the mass of people. The crowd had increased in size since I'd gone outside. I could sense Shaz, but he was nowhere to be seen.

Jez' golden hair stood out on the dance floor where she danced with a couple of girls dressed as naughty angels. Surprisingly, Kylarai was dancing with them. Julian and Zak were still shooting pool across the room. Didn't they have anything better to do?

I made my way towards Jez and Ky, shaking my head *no* when a waitress intercepted me. By the time I reached them, they had taken a seat at a nearby table. Jez' expression was knowing and amused, but Ky looked astonished. I pulled out the chair across from them and sat down, a silly smile on my face.

Kylarai gave me a more pointed, raised eyebrow look. "I'd ask where you were, but I already know." She smiled and winked before sipping from some ice water.

"What can I say?" I shrugged, trying for casual. "I couldn't resist."

"And, so you shouldn't." Jez leaned over to nudge me; an approving smile revealed tiny fangs beneath her ruby red lips.

"Where did Arys go? He took off out of here in a hurry." Ky looked curious, and I frowned in response.

"He just left?"

"Yeah, right before you showed up. Weren't you with him?"

"I was. I went to the ladies room." If I thought about Arys hard enough, I could still feel his presence in the vicinity.

A strange sensation began to unravel as I grew suspicious. Where was Arys and what was he up to? He had been acting a little sketchy since he arrived. Something told me I wasn't paying enough attention. The intensified power running through me was trying to come to the forefront of my mind, trying to make me aware of something.

"Speaking of the ladies room," Ky interrupted my thoughts. "Is it insanely busy?"

"Not when I left."

"Good. I'll be right back." She grabbed her purse from the tabletop and got up from her chair. She was soon just a green figure among the rest of the crowd.

I scanned the crowd but saw no sign of Arys. I could still feel him when I concentrated, but that didn't tell me much.

I pushed my chair back with a loud scrape. "I think I'm going to go hunt down Arys. If I miss him and he comes back, tell him I'm looking for him," I said to Jez.

She waved a hand at me dismissively before sipping from her bright blue drink. "I'll keep an eye out in case he comes through here."

Just to be sure, I went around the building once to confirm that he was not inside. I even ran up to the second floor where the atmosphere was more laid back. TVs hung from the ceiling, each playing the same hockey game. My vampire wasn't up there either. I hadn't thought so.

Kylarai said she'd seen him leave the building. I didn't think twice about going outside in search of him.

Exiting the building brought a welcome relief from the noise. The front entrance was packed with people milling about, most of them smoking cigarettes. A small group of girls whined about the cold fall night as I passed. I didn't find it too bad.

I lingered near the front of the bar for a minute, searching mentally for Arys. I was certain I felt him down the alley to the left of the building, on the way to the parking lot.

That alley intersected with the one at the back of club, where we'd been such a short time ago. Arys was known to sneak away down the alley when luring a victim into his grasp. Though he hadn't done that as often since we'd become involved.

Despite being drawn to the alley, my gut instinct was telling me to stay away. I was confused and not liking this one bit.

I stared down the dark alley but made no move to venture further. My senses were straining to discover what it was that was eluding me. I could feel it nagging at the back of my mind, something I couldn't put my finger on.

Feeling like the first ditzy girl to get murdered in a slasher film, I took a few steps down the alley, then a few steps more.

"Arys?" I called, careful not to raise my voice.

I stopped when I had left the safety of the parking lot lights. I looked up at the moon and tried to use its calming serenity to focus harder. I was able to tune out the rest of the night, staring up and seeing only that glowing silver light in the sky.

The energy of everything around me grew more pronounced and I was able to identify everything from the ground beneath my feet to each star overhead. And that's when I felt him. I sensed the sudden approach behind me and whirled to face the unwelcome vampire.

"You smell absolutely divine." The melodious voice was rough, yet dangerously attractive.

It caused my stomach to tighten, a wave of nausea sweeping me. I was suddenly breathing too fast. My mind raced with several thoughts at once. I was already defensive, but I couldn't see an immediate way out of this.

I stared at Harley with horror etched on my features. He grinned, my worst nightmare come to life. I swallowed hard but didn't dare speak.

"Why so surprised wolf? Surely you've been expecting me."

Chapter Sixteen

"Where's Arys?" The words just came out. I hadn't meant to ask.

Harley took a moment to look over my attire, successfully making me feel like a piece of meat. I was silently praying that he was not enjoying what he saw. The slow grin that spread across his face caused my hope to die.

"That's a great question." His dark eyes glittered in the moonlight as they bore into me. "You're bonded to him. How is it that you don't know?"

I shifted uneasily, knowing I'd never make it far before he caught me. "It doesn't work that way." Energy danced along my fingertips, summoned by fear and instinct. Like before, Harley paid it little attention. He didn't fear me in the least. I wished I could say the same.

"So tell me more about how it works." He feigned casual very well, crossing his arms over his impressive chest. He wasn't as well built as Arys or as firm as Shaz, but he could do a lot of physical damage if he wanted to.

"What do you want?" My voice was as shaky as my legs were in my heels. I was regretting my decision to wear them.

Abandoning any semblance of a smile, Harley allowed for a dramatic pause before he said, "You."

I felt faint, and all of a sudden, I couldn't breathe. I risked a glance behind me, hoping the entrance to the alley was closer than I remembered it being. He cleared the distance separating us before I could take a step.

I expected a lot of things from him, but a total cheap shot wasn't one of them. He thrust a rag in my face that reeked of chloroform, and I gagged, trying not to inhale. Eventually the need to breathe won out, and I had no choice but to draw the harsh fumes into my lungs.

Despite how hard I struggled, I couldn't break free of him. It wasn't long before the darkness closed in on me.

ഌഌഌഌ

My hands were tied. I was aware of that before my eyes even flickered open. I also knew where I was. The strange, eerie energy of The Wicked Kiss stabbed at me like needles, and I resisted the urge to groan.

I didn't want to open my eyes, not when I could feel my captor's heavy gaze on me like a weight. Part of me was hoping that this was all a bad dream and I would open my eyes and be in my bed at home. Fat chance.

There was no point putting off certain death. It was inevitable, right? I finally looked up at Harley, acceptance settling in far too soon. I wasn't usually one to give in without a fight, but my stomach hurt, and my head pounded from the chloroform.

"If you're going to kill me, would you at least make it quick?"

He chuckled, drawing my attention to his dark eyes. He looked more amused than anything else. I was confused. What did this crazy ass vampire want with me?

"Don't be ridiculous," he scoffed. "I'd be a fool to kill such a rare creature as yourself. That would be much like killing a unicorn."

"Unicorns don't exist." I stated, daring to look at my surroundings.

"Exactly." He let that word hang in the air between us while I absorbed the reality of the situation.

The room we were in was similar to the one where I'd found Kale with its hotel room set up. This one however was twice the size and had a different décor. The carpet was a soft grey; the walls, warm tones of tan accents. Unlike Kale's room, this one had a full-length sofa and matching easy chair. Wall sconces held candles that flickered away brightly as they were the only source of lighting other than the fire that blazed in a fancy iron fireplace near the sofa and TV.

I was propped against the couch but sitting on the floor. When I glanced down at myself, I noticed that it almost looked as if he had tried to arrange my cape so my underwear wasn't visible due to my position and short skirt. That was mind-boggling. Was it possible that Harley had a sense of respect after all?

"So what do you want? It must be good if you were willing to take me by force." I glared hard, uncertain but refusing to let him cow me. Now that I was pretty sure I wasn't facing immediate death, I was ready to fight.

Harley was sitting at the small two-seat table near the mini bar and the only door in the room. How convenient.

"Honestly, can you blame me for wanting to get a better, more personal look at you?"

"I'm not a fucking museum exhibit." I spat the words, and he merely smiled. It was beyond aggravating.

"Certainly not." He stood and approached me, a pocketknife held in one hand. "It's up to you if I cut the ropes on your wrists or not. I'm not in the mood to play games. Yet."

I sighed. What choice did I have other than to play along? "Fine. I'll behave myself. What can I really do anyway?"

"Indeed."

His approach was slow as if he was trying not to spook a skittish animal. He went down on one knee, knife held ready. I struggled to remain still when I felt the cool steel blade slide between my wrists and the rope that held me.

His close proximity gave me the opportunity to study him. If I had to guess, I'd say he had been mid-forties when changed from human to vampire. He had reached that golden age for men when they start to look better with the onset of years. The lines around his eyes were visible but faint. The hard set to his jaw spoke of more experience in his mortal years than I had had so far in mine. He was astonishingly handsome. But, there was a deep darkness in him. I could feel it like a suffocating blanket, like a spider web I could not shrug off.

When my wrists were free, I sat very still on the floor, waiting for him to move away. Instead, he surprised me by holding a hand out as if to help me to my feet. I stared at his outstretched hand as if it would bite. The look he gave me indicated that I really could trust him not to trick me with something as trivial as a hand up.

Regardless, I chose to ignore his hand and struggled to my feet

193

on my own. I tugged my skirt down and flushed, suddenly wary that he would be aware of my scent. If I thought about it, I could easily smell both Shaz and Arys all over me.

"Here." Harley strode to the mini bar fridge, pulling a bottled water from inside. "Don't tell me you don't need this."

The bottle was sealed. I was sure it was safe so I accepted it gratefully. My throat was dry, and after the wine I'd drank, I really needed some water. He waited patiently while I soothed my thirst, but I felt the eagerness emanating from him.

It was hard to shake the images I had of him from Arys' memories. Bloody images of fun-filled torture sessions, his attack on Arys that brought him to the brink of death and back again, all of it swam behind my eyes. I stared at him unflinching, preparing for anything.

"Thank you," I murmured, indicating the bottle in my hand. I was uneasy and unable to hide it. Of all of the places for me to end up on Halloween, it had to be here with him. What was with my luck?

"How much do you know about me?" His question caught me off guard. It wasn't what I'd been expecting.

My answer was automatic. "Enough to know that I don't want to know any more."

His look became appraising, and I glared in response. I had expected his anger, and the fact that he was enjoying this was driving me crazy.

"I'm afraid you have the advantage over me. I don't know nearly as much about you as I'd like to."

"And, what is it that you want to know?" My voice was weak, and I coughed. I wasn't feeling nearly as on the ball as usual, and it nagged at me. I had to get it together.

There was a long pause as we stared at one another. I could only imagine what kind of a fit Arys would pitch if he knew where I was. He must have noticed I was missing by now.

Harley's dark eyes sparkled with an evil glint that told me I was about to regret my question. "I want to know if you're a screamer. I want to know if your blood tastes as good as it smells. And, I would love to know if you would beg me to stop or beg me to bite harder."

I don't know what I'd been expecting him to say, but it wasn't that. The look in his eyes had grown hungry and even though he stood six feet away, I felt like he was too close.

I gaped at him incredulously. I had no words for that. I was filled with terror, something that only fed his fire. Try as I might, I could not force my pounding heart to slow back down to a normal pace.

With nothing more than a blur of motion, Harley had a handful of my hair tight in his fist. My breath caught, but I didn't shriek like I wanted to. I knew that's what he wanted. I couldn't give him that kind of satisfaction.

He exposed the bite on the left side of my neck, and a new panic gripped me. His eyes lit up, and before I had even formed a coherent thought, he leaned in closer, scenting the tender wound.

"He must be hopelessly in love with you." Those whispered words brought the barest touch of his lips against my skin, and I shuddered. "To be able to stop without draining you dry. Blood this heavenly is so hard to resist and even harder to come by."

I couldn't prevent the small shriek that did break free when the moist tip of his tongue touched Arys' bite. I closed my eyes and prayed that he wouldn't dare bite me. Against my will, the power rose up inside me as if curious about this close new source of strength. Along with it came the gratifying rush of sexual excitement. It was as unwelcome as it was confusing.

"I can feel him all over you, inside you." Harley suddenly released me, and I hurried to put distance between us. The way I physically reacted to him wasn't right. This kind of desire was unnatural.

"Stop that," I muttered. "Whatever you're doing, just stop."

"Come now, Alexa. Surely, you are used to the touch of an incubus vampire. You belong to one."

Why did I always feel like the perpetual student? "I thought demons were succubus or incubus."

"What do you think a vampire is, my love? We're all demons in our own way." His wicked tone dropped, becoming more physical rather than solely audible. "Some vampires use straight up fear to get the blood and energy pumping for a good feed. Others rush right to the finish, unable to prolong that powerful moment. And, many like myself and those created by me tend to draw out the energy by using sexual influence as well as fear."

He paced the length of the room near the door, always so close to the door. "If you can withstand the hungers of an insatiable vampire like Arys, then are you more powerful than any other mortal I've ever encountered.

"You are young still but I'm amazed you don't know more about what you are. That explains why you haven't effectively turned me to dust already."

"Yeah, well I don't know a lot of people quite like me. None to be exact." I shouldn't have bothered talking to him, but the silence seemed to enhance his eerie qualities.

"Does that make you realize that you possess something that nobody else does? I don't think you know what you're capable of."

I had to agree with him there, but I couldn't voice the words. In the last few months, I'd learned a lot about my abilities. Clearly, it wasn't enough.

"You must have some kind of weakness, though," he continued. The new and darker tone to his voice instantly put me on red alert. "And, finding it is a challenge too good to pass up."

Anything I said or did would set him off. I could feel it. I stared at him in wide-eyed terror, waiting for him to make a choice. The undead power inside me combined with the power of wolf to fill me as everything in me prepared to fight for my life.

His lips peeled back to reveal fangs. I swallowed hard and braced, expecting an attack. I wasn't sure if it was possible, but his eyes appeared to be two black pools, beckoning me to fall in.

"You're supposed to be mine," he hissed, catching me by surprise. "I was everything to that son of a bitch and all he ever did was punish me for it. He took so much from me."

"That has nothing to do with me. I wasn't part of your past with Arys." The terror was evident in my voice.

One step closer, and then Harley stopped. The hunger in his eyes was hypnotizing. "He loves you, and you are bound to him. It now has everything to do with you. You make him more than a vampire. More than I am."

I watched Harley take yet another step toward me. He was backing me into the corner between the couch and the bed. As if I were prey. I planted my feet, refusing to move another step.

"Are you going to hurt me then? Is that your big revenge?"

Damn my big mouth and quick tongue. Why did I not know when to shut up? I felt the blood drain from my face as instinct told me to brace.

With a ferocious, animal-like sound, he lunged at me. I reacted by blasting him with power that burned my hands with its intensity. He barely raised a hand to deflect it before taking me down so that I hit the floor hard. He was on top of me, trapping me with his weight.

"Can you imagine dying in my arms as I drink your life away?" Harley pinned me effectively and glared down into my face. It was impossible to shield his energy, to prevent it from mingling with mine. A sexual glow enveloped me, and I wanted him to keep talking.

"It would be too easy," he purred in my ear. I bit my lip to keep quiet as I shook my head furiously from side to side. "Why don't you give me a challenge, Alexa? Show me what it is that you have with my vampire."

His reference to Arys was enough to break the spell, and I focused on driving power into him as hard as I could. The force sent him reeling twenty feet or more until his back slammed against the wall near the door. I was on my feet in one leap, following the burst of power with another. As soon as his touch fell away, so did the desire.

His laughter was richly melodic as he regained his composure. My attack hurt him; I could sense it. However, it seemed to drive him at the same time.

I yelped when his power hit me before he did. I was ready for the physical impact, but the metaphysical caught me in a moment of poor preparation.

Harley's icy hand closed around my throat, and he slapped me hard with the other one. The side of my face stung, and I tasted blood. His eyes were completely insane, like he'd slipped into another state of mind.

"That's right, wolf. You can't hurt me. You have power, alright, but I have experience. Something that you are obviously lacking. Anything you throw at me, I can easily use to my own advantage."

I fought hard, slashing out with a clawed hand. He easily met each of my efforts with one to outdo it. His grip on my throat allowed me to breathe but held me immobile. Panic caused my heart to beat so hard I thought it would burst. My instincts had me fighting for my life, but my every struggle was feeding his fire. Even though I knew this, I couldn't stop.

"Oh, I can certainly see what made you so appealing to Arys. There is just so much fight in you. Irresistible." Hooking a foot behind my ankle, he tripped me so that I fell heavily against him. Harley's arm went around my waist and releasing my throat, he tilted my head to bare my wounded neck.

He leaned down to taste my bitten neck again, and I gagged when the unwanted desire came back with a greater impact. I wanted him so bad physically, but mentally, I knew it was all false.

I moaned in both pain and pleasure when his tongue probed the edges of the wound. I was desperate to make it stop. Right then, I would have rather been dead than loving Harley's unbidden touch. My power ached to taste his, to draw it into me.

I couldn't resist as I opened myself up to him metaphysically, drawing in what he was giving off. It was sweet like butterscotch and seemed to coat my insides in warmth. It felt amazing, like a spiritual experience made flesh. And, I hated that I loved it so much.

"Do you feel betrayed by your body, wolf? Does it sicken you that I can command you despite the fact that you are more powerful than I am?"

Through my desire-induced haze, I fought to make sense of what he'd just said. How in the hell could I possibly be more powerful?

I knew that my reaction to him was driving him further into insanity. However, I could not alter the beat of my heart or prevent the flood of fear that claimed me. I was running a series of options though my mind. If worse came to worse, I'd fight as dirty as it gets. And, he'd be sorry he tried this.

My entire body was buzzing with an electrical charge. I was ready for anything. The crazed vampire pulled back, looking down at me with surprise. "My God," he breathed. "Your eyes ... they're his."

I didn't count on the extreme enjoyment that was written all over his face. I was learning very quickly that Harley was the type of guy that would laugh all the way to hell.

"I love it!" He exclaimed enthusiastically. "I never would have dreamed this to be possible. Nothing living should have the kind of power that you have."

His comment was not so different from what I'd already been told by Arys. The evil shining like a dark light in his eyes made my stomach hurt. Even if I managed to hurt him, it would likely have the opposite effect and would only serve to empower him.

"So I've been told. And though I may not know as much as you do, I am always willing to learn through action." My fingertips sparkled with deep blue energy laced in gold. I knew when I slipped into a different mindset that Arys' influence was strong in me.

I smiled ruthlessly, waiting for Harley to decide how this was going to play out. Feeling trapped, the wolf in me was fiercely aggravated at his attempt to dominate me.

"Oh, my dear wolf, you surely do coax the hunger within me." Those dark eyes fixed on the pulse leaping in my throat.

An image flashed through my mind, one from the dream I'd had while at Raoul's. Oh please no, this couldn't go down like that. I would force Harley to kill me before I'd let him bond me by blood. I couldn't let him bite me, anything but that.

I was facing a decision, a reaction to his action. Time seemed to slow down, and I became aware of another undead presence just as Harley turned his attention to the door. I identified Kale's energy before he called my name. He couldn't come in here. He'd get us both killed, or worse.

The door burst open with an ear-shattering screech of wood and metal. Kale's energy was livelier than I had ever seen it when he burst into the room. His different colored eyes were entrancing, and I stared at him in wonder.

Harley waved a hand dismissively and hissed, "This had better be good, Sinclair." Then to me he said, "Don't tell me he's another one of yours."

I was numb. I stared at Kale, afraid that he had just put himself in very great danger for me. It wasn't worth it.

"Kale, what are you doing here?"

"Are you alright?" Looking to Harley behind me, Kale strode into the room. "Get the hell away from her."

Harley barely twitched a hand, but it was enough to take Kale down. He writhed on the floor near my feet, anguished sounds coming from him.

"Stop it!" I stepped between them, attempting an energy wall that I expected to fall flat. It didn't. It held, effectively stopping Harley's attack.

Adrenaline crashed through my veins, and I whirled on Harley, fangs bared, a growl rumbling in my throat. "This is between you and me. You want me? Then come and get me, but I'm not going to let you hurt anybody else."

Harley glanced at Kale as he struggled to his feet. I could feel him analyzing the connection between Kale and I, trying to determine how deep it went. I spoke to Kale but didn't dare take my eyes from Harley or drop the wall I held strong.

"What the hell are you doing here?"

"You know what I'm doing here, Alexa. I'd know your energy anywhere. Are you ok? Did he hurt you?"

Kale began to look me over, blatantly ignoring the other vampire. When he touched me, I couldn't help but flash back to the kiss we'd shared and a fevered heat stole over me. Harley was smirking as he made a show of dusting off his suit jacket. I was sure I didn't want to know what he was thinking.

"Kale," I said breathlessly, pulling away from him before the tension could grow between us. The entire room was filled with way too much vampire energy. It was overwhelming my senses. "You shouldn't be here."

"Too late." He shot a dark glare at Harley who laughed wickedly and eyed my barrier. "Where's Arys?"

"Good question." Harley piped up. "I notice that he hasn't come riding in to save you yet."

"Kale, please." I shut out Harley's words, refusing to allow him to get to me. "You have to get out of here. I can handle this. I swear."

"I'm not leaving you, Alexa. We're partners, and this is just another dirty vampire to be wiped out."

Harley quirked an eyebrow in interest at Kale's words, and I cringed inwardly. "Is that so? Well, I'm sorry to have to disappoint you ... friend."

With a flick of his wrist, Harley destroyed the wall of energy I held steady. He literally jerked the power that fed it, and I stumbled, pained as the sensation became physical. He downed Kale with another powerful blast before stepping over his unconscious form to capture me in his arms.

Harley was done playing around. I cried out as he aggressively bit into my flesh, his fangs sinking deep into my neck just inches from Arys' bite. It hurt immensely and yet, my body was still flooded with that sexual need for him. Just that easily, I had lost.

Chapter Seventeen

Pleasure flooded me, and the moisture grew between my thighs. I clung to Harley as he fed from me, wanting to feel more of him. More pain, more pleasure. My thoughts were dominated with the aching need to have all of him.

As Harley pressed deeper with his fangs, I squirmed against him, unable to fight the amazing sensations. There was a small sense of rationale left in me that urged me to fight back. If only I actually wanted to. The vampire energy in the room was too strong, and it literally swept me away. When he lifted me in his arms and carried me to the bed, I barely even noticed.

I moaned when he placed me on the soft mattress and slipped his fangs from my body. He licked and sucked at the oozing wound as my blood flowed. I wrapped my arms around his neck, holding him close like a lover.

With one hand, Harley stroked the inside of my thigh, and I shuddered in his embrace. His power called to mine, encouraging it to grow and to envelope us in a heady glow. It was electrifying, and yet it was nothing like anything I'd experienced with Arys. My power didn't try to bond with Harley's. Instead, it seemed to roll over and around his energy, tasting and enjoying it, but never becoming one.

He brought his head up to look at me, and my intentions wavered. His eyes were absolutely jet-black, and my blood smeared on his lower lip reminded me that I should be afraid. Very afraid. I was an idiot. I had played right into his hands and proved to be less than a challenge.

"My God, you taste divine." Harley licked his lip slowly, sensually. He smiled as if intoxicated. I tried to get up, and he pressed me back against the bed with a hand on my chest. "I have to do it, Alexa. I must make you mine."

His words hit me like a punch in the guts, and I shook my head, confusion slowly becoming clarity as I fought to see through the desire he ignited in me.

"No," I whispered, struggling to find my voice. I looked to Kale, unconscious on the floor, then back to Harley. "Get off of me."

"I was hoping you'd fight. In fact, I was counting on it." Kneeling over me, he pinned my wrists above my head in a move too smooth to have not been practiced. "This is going so much better than I'd anticipated."

My stomach turned as a wave of nausea hit me. If his intention hadn't been clear before, it certainly was now. I knew what he wanted, and I couldn't let it happen. He was going to try to force me into a blood bond. And, if I kept succumbing to the false sensations of pleasure, I wasn't going to be able to put up a fight.

I tried to tap my power, but I couldn't maintain focus as I wrestled to free my hands. "You don't want me, Harley. I am a werewolf, a mated Alpha. I can't offer you anything."

"Don't insult my intelligence, sweetheart. You're going to take my blood and complete this bond one way or another. I've taken more than enough from you. It's already begun."

Hot tears stung the back of my eyes as I furiously tried to blink them away. Though I couldn't recall exactly how I'd gotten myself into this situation, I was pretty sure it had to be my fault.

Harley never took his eyes off me as he raised his wrist to his mouth. He bit into it with a warm, wet sound that both tantalized and horrified me. The scent of his blood almost caused me to salivate as the bloodlust rose up inside me. I licked my lips, the temptation to taste it commanding me to reach for his arm.

Everything inside me that was wolf warred with Arys' undead needs. The wild animal in me refused to be dominated by this male. Two men could take that role with me, and he was not one of them. The two powerfully opposing sides of me faced off, and I whimpered in confusion.

He brought his bleeding wrist closer, and I leaned as far away as I could. He'd have to drain me to the point of death in order to turn me into a vampire this way, but that wasn't what he sought. Harley wanted to blood bond me so that Arys never could. And, by doing that, he would seal my fate. Upon my mortal death, I would rise as a vampire, bound to him forever.

The thought truly was worse than death itself. I'd rather he killed me then and there. As badly as I wanted to run my tongue along the bleeding punctures in his wrist, I was wolf first, and that ruled me. I made the decision consciously, and something inside me snapped.

With a snarl, I jerked my bound hands free and sat up with my fists flying. Harley's head snapped back as I caught him with a mean right hook. He was momentarily stunned, giving me just enough time to roll off the bed as he grabbed for me. I hit the floor hard and scrambled to my feet.

He lunged off the bed at me, blood dripping from his self-inflicted bite. The scent hit me, and my will started to crumble. I wasn't going to be able to hold out much longer, but I'd be damned if I would go down without one hell of a fight.

My instinct told me to run for the door, but I couldn't leave Kale behind. Harley threw me into the wall with my head hitting hard. For a moment, I saw stars, and the next thing I knew, he had thrust his bloody arm in my face, filling my nostrils with the intoxicating scent.

I growled and snapped at him, driving him back but just for a moment. He avoided my attack and came at me again, trying to pin me so that I couldn't move. I couldn't use metaphysical power, not when he could simply use it against me. I was strong, but he was stronger, and my heart sunk when he caught my right arm and twisted it behind my back.

It was all over for me. When Harley brought his deliciously crimson wrist to my lips, my mind cried out in protest, but the blood hunger swayed my intentions.

Arys was just suddenly there with Shaz at his side. His blue eyes filled with rage as he took in the scene before him. Three strides and he reached Harley, grasping him tightly with both hands and jerking him away from me.

"Alexa! Are you ok?" Shaz smoothed my messy hair back from my face so he could peer into my eyes. I could feel the crazed expression I wore as I gaped at him, wondering if he were real or just a torturous figment of my imagination.

Across the room, Arys had Harley pressed against the wall, gripping him tightly by the lapels of his jacket, letting fly with the shots. Harley didn't hesitate to retaliate, and I winced when the two vampires collided in a mash of fists and fangs.

"Tell me, Alexa," Shaz said, giving me a slight shake as I continued to stare over his shoulder at Arys and Harley. "What happened?"

"Nothing," I gasped. "I mean, other than the obvious."

His eyes narrowed, and he studied the fresh wound in my neck. "He hit you. Don't deny it because your face is bruised."

The glance he cast over at Harley was pure venom, and I started to think I'd have to stop him from jumping in. The vampires were on each other like two rabid dogs. I didn't want to watch, but I couldn't look away.

When the first blast of metaphysical power was thrown, I felt it in my guts. Every time Arys lashed out, he drew on my power, too, and it felt like a cold fire burning in my core.

They were out of control, each vampire fighting to get leverage over the other. The scent of blood filled the air, thicker now as it mingled with mine. It was empowering, and I embraced the rush that filled me and let my instincts take over.

I had to separate them before they killed each other. I was terrified for Arys, and I wanted this madness to stop. I lashed out with enough force to knock each of them off their feet without serious injury. It happened so fast. They were both abruptly on their asses, staring in confusion.

Blood spilled down the side of Arys' face from a gash in his eyebrow. It ran down his strong jaw, dripping steadily. Though Harley sported a hell of a shiner, he also carried a natural air of menace and twisted joy. A streak of blood marred his left cheek beneath his eye running to his upper lip. His malicious grin spoke nothing of pain or upset, only anticipatory intent.

With a scathing glance at Arys, he said, "Who invited you?"

"Stick it in your ass, Harley. This is the last time you make trouble for my wolf. I'm ready for you. But, Alexa is off limits."

There was no mistaking the widening of Harley's eyes as he took in Arys' hate filled expression. Was it just me or did fear flash behind his gaze? He dismissed it in a blink, recovering his malicious smile.

"Your wolf?" Harley questioned. "The one that you will not claim?"

I instinctually reached for Shaz' hand. The action wasn't missed by Harley who raised an eyebrow and smirked. "Or, could it be that you cannot claim her, because someone else already has?"

When Arys spoke, his tone was low and menacing. I could almost feel the quiver in it as he pleaded with the other vampire. "Please, don't make me kill you. You know I don't want to do that."

Shaz' predatory stare looked back and forth between Arys and Harley. He was ready for a fight. The intent in his stiff stance and expression was unmistakable. I squeezed his hand, willing him to stay calm.

"You seem to have quite the quaint little ménage à trois going on here. I didn't realize you liked the beasts so much." Harley paced casually on his side of my barrier. "If all you wanted was to do a werewolf, we could have explored that centuries ago."

As Arys and Harley stared at one another, the atmosphere grew painful with the strength of their animosity. I knew there was no way this was going to go smoothly. I was awash with power, instinctually reacting to their unspoken threats.

"If you want to finish this now, then by all means, let's do so." Arys' jaw clenched tightly, and he angrily wiped the blood away from where it ran near his left eye. "I've tasted your death for decades. I'm not ready to kill you, but I will do anything to protect her."

Terror filled me, and I turned to him, ready to beg him to stop this. But, he had eyes only for his sire, and the look in those inky blue orbs chilled me to my very soul.

Harley's smile had vanished. He now wore a look of utter calm, but it was disturbing in its serenity.

"I am not negotiating with you, Arys. Kill me if you will, but see if I don't do my damndest to take her down with me." He nodded in my direction as he spoke.

A growl immediately rumbled in Shaz' throat, and his body tensed beside me, ready to fly into action. I maintained my hold on his hand, refusing to let him go.

"What do you want with me anyway?" I finally spoke up, hoping to bring a sense of rationale to the situation. "I can't imagine what I have that you want."

He stared at me curiously for a long moment until I felt extremely uncomfortable. "No, I don't suppose you would." Looking at Arys he added, "You don't even know what you have here. She is completely wasted on you."

Arys frowned, assessing the statement. He didn't seem to know what to make of it any more than I did. "This isn't the old mine versus yours game, is it? Aren't we beyond that? I tired of it so long ago." He looked exasperated, like one dealing with an unreasonable child.

"Everything is a game to you." Harley began to pace, taunting Arys openly. "Do you even know any other way to play? We both know she's just the latest in your lengthy history of conquests. And, we both know what happens to those conquests when you're finished with them."

I didn't take my eyes off the finely dressed vampire, noting how he moved. Arys moved in response to him, closing the distance separating them. His fingers danced with energy that was bright gold with only a hint of blue playing around the edge. I felt the power call to me, too, wanting to join through us. I continued to resist, fearing it would push the boundaries of my control.

Even though Shaz couldn't visibly see the brilliant energy, he immediately reacted to it. There was no way to avoid feeling something so strong. His eyes closed for just a moment, and a shudder caused his body to convulse.

"I'm not here to rehash the good old days with you. I'm here to make sure you never make the mistake of touching Alexa again." The growl that came from Arys astonished me. I wasn't the only one. Shaz and Harley wore similar questioning looks, but Harley recovered first.

He appeared absolutely bored and uninterested when he crossed his arms and simply said, "Then, stop me."

Shaz responded rather than Arys. My heart exploded with adrenaline when he said, "I would love the opportunity to finish you off." In a move that was not usual for Shaz, he taunted the vampire with a beckoning motion that promised pain. "You dared to force yourself on my mate. You can't be allowed to think that's ok."

The intrigue written all over Harley's handsome face when he looked at my wolf had me on the defensive. He didn't seem opposed to the idea of taking on a werewolf.

Was Shaz out of his mind? The thought of my wolf getting physical with Harley was enough to make my skin crawl. The vampire surveyed the room, taking in all three of us. I could almost see the strategic thought process going on inside him.

"So it's three on one, is it? I thought werewolves were more honorable than that. Though I expect as much from you." Harley's eyes shot daggers at Arys who snickered in response.

"No, not three on one. Just me and you." Shaz took a step toward Harley, and my inner voice cried out in protest.

"Don't be a fool, kid," Arys hissed, his eyes darting between the other two men. "You don't know what kind of monster you're dealing with."

Kale groaned and sat up, a hand holding his head. I wondered what Harley had done to him with that shot of power. He gazed up at us, confusion dancing in his brown and blue eyes.

"I'm touched by your heartfelt words ... lover." This from Harley who added a suggestive inflection to his tone. It must have had the desired effect because he grinned when Arys swore. "But seriously, if the kid thinks he can take me..."

"No." My voice was low, but they all heard it. Shaz' silence was as good as ignoring me.

"Would you prefer to turn this back into a private party?" Harley smiled widely at me so that his sharp fangs glinted in the dim lighting. "I only want you anyway."

Shaz stiffened behind me, bracing for action. Knowing it was his only chance, Shaz launched himself at Harley before I could stop him. A sound came from me that was a combination of a cry and a growl.

Harley was poised, ready to meet him. As Shaz sunk claws deep into the vampire's upper arm, he grappled for the opportunity to use his vicious fangs. With the other hand, he delivered blows so hard and fast I couldn't keep up. But, Harley had been in tighter spots, and he easily lifted Shaz off his feet, slamming him against the wall.

The bedside lamp shook from the impact and toppled to the cushion of the carpeted floor. The blows never stopped coming from Shaz, and I flinched when one of them connected dead on with the vampire's lower jaw. The resulting crunch sent a shiver down my spine.

Arys wasted no time leaping into the fight. He tried to get between them, but they were so intent on each other that it was impossible. Harley barely glanced at Arys as he threw power into him.

My dark vampire was on his ass across the room in an instant.

Kale was suddenly behind me, a hand on my elbow as he held me back. "Don't jump in there, Alexa. It will only make things worse." I stared at him, wanting to ignore him but knowing that he was right.

Shaz' enraged wolf sounds filled the room. Blood ran from a slash in Harley's throat. Shaz was fighting full out; no sign of human thought flickered in his enraged eyes as he fought for his kill.

I watched in horror as everything seemed to slow down like a sports replay. Despite the illusion, it all happened so fast. The power in the room rode us all, but it drove those that embraced it.

The two of them were face to face, locked into a violent embrace. As close as lovers, Harley and Shaz were engaged in a battle for the other's blood. They each struggled to gain a stronghold.

Blood sprayed as Shaz took a hit when Harley had caught him off guard. Red rivulets ran down his chin from his split lip. It seemed to fuel him, and he unleashed on the vampire with a flurry of shots that had Harley on the defense.

It only took one flaw in Shaz' attack for Harley to gain that split second edge he was seeking. I saw it coming, and I was powerless to stop it.

Harley feinted left, lingering long enough for Shaz to make a counter move. The moment he did, Harley attacked from the right and scored a clear shot on Shaz' unguarded throat.

I didn't breathe as I watched his fangs pierce the creamy white flesh of my mate. The wolf in me cried out in a savage roar, rising up to break free. Shaz struggled against him, but it was too late now that the vampire had sunk fangs.

As he sucked the lifeblood from my white wolf, I focused hard and tapped the waiting power in my core. It came forth in a mad rush, victorious as I set it free and relinquished my hold. The sensations had me gasping as my veins burned with a heat that grew hotter. It quickly became painful, but once I directed it, the pain was pleasure.

From deep inside a memory came, playing behind my eyes. I simply drew on the pained memories Arys had of Harley to inflict pain on him. It was a matter of projecting the thought through the power.

I pushed that sensation into him with everything I had in me. My concentration was easy to maintain, taking far less effort than the last time I did something this extreme.

He let out a noise of pain and frustration but did not release his hold on Shaz. He tried to shield against me, a resistance forming that had me struggling to call more power.

Arys stood nearby calling my name, clearly unwilling to touch me and feed my fire. That was fine. I could do this without physically touching him. I had all I needed inside me.

I was moving before I knew what I was doing. The force behind my action sent me hurdling into Harley. I could do nothing that would physically move him; one wrong move would turn those punctures into a gaping hole. So, even though my wolf side wanted to take Harley apart in little bits, instead I grasped his hand tightly. The physical contact connected me to him in a deeper way, and I punched through his shield without a problem. It was like putting my mental hand through an open window.

I knew I was smiling as I pushed everything I had inside me into Harley. It burned as it rushed through my fingertips, out of me and through his cool, undead form. I groaned from the exertion and fought to stay on my feet as the power swirled and roared all around me.

With a loud wail, Harley released his hold on Shaz and jerked away from me so hard I stumbled. His head in his hands, he went to his knees a few feet away. I made as if to pursue him to continue my assault. Arys was suddenly there, sweeping me off my feet with an arm around my waist, pulling me away.

"Alexa, no. I can't let you kill him. See to your wolf." He gave me a push towards Shaz who was slumped against the wall with a hand pressed to his bleeding neck.

Though I was ticked at my vampire's interference, it wasn't hard to turn my attention to Shaz. I dropped to my knees before him and pulled his hand from the bloody punctures. He didn't resist me, letting his hand fall away. The bite was deep, as bad as it could be.

Shaz fixed me with a brilliant green stare. "I could taste his death. It was mine."

"Have you lost your mind?" I stared at the wound, careful not to let my feelings show on my face. It was nasty, pumping the blood out in accordance with the beat of his heart. "You've got to calm down, babe. Please. There's a lot of blood."

It wouldn't take much to heal a wound like that, but if he didn't calm down, it was going to bleed out.

"I'm not going to die on you. I promise." He reached to touch my face, streaking blood along my cheek in the process. "It will never be that easy to leave you."

"Don't talk about leaving me. We're going home. You need to shift." I tugged at what remained of his clothing. Shifting would speed the healing process, and near the full moon, that would be even more effective.

He didn't fight my attempt to unclothe him. His eyes rolled from me to where Arys stood over Harley who continued to howl like a wounded animal. I wrapped my hand around Shaz' forearm and pulled him to his feet.

"You know I love you, right?" He tried to give me his amazing grin, but it was pained and said more to me than he would ever admit.

"Is that why you dared to get yourself slaughtered? He isn't worth it. I need you. Alive."

Shaz was so far gone already. It was eating him alive to resist the natural pull to be wolf. His eyes shone with pain that echoed inside me.

"Shift dammit! You need to. I'm getting us out of here."

I turned to find Arys hovering over his injured sire. To my utter surprise, he held Harley's face cupped tenderly in his hands. As I stared in wonder at the two vampires, Shaz was a burst of white fur beside me. I really hoped I wouldn't have to restrain him. In that form, he had a very distinct weight advantage over me.

A long, angry growl rumbled from his chest, but he didn't move. I reached a tentative hand out to touch his resilient yet impossibly soft fur. His cold, wet nose nuzzled my palm as if assuring me that he was calm enough, but the low growl never ceased.

A small bloodstain stood out on his shaggy white coat but already the flow from the vampire bite eased. Without doubt, he would be fine.

"Arys?" I spoke softly, aware that his focus was elsewhere.

With Arys gazing deep into his eyes, Harley grew calm. His cries stopped, and I knew Arys was doing that soothing thing that he did so well with me on occasion. In addition to the rush of power enveloping us, the calm emotion was somehow lulling.

I watched, curiosity silencing me, as Arys leaned in so close I thought he was going to kiss the other vampire. Inches away, his lips moved. He spoke so low that even with my enhanced hearing I had to strain to make out the words.

"Never again will I stop her. Next time, you die. And, though a part of me loves you still in some perverse way, I will have no regrets." And then, he did kiss Harley. The barest brush of lips so brief I had to question if it had been imagined.

Kale stood a few feet away, watching silently. He was an amazing friend. It's too bad that Kylarai hadn't been able to love him the way he needed.

When Arys rose to his full height, there was no missing the red tears that filled his blue eyes. I realized more had just passed between them than I was really aware of. Harley never budged from where he knelt. His head bowed and hands clasped, he seemed to be awaiting our exit.

In just a matter of mere moments, the entire dynamic had shifted. When a crimson tear hit the carpet, I took an involuntary step backwards, into Shaz. Ignoring Shaz' noise of protest, I grabbed my purse and pushed him toward the door; Kale followed with soundless footsteps. The hallway beyond remained eerily quiet.

Of all of the things I wanted to bear witness to right then, Harley Kayson in emotional distress was not one of them. I was simply too sensitive tonight, and I hated him. I couldn't allow myself to be swayed by his much deserved personal torment. I wanted him to suffer.

When I stood framed in the doorway, I looked back over my shoulder. Each vampire remained as I'd left him.

A strange energy tickled along the back of my neck. The feeling was unexplainable, like I was waiting for the other shoe to drop.

"I want her, Sindarys." There was a noticeable tremor in Harley's low voice. "And, you owe me. What's one werewolf to you?" His words ignited the fire in Shaz, and I had to throw my arms around his neck to keep him from barreling back in there.

The chill that ran through me at Harley's calmly spoken words almost hurt. I didn't like being spoken of like a possession. An object. A power source.

"You never learn, do you my friend?" Arys' reaction was nothing like Shaz'. He merely regarded Harley with a look filled with scorn and pity. "I'm sorry it always has to be this way."

He wanted to say something else; I could feel it. With a glance at Shaz and me in the doorway, he shrugged his wide shoulders and turned his back on the vampire that made him.

Chapter Eighteen

The sound of water running upstairs was the only noise in the large house. Shaz had gone to clean up, leaving me alone with Arys. We sat on the bed in the guest room downstairs. After calling Kylarai and Jez to tell them I was alive and at Raoul's with the guys, I had gratefully kicked off my painful boots.

Worry nagged at the forefront of my mind. The entire trip home, I had been plagued with anxiety and questions. So many questions. What was I supposed to do now? I was a vulnerable, tasty power source with no true protection from a vampire powerful enough to force me into submission. Harley was that powerful. And, how many others?

If he didn't come for me again, which I knew he would, then who would be next? A chill shot down my spine, painful in its intensity. I had to make a choice. One that would enable me the protection that I currently lacked. It was just so huge. It was my whole life. I didn't know what to do. I'd never felt so lost.

I didn't have any clothes at Raoul's so I had been forced to settle for one of his robes. Arys had fetched it from the bedroom closet. I still wasn't comfortable going into his bedroom. The robe smelled faintly of Raoul, but it was soft and cozy so I snuggled into it anyway. After leaving The Wicked Kiss, I had just wanted to be here, in this house. It felt right.

Arys sat close but not quite close enough to touch. He was kicking himself, guilt riding him hard as he blamed himself for what Harley had done tonight. Try as I might, I could do nothing to console him.

"I wish you would stop being so hard on yourself," I said, reaching to touch a bruise near his eye. "None of this is your fault."

He gave me a studious look, long and hard. "And, I wish that you would start being a little harder on me. When did you get so soft, Alexa? You're usually such a hard ass."

I frowned and pursed my lips. "Thanks, I think. But, I'm serious."

"Yeah, so am I. He hurt you and your wolf. Because of me."

A sound in the hallway caught our attention as Shaz rounded the corner. He paused in the entry, an anxious look on his beautiful face. I hadn't noticed the water in the shower had turned off.

He was clad in only a pair of grey track pants from a stash in Raoul's bottom dresser drawer. His skin was exceptionally white, making the vampire bite stand out starkly red in contrast along with the facial cuts and bruises from fighting. The mess of white hair on his head stood up in every direction. I found it as endearing as it was sexy.

I held a hand out to him, beckoning him to come to me. After a fleeting look at each of us, he slowly made his way across the room. Going down on his knees before us, he threw his arms around my waist and put his head in my lap.

A glance at Arys revealed a mask of guilt where his enticing grin should have been. His eyes were fixated on Shaz, and for once, there was no animosity behind them. Call me crazy, but I got the strangest feeling then that the vampire had the urge to touch the head of soft platinum hair resting on my thighs.

The moment should have been awkward, and I kept expecting it to be. Yet, it wasn't. It felt strangely peaceful despite the fact that we all seemed to be waiting for the weirdness.

I stroked the side of Shaz' face as I scrutinized the cuts and bruises from his round with Harley. It could have been much worse, but he still looked pretty damn rough. Arys sat tensely beside me. Arys broke the silence first.

"I should have let you kill him, Alexa." Regret, so much regret, filled Arys, and there was nothing I could do to ease that ache.

"No, you shouldn't have. You have your reasons, and you don't owe me any explanations."

"He's right, Lex," Shaz' voice was so low it was almost inaudible. "He shouldn't have stopped you."

I opened my mouth to protest but was interrupted by Arys' velvet smooth chuckle. "This is one time I agree with you whole heartedly, wolf. Let's make a note of it. It may be the only time."

To my surprise, Shaz laughed lightly, and there was a strange sense of camaraderie between them. I was reminded that they'd obviously had their time alone together lately while saving my ass ... twice.

Arys shifted closer on the bed so that he could slip an arm around me. The touch of both my wolf and my vampire brought forth a flurry of memories as I flashed back to the sensation of both of their hands on me in the same moment. I flushed with heat and prayed neither of them would notice.

"I'm sorry," Arys said before daring to briefly lay his free hand on Shaz' bare shoulder. "I know it's my fault for what he did to each of you. There is no excuse for what happened tonight."

At first, Shaz was silent, and I assumed he was trying to keep quiet because he had nothing nice to say to that. I leaned into Arys, resting my head against his.

"Nobody is blaming you for Harley's actions, Arys. He is his own person. Albeit, a disgusting and pathetic excuse for one."

"It's over," Shaz said then, lifting his head to meet the vampire's gaze. "Let's just call it water under the bridge."

Something passed between them, and I started to feel like I was the odd one out. Then Arys simply gave a nod of his dark head, and that was that.

"If I don't get out of here, I'm never going to beat the sun." His arm tightened around my waist as I ran my fingers through Shaz' tousled hair. "But, I don't want to leave your side."

I didn't want him to go either. The tightness in my gut made me never want to allow either of them out of my sight again. How unfortunately unrealistic.

"Then stay." The words just kind of fell out of me before I could censor them. "I mean, you don't have to go. You're safe here."

He seemed to consider this while I felt awkward and silly. Shaz remained expressionless, waiting for Arys' reply. They stared at one another, and I realized Arys was awaiting the white wolf's permission. Uncanny.

My throat was dry, and it hurt when I swallowed. I didn't notice that I was holding my breath until Shaz spoke.

"You're more than welcome to stay with us."

As I exhaled, I was awash with relief. I'd been worried Shaz would leave if Arys stayed. I didn't want anyone to feel uncomfortable, but I couldn't choose between them, either.

The sudden change in their behavior had me on edge. It wasn't normal. I think I preferred them to be at one another's throats. At least it was expected.

Needing a moment alone, I excused myself to the washroom to step into a hot shower. I needed to wash the remnants of Harley from my skin. The shower was heavenly. I easily got caught up in the relaxing sensations as the hot water beat against me. However, there was no forgetting that my two lovers both awaited my return.

Upon exiting the shower, I took a moment to scrutinize my injuries in the mirror. Arys' was perfectly formed and not too deep. It barely hurt. The one Harley had left on me burned. It wouldn't take long to heal, but in the meantime, it hurt.

I couldn't help but think about Harley's assault. Being blood bonded to Arys may have prevented the entire scenario. Since it had first come up, I didn't pay it much thought. Now, I knew it was something I seriously had to consider. It was all I could think about.

The scent of fresh coffee reached me as soon as I left the bathroom. Shaz must have known how bad I'd be needing a caffeine fix. I wandered down the stairs, listening to the sound of two male voices low in discussion. I shook my head in amazement when I detected no trace of animosity in either.

They each looked at me when I re-entered the guest bedroom. Shaz leaned against the dresser with a coffee cup in hand and another on top of the dresser, which he quickly handed over. Arys lounged on the end of the bed. I gave them each a suspicious glance as I accepted the cup of steaming hot java. Precious caffeine.

I was nervous, and try as I might, I couldn't it from either of them. Did they share a smirk, or was that just my mind running away with me? The approach of dawn instilled an anxiety in me like no other.

"How are you feeling, Alexa? You look pale." Arys' lips twisted as he tried to hide a smile. "And you smell like frightened prey."

"Thanks." I flashed him a middle finger before sipping from my coffee. "I wonder why that might be."

"If you're worried about the sleeping arrangements, I have no problem crashing in the living room." Shaz looked dead serious, but the glint in his eye indicated that he was teasing.

I tilted my head to one side, appraising him studiously. "Is that what you would prefer, my love?"

The blush that colored his cheeks and sped up his heart rate made me laugh. I raised an eyebrow though when he boldly stated, "Of course not."

"Then I guess we'd better get settled in." Arys beamed a sexy smile at me, and my pulse hammered in my veins. He'd abandoned his suit jacket and shirt and began to unfasten his pants. I was left standing there staring at Shaz. I'm sure our anxious expressions matched.

I wanted to ask him again if he was sure about this, but before I could, he raised a finger in warning. "Let's just get some sleep, ok? Whatever you're about to say, don't say it."

Arys smirked but said nothing. I nodded. I got it. Shaz didn't want to make this any weirder than it was by talking about it. And, after what happened outside Lucy's Lounge, this shouldn't be all that panic inducing.

"Fine," I said. "But, if you feel uncomfortable-,"

Shaz grasped my hand and pulled me along with him towards the bed, almost causing my coffee to spill. The wicked grin plastered on Arys' face revealed fangs and sent a shock of excitement to my nether regions. Shaz nudged me from behind, causing me to notice that I'd stopped moving. I took a shaky step, feeling like my legs would buckle before I made it any further.

"Is there a reason why you're looking at me like you've just caught a snack unawares?" I gave Arys a dirty look when his smile became a sexy laugh.

"Possibly. Is there a reason why you look like a nervous virgin on her wedding night?"

"Perhaps." I approached the bed, setting my coffee down on the nightstand while double-checking that my robe was tightly secured. "Don't try any funny stuff, mister. If you freak Shaz out-,"

Arys reached out in blur of motion, grabbing me and pulling me down on the bed with him. He rolled me so that I was beneath him, his bare chest pressed to the front of my robe. I gave a little squeal as he did so.

"Is it really Shaz you're worried about? Or is it you?" He

nibbled my bottom lip ever so lightly. "Because something tells me that your wolf is probably more game than you realize."

Shaz coughed lightly, drawing our attention to him. He stood beside the bed, a strange smile playing along his lips. "Actually," he began, his expression growing serious. "I do have something I want to say, to both of you."

Uh oh, I thought. Here it comes. I wasn't sure what I was expecting from Shaz, but it was not at all what came next. Setting his coffee down on the night table, he sat gingerly on the edge of the bed. Arys let me up so that I could face Shaz, my heart in my throat as I expected some kind of bad news. Clearing his throat, Shaz took a deep breath and ran a hand nervously through his hair.

"Lex, I think that you should let Arys blood bond you."

Chapter Nineteen

Shaz paused, allowing the meaning of his words to sink in. My jaw dropped, and I gawked at him incredulously. "Have you lost your mind? Is this a joke? No, forget I asked. You have to have lost your mind."

He gave me a small smile, as if he'd expected my reaction. "No joke, babe. I'm dead serious. You're clearly not safe anymore, and it will protect you from Harley and anyone else like him."

I turned on Arys, glaring hard. "Was this your idea? Manipulate Shaz into your way of thinking so you can make me more of a vampire than I already am?"

"Of course not!" Arys' blue eyes widened, and he drew back, shock written all over his face. "I didn't know what the hell he was going to say."

"Lex," Shaz gave an exasperated sigh and reached to take my hand in his. "This is all me. Look, I know that there is a side of you that is all wolf and all mine. I cherish it more than I could ever express. But, we all know there is a part of you that has never been human or wolf. A part that is closer to vampire than anything else. It just makes sense."

"It would join her to me forever," Arys interjected, forcing Shaz to meet his piercing gaze. "Beyond death, she would rise again. Do you understand that, wolf?"

Shaz looked down at the floor, and I noticed that his lower lip trembled ever so slightly. My heart broke and I gravitated closer to him. He fixed Arys with intense green wolf eyes. "I do. That's why I'm saying this." To me, he added, "It's your choice. Imagine what could have happened tonight if Harley had been the one. I just ... I fear for you."

Arys shifted uncomfortably, and I knew that he agreed, despite what he had said before about not wanting to be the one to take my mortality away. I looked back and forth between the two of them. It became clear to me why neither of them wanted to tell me what they'd talked about the night I was attacked in the park. They had talked about this very moment. Without me.

It stung in strange places. Not that I planned to admit it to them. I avoided eye contact with either man by picking compulsively at the fluffy bedspread. Of course, I couldn't really hold it against them for discussing my well-being. But, I was anyway, just a little.

I didn't want to be bound to Harley, but the real question was about my mortality. There was definitely an advantage to being able to die twice, but to live as a vampire, for God knows how long, could I face that? Did I want to?

When Arys looked at me, I saw fear lurking in the depths of his ocean eyes. "I don't want to influence your decision in any way. It has to be entirely up to you. I'm afraid that Harley will never give up his infatuation with having you for himself. Not if he feels he's entitled to you."

I couldn't help but remember the sensation of Harley's hands upon me and then his fangs. I had been unable to defend myself. I'd been helpless, and as I recalled how it had felt, I knew I could never allow Harley or anyone else to put me in that position again.

He had enlightened me to one thing though, I had to get more comfortable with my power and learn how to use it to the fullest extent. Harley had so much on me in that regard.

"Would you really want that, Arys? To be blood bound to me until one of us finally bites it?"

It was a crude way of saying things, but I was an anxious ball of nerves. I hadn't realized I could be faced with a choice like this, at least, not so soon. After tonight with Harley, I couldn't escape making a decision.

Arys' voice was softer than I'd ever heard it. "You know I do."

Shaz sat stiffly beside us. He didn't seem at all put off by the vampire's admittance. Worry and love emanated from him, and again, I wondered how I had gotten so lucky to have someone like him in my life.

I could see Harley in my mind, his fangs sunk into my white wolf. Shaz was Alpha now, and I knew he was everything that meant and more. I had to accept that Shaz was as much a part of the supernatural and its dangers as I was. Doing this would be good for all of us. It wasn't just about me.

"I said what I had to say. I didn't mean to upset you." Shaz pulled me close, pressing the warmest kiss to my lips. The love that filled me was unlike anything I'd ever known, and the power of it brought tears to my eyes. A few spilled over before I could blink them away, and I quickly wiped at them.

"I'm not upset. I'm just overwhelmed by the affection you have for me." I smiled and kissed him back with the intensity of what I was feeling. "I haven't been able to stop thinking about it. Ever since Harley told me there would be others coming for me ... I think I should do it. Now. Tonight."

Arys looked up sharply, a combination of fear and relief in his eyes. "Are you sure? You should take some time to think it through."

Shaking my head, I forced back any second thoughts before they could infect me. "He won't stop, and there will be others. We started this Arys, and we have to maintain it. I want to do what I have to, to protect ourselves and everyone in our lives. Let's do it ... now."

Arys was a total fit of nerves, and I couldn't help but vibe off him. His energy tickled me so that I wanted to scratch, but the feeling went beyond the physical surface of my skin.

I frowned in uncertainty. "Arys? This choice is yours, too. You don't have to do this if you're having doubts. We're only bound by power; we don't have to come full circle and make it blood and body as well." It wasn't like Arys to show this type of anxiety. He was always so cool and pulled together.

"Oh, I'm not having any doubts." The surprised expression on his handsome face had me shaking my head in wonder. "I've never wanted any creature the way I want you, Alexa. It's my control I'm worried about. I don't want to kill you."

I couldn't have been any more astounded. Shocked didn't begin to describe what his words made me feel. I had no control over the sudden increase in my heart rate. "Excuse me?"

His face was a mask of anguish. "The blood bond is so much deeper than anything we've ever done before. It's called the wicked kiss for a reason, Alexa. To bond you, I have to take all you have to give but not so much that it takes you to the point of death. It's very precarious, and I don't trust myself to stop if I take it that far." He gazed down into my eyes, and I saw the predator in him, the one I had seen every time I looked at him before we'd become intimate.

Was I so blinded by lust and power that I had failed to remember that he was a vampire? A killer. When had I stopped fearing him?

"Why are you afraid?" Arys asked with concern in his voice, but there was a new hunger in his eyes. Shaz was silent, but I knew he was watching us with a keen awareness.

"I'm not." I had to force myself to meet his eyes. "I mean, I don't know. I think I just realized that even though there's something between us, you're still a vampire."

He chuckled, a soothing sound that manipulated my fear into excitement. "That's what you love about me. The ruthless killer ... the darkness. You need that in a lover, because it's what you are."

His comment left me unsettled. Shaz stirred uneasily, and I flushed, hating the side of me that went beyond a natural predator. Capturing my hand in his larger warm one, Shaz turned to Arys. "Once you do this, there is no way that he can bind her. Right?"

The vampire stared at Shaz until he appeared uncomfortable. Then he gave a slight nod. "She will be mine, and no other vampire can bind her."

"Why do I sense a 'but' coming?" I asked, watching Arys. His strange mood piqued my interest.

"But," he flashed a smile at me that made my knees weak. "You will still be a mortal werewolf with more power than you know what to do with, and therefore, still a target. And, don't forget, my love; we will be bonded on every level, not just metaphysically. Mind and body will also be bound in many ways, some of which are unknown to me. I've never bound any mortal."

I touched Shaz' face, forcing him to meet my eyes. "Are you completely sure of how you feel about this?"

"No," he admitted, chewing nervously on his lower lip. "It's not easy for me to be part of this, but this isn't about making me comfortable. This is about what's best for you. And, as much as it does kill me a little, I'm a nervous wreck knowing the kind of danger you're in." He glared in Arys' direction then, and I realized he blamed him for Harley's intentions. Of course he did.

Arys returned the dark look with one that was carefully neutral. So, their fragile understanding had dissolved. That didn't take long. Was it wrong that I preferred that?

My discomfort grew when neither of them broke eye contact. The negative energy grew thick with animosity. As if this wasn't already difficult enough.

"Is there something that you'd like to say, Shaz?" Arys' voice was low, menacing.

Shaz gave his platinum head a shake. "It's already been said."

"This is never going to end, is it?" I asked, looking back and forth between them.

With a toss of his head, Shaz assumed a casual expression. Feigned nonchalance wasn't one of his strong suits, and I wasn't buying it. "It's all good, Lex. This is about you, not us."

Arys sat back against the headboard with his arms crossed, glowering at nobody in particular. "Don't let me kill her," he said suddenly. "I've never had to stop myself before. I've never wanted to. This won't be easy."

The silence was heavy, and the atmosphere, thick with tension. Shaz looked at me so hard with so much emotion in his jade eyes that I started to come apart inside. He would go to the ends of the earth for me. I felt it, without a doubt when he replied, "Not a problem. I assume that means I can do whatever it takes, if it comes to that."

Shaz gave me a wink and a grin, which was missed by Arys, who frowned. "Of course. No cheap shots, wolf."

I was calmer than I should have been with the stimulating sensation of each man's high-strung energy assaulting my senses. This was something I had to do. I grew more certain of it with every passing moment.

Arys moved quickly, jerking me up against his hard chest. I gasped and adrenaline crashed through my veins. "Listen closely to her heart," Arys told Shaz. "It will be your guide. Don't let it grow too faint before you stop me. She can take more than a human, but it's hard to say how much more. She's already lost a fair amount of blood." He peered at both of us through those midnight eyes. The hunger already filled him as the bloodlust fought for control.

Shaz flashed him a dirty look. "I'm not going to let her die. Not unless you intend to kill me first."

The Wicked Kiss

Oh, that was just what I wanted to hear before putting myself completely into their hands. I needed to be able to trust both of them to hold it together. "Do you think you guys could lip each other off after we do this, when I'm not dead?"

"Sorry, Lex." Shaz shifted so that he was closer to us, almost touching. His pure werewolf energy was calming.

I looked up at Arys, expecting him to ease me into this. I had no second thoughts; I just wanted it over. When he gazed down upon me, I felt more like food than I ever had before, including when walking into The Wicked Kiss. The anticipation of feasting upon my blood was quickly stripping his control away. It was that awareness that instilled the first trace of true terror within me.

I struggled to control my breathing as the adrenaline flooded me. Fear would drive him harder and faster, and yet, knowing that made me that much more afraid.

"Ready?" One word, one chance to turn back. At my stiff nod, he tilted my head to reveal the smooth, unbitten side of my neck. Physically, I felt pretty good after my encounter with Harley though I was reluctant to find out how much more I could take.

Had I expected Arys to hesitate? Possibly. What I hadn't expected was the rough way he grasped my upper arms, holding me immobile. I couldn't even open my mouth to complain before his mouth was on my skin, his fangs plunging deep.

My blood spilled, and a strangled cry filled the room that I vaguely knew was me. It was nothing like it had ever been when he'd fed from me during our lovemaking. This was pure agony. Every vein and artery in my body seemed to seize as he pulled my blood into him. I went cold inside; the chill forming in my core spread throughout my limbs.

I never could have imagined what being Arys' victim truly meant. Not until that moment. With his razor sharp fangs buried in my flesh and the intent to drain me, I had never feared him so thoroughly.

I heard Shaz' voice, but it sounded fuzzy and far away. He didn't make the mistake of intervening, instead watching helplessly as my vampire lover sucked me dry right before his very eyes.

Arys held me tightly to him; a low groan reverberated in his throat as he pulled hard at the wound. A jolt of searing hot pain burned through me, and as instinct kicked in, I struggled against him. He forced me back so that I lay flat on the bed and ground his fangs deeper until I thought that the pain would surely kill me before the blood loss did.

When he withdrew his fangs to let the blood rush freely against his tongue, I convulsed and shuddered amidst the sudden pull of power blanketing us. It rose up like a thunderstorm, crashing over us. Even as he stole my life source, our bond was as strong as ever.

The room began to spin, and I had to close my eyes as a wave of nausea threatened me. Every second brought me closer to certain death. I could feel it. Maybe this hadn't been such a good idea after all.

The audible beat of my heart grew louder in my ears until it was all I could hear. Though I physically struggled uselessly beneath Arys, our power seemed to dance all around us. I knew Shaz was reacting to it when he reached to touch us both. One hand gripped Arys' forearm, ready to drag him off me. The other stroked a few long blonde tendrils that streamed out on the bed spread behind me.

I wanted to beg Arys to stop, but the words wouldn't form properly. All I could do was gasp for breath amid the pain. Forcing my eyes open, I was saddened to see that Shaz' face reflected my anguish. I saw his lips move but couldn't make sense of what he was saying.

It wasn't long before I was too weak to do more than listen to my heart slow. That's when everything went from slow motion to full speed ahead. Shaz jumped like he'd been electrocuted. He grabbed Arys and threw him in one solid motion. The sound of his body hitting the opposite wall caused a reverberation throughout the house.

My eyes rolled back in my head, and I battled to maintain my focus. Arys came back at Shaz fast, instinct driving him. Shaz was ready though, delivering a body slam that had Arys on the floor blinking up at him in shock.

"Finish this!" Shaz reached to drag him up, and Arys smacked him away. "Finish this now, before it's too late!"

I tried to roll over onto my side, and the exertion caused me to cough raggedly. It was enough to draw their attention to me. I couldn't move, try as I might. Everything was slowing inside me, and I was terrified, not that I would die, but that I would die here with each of them watching.

Arys was at my side in an instant, offering his wrist to me. "Take my blood, Alexa. You must." When I simply stared transfixed at the smooth alabaster skin, he grew panicked. "If you come any closer to death, you will rise as a vampire a lot sooner than intended. Or just be another victim." His voice broke on the last word, and his unusual display of emotion was enough to break through the fog that clouded my brain.

When the bloodlust hit me, it was with full force. I had no physical strength to resist. I didn't want his wrist though. The stark contrast between Arys' ebony hair and the pale skin of his neck drew my eye. All it took was a look, and he knew. Bending to bare his throat to me, I peeled back my lips to expose my ferocious fangs.

They were made for tearing and shredding, not piercing pretty little punctures like Arys'. I bit him quickly in an attempt to avoid doing serious damage. His blood hit my tongue, and it was like a rebirth. The power soared through me in a rush of electricity and fire.

It was so much more than a taste. His jugular slowly but steadily pumped the hot crimson fluid into my mouth as I licked and sucked at the gash. The return of my strength was immediate. I wrapped my arms around him, holding him as close as physically possible. Shaz now stood by the bed watching us. As I fed from Arys, my power reached for my wolf.

His energy was alive and taunting; I itched to taste it again. With a finger, I beckoned him closer, something driving me that I wasn't controlling. Shaz eyed me warily, but he responded by kneeling on the bed near Arys and me.

Arys grunted and attempted to disengage himself from my grasp. It encouraged my hunger, and I resisted, clinging to him when he sat up. The strength with which I held him was unnatural, even for me, but he was still stronger. Gripping each of my wrists, he forced me back against the bed.

I felt the vicious grin that stole over my features, felt its evil to the root of my being. I loved it. Arys' blood on my lips was warm and delicious as I ran my tongue over it. Despite being pinned down by him, I had the sneaking suspicion that I could escape him if I really wanted to.

"Alexa?" Arys stared into my eyes, searching for a sign of sanity. He turned my head to examine the bite on my neck.

Shaz swore softly and gravitated closer to me on the bed. "It's already healing."

"Yes. Thank God. I thought I'd gone too far." Arys' voice held a tremor.

I rolled my head so that I could look at each of them in turn. Their expressions couldn't have been more different. Arys was hard to read, his careful mask back in place. He stank of guilt though, and it turned my stomach. A glance at Shaz revealed curiosity and concern. He reached for me, and Arys released one of my arms.

"Shaz?" My voice came out hoarse and scratchy. "I can't..." I longed to warn him, to tell him what I was feeling, but all I saw and felt was the hunger.

When I lunged at him, Arys was ready for it. He jerked me away from Shaz hard enough to make me cry out. My shoulder burned, and I turned on him, snarling and snapping. Like the first time I'd experienced Arys' bloodlust, I saw through a red haze. Blood and death. It was all I cared about in that moment.

It took both men to wrestle me down, and I didn't make it easy for them. The need to feel something die as I bathed in the heady glow of blood and power consumed me until I was lost inside it. I fought them until I was exhausted.

"I'm sorry," I whispered, unable to take my eyes off my beautiful white wolf. I knew by the look on his face that my eyes were Arys' sensational blue. "It just aches so bad inside."

"What the hell is happening to her?" Shaz directed his words at Arys, but he had eyes only for me.

Arys sounded defeated when he replied. He held my arms at an incredibly painful angle but it was helping me see through the blood hunger. "It's the bloodlust driving her. The bond has been formed, and she's experiencing her own hunger, not just remnants of mine. The worst of it will pass ... eventually."

"I'm ok. Don't talk about me like I'm not right here." That had been snappier than I'd meant for it to be. "Please let me go. I feel like a prisoner."

Instead of doing as I asked, they looked at one another to decide. That infuriated me, stirring the power inside me in a negative way. Arys studied me with a look heavy with contemplation. Shaz just appeared confused.

Nodding to Shaz, Arys slowly began to release his hold on me. "Get into bed with her, but keep your guard up. She may not even know what she's saying."

Like hell I didn't. I knew what I said. And, I knew what I wanted, needed. I eyed Shaz hungrily as he slipped back into the bed next to me.

Shaz drew me back against his chest so that he spooned me. Arys wasted no time pressing his nakedness against me, eliminating any possibility of space between us. He was careful not to reach into Shaz' personal space when he laid a hand on my hip.

"Alexa," his velvety smooth voice was barely a whisper. "The hunger can be fed by more than blood."

All it took was the touch of my two lovers to stir the hot embers of the fire simmering in my core. The hunger refused to fade, but it wasn't averse to taking a new direction.

Arys' eyes were heavy upon me. My breath caught, and I waited in eager anticipation as he slowly brought his face towards mine. My eyes closed and vision ceased to be my main sense. Scent and touch took over as he explored the inside of my mouth with his tongue. He tasted slightly like blood and spice, which triggering a yearning in me for more. I instinctually reached to bury my fingers in his thick, glossy hair.

There was the barest movement at my back as Shaz pulled my long hair to the side, baring the back of my neck. When his mouth came to rest against my sensitive flesh, I quivered between their two firm bodies. His lips and tongue traced hot, wet circles along my sensitive skin, and I became flushed with heat and desire.

Both my body and power eagerly anticipated the joys of two men. I couldn't hold back the urges that drove me to consume, to take what they were giving and more, should I so desire.

Arys deepened the kiss, and I fell into his seduction. There was possessiveness to his touch that spoke volumes of need. When he nipped and bit my tongue and lower lip, Shaz did the same along the back of my neck. It was a hot spot for me that he knew would bring about the desired response.

A throb began between my legs as Shaz ran a gentle hand down to my thigh where my robe parted. His fingers grazed my skin, stirring the nerve endings to life. A tingle spread from where he touched until it filled my entire body with a warm glow.

Arys' lips moved to the corner of my mouth in a slow, lazy

motion. Tipping my head up ever so slightly, he kissed the soft spot beneath my chin before lavishing my neck with moist little love bites.

My breathing grew heavy as the burning hot power built along with the physical lust. As I tuned into my metaphysical side, I was able to clearly taste and feel each of their differing energies: warm and cool, life and death, the power in my core was ravenous, with a viciousness I'd had yet to experience. I was intrigued by what they had to give, and I couldn't help but want it all.

I moaned softly when I felt Shaz press against my ass, rock hard and persistent as his lips traveled down the curve of my neck to my shoulder. The hand on my thigh grew painful as his fingernails became claws. It was a delicious pain though, one that made me itch for more. I ground my butt against him so that his breath came in a hot pant against my skin.

My hands glided over Arys' taut chest and abdomen, feeling the muscles ripple beneath my fingertips. There wasn't a lot I could do caught between them the way I was. It was both intimidating and exciting as they dominated me together.

As Shaz alternately stroked and clawed his way to the lacy string of my thong underwear, Arys boldly slid a hand inside my robe and deftly parted it completely. His cool hands on my naked flesh fed the growing desire, and I arched my back with a sigh when he cupped my breasts.

A sexy, low growl rumbled in Shaz' throat, increasing my need as the sound touched me in intimate ways. With each one of them kissing, licking and touching me, I grew weaker willed by the second.

The first shock of anxiety resurfaced when my dark vampire moved so that he could take one of my nipples into his mouth. I tensed, waiting for Shaz' reaction to such a private act. I was astonished when Arys disrobed me with an aggression that defied my halfhearted attempt to resist. My robe hit the floor, leaving me thoroughly naked.

My blood rushed, and I felt lightheaded. It was surreal, like a dream. I almost doubted this was really happening. Those doubts were banished when Shaz gently turned my head so that he could kiss me while the vampire feasted on my breasts. The musky taste of wolf was heavenly. He was my mate, and I longed for him desperately.

I moaned into Shaz' mouth when Arys plunged a hand between

my legs. He rubbed his fingers back and forth over my wet opening before forcing two of them inside me with the roughness I'd come to know and love from him.

The power that commanded Arys and I once again expanded to include Shaz as his Were energy enticed it to take note of him. As the physical pleasures grew, so did the blinding rush of power that had never taken no for an answer.

I kissed my wolf with a passion that knew no limits. Our tongues seemed to dance together. No sooner had Arys abandoned my breasts than Shaz had his hands full of them, kneading and pinching. Small noises of contentment came from him. His energy was wild and delicious, and I savored it.

Arys continued to work me with his hand; his intense gaze rested heavy upon me. The hunger in his eyes was raw, frightening. The rush of power in the room was near deafening.

I moaned as the waves of an approaching orgasm began to stir inside me. Arys' slick fingers slid in and out of my body, pausing to rub the little sensitive nub that had me writhing between them on the bed.

The combination of their hands and mouths upon me was more than I could take without my sanity collapsing into fragments. The orgasmic sensations built until I reached the breaking point.

I cried out in ecstasy as I exploded with climax. The intensity nearly brought tears to my eyes as my body spasmed uncontrollably. Shaz showered my face with kisses as I clung to him. I could feel the vibration as he shuddered under the pull of so much high-strung power.

His arms went around me in a tight embrace. Arys curled up on the other side of me so that I was locked between their bodies. It felt so perfectly right. I clutched Shaz' hand, entwining our fingers together.

The afterglow was sensational. I snuggled into the feeling as if it were a warm blanket on a cold night. Despite the power humming all around us, I was calm and peaceful.

I was overdosed on everything they'd each given me, most all, love. I sunk into blissful slumber with a smile on my lips. My vampire's cool body conformed to mine as if it had been made to do so. And, though I was drunk on the two of them, I wasn't so far gone that I didn't notice the desperate need in Arys' touch as his arm wrapped firmly around my waist.

I lay between them, listening to Shaz' even breathing, as sleep claimed me. Even with the uncertainty and danger that had become a regular part of my life, there was nothing better than being a werewolf in love.

Chapter Twenty

"I think you were right to do it. It's obvious that you had to do what's necessary in order to protect yourself and those you love." Jez absently stirred her gourmet coffee with a stir stick, but her serious, green eyes were fixed on me.

Kylarai sat across from me, her eyes downcast as she picked at the apple pie on her plate. She didn't agree with Jez or Shaz as far as the blood bond issue was concerned. She thought it was a huge mistake.

It had been four days since I'd entered into the blood bond with Arys. Honestly, I had felt incredibly out of sorts since then. I'd learned quickly that I couldn't handle the mid-afternoon sun any longer. It burned both my skin and my eyes. The bloodlust had been my constant companion every night since. Without Arys to ease me through, I never would have succeeded without going on a murderous rampage.

He promised that the worst of it would wane and I would gain control of the many vampire tendencies that now ruled me. If I thought experiencing Arys' weaknesses before was bad, this was a whole new ball game. They were my very own vices now.

I had asked my two best friends out for dinner, wanting to share with them the decision I had made. I wanted their opinion, knowing they would each be completely honest with me about what they thought. I valued what they had to say.

"I just don't think you should have rushed into anything, Lex," Ky's voice was soft, and she beamed a shy smile at me. "You altered your own death."

Things had been better between us since I'd starting spending more time at Raoul's. It gave her and Julian time together without

233

taking chances on having Shaz in the house as well. That would just get incredibly ugly.

I had barely touched the Alfredo pasta dish I'd ordered. It was the best in town, yet it wasn't encouraging my weak appetite. "I know that. I was confused and scared. But, I can't help but feel that it's what I needed to do. Especially after what happened with Harley."

"That's just the thing," Jez piped up again. "He won't stop until he has you. And, it's only a matter of time until other power hungry vamps seek you out." She gave me a pointed look, one that Kylarai missed. I knew what she meant. Kale had already developed an attraction to my power. How many others would?

Would Harley give up once he discovered Arys had bonded me after all? Lord, how I hoped so. I felt like a weapon that I didn't know how to use, that could go off at any moment.

Kylarai reached over to pat my arm affectionately. "You know I love you no matter what you do. That's just my opinion. I don't want to see you regretting this decision. Regret is a hard thing to live with."

I felt like I would have some kind of regret either way. Choosing to bond myself to Arys through blood had completed the bond we'd begun when we joined our power. My life and death would never be the same again. Yet on the flip side, it was already so beyond any semblance of normal. I couldn't help but feel empowered in a way, knowing that Harley wanted me as badly as he did. I didn't even really know why.

"I appreciate you both coming out tonight." I swirled the ice in my tea and took a sip of the too sweet juice. "It feels good just to hang with the girls sometimes. I need more of this."

"I'd say you do. I miss killing things with you. It's not as fun with Kale." Jez' voice was loud enough to carry, and I blushed and hid my face when a lady at the next table stared open-mouthed at her.

"I hate having to cut and run, but I'm meeting a source that's helping me out with a case." Kylarai reached for her wallet, and I stopped her with a gesture.

"Forget about it. I invited you out. I'll pick up the tab."

"Fine, I'll get the tip then." She tossed down a few bills and pushed her chair back. "Will I see you at home later or are you going to Raoul's?"

I had to think about that. I'd been pretty much living there over the past week. "I'm not sure. I may have to come by the house to grab some more of my things. Feel free to have Julian over."

"How's he doing anyway?" Jez asked with interest.

Kylarai shrugged and forced a smile. "Let's just say that his ego took the worst of it." She rolled her eyes and to me said, "I think it's great that you're staying there. You need to face that part of you and find peace with it all. Let me know if you want any help redecorating."

"Actually, now that you mention it, I do." I grinned when her face lit up in excitement.

"Sounds great! I'll give you a call later, and we'll talk about it." She stood and slung her purse over her shoulder. "It was nice seeing you again, Jez. Have a good night, you two."

After she'd disappeared out the door, I turned to the leopard, finding her staring at me with an expectant expression. "What?"

"I have something to tell you." She raised a brow and her ruby lips curved into a smile.

"Please don't. I'm sure I don't want to know."

"Kale's been dreaming about you. He told me. I just thought you should know. You've had one hell of an effect on that man."

Why did she have to look so pleased when she said that? "What do you mean, dreaming about me?"

She shrugged and sipped from her coffee. "I'm not sure. He didn't go into detail. I think he just needed to say it out loud to someone and that happened to be me. I just wanted to let you know."

"Shit." I let out an exasperated sigh and reclined in my chair. "That's just what I needed to hear."

"Sorry."

Kale meant a lot to me. He was more than a colleague; he was a friend. And, because of the power I had, I now had power over him. There was something so wrong about that.

"Anyway," Jez quickly changed the subject. "Kale and I have been taking out new vampires all week."

That caught my attention. "New ones all week?"

She nodded, and her golden waves bounced. "Yeah. We haven't been able to determine where they're coming from yet. So ... you want to come out tonight?"

That was intriguing. After the past couple of weeks I'd had, I was certainly up for a challenging hunt. "Definitely. Count me in."

ഇ൸ഇ൸ഇ൸ഇ൸

The evening had been going splendidly. Hunting down a coven of new vampires with Jez and Kale had been a release that I'd desperately needed. It had taken no time at all to locate a handful of new vampires lurking in a local cemetery. It was typical really. Many of them wound up in such places, either from seeing it in Hollywood films or because it was guaranteed to be free of anyone else.

It had been almost too easy to take out the two we had followed to the cemetery. Upon arriving we had discovered another four of them nesting there. From the looks of it, they had been up to no good. There was more than one old corpse decomposing beneath some trees. Nasty.

The last two put up a nice fight that had Jez smiling as she slashed her way through one of them with clawed hands as he shrieked like a little girl. After slashing a hole in his throat the size of her fist, she pulled out the stake she carried strapped to her wrist and plunged it deep into his chest.

No sooner had she done so than the last one escaped me and rushed her head on. She had just a split second to defend herself. Throwing her arms up in front of her, she took the brunt of his force as they tumbled and rolled as one.

I moved abnormally fast as my legs carried me across the distance. I snapped his neck with a powerful twist; the resulting crunch echoed as I went for the heart, stake in hand. He had already succeeded in lashing out at Jez, drawing blood from a deep cut above her eye. The scent of her living and highly potent blood caused a tightly wound string inside me to snap, and I lost all control.

One moment, I was focused on the pathetic vampire on top of Jez, and the next, I was tossing him aside so that I could get to her myself. I shudder to imagine how that would have played out if Kale hadn't been there.

Being as in tune to my energy as he was, he felt the shift in the atmosphere when the blood lust dominated my actions. All of a sudden, he was just there, throwing me off her so that I landed in a sprawled heap not far from one of the decomposing victims. As I leaped to my feet, there was no conscious thought in my mind. I was acting on instinct.

With a snarl, I turned on Kale. I didn't want him though. I wanted the natural born Were blood, the blood that had never been human. I practically salivated as the scent drove me into a frenzy.

The pain was like a punch right in the guts when Kale knocked me on my ass with a blast of power. It didn't hurt me otherwise, but it successfully knocked the breath out of me. Before I could get up, he was on top of me, straddling my body with his strong frame, a silver psi ball burning in the palm of one hand.

It was as if a cool breeze blew through my mind then, bringing with it the presence of my dark vampire. Arys' voice was soothing, snapping me back to myself as if I was jolting awake from a nightmare. *My wolf, what's happening? I knew I never should have left your side.*

I stared up at Kale, struggling to reply with something sensible to Arys. Kale's sweet energy was alluring in its own right, and I found myself falling into his enchanting eyes.

"Alexa?" Kale lightly slapped the side of my face, a frown creasing his fine features. "You never should have done this. The blood bond is not meant for one as free spirited as you."

I was confused by his words. All I could think about was reaching to touch the lock of dark brown hair that fell in his eyes. As I remembered the taste of his blood, I licked my lips seductively. "Kale..." The word fell on a hushed whisper, and I knew that he was mine if I wanted him.

"Don't do this," he pleaded, and I could feel his resistance crumbling. "I'm trying to stop you from making a huge mistake here. Don't draw me into another one. You know I can't deny you."

Jez came to stand nearby, careful not to get too close. I concentrated on Arys, on his cold blue energy raging inside my mind. *I'm going to self-destruct before I can begin to have regrets.*

It was strange, knowing I could share my thoughts with him and finding that I could also shut him out. I wondered if I would ever get used to it. Arys could feel my edgy emotion, yet he could only know what I revealed to him. There was something very reassuring in that.

Wrapping a strong hand around my wrist, Kale jerked me

upright and pulled me to my feet. He didn't let me go, though. As much as it killed him to touch me, reaching right into my personal energy, he did it anyway.

The blood hunger didn't leave me, but I was in control now that Kale had stepped in. He was an amazing friend, one that I owed dearly. Despite that, the sinister vampire essence within me couldn't help but want to toy with him. The look he fixed me with insinuated that he wasn't new to this game. Of course not. The guy had centuries on me.

"Cut it out, Alexa. Don't you understand that you're playing with fire?"

"Why? What am I doing?"

"You know damn well what you're doing."

Kale and I faced off, and I couldn't help the grin that spread over my face. Regardless of how wrong I knew it was to continue down that path, I didn't want to stop. However, I did know what I was doing. I couldn't help but think about what Jez had said at dinner. Kale had been seeing me in his dreams, unable to escape his attraction to my power. Knowing his history and his dependence on The Wicked Kiss, I knew I couldn't be just another power hungry female that would use and abuse him. He'd had enough of that in his past.

It actually hurt to deny the many hungers and urges commanding me. Yet, it wasn't as if being a werewolf hadn't been much the same in its own way. This was just a new kind of pain. I was able to make it back to the office without eating another silver blast from Kale.

Arys' presence lingered in the back of my mind, but I didn't acknowledge it. It was still too strange, and I didn't want to share my thoughts with anyone. Jez laughed and joked as if I hadn't been ready to bite into her jugular vein, already brushing it off like no big deal. I wished I could roll with the punches as easily. Although, it was refreshing to have someone in my life who could so simply shrug it off, knowing it wasn't worth altering her life. I could learn a lot from Jez' take on things.

Despite her attempts to loosen Kale and me up, the tension between us couldn't be dismissed. I watched the clock tick past one am in the kitchen of our office building. Jez wasted no time closing up her office and heading for the door.

"Since I have made it through yet another night without facing certain death, I will be celebrating by sipping wine by a crackling fire with a smoking hot redhead." She announced. "I assume you two will be out of here right away?"

I knew what she was really asking. Was it safe for her to leave us alone together? All I knew was that it was safer for me to be alone with Kale at that moment than with her. The cut on her head wasn't critical, but the blood drying there was taunting me.

"Yeah, I won't be here much longer." I gave her a look, one of those that women share, which enables them to have an entire conversation with others present, with no more than the right expression. Without batting an eye, she quickly bid us goodnight before sashaying to the exit.

I couldn't shake the feeling that Kale was waiting for us to be alone. He had something to say. I leaned against the small kitchen counter and considered but then abandoned the notion of feigning nonchalance. Why bother? He would see right through it anyway. So instead, when the door had closed behind Jez on her way out, I looked at Kale expectantly.

"How's Kylarai?" He asked, crossing his arms over his chest. A moment later, he uncrossed them and stuck his hands in the pockets of his black leather duster. He didn't seem to know what to do with himself.

I could see by the look on his face that he already knew about Ky and Julian. I could attribute that to Jez and her willingness to talk. He really wanted to know though. There was no faking the concern in his eyes.

"Are you really asking how she is, or are you asking about him?"

"Both."

That was fair. "She's good, although, I'm not sure that she's really happy. I don't think Kylarai really knows what she wants right now."

"I heard Shaz kicked his ass." He didn't have to say Julian's name, and I understood why he chose not to.

I nodded and thought back to that night. It had been an intense scrap. "Hell yeah, he did. It's been a little awkward at home since. Shaz and I have been spending a lot of our time at Raoul's."

"If he hurts her, I'll tear him to pieces." Kale promised with a glint in his eyes as if he was hoping to get a shot at Julian himself.

"He's all yours."

Kale studied me, and though his gaze was heavy, I didn't flinch beneath it. I merely waited calmly for him to speak. I knew him well by now, and it wasn't hard to tell when he had something to say. When his eyes fell to my wrist, I knew he was thinking about the night in the car when he'd bitten me. Though the bite was long gone, I had to resist the temptation to rub the place where it had been.

He looked away before he spoke, as if suddenly intrigued by the pattern on the linoleum. "I understand why you made the choice that you did, but do you really think it was the best option?"

"Honestly," I replied. "I don't know. It feels very surreal right now. If I didn't bond myself to Arys, it would have been anybody with enough power to force me."

Kale nodded, his gaze coming to land on me again. I felt the weight of his analysis as he truly studied me. "It's going to change you, you know. Tonight ... that kind of thing isn't going to end, even if it gets easier to deal with."

That wasn't really what I wanted to hear though I couldn't say I was surprised. "Thank you. For being there and making sure I didn't do anything stupid. And, for intervening at The Wicked Kiss." What else could I say? Kale was bush beating, and we both knew it.

"That gossipy little leopard told you, didn't she?" He gave me a knowing look, and I had to laugh. He knew Jez just as well as I did. "Well, whatever she said, I'm sure it was exaggerated."

"Was it?" I raised an eyebrow, my smile fading. "She told me that you've been dreaming about me, Kale."

He didn't appear upset. If anything, he'd fully expected her to tell me. When at last he made direct eye contact, it was forced, as if he didn't trust himself to look at me. Nervous energy trickled from him to tease my senses.

"I'm sorry." His face crumpled, and he looked ashamed. "It was bad enough after I took your blood, but then we killed that she-wolf together ... I kissed you ... and everything went to shit."

As his agonized energy marched along my skin like red ants on their way to a picnic, I picked it apart to determine what it was made of. Kale was filled with regret and more than enough guilt for both of us. Despite the urge to soothe him, I bit back my response when he slowly crossed the small kitchen until he stood before me.

I looked back and forth between his brown and blue eye, entranced by the difference. This was so much more than a power trip between two friends. He was getting something from me that he hadn't had in years, possibly more than I even realized. Though I knew that, his next words shook me to the center of my being.

"You have awakened something within me, Alexa. Something that has been cold and buried for decades, centuries. It's dark, it's deadly, and I have only known one other who could ignite within me the sensations you do."

He didn't say who because we both knew and to mention the one who made him could bring out the predatory side of Kale that I'd encountered in the car. I was all for avoiding that at all costs. Like the last time Kale had made a confession to me, I didn't know what to say. So, I said the first thing that came to mind.

"What is it that you want from me, Kale?" The urge to touch him played with me. "Let's just be straight up here. Friends or not, there is something bigger that we have in common. And, if we can just talk openly, it will be a lot easier to deal with."

"I don't know." His answer came quickly, suspiciously so. "The things that I want from you are new to me. It doesn't feel right." He actually looked embarrassed. "You're a friend, almost a little sister that I drag into trouble. I've never wanted you like this before."

The heat in his dazzling gaze had me tingling with adrenaline. My heart jumped, and my lungs deflated of air. I'd be nothing but a filthy liar if I tried to say that I hadn't wanted him the night we'd kissed. I had wanted to devour him.

"I understand what you mean by that better than you might assume. Most of the time, I feel like I'm being pushed along by this tidal wave that I have very little control over. It seems to have the snowball effect, getting bigger and bigger by the day." A sigh escaped me as I said to Kale what I never said to Arys or Shaz but probably should. "I'm afraid it's going to consume me, and I'll be a total maniac, feeding off the blood and energy of everyone I love."

Kale chuckled humorlessly and nodded knowingly. "It's not all bad. Not when they're willing." He flashed fangs at me, and I shivered when he added, "In fact, it can make the transition a little smoother."

"I'll bet." A swirl of undead power spiraled like a tornado inside me. My next words came unbidden. "Is that an offer?"

The atmosphere thickened and pulsed, much as it had the night of our strange kiss. I felt that shift in my brain, the one that brought the vampire power alive. A teasing smile graced my lips. I felt Kale's hunger like a storm coming on the wind.

He took a step back and then another, each one looked like it was killing him. Instinct commanded me to advance on him, to back him into a corner. Would it really be so wrong? I just wanted a little taste.

"If I do what I want to right now, I won't be able to let you out of this building without bleeding you." His eyes were wide as panic gripped him. "You barely even feel like a werewolf anymore. Without your wolf scent, I would think I was in this room with a vampiress. A damn powerful one."

That was unsettling. I held myself in check, the warmth of my wolf balancing the cool undead urges. It was a constant battle inside me. I had to get out of there, or we were both going to lose the struggle for control.

"I'm going to go before we do something we really regret." Pushing away from the counter, I aimed to fly past him on my way out of the room. When his hand snaked out to grasp my arm, jerking me to a halt, my power instantly reached to touch his.

Like with Harley, there was no bonding. That was with Arys and no other, which was defining all on its own. Yet there was no escaping the way my power sought to taste his, feel it and draw it into me.

"Wait," Kale gasped, his voice low and strained. Whatever it was that he craved from me, it had him trembling. I could have stopped him; his control was pushed to the limit, not mine. "There is nothing that I wouldn't do for you. Remember that."

Pressed against him, the scent of leather toyed with my sense of smell. His eyes held hunger, but they also possessed a wealth of knowledge and genuine affection. I allowed myself a moment to enjoy touching his exhilarating aura.

"I will. Probably sooner than you'd like." I managed a friendly grin as I disentangled myself from him. I paused to give his hand a squeeze. "I'll tell Kylarai you asked about her. I'm sure she would appreciate it."

I adore Kale. He is easily one of my most favorite people. But, he had a longing I couldn't begin to dream of and something in me spoke to that yearning need. As I headed for the door, I felt the weight of his gaze upon me. It would be best to avoid feeding those hungers, for both of our sakes.

Chapter Twenty-One

The house was quiet when I slipped in through the sliding door. I was glad to see that the railing had been fixed and looked better than ever. No thanks to Arys of course. Shaz got the credit for taking on the task.

Kylarai hadn't been around when I'd come by the house to go for a much needed four-legged run in the forest. It had been quiet, and when I'd first stepped into the house, it hadn't felt like my home anymore. My belongings had slowly been disappearing, taking up residence at Raoul's. I had been putting off moving my furniture. Raoul's place was fully furnished, and I hadn't the need to do so. It also made me feel like I wasn't completely leaving the house I shared with Ky.

The rush of sexual energy slapped at me when I came inside, pulling my robe closed around me. I padded down the hall towards my room to get dressed when the hush of murmurs and whispers carried to me. Aw, crap. Maybe I could change fast and bail out before I had to hear much more.

Despite closing the bedroom door behind me, I could still hear Julian's animal rutting sounds, and it creeped me right out. They clearly hadn't known I was here or hadn't expected me back for some time.

I got busy jamming my legs into my jeans in a desperate attempt to get dressed and get out. Pulling a t-shirt over my head, I headed for the door with my robe in hand so I wouldn't have to keep wearing Raoul's. I slid my feet along the hardwood floor so that I made not a sound on my way out.

Today they were going at it like bunnies, but three days prior, they had been having a shouting match in the kitchen when I'd arrived. It really was none of my business. I wanted Ky to be happy, but I was starting to appreciate having another place to call home. It was evident that she was enjoying my absence in her own way, as well. Since the beautiful stretch of forest was outside her back door, I would likely be here often enough regardless of where I spent my nights.

I took a moment to admire my car as I approached. After two days in the shop, the damaged driver door was now good as new. My smile turned into a glare when I noticed how close Julian had parked his SUV to my Charger. There was no way he could have gotten out without dinging it with his door. I stalked around it angrily until I was sure that he hadn't scratched my car. It was the principle of the thing.

Raising my face to the fall night air, I inhaled deeply. I couldn't detect anything, but I knew I'd picked up a trace of Zoey's scent while running. I hadn't seen her though. Raoul's daughter had crossed my mind recently. I'd been asking myself if it would be a bad idea to track her down and try to communicate with her. If that was even possible. One could only guess as to the state of her sanity. Still, I couldn't shake the feeling that I should seek her out ... one day anyway.

When I turned onto Raoul's street, my heart soared at the sight of Shaz' little blue Cobalt parked in front of the house. Would my heart ever stop fluttering in anticipation of seeing him? I hoped not.

Arys and Shaz both had a key to the house, but they rarely came by at the same time. Since Halloween night, when we'd formed the blood bond and the three of us had been intimate not once but twice, they didn't spend much time in close quarters.

I pulled into the driveway and ducked into the garage where Raoul's Jaguar was parked. I made it a habit to check over the property regularly. I couldn't afford not to be careful. I paused to run my hand over the smooth black finish of the expensive car. I hadn't driven it yet, but I intended to use it for my evening hunting excursions. It wouldn't stand out like a bright red beacon the way the Charger did.

Surveying the cold, damp garage, I was again enveloped with the feeling that I was right where I was supposed to be. I was greeted by the heavenly scent of dinner when I entered the house. Shaz called out from the kitchen, and I smiled to myself. He was simply amazing. If the scent of chicken and baked potatoes indicated anything, I was in for a treat.

When he met me at the entry to the kitchen, he held a glass of red wine in one hand and a single long stemmed red rose in the other. Though it was simple, it was easily the most romantic gesture I'd ever received. My heart melted, and I blushed.

"You rock my world, wolf boy." I accepted the wine glass and took a grateful sip before pulling him close for the hot kiss that I craved. Shaz didn't get many nights off, and I tried to take advantage of every one. "You take such good care of me. Thanks for fixing the railing at Ky's. It looks great."

He teased me by tracing the outline of my lower lip with his tongue before dipping it inside my mouth to taste me. I pressed against him, careful not to spill the wine. When at last he pulled back, he raised an eyebrow quizzically. "Ky's? Have you officially moved out, or are you still on the fence with that?"

"I'm not sure. I do know that being there when she and Julian are going at it is a nightmare I don't want to face again."

Shaz chuckled and pressed the rose into my hand. I followed him into the kitchen, watching with admiration as he attended things on the stove. The temptation to rub the soft petals on my face was too strong to resist, and I gave in happily. It was less than an hour later when we were lying in those petals on the living room floor before the fireplace.

I pulled a throw blanket off the nearby sofa, and we got comfortable in front of the blazing flames. I couldn't help but flash back to a time when I'd lain naked in this very spot with Raoul. I couldn't deny how much I missed him, even as I shoved the memory from my mind.

Shaz fed me dessert from a platter of strawberries and chocolate sauce while I played with his near white locks. The night couldn't have been going any better. So of course, it had to get worse. When Arys projected his thoughts to me, it was loud and clear, setting off a domino effect reaction in me.

Wherever he was, he was hunting. His victim's screams drove him over the edge, and the walls between us came down as he tore into her with a savagery that had me shaking. If I closed my eyes, I could almost see through his as images swarmed me.

She was bleached blonde, middle aged and heavily made up. I had no way of knowing why he'd chosen her. She fought hard, and the thrill that raced through Arys in response was easily transferred to me. Like a rabid dog, he tore into her without holding back. She didn't make noise for long.

I could hear Shaz asking if I was alright as I sat frozen stiff in his arms. Arys' strong emotions were flooding me with more than I could take. His excitement as the blood spilled was what pushed me over the edge. Snapping into action, I scrambled away from Shaz and focused on forcing Arys out of my mind. It was easier than I expected, but the damage was done.

I forced myself to concentrate on the sound of the fire crackling and the smell of logs burning. Anything to combat the bloodlust that rocked me. I closed my eyes so that I wouldn't look at my wolf mate and see food. He wasn't prey to me, but he was still a blood source. It hurt in places that never should feel that kind of agony.

Shaz was no fool, but he approached me anyway, hands held up cautiously. "Whatever that was," he said softly. "You can't run from it, Lex. We can deal with it."

I whimpered softly and hid my face behind a curtain of my hair. The closer he drew, the stronger the beat of his heart sounded in my sensitive ears. I didn't realize I'd started growling at him until he told me to stop. Shaz wasn't afraid of me though, not in the least. Not a trace of fear emanated from him.

When I bared my fangs at him though, his demeanor changed. The look in his eyes was fierce when, with a solid motion, he grabbed me and flipped me so that I landed hard on the floor beneath him. He used his body to pin me, and it came as a shock to find him dominating me like the Alpha male that he now was.

I grunted when I hit the floor. My wolf was instantly subdued as Shaz commanded respect from me with the action. Though the wolf in me was calmed, there was a part of me that was enraged and then ashamed. I was roiling with emotions, each of them leaving confusion in its wake. I choked back a sob and bared my throat to Shaz, submitting to him completely.

He didn't hesitate to bite me, and it was nothing short of astounding. I hadn't expected him to go Alpha on me. His teeth didn't break my skin, but the act spoke volumes rather than the injury. I was awed and also madly turned on.

"I'm sorry, Lex, but I'm not going to let you worry about making me a victim. I'm your mate. You should never be running from me because you think you're going to hurt me." With a strong hand wrapped around my arm, he jerked me to my feet. "Call it tough love, baby, but I have to stop this now, before it spirals out of control." I stared at him with wide-eyed astonishment. I thought I was hearing things when he said, "You're just going to have to take my blood. It's the only way for you to realize you can handle this."

I swallowed hard and tried to say no. My lips formed the word, but nothing came out. He smiled down at me, clearly enjoying his moment of power. When at last I could speak, I squeaked out, "Why?"

Shaz' hands were rough where he gripped my arms. "You know why. I'm not letting you do this by yourself. You're only weak if you don't let me help you."

Awe filled me, as well as complete adoration. He was everything I needed in a man and more. But, when he held his wrist out to me as an offering, I paled and shrunk back, shaking my head. "No, Shaz I can't."

"You will." His tone held no room for argument, and I did a double take. If Arys had said that to me, I would have told him to shove it up his ass. This was Shaz, though, and all I could do was stare stupidly. When he saw my face fall, dismayed, his expression softened, and he added, "Trust me."

Was he serious? Trust him? I trusted him more than I trusted any creature on the planet. It was me that I had little faith in.

"I don't want to hurt you." I peered at him through strands of blonde and red hair as a lock fell in my eyes. He reached out to brush it away, the gesture filled with tenderness.

"It hurts me more to watch you suffer like this. For months now, I have kept quiet about this side of you, but things have changed. Let me be part of this. I'm your mate, Lex."

There was no changing his mind. I knew that look in his jade eyes. He had made up his mind, and he was taking a stand. I should have been overwhelmed with emotion at his words, but instead I was stricken with terror.

With the bloodlust eating away at me, I was unable to cling to that terror. It fell away from me like abandoned clothing. The pulse beating in his offered wrist drew my eye, and I licked my lips hungrily. We faced each other in all of our naked glory, completely at ease with the naturalness of it.

I watched him pensively, a question in my eyes. Without

words, Shaz merely nodded, waiting with acceptance and even a hint of excitement. Because it was him, I didn't snap in a frenzy of blood hunger. However, I was clinging to sanity by a very thin rope. And, I could feel that I was slipping quickly.

I had to do this. It was vital to preventing my quick descent into blood madness, and it meant something to Shaz. If I didn't act soon, I was going to lose it.

With shaky hands, I encircled his wrist with my fingers. I was virtually salivating when I drew in the clean wolf scent of him. I indulged in the urge to rub my face against that perfect skin. Pressing my lips to his pulse, I closed my eyes and savored the sensation of his life force pumping just beneath the surface.

That was all it took, and there was no going back. I bit into his wrist fast, hoping to ease the pain. When Shaz gave a small gasp, I thought I had hurt him. The pleasure that oozed from his energy indicated otherwise.

Once released, the blood dripped fast and steady. I rushed to catch it with my tongue. The scent, taste and feeling of it in my mouth hit me like a tornado. Everything around me seemed to fall away. Nothing was left in the entire world but Shaz and me in that moment.

Along with the hot, flowing, crimson stream, I took in the freely exuded energy of a male Alpha wolf. It was like having electricity poured over and through me. Tasting Shaz was like sipping from a fount of lively power, one that I couldn't get enough of. He tasted like heaven.

It didn't take much to satiate the hunger for blood. I didn't need it to survive. Not yet. The craving for the energy high that was building had only just gotten started. My need for my mate was immense, and giving the slowing bleed a long satisfying lick, I began to kiss my way up his arm.

Shaz reached to pull me close. The power ruled us both as we fed it with our voracious desire. He kissed me roughly, his tongue delving into my mouth between my fangs. Tasting his own blood, he shuddered and reached between my legs.

I was ready for him, already slick with feminine moisture. The wolf in me was impatient, needing him now. I needed him to claim me as I had claimed him in taking what he gave. He pressed his shaft against me, long and hard, throbbing in time with his heartbeat. That was all I needed to set off a series of small explosions in the pit of my stomach. I wrapped my arms around his neck and, at his encouragement, my legs around his waist.

He put me down against the soft carpet so that he was above me, peering down at me with eyes that had gone full wolf. Shaz thrust his way inside my warmth, and my body instinctually hugged him close in response. He plunged deep in one long stroke, bringing a small yelp from me that was both surprise and pleasure.

Something had changed between us, something that transcended everything we'd known so far. His devotion was strong enough to move mountains. Allowing him to meet one of my needs had enabled him to be my mate in every sense. He needed it as badly as I'd needed to be dependent on him; my trust spoke louder than any words.

Every one of my senses blazed like an inferno. I clung to him desperately. The sweat rolled from each of us to create slick, wet sounds as our bodies danced and united as one.

Epilogue

The taste of human blood lingered on my tongue like sweet copper. With a pinky finger, I wiped a minute trace from the corner of my mouth. Breathing hard, I glanced at Arys, who watched me like I was the most delicious thing he'd ever seen. The dead pimp at my feet stirred no emotion within me. He'd been a peddler of teen girls barely old enough to drive a car. Worthless.

How I had managed to avoid slaughtering an innocent was beyond me. The bloodlust was a strange and funny thing. It no longer assaulted me when Arys neglected to feed. It assaulted me on a nightly basis. My hunger was my own, yet, his neglect reverberated through me when his energy infected me with his inner desires. That's when it became too much for me to bear, and my control was stripped away in layers until I was a maniacal mess.

On the flipside, nothing had changed for Arys as far as my personal weaknesses go. My wolf lurked inside him due to our metaphysical bond, but Arys was long past mortal afflictions, and he experienced nothing further in that regard. Though as far as connections go, ours had undergone many transitions.

We could now open a telepathic link by will and tap one another's power when we were nowhere physically near each other. If Arys had been packing a loaded weapon before ... well now, we were really something to be feared. Of course, that would be more accurate if I knew how to handle half the power I possessed.

Arys insisted that we could command this power ourselves, wield it as needed, however needed. Lena once told me that we were two souls cut from the same magical cloth, destined to unite as one regardless of our physical forms. If this power is to be of any real use to me, I need to be the one in control, and that is something that I intend to focus my strength on.

It nagged me to no end knowing that Harley has the valuable information that I seek. He can't possibly be the only one. Finding a source willing to share was among my priorities.

I wasn't naïve enough to believe that I was safe because of sharing the wicked kiss with Arys. Harley's warning continued to haunt me. If he wanted a piece of me so bad, who else out there did? As a mortal with this kind of power, I was a walking snack to bigger, badder predators than me. My biggest fear continued to be endangering those I loved. Though they can all protect themselves, there are things out there that may not hesitate to use them to get to me.

"Alexa..." Arys murmured, pulling me into his arms. He nuzzled my hair, inhaling my scent before tasting the blood on my tongue with a deep kiss that had me swooning.

My heart pounded until I thought it would burst. The exhilaration of the feed along with the rush of the hunt was better than any drug known to man. This was why vampires and Weres lost it. It was why I took them out before they did something stupid to expose the rest of us. Control was not an option; I had to have it.

I was curious as to what Veryl would say when he returned from out of town. After the secrets he'd hid from me for the past ten years, I didn't feel that I owed him anything, least of all explanations regarding my personal life.

If Arys and I hadn't been standing in a dirty back alley behind a filthy nightclub, I would have been tempted to hike my skirt up and take him right there. The high that I was flying was that spectacular. Instead, I took his hand and led him down the alley, towards the light at the far end. I wanted to go home.

It was strange still to think of Raoul's house as home, but that got easier the longer I stayed. I still hadn't braved his bedroom, but I had been thinking long and hard about what I was going to do with it. Though I missed having the stretch of forest behind my house, Kylarai's was just a short jaunt across town. Easily accessible.

Strolling down the dingy alley with my vampire lover, my senses were working on overdrive. I was informed of everything from the sound of each and every separate car on the parallel main street to a couple having sex in the bathroom of the nightclub we'd just walked away from. The smells were a whole other world unto themselves.

Perhaps the best part was that I could now feel every supernatural creature in the surrounding vicinity. Like a hot red glow, I could sense two vampires four blocks to the west and a werewolf sitting in a coffeehouse at the end of the street. If I really concentrated, The Wicked Kiss stood out like a blinking beacon in my mind, ablaze with the energy of all those inside.

I couldn't help the satisfied smile that curled my lips. There were certainly perks to this blood bonding thing. The increased psychic awareness was almost worth the occasional agony. It gave me great peace of mind to know that Harley wouldn't so easily catch me off guard again. There is more to being empowered than an increased arsenal, but nobody can say it doesn't make a difference.

"So," Arys began hesitantly, drawing my attention. "What do you think the point is to all of this?"

That was random. I frowned, pondering what he was getting at. "What do you mean?"

"Uncanny abilities don't just happen. Isn't there usually some reason, some purpose for the greater good?"

That drew my eyes to him, and I gave him a studious look that had him glowering in response to my scrutiny. Was Arys feeling the need to justify what we had, or could he possibly be seeking a greater purpose to his existence? I was baffled. I'd never heard him give any thought to the meaning behind everything.

"Maybe it's up to us what we do with it. That whole good versus evil kind of deal." I'd asked myself the very same question that Arys was voicing now. I had no answers for either of us.

"Yeah ... maybe."

We ambled along in silence, each of us lost in our own thoughts. Walking in darkness didn't mean having to become one with it, did it? Could we not live with our inner natures without embracing the true evil we all are privy to? Humans are no less evil than the worst of vampires at times. Surely right and wrong couldn't be so perfectly cut and dried.

Reaching the end of the alley, we stepped out into the glow of the streetlights. The city traffic flew past us as those out and about for the evening sought entertainment, companionship or things unknown to the rest of us.

A homeless man on the corner began to shout, "I see you,

bloodsuckers. You ain't gonna get me. No sir, I know your kind."

It was somewhat expected. The mentally ill had a tendency to see right through our human appearance. Thankfully, nobody paid them any mind when they ranted and raved about it.

We strode past him without a second glance. I didn't want to encourage his shouting by making eye contact. The heavy stare of a young woman waiting for the bus drew me. She wore a knowing expression but quickly averted her eyes when I met them. Psychic? Possibly. Those with sixth sense abilities could often detect our inhuman energy. For the most part, they were smart enough to keep their mouths shut.

The werewolf I'd sensed in the nearby coffee shop watched us with little interest from his place in the window. He held a coffee cup in one hand and a book in the other. I chuckled to myself, finding it amusing that so many supernatural creatures were nothing like the average person would assume. Of course, I was probably exactly how they would assume: blood hungry and power tripping.

Arys reached for my hand, stroking my fingers gently with his thumb. The zap of our energy making a sudden physical connection tingled all the way up my arm like a bad static shock. It created a warm feeling in the pit of my stomach, which spread to encompass my limbs. The sexy grin he shot me stirred the sensations into a fire that blazed just for him.

As we drew closer to the car, my anticipation grew. I hungered for many things, but my need for Arys and Shaz was something I was happily learning to live with. I'd just opened the driver's door when the strange awareness struck me.

That glowing place in my mind, The Wicked Kiss, had just spawned another vampire. I felt the new undead existence as surely as if I'd been inside the club. Perhaps I should look into how often that was occurring in the blood bar. I wanted nothing more than to chase Harley back to Vegas and out of my domain. Maybe that would get the ball rolling.

"Did you feel that?" I asked Arys, afraid I was the only one.

"Yes." Arys stared off into the distance, as if seeing The Wicked Kiss in his mind. "Somebody has just awoken as a vampire."

One thing was for sure, I would be keeping a close eye on the vampire bar. The Wicked Kiss was definitely on my radar; however, it would have to wait for another night.

Tonight, I wanted nothing more than to go home to a hot bath and curl up in front of the fireplace. A glass of red wine and my two favorite men in the world would make that a much more pleasurable experience. If Arys' libidinous energy was any sign, he was thinking along the same lines.

As we exited the city onto the highway that would lead us the short distance home, I felt surprisingly peaceful. The stars twinkling overhead called to my wolf. Though I wasn't so foolish as to believe that everything was perfect, I was content, and that's what mattered.

My heart was shared by two men, each of them I desperately ached for. They completed me in ways that I still could barely comprehend. With them in my life, I had learned how to trust again and discovered the true meaning of love.

Their acceptance and encouragement meant the world to me, and I knew that I would never have come this far without either of them. I have gained so much: strength in both mind and emotion, the comfort of their unconditional love and a desire for more from this world.

Now ... I'm ready to take on anything.

Trina M. Lee's Alexa O'Brien Huntress Series

continues with

Only Vampires Cry Blood

Power. Werewolf Alexa O'Brien has more power than she can handle. Learning how to control and use it effectively is at the top of her priority list. The one man who has the knowledge she needs is the vampire she loathes, Harley Kayson. He just so happens to be the sire of her vampire lover, Arys Knight.

Alexa's wolf mate, Shaz, wants her to feel secure with the power she commands, especially with unwelcome new werewolves in town. Despite sharing some steamy encounters with Alexa, Arys and Shaz rarely see eye to eye. This time is no different.

Arys doesn't want Alexa anywhere near Harley. When desperation drives Alexa to make a deal with Harley, Arys is livid. Conflict threatens to destroy Alexa's relationship with Arys, but due to their eternal bond, they can never truly walk free of each other.

When Arys teams up with his sire to revisit their sordid past, the pain he and Alexa inflict on one another rises to a scathing boil. Alexa comes to realize that her only solution is to fulfill Arys' greatest wish and worst nightmare, regardless of the consequences.

Excerpt at: www.TrinaMLee.com

About the Author

Trina M. Lee has walked in the darkness alongside vampires and werewolves since adolescence. Trina lives in Alberta, Canada with her fiancé and daughter, along with their 3 cats. Trina is a big fan of the UFC and is more than a little obsessed with her Dodge Charger. She loves to hear from readers via email or Twitter.

For news, contact information and more on her books, please visit:

www.TrinaMLee.com

7143736R0

Made in the USA
Charleston, SC
26 January 2011